DARKLING PARK

For Canbury
school, English
department
enjoy My book,
keep reading
and writing,
best wishes,
elisa x x x

For Cadbury
School, English
experiment

enjoy my book.
keep reading
are writing
Best wishes,
Alischer

DARKLING PARK

ELISA MARCELLA WEBB

Elisa Marcella Webb created and managed the Department of Sociology, Psychology and Law at a top London School for eight years. She then took a gap year graduating with an MA in Creative Writing in 2013. She is currently a part-time Ph.D. student at Kingston University. Her special interest is Southern Gothic literature. She has two daughters. *Darkling Park* is her first novel.

Published by Pudding Press, an imprint of Patrician Press, 2016
For more information: www.patricianpress.com

First published by Pudding Press, an imprint of Patrician Press, 2016

E-book edition published by Pudding Press 2016

British Library Cataloguing in Publication Data. A catalogue record for this book is available from the British Library.

ISBN 978-0-9934945-3-6 paperback edition

ISBN 978-0-9934945-2-9 e-book edition

Printed and bound in Peterborough by Printondemand-worldwide

www.patricianpress.com

For David, Phoebe, Tatum and Andrew

FIN MOVES HOUSE

Fin stared at her face in the bathroom mirror. She looked like a badly drawn girl. Her face was definitely lop-sided. Like someone started a sketch and ran out of time. She was trying to ignore her sister. Ermine was banging on the bathroom door as usual.

"Hurry up, Freak. Time to clear out." Ermine was right. Since Fin got sick and Gran cut her hair, really short, she did look like a freak. Ermine called her Freak all the time, as if Fin had changed her name when she was in hospital. Fin didn't care, mostly. She had bigger problems in her life. She'd made a list in a new notebook:

1. Why are Pop and Mop so secretive about our new house?

Conclusion: there must be something very, very wrong with it. Fin didn't want to leave her snug bedroom. Despite the fact she'd spent the last three months there, lolling in bed, ill.

2. Will I have any friends left at school after being away for so long?

Conclusion: probably not.

3. Will *ex?* best friend Zelda ever be in touch again?

Zelda had moved to a chip shop in Australia. Well, it wasn't exactly a chip shop more a *fish and chip supper restaurant and Bar-B-Que* according to Zelda's only email. Zelda lived in a wooden house with a corrugated iron roof, next to the *fish and chip supper restaurant and Bar-B-Que*. There was a big sign. A boy called Tod lived next door. He had a swimming pool, well not Tod, but his mum and dad. Zelda was full of Tod *this* and Tod *that*. She attached some photos of the pool, her and Tod splashing about, showing off. Zelda even added a copy of a school project on something called extinct thylacines by *her and Tod*. Fin didn't bother to open it.

4.   When will I be better?

Conclusion: not for a while.

Fin had Heinoch Shonlein Puerpera. She was still impressed with the name of her illness but pleased it wasn't a killer. The only thing interesting about it was its name. It was a boring spend-all-day-in-bed-no-school illness.

Ermine banged on the door again.

"This is a parole violation, Freak. Get out, I need the lav."

Fin unlocked the door slowly. Ermine pushed past and slammed it shut. Fin walked down the stairs. She didn't want to leave their cosy house. Mop had painted each tiny room a different colour. The sitting room was yellow, the kitchen blue and Fin's bedroom was lime. Ermine said her room was puke. Mop called it puce. The little house was always warm. It smelt of toast. When Fin got sick, she had to stay in her room for a very long time. Pop spent a whole day off work fixing fairy lights up and down Fin's bedroom walls and around her window. Fin liked the long twilight. The bulbs glowed blue and pink. Pop promised to do the same in the new house. Mop said that might be inappropriate.

Gran had chipped in: "The whole move is *inappropriate* if you ask me, but no-one has."

"It'll be fine, fairy lights will cheer the place up, the..." here Pop paused, "the visitors will appreciate some cheer. I know I would."

Gran shook her head and asked: "And what about your *new neighbours*?"

Mop jumped in to defend Pop. "There aren't any neighbours."

Gran straightened up: "Oh well, don't come crying to me when one of *them* sneaks up on you in the middle of the night."

Mop glanced at Fin, who was sitting on the sofa wrapped in a blanket, chewing her nails. Mop frowned at Gran and said "It'll be *fine*, if I see anything odd, I'll..." she paused, "I'll tell it to sod off." Fin didn't understand what they were talking about but she knew she was going to find out pretty damn soon and it didn't sound good.

It was cold and dark in the street. Pop rubbed his hands together, they made a dry sound. Ermine said he was trying to make fire. Pop unlocked the van door.

"Come on, love, hop in," said Pop. Fin squeezed herself into the passenger seat amongst bin bags and boxes bound for the new house. Ermine popped bubble gum, in the back, but didn't offer any to Fin, as usual. Pop rearranged some of the bulging bags, so he could get in. Fin remembered the time Ermine stuck bubble gum in her hair. As Gran had cut it out she told Fin a story.

"Once upon a time a little..." here Gran paused, for dramatic effect. "A little creature was born called Ermine. She was called Ermine because her skin was as white as the Arctic fox and her eyes were as black as coal. Her parents: a poor woodcutter, turned plumber, and his wife, were worried that Ermine was so pretty that she wouldn't need to grow a personality. One day while walking and wishing very hard for a personality, Ermine didn't notice a deep well. She tripped and fell headlong into its green-slimy water. By the time the villagers heard her shrill screams and dragged her out she'd found a personality. Deep but unpleasant, like the well. And to this day Ermine covers her face in white powder and black lipstick, so no one knows about her old pretty face any more."

Every time Ermine stormed in and out of the little house, pink dreadlocks flapping behind her, Gran would wink at Fin. As if to say what do you expect she found her personality at the bottom of a well.

Pop was excited. Fin could tell, he kept repeating himself.

"Seat belts on, seat belts on."

Fin tried to get comfortable but the van was rammed with stuff. She never liked being in the van. The diesel fumes made her feel sick. Ermine blew a large bubble, popped it and thrust an empty carrier bag over Fin's shoulder.

"Sick bag, do *not* throw up on my stuff." Fin took the bag and watched their house disappear behind them. Pop turned into the Avenue and then out onto the High Street. After the roundabout Pop slowed down and pulled over at the side of the road. Fin thought he was going to look for his *A to Z*. Pop never went anywhere without a map.

"You never know, we could get lost," he always said.

"What and then we'd eat the map?" Ermine always added.

Pop leaned over, rooted around on the floor and hauled up a torch.

"We'll need this, ladies." And with that he leapt out of the van and bounded towards some tall iron gates.

"Why have we stopped?" said Ermine, dragging her eyes away from her phone. "We're here, idiot," said Fin, leaning forward to peer out of the dusty windscreen.

"Get out then, Freak," said Ermine. Fin eased herself out of the van. Her legs were stiff and cold. She stood on the pavement, looking at the gates. There was a high brick wall that stretched as far as she could see to her left and right. Everything looked orange under the sodium street lights, even Ermine's pink hair. Pop was rattling at a chain wrapped tight around the gates.

"Can't believe it. I took a chain off this morning and now there's another one, don't have a key. Ermine, phone Mop, ask if she knows anything about it," said Pop.

"Can't," said Ermine. "No signal."

"Just try, cross over the road," said Fin, even her head was getting cold.

Ermine sighed and crossed the road. It was quiet now, the rush hour was over. Fin leaned on the van, ramming her hands into her hoody pockets. She pushed the stretchy cotton down to her thighs. Pop put a cigarette in his mouth but didn't light up. He was giving up. Fin couldn't see through the gates. There were no lights the other side, only darkness. The wind clattered an empty vodka bottle along the pavement.

A gate banged down the street and a boy about Fin's age appeared; hood up, heading their way. Fin ignored him. However, he walked right up to Pop, thrust out a key, mumbled something and walked away fast. Pop raised his eyebrows to Fin and tried the key.

"Woo hoo," he shouted and waved the chain like a snake trophy. "We are in. Wait here, I'll drive the van and park behind the gates."

This was easier said than done. Pop had to lift and push one gate, while Ermine and Fin had to work together to lift and push the other gate. Flakes of old paint prickled their skin. Fin rubbed rust off her hands, onto her jeans, as Pop drove into the darkness. Ermine began to swear.

"Look," she said, pointing her phone towards a battered sign stating: Darkling Park. "I've been here before on a sodding art trip. Park, my arse."

Fin thought the wall looked familiar but like something in the background she'd never really noticed. They'd probably driven past and walked past hundreds of times before. It was just a big wall. Pop emerged from the van with another torch.

"You've gotta be kidding me," spat Ermine.

Pop smiled. "No, popsicle. Welcome to your new, and very grand, home: Darkling Park."

"But it's a graveyard," wailed Ermine.

Fin was shivering but she felt as if she was getting hotter and hotter. She wiped her greasy forehead with her sleeve. Her stomach wobbled. She was going to be sick. The rushed tea of baked beans and plain chocolate biscuits churned. Fin didn't even like plain chocolate biscuits. She bent over: spurt, splatter, another splatter bigger than the first and a dry heave. She felt better. She didn't feel queasy any more, just hungry and shaky. Pop put his hand on her shoulder and passed her a grubby hanky. He looked sad like it was his fault. Ermine screamed and jumped about. Fin thought she'd been stung.

"Now look what you've done." Pop and Fin looked at Ermine. Ermine stuck a boot out towards them. Her new black 18 buckle boots were coated in sick.

"We'll clean them up later, in the great scheme of things this isn't a..." Pop didn't finish. Ermine wasn't listening. She'd turned her back, prodding her phone. This gave Fin a chance to smile in the darkness.

"Jeez, no wonder you kept this a secret," said Ermine. Pop smiled and passed Fin a torch. Ermine continued to complain.

"I came here in Year 10; never in a million years thought I'd end up living here. Karma's a bitch... *where exactly* are we going to live?" Ermine frowned. "It's not a tent is it?" Pop and Mop had lived in a tent in Spain when they first got married. They'd laugh about no water and a loo made out of plastic bags.

"No, it's a house, over there," Pop pointed into the darkness. "Come on, we'll walk. I'll come back for the van after dinner." Fin smiled again *if* Ermine hated it so much maybe she would *have* to like it. Really, really like it. Though, as they walked down a cracked road into the darkness she wasn't so sure.

The brick wall blocked most of the orange street light. There were trees on either side of the narrow road. Fin could hear them rustling and settling in the breeze. Ermine walked closer to Fin than she had in a long time. The torch light was feeble against the black empty space. It was cooler here. Fin could smell damp earth and rotting leaves. The hum of buses and cars faded. It was like being tipped out of London into the countryside, as if a forest had sidled up to the main road after dark.

"I can't get a signal," Ermine muttered.

"That might be the hospital, it's over there," Pop pointed into the black. "This used to be a country estate about 200 years ago."

Ermine groaned. Fin sighed, not only were they in for a long walk, by the look of things, but Pop was launching into a history lecture. The wind picked up and they were sprayed with some dead twigs.

"Ow!" shouted Ermine. Pop continued, oblivious: "Lord Basel's family built the estate, but when he died, he left no heir. His son died of cholera, when he was your age, Fin. Anyway, he left his estate to the London Board of Works for a hospital and cemetery. Now this is really interesting..."

Fin and Ermine looked at one another. Ermine rolled her eyes.

"Lord Basel had a grand scheme to build a Workers' Spa with fountains..." Fin and Ermine both slowed down so they heard less of the lecture. Pop forged ahead talking and waving his arms about for emphasis. His torch caught headstones and large marble plinths carved with letters and dates. Ermine tried to ignore the graves; hissing at Fin if she dared shine her torch left or right. However, Fin was interested *and* she was annoying Ermine, a win/win situation.

"I just want to read what they died of," she said to Ermine.

"That's not on the graves, but it should be," said Ermine, taking up the challenge.

Soon both Fin and Ermine were zigzagging across the narrow road, pushing past spikey bushes to read the graves. Most of them were pretty boring. People like Vera and Ivan died in 1871 and were sadly missed. Sometimes they found whole families, as their eyes adjusted to the dark, they read about children buried long before their parents. They began to suggest suitable deaths depending on names and ages: miner's lung, the pox, a terrible drunken fall, crushed to death by a falling drunk, terrible.

Pop stopped up ahead and called them. He was standing in front of what appeared to be a grassy mound like a traffic island. As they caught up with him, he swept his torch beam across the island. Ermine and Fin stared as the yellow light caught a weird collection of palm trees and bulbous firs. White stone statues leaned towards them. Angels with broken wings gazed up at the night sky. Ugly chubby faced cherubs smirked. Fin took a step closer using her torch to make a path up the overgrown bank. Some of the statues had lost arms or heads. These lolled in the ivy. Fin stepped over them. She tripped up now and again as brambles snagged her jeans. At the top there was a stone zebra standing on a marble plinth. Before Fin had time to find death clues about the zebra, Ermine caught up with her, puffing.

"I remember this. Art trip, Miss Tolstoy got us to photograph broken limbs and headless torsos. Weird. That's not a zebra by the way." Ermine stopped. She was interrupted by a low growling sound coming from the other side of the not-a-zebra. Fin and Ermine stood very still. Fin felt her short hair stand up on the back of her neck. Pop glanced about, grabbed a thick stick and walked towards the sound, making as much noise as possible. The growling stopped. They all held their breath. Pop sprang forward, banged his stick on someone's grave and shouted: "Get out of here." Something large crashed away through the brambles.

"Probably just a fox... or a lost dog" said Pop in a loud voice, frowning. Ermine and Fin walked quickly back to the cracked road. Whatever it was had gone, for now.

They all began to walk faster. Up ahead Pop's torch caught two stone angels; both had lost a wing. Pop handed his torch to Ermine and rooted about in the undergrowth. He only took a few seconds but to Fin it felt like an hour. She stepped closer to Ermine and tried not to look beyond the yellow torch light. Pop gently lifted a wing from the damp earth and laid it down at the edge of the road.

"This is why we're here. I'm going to be caretaker and fix this lot, protect them from harm, well vandals," he said. "You guys can help." He picked up a marble hand and passed it to Ermine.

"Yuck," said Ermine and passed it straight to Fin. It was heavier than it looked but Fin liked its cool smoothness. The fingers curled together as if they were meant to be holding something. She decided to wash it in hot soapy water whenever they arrived at their new house. It might be useful.

"Onward comrades, this way" said Pop. And instead of following the road ahead they turned right down another narrower road, only just big enough for the van.

"Is it far?" said Fin. She felt tired and queasy again.

"No, just down here, past the tree line, Mop's got the dinner on." At this news both sisters groaned. Mop's cooking was awful. Gran and Pop usually cooked while Mop washed up. However, recently Mop had taken over at the stove as Gran was moving to her own place, Sheltered Accommodation it was called. So far they had been treated to brittle pasta, burnt toast, vomit trifle and mutant stir fry.

"Come on, not far now, guys," said Pop.

This road was muddy and uneven. It undulated under Fin's trainers. She stumbled twice. Her torch battery began to fade. Her hands were numb. Both Fin and Ermine started to walk closer to Pop. The wind was noisy in the trees above their heads. A fox hurried across the path ahead. The headstones were smaller here; some had given up and fallen over. Fin couldn't see very far but she kept checking behind. What if the thing that growled came back? She turned again and nearly jumped out of her skin. Her torch caught two glowing eyes. But it was only the fox watching them.

Fin puffed in relief and stopped to tie up her trainers. Their loose sloppy feeling had been bothering her since they left the van. She put the marble hand down on some mashed leaves. As she retied her right lace there was a loud thrashing sound in the bushes to her left. Ermine and Pop seemed very far away. Fin stayed low, near the path and waited. Her heart pounded in her ears. She didn't have to wait long. There was a crash when something large burst through the bushes and shot across the path. Ermine shrieked. Pop spun round trying to point the torch towards the noise. Fin knew it was way too big to be a fox. The giant shape reappeared; it was easily as big as Fin. It barged back through the undergrowth, leapt across the path and vanished in to the night. Fin stood up.

"What the?" Ermine shouted.

"Some sort of dog?" asked Pop. Fin looked for the fox, it was gone. Whatever it was it had a very long tail. And maybe stripes across its back? Fin didn't know much about dogs. She was frightened of them when they barked. But she had never, ever seen a striped dog. Fin forgot all about the marble hand. They began to walk away, very fast.

2

BLIND TWIN HOUSE

There was a squeaking sound up ahead. Pop shone the torch towards another sign, on a pole, high above a low brick wall. The sign swung back and forth in the breeze as if it was repeating itself: *Blind Twin House* it read.

"Is that the name of our new house?" said Fin. She expected it to be a practical joke, this couldn't be real. Or could it?

Ermine rolled her eyes and jabbed at her phone.

"Put your phone away and follow me," said Pop. There was another iron gate but this one lent against the wall, its hinges rusted through. They walked under the tall trees. A door-shaped hole appeared in the blackness, revealing Mop with another torch. She was wearing her spattered cooking apron. Mop's torch was covered in chocolate dribble.

"Come in. I've made a cake for our first night in our new house."

Before they could step into the hole Pop cleared his throat in a theatrical way. He smiled and shone his torch up the brick façade. The house towered above them; layers of bricks and boarded up windows.

"Welcome to Blind Twin House." Fin was glad Pop was smiling; he had been frowning since he was made redundant. Now they had a new house and Pop had a job, sort of. "Desperate," muttered Ermine as she stomped into the hall.

Pop wedged the heavy door shut. The square hall was as big as their old house. The walls were bare plaster. The cold floor was covered in red Lino, some of which had been ripped up to reveal black and white stone tiles, like a chess board. Stairs snaked up into a dense darkness. Fin shivered. She didn't want to look there for too long. What if a face appeared? There were five tall doors; they all looked like they had been dyed with black ink.

"Come into the kitchen, our new kitchen," said Mop. Mop was grinning. "Fuses have gone again, so I had to get more candles. We don't have that many so I think early to bed." This was one of Mop's favourite phrases.

"Whoa, whoa, whoa, I'm not spending a night in a dump called Blind Twin House," said Ermine. Fin felt the same but guessed it was their only option. Perhaps the kitchen would be more like a normal house?

Pop and Mop ignored Ermine's protest. Fin held her breath. Would Ermine storm out and risk being attacked by whatever was lurking outside? Instead they both followed Mop towards the second door on the left. It led to a long narrow kitchen. The kitchen table was covered in cutlery and piles of plates and scrumpled newspaper. A burning smell came from a battered stove.

"Oh damn," Mop said, grabbing a tea towel to rescue the cake.

Mop cut the burnt top off and smeared it with jam. Pop, Ermine and Fin washed their hands at the chipped enamel sink. Then they sat down on their wooden chairs from home. Mop pushed mugs of scalding tea across the table. She began to point out some original Victorian fixtures, as she called them, from Lord Basel's time. It was difficult to appreciate the ornate plaster ceiling because it had been suffocated by layers of paint. Three candles rammed into cups and two torches didn't give much light.

"The wall paper's probably from the 1950s" said Mop pointing at the mottled pattern: knives and forks lined up next to onions and grapes.

"It's vile," announced Ermine. "God, look, there's even a cabbage."

"So why's it called Blind Twin House?" asked Fin pouring herself more tea, before it stewed "And why are all the windows boarded up?"

"That's a surprise for tomorrow morning, let's show you round," said Mop, picking up her torch.

"And I'll try to fix the fuse box," added Pop. Fin worried he might go back to the van alone. But Pop began to rummage about picking up screwdrivers and duct tape from some of the half unpacked boxes on the kitchen floor.

"Things just keep getting better," Pop said fishing out his camping headlamp and snapping it on his bald head. Mop led the tour. At first it was difficult to see. The torch was too small for the big rooms. Mop got excited and kept pointing in different directions. Pop had already unpacked most of their furniture. Mop and Pop had created islands, as they called them. This meant pushing all their cheap, rickety furniture into a corner or around the giant black fire places, or in the oval dining room, in the middle. Ermine said it looked like an amateur theatre production of failed family life. Downstairs there was a basement with a sink and shelves covered in battered tins wrapped in cobwebs. They left Pop there humming and rattling away.

There was a small room Mop said she was going to turn into a study, the oval dining room and a huge room that could be a grand sitting room, *if* they could afford grand sitting room furniture. They couldn't. With their crappy furniture it just looked sad, thought Fin. Each room was colder than the last. The feeble torch made weird shadows like something was moving towards them, then quickly away again. The walls were covered in old fashioned wall paper: urns and ivy, mutant flowers and weird shapes like giant magnified insects squashed flat for some awful experiment.

"This is beyond creepy," said Ermine, going up to the walls for a closer look.

Fin didn't want to go anywhere near the patterns, they looked like they'd start to move.

"Is it like this upstairs?" asked Fin.

Mop smiled. "Not exactly, you'll see."

Fin didn't want to see. The house smelt sad like rainwater.

Ermine shot ahead up the stairs, clomped round the first floor, and found another staircase. Fin could hear her boots moving fast above their heads, like a giant rat in clogs. "Mine," shouted Ermine, before Fin could say whatever it was, was unfair. But Mop put her hand on Fin's arm and said "Wait and see. We've already set your room up."

On the first floor there was a white and black tiled bathroom with a giant bath. Next to it was a square room with Mop and Pop's bed leaning against the bare wall. Next to this was a narrow corridor sort of room.

"This is odd, really odd, it looks like a linen cupboard but I think it might have been a playroom. Maybe, after Lord Basel's son..." said Mop. "Anyway, someone put up shelves."

Fin peered in. It was more like a corridor with shelves on either side. It felt warmer than the rest of the draughty house. Behind the shelves someone had painted a landscape of flat green with a sliver of blue sky. There were animals dotted here and there: a leopard, a black bear, a fierce looking pig, an owl and a black stork. Fin couldn't see more in the torch light; some animals were half hidden behind the shelves as if they were hiding. The painter was quite good, except each animal looked like it was smirking. Fin wondered if that was the intention. It was creepy.

They walked past a wide wooden window seat.

"This is for you," said Mop pausing at a narrow white door. So this was her new room. Mop twisted the door knob back and forth and pushed open the door.

"Best not shut this door. It's difficult to open again," she said. It was long and narrow, but mostly long. There was a fire place. Fin's bed was made. There was a new anglepoise lamp on her bedside table for reading in bed. Some cardboard boxes were piled against another white door. The only light was a candle in a clean jam jar, so the room had no colour but Mop assured her it was pale blue, sort of faded, she said with a faraway look in her eyes.

"When the chimney's cleared you can have a fire," said Mop, turning to go down stairs. Fin sat down on her bed. Her legs ached. Her bed smelt like their old house. Fin felt sad, her eyes were sore. She shone her torch up and down the walls. She was too tired to figure out the silvery shapes: clouds or maybe shells? At least it wasn't cockroaches.

She just wanted to lie down but a victory yell broke the silence.

Ermine had won but Fin wasn't sure what. She decided to find out. It was the attic, now Ermine's new room. Fin pulled herself up another steep staircase. The walls pressed in around her. It was almost as if the stairs were carved into the bare plaster. There was a short door at the top leading into darkness. Ermine laughed and clicked her torch on, under her face. However the scary effect was ruined by the house lights flickering on, then off again. For a moment Fin saw a white room with round windows like portholes on a ship. This of course was the best room.

"Bet you can't see the graves from up here," said Ermine, bouncing up and down in her giant platform boots. Fin's eyes slowly adjusted to the dim torch light. The walls were black but the portholes were even blacker, like a ring of spider's eyes.

"It'll be like sleeping in a spider's head," she said. Ermine paused in her bouncing. Fin slipped out and down the stairs. Ermine followed Fin quickly, slamming her new bedroom door behind her, muttering "I'm not sleeping anywhere until we get electricity."

After the tour Fin sat down on the stairs, listening to the wind in the trees outside. She could hear the enamel sign squeaking in the breeze. She hadn't decided if it was annoying or spooky. Mop passed now and then with more boxes and bin bags. Fin wanted to cry but she was just too tired. What was the point, they were never going back to their old house. The new owners were probably already demolishing the garden for their off street parking.

"Cheer up," Mop sang as she hurried past wearing rubber gloves and a manic smile. "You've got your own room now." Mop stopped lower down the stairs so her face was level with Fin's. She looked tired and her big hair was covered in plaster dust.

"No more sharing with Gran and the Imperial family."

Fin trudged back to her room. She took off her trainers and lay on the bed looking at the plaster shapes on the ceiling. They'd once been flowers she decided, but now looked like dollops of melted ice-cream. Her tired eyes rested on the faded wallpaper. It might be a coronet. It was difficult to tell. There was a tap on the door. Fin's Grandmother blocked the doorway.

"Gran!" Fin got up and ran to her Grandmother. Gran wrapped Fin in a big hug. She smelt of cigarettes and Parma Violets.

"I got a cab, got a funny look coming here. Cabbie helped me open the gate, then took off. Look, doll." Gran waved a hammer in Fin's face. She then strode towards one of the bigger boxes wedged in front of the other door in Fin's room.

"Contraband," Gran snickered. She used the hammer to prize open the box. She slit the inside with her long nails. She rummaged about through her second-best-scarves and started to take out small silver photo frames; laying them on the bed where they gleamed in the torch light. She drew a chocolate bar from her coat pocket and passed it to Fin. "Supplies."

Fin unwrapped the chocolate sniffing its deep burnt smell: plain with crackle toffee. This one was a bit rich for Fin so she broke off a small piece and sucked it slowly to build up her tolerance. Gran looked over her shoulder to make sure the coast was clear, before starting to take out her homemade door-stops. Each one was a little bit bigger than the one before. The largest was as big as their family cat, Fat Bastard. He hated the doorstops and had once been caught trying to scratch their faces off. It was Gran who renamed him Fat Bastard after that incident. Now no-one remembered his real name. Gran set them all out around the room, like sentries. They were made of newspaper with something heavy and secret inside. Gran would never give away this secret.

"When you need it, you'll know," Gran said, usually after she told the story of how the Tsar's daughters had diamonds and rubies sewn inside their clothes. The doorstops were covered in yellowing sellotape but the photocopied faces were still clear: Tsar Nicolas II, his daughters: Olga, Maria, Anastasia, Tatiana Livadiya, (very good at maths, insisted Gran), little Alexei and the Tsarina Alexandra Fyodorovna.

Fin felt better. The Imperial family were like old friends. Since Fin was little, Gran had been telling her bedtime stories about the old country, mother Russia. Gran had left as a baby but she said she was scarred by folk memories, seared into her DNA. When Fin got sick and Gran came to stay she'd brought the Imperial family to keep Fin company. They now circled her bed on the floor, on the mantel piece and on packing crates. Fin hoped they'd keep any ghosts away.

They finished the chocolate and stared at their Imperial friends as the torch battery began to flicker and fail. Fireworks popped in the distance. Fin leaned back on her pillow, her eyes began to close. Gran rattled the other door knob. The door did not open.

3

THE FIRST NIGHT AND THE NEXT DAY

Fin was woken by Mop rubbing her shoulder. Her mouth tasted cacky after the chocolate. She was very thirsty. She pushed Mop away and staggered to the bathroom. It was very cold. She could see her breath. She washed her hands but couldn't see her tooth brush or any toothpaste. She scooped up a handful of water and sloshed it round her mouth. It tasted like old pennies. The mirror had black patches as if it was rotting from the other side. Fin hurried back to her room. Mop pulled back the quilt and thrust in a hot water bottle. Fin climbed into bed listening to the wind moan down the chimney. She shivered, branches scrapped at the boarded up window.

"Blimey, it's like moving to the countryside," said Mop. "Without the pigs and potatoes..." This was no consolation to Fin. At least that sounded normal.

"Where's Gran?" said Fin.

"Pop's taken her home. Ermine went as well, probably just to use her phone. We've no signal here, could bugger up my internet business plan. But hey hoe." Mop always said this when something cracked and broke beyond repair. Before Ermine became too grand for Fin, they had a joke that got more extreme. They would end up giggling uncontrollably into the night. Pop's been made redundant but hey hoe, Mop's gone mad but hey hoe.

"Correction, Mop's got a mental illness," Ermine would interject putting on a serious voice. "Fin's got Heinoch Shonlein Puerpera. The cat's eaten next door's baby and school's collapsed leaving 16 children minus 24 limbs but hey hoe and by the way there's been an explosion at a nuclear power plant, hey hoe." Sometimes the list helped. Ermine was very good at thinking up awful illnesses and disfigurations for anyone who'd been mean to them in the week.

Eventually Pop would yell up the stairs: "For crying out loud go to sleep."

Fin would wait holding her breath then whisper "Hey hoe," setting Ermine off in loud, getting-into-trouble guffaws.

"So we're alone?" asked Fin, sitting up in bed.

"Yep, just us girls."

Fin stared at the open door. The hall beyond was black. Mop followed her stare. She went over and shouldered the door shut. She came back and sat on the bed. She touched Fin's cheek.

"I was going to clear up but why don't I stay here for a bit? Remember the first night you were in hospital. We got to the ward at 4 a.m. I slept at one end of the bed with you at the other, wondering who was behind the other curtains."

Fin remembered waking up in the morning confused. Mop was talking to a man in a green plastic apron. There were three other beds with kids in pyjamas leaning over tables shovelling up cornflakes.

But that was months and months ago. Fin lay back on her pillows. They smelled of her old room: Ermine's hairspray, bath bombs and cigarette smoke. It was weird to finally have her own room. Mop slipped off her battered crocs and pushed herself against the end of Fin's bed. Rain tapped at the boarded windows. Fin's eyelids began to twitch. There was something she needed to do before she fell asleep. She shut her eyes. They were sore. When she opened them again, Mop had gone. She looked at the pile of boxes for a moment. Was she still in the hospital? Had they moved her bed again? Then, she remembered. She was in her own bed. She was in her new *very old* bedroom with two doors.

Mop had turned off the torches leaving them out of reach on the black mantelpiece. A lone candle flickered in a jam jar on the window sill. The fireplace looked like an empty mouth. The door was open.

There was a cold draught across Fin's face. It blew out the candle. Fin was too tired to be scared. She could see a dim light in Mop and Pop's room. Their door was wide open. They were moving about quietly, trying to reassemble their bed frame. Fin watched their shadows stretch and yawn until she fell asleep.

The bang of a hammer hitting the floor woke Fin up. It wasn't Mop and Pop and their bed frame. That task had been abandoned around 2 am. They'd spent the night on the mattress, on the floor.

Pop was grinning at Fin. "Sorry, love, but its past 10, time to get cracking," he said passing the hammer back to Mop. Mop was standing on Fin's window sill. Mop used the hammer's claw end to pull out long nails holding the mouldy boards across the window. Daylight flashed in, then disappeared. Mop wrenched the board back and forth.

"Don't try to pull it off in one go," said Pop. "You need to loosen it all the way round first."

"That'll take all day," puffed Mop, wiping her face.

"Better all day than a broken window," answered Pop.

Fin decided it was way too dangerous to stay in bed. She was likely to be sprayed with nails. She got up and went to the loo. The Victorian flush was loud, the pan filled with a cascade of rusty brown water. When she returned Mop and Pop were holding both sides of the board.

"Ready?"

"Ready."

Together they levered the old board down to reveal a large window made up of small pains of coloured glass.

"Wow," said Pop standing back. Fin stared. The window was so big it filled half the wall. Each pane gleamed through the dust. Fairy tale colours: blood red, midnight blue, poison purple. Bright shafts of coloured sunlight filled the room. Mop rushed out and returned with a plastic bucket filled with hot soapy water. She tore open a new pack of yellow sponges; flinging one at Fin. Fin pulled her sweatshirt over her head to hide her surprise. Mop usually moved so slowly these days. Together they rubbed and soaped, and rubbed and soaped again until their hands were raw. Then after an hour they stood back.

"I counted 18 different colours," said Mop.

"I've got 24," said Fin. "The pinks look the same but they're different, sort of watery, then a bit Barbie..." Mop smiled. Fin smiled. Mop didn't often smile. Sometimes Fin worried it was her own fault for being sick.

"I want to sit down and just look at it but there's so much to do..." said Mop. Fin leaned back on her bed. The sun warm on her arm. Mop sat down next to her and surprised Fin with a hug. They could hear Pop working his way round the house, boards and nails falling. The odd swear word thrown in. The outside of Fin's window looked like it had been sprayed with cow dung. It would need quite a clean by ladder. Fin wondered if Pop would let her do it?

Pop came back and peered through the smooth blue panes then the bubbly orange ones. He turned and looked at Mop.

"Come on let's stop for elevenses," he said. "I'll ask Guy to do the outside, later."

"I'll do it," said Fin. She didn't really want to spend the rest of the day scrubbing windows but it annoyed her the way Pop hadn't even considered her for the job. OK Guy was Ermine's 7 foot tall boyfriend but girls could use ladders too. Pop raised his eyebrows and glanced at Mop.

"Well, OK but no stunts, I'll set you up after you've eaten a proper breakfast."

By 11.30 Fin found herself outside up a ten-foot ladder, with a bucket of water, filled with Fairy Liquid and vinegar. She created a foul smelling cream she rubbed all over the panes. It was hard work. She couldn't just sweep her hand across the window. The lead got in the way. There was no way she could reach the top of the windows without asking Pop to extend the ladder, she was nervous enough as it was. And she would need a hose to remove the cack. It began to rain. Fin estimated it was about lunchtime and she'd only done half of her own window. She stopped to rub the back of her neck.

She had to keep squeezing round tree branches. She wanted to turn round and break them off. When a tree branch caught her again in the back of her head she did turn round; catching it in both hands bent it back and forth in a mighty temper. It didn't snap just bent about. Fin shouted at the tree. The tree didn't respond. She grabbed the bucket and hurled it at the tree trunk.

"Watch out," came an angry voice from below. Someone had been watching her performance. Fin peered down through the branches but couldn't see anyone. Then she caught the back of a boy? He was moving fast up one of the brick paths, long black hair swinging round his neck. A big brown dog lumbered after him. Fin had a feeling he was laughing at her but he didn't turn, so she couldn't be sure.

"And you can feck off, Stig," yelled Fin. Ermine opened Fin's window and leaned out. "What are you doing, Freak?" she asked. Fin was about to order Ermine out of her room when Guy appeared behind her.

"We'll help," he mumbled, staring out through the trees.

"Yeah, after lunch," snarled Ermine, banging the window shut. Fin wiped sweat off her forehead with her sleeve. She twisted round as far as she dared to see if the boy was still around. Fin wanted to wait until the dog had gone before she climbed down the ladder. The boy and the dog had vanished. Fin felt vaguely disappointed. All she could see was trees, more trees and long grass, criss-crossed by brick paths. Branches and brambles hid most of the graves from this angle. Fin was relieved her bedroom window didn't look directly into the graveyard.

Fin was starving. She stepped down the ladder and hurried into their new kitchen. She washed her hands and dried them on a spare tea towel. She helped herself to an open box of cornflakes on the table, sticking her hand in and dragging out a crunchy handful. Mop didn't notice. The kitchen was crowded and she was still unpacking cutlery. Fat Bastard growled from his cat box.

"I'll let him out at night, just in the kitchen, too early for outside," said Mop, dropping some knives. Fat Bastard swore. Mop leaned across the sink and pushed open the window. It was stiff. This window was just two colours, a sort of burnt orange and faded yellow. "Is that why it's called Blind Twin House?" asked Fin. Ermine stopped stirring tinned soup and looked at her.

"Well it's sort of blind, isn't it?" continued Fin. Guy nodded, laying out bowls.

"Yeah, s'ppose," he said, or something like it. Fin was never too sure what Guy said through his floppy hair.

"We can't see out and people can't see in," said Fin.

"Shouldn't there be a Twin House then?" said Ermine, sloshing tomato soup into the bowls and onto the table. Fin decided to stick with brown bread and butter, she hated tomato soup. She pulled open the bread bag and scanned the table for a clean knife. Mop couldn't find the spoons so everyone else had to hold up their bowls and slurp.

"There's another caretaker, perhaps there's another house?" said Mop. She went back to the window and tried to peer through the grubby glass.

"This colour blindness could get annoying. I can't see a bloody thing." Fin was glad the window didn't open very far. The big dog might still be outside.

"I saw someone," said Fin, buttering her bread.

"What d'you mean, you saw someone?" asked Ermine. She was always on the lookout for what she called perverts who might be staring at her. She seemed oblivious to the fact her pink dreadlocks and black Goth clothes attracted everyone's attention anyway.

"When I was up the ladder, I saw a boy with a dog." Ermine frowned and put down her slippery bowl. Mop began to clear the table, then stopped. There was nowhere to put the dirty dishes. There was still stuff everywhere.

"People walk their dogs here. It's like a park I suppose."

"What?" said Ermine "Like a park? Really? You're whistling in the dark."

After lunch Mop and Fin visited each room to make a to-do-job list. Fin took charge of the note book. She liked writing, she felt in control.

Her best friend Zelda said she was a control-freak but Gran disagreed when Fin told her.

"Your friend," Gran made the word friend sound like she was really saying the word enemy. Gran was good at that. "Your friend, *Zelda*" she made Zelda sound like a ridiculous name, "probably got that from the television; a lot of ignorant people think they learn from T.V. They don't." This was the end of it as far as Gran was concerned.

The rain continued softly for most of the afternoon but Guy and Ermine pressed on with the windows. Pop hammered around the house.

"Right, kitchen," said Mop. "Finish unpacking, wash up, find spoons." Fin added buy food, URGENT: bread, more soup, *not* tomato, Jaffa Cakes and Oreos. Since Mop was tired most of the time, Pop would pick up lists and plough through them. Several times he'd returned from the supermarket looking bemused with a box of black icing sugar or tinned lychees, Ermine had added to the list to test their fence for weak spots, as she called it.

"Important to know where the blind spots are, Freak," she explained to Fin in a friendly moment.

Next to the cooker was another tall black door leading to some rickety stairs down to the basement.

"We'll leave that for Pop," decided Mop. Fin wrote basement equals Pop. As they made their way into the hall Fin had an idea. She could use the list in her email to Zelda. After all Zelda was bragging about her new house in Australia. Maybe Fin could do the same? It wasn't just Zelda who had moved on.

1. Hall, very large, big enough to park a double decker bus.

To-do-job: pull up skanky lino, clean chess board floor.

2. Sitting room... Fin was enjoying herself. Later she could add how the rooms might look after a luxury make-over. Zelda wouldn't know they had no money for that.
3. Other sitting room, f'ugly green wall paper.

To-do-job: set up computer. Pop had placed Mop's desk in front of a long pink and green window.

"We need to find my chair," said Mop, looking into the crackly mirror above the fireplace. Pop appeared in the doorway.

"I need to inspect the taps," said Pop. "Fin can help. You put your feet up until we get back." Pop slipped on his wellies. "Get your trainers; we're going on an expedition."

Fin realised he meant outside. She passed the note book back to Mop. Fin preferred to stay indoors. She had been ill for so long she expected to spend her mornings in the kitchen wrapped in a quilt and her afternoons dozing in front of the television, her book sliding off her lap. But the television hadn't been set up. Ermine and Guy had de-boarded and cleaned most of the windows, but the rooms were cold and dark. The stained glass looked more like wine gums glued together, blocking the feeble winter light.

Fin couldn't find her coat. There were several heaps in each room to be sorted, ideally before Gran returned. Gran was a brisk helper, throwing out anything she thought was unnecessary. If she found a toy on the floor she binned it, she claimed to have learned this from Madonna.

"You're not telling me you knew Madonna, are you?" Ermine had shouted, after Gran binned her nail polish and eye-liner.

"No you daft cow, I read it in a magazine. Madonna said if you throw it away, you don't have to pick it up again. Sorted." Gran believed in throwing stuff out that stopped her travelling fast: hair-dryers, knick-knacks, umbrellas....

Mop passed Fin her old fleece, it smelt of Fat Bastard but it was warm. She followed Pop out into the drizzle. It was strange being outside in daylight. Last night, she sort of thought it would always be dark here. The trees were starting to lose their leaves. The sky was the usual London grey. The path was wet and covered in small twigs and leaves from a storm. Pop stopped at the gate and turned to look up at the house. Fin did the same. It was red brick with big dark windows. The stained glass looked almost black from outside.

"If we come back after dark those windows will be really pretty," Pop pointed out. Fin shuddered. She didn't want to come back after dark with something roaming about growling. Fin decided a practical plan was needed otherwise Pop would hatch some scheme that would involve them wondering here, there and everywhere to get the best view of the windows, after dark. His approach meant their family had an almost forensic knowledge of Kew, Battersea Park and Crystal Palace.

"When we visit the taps perhaps we need to look out for the... whatever it was, so it doesn't attack us again," said Fin.

Pop frowned. He'd forgotten.

"Eh? Attack's a bit strong, probably as frightened of us as we were of him, it... but you're right. If we've a feral dog on our hands we need to..." They both picked up a large stick, just in case. Fin could hear her heart beating.

They turned right at the weird roundabout. The path led up a gentle slope. There were fewer statues and more mausoleums here. Stone and marble temples the size of garden sheds. Some had urns; some had rusted metal doors with holes in. There was one near the top of the hill with no door. They were able to stand inside. Names coated small stone drawers running from floor to ceiling. Spiders' webs made hammocks in every corner and dry leaves crackled across the floor. There was a purple window overlooking the hill. Fin looked out across the broad field of graves. There were trees lining the paths with the odd cypress and palm dotted about. But no people or dogs as far as Fin could see.

Pop made some notes in his notebook and left, heading up towards a dripping tap. He fiddled about and then darted along the ridge towards another tap hung with three plastic milk bottles. Fin enjoyed watching the rain clouds, now purple because of the glass, but as Pop scurried further away she decided to catch up. The Mausoleum was very quiet and the spiders' webs were pretty big.

After an hour of following Pop from tap to tap, Fin decided to head back zigzagging along worn brick paths trying to avoid the bigger puddles. She left the stick in a rusty bin. Her hands were cold and muddy. The drizzle had stopped. Fin tried to find their house beneath the trees. It was difficult from up on the hill. It was like looking down onto a forest. She guessed the dense clump of trees to her left hid Blind Twin House. There was another dense clump to her right, near the boundary wall. Maybe there's another house? Fin headed down to have a closer look. At least she'd be out of the wind.

4

TWIN HOUSE

Fin was tired, her legs ached. She decided to cut across the yard through the graves. But the grass was spongy and uneven. It was also very long and wet, so her trainers kept getting caught. Once or twice she almost tripped on a headstone. Ermine would howl at that. Fin imagined the headline: Kid Killed by Grave. The graves were smaller here, just headstones really. Some had faded plastic flowers jammed into cracked jars. Some had enamelled photos stuck next to a name. Fin thought it odd, the black and white people smiled as if they were pleased to be there.

Why don't they say what they died of? Why? That's the most interesting part, thought Fin. Finally, she got back on a brick path, slick with rain and leaves. She followed the crisp packets swirling in the breeze to a bin and another tap. She was still high enough to look down on the traffic island or the grassy knoll as Pop now called it. She scanned the rest of the yard and then she saw it, another house. Fin had to investigate. She hurried down the path trying not to slip. Soon she was outside a house identical to their new, old house, except the windows were clear glass. It looked empty. There were no curtains, no lights, no people. She decided to peer in. It was difficult to see in the gloom, there was some furniture and in the kitchen a box of cornflakes obscured part of the window. Typical, her parents had managed to rent the weird place.

Fin heard a car. She leapt away from the glass but it was just the start of a funeral cortège. A long black limo slid past. The driver wearing a cap, nodded. It was followed by two more limos and then about five scrappy cars all rammed with overweight people. They all stared at her as if they didn't want to look ahead. Fin was trapped on the grass verge until the cars passed. Someone banged on the window behind Fin. She jumped, then decided she should pretend she hadn't heard. It was probably the other caretaker, a grumpy git who'd hate kids. Whoever it was banged again. Fin hunched up her shoulders offered a weak smile at the last car and darted behind it towards Blind Twin House.

A door opened behind her. A woman's voice called "Wait, *wait a minute.*" Fin scuttled under the trees. She felt bad. Her cheeks glowed. She waited under a dripping fir tree. A small woman emerged from the house in a blue boiler suit, she was frowning. Her hair was wrapped in a red scarf; she looked Chinese no Japanese Fin decided, though she wasn't sure why.

The woman called out something, looking towards the gate. Fin caught sight of the boy again with his dog. It was big. It came up to his waist. It had a long tail and a stripy back, stripy? Weird. The woman pointed to the dog and the house. The dog bounded in. The boy trudged in after it. Phew, Fin breathed out as the door shut. But now she could hear Pop calling. Despite the bereaved families heaving themselves out of the cars and adjusting black nylon skirts and brollies, Pop was yelling her name. Fin had no choice but to leave her hiding place and wave to make him stop. He smiled and waved, as if he'd just found her on a beach. Then he pointed towards the gate. Fin walked over to meet him. But he wasn't indicating the gate, he meant the house. Fin's stomach churned. She was bound to get told off for rudeness now. She arrived at the front door at the same time as Pop. It said Twin House in tile letters above the door. Pop rattled the letter box.

"Our new neighbours and my new boss," Pop pulled a face. The big dog ran towards the door, she could hear its nails scraping along a bare floor. It didn't bark as Fin expected. But she took a step back just in case. The dog waited, getting bigger in Fin's mind. When the door opened the woman in the boiler suit looked as scared as Fin. Pop thrust out his grubby hand. The woman took it more in surprise than courtesy.

"Hello, Hello. I'm the new caretaker, Jim Laurel, this is my daughter Fin... we moved in *Blind...*"he said, noticing the giant dog. "We moved in last night, well more last week really." The woman smiled blocking the doorway to stop the dog escaping.

"Zen," she yelled and looked behind her. Fin wondered if the boy was being called to translate. The boy sauntered down the hall and pulled the giant dog out from behind the door and dragged it into a side room, slamming the door behind him. The woman winced and gritted her teeth.

"Come in," the woman grimaced. "I too am caretaker. I am Hatsumi from Tokyo, Japan." She added. They followed her in. Pop put his hand on Fin's shoulder, letting her know he knew she was nervous about the dog, but that he was there. Fin's cheeks were red. She was sure both Hatsumi and the boy saw her run off. Odd name Zen but then he wasn't really going to be called *Stig of the Dump* was he?

Fin glanced at the shut door. It was covered in deep scratches made by big claw marks. She held her breath as she walked past, just in case it opened and the giant dog reappeared. At least the beast wasn't barking. The hall was the same as Blind Twin House except all the plaster cracks had been filled, creating soothing rivers and streams that snaked across bare walls.

The kitchen was warm. Twin House was the same as Blind Twin House except smaller. It felt cosy. Fin wondered if there were other houses, each one smaller than the last, like a set of Russian dolls.

"Miso or Tea?" said Hatsumi waving a silver kettle under the tap.

"Oh tea's fine, isn't it, plum?" said Pop. He was admiring the walls by rubbing his hand along them. "Professional job," he muttered.

Hatsumi opened her mouth as if to say something, then stopped. Fin was disappointed she had no idea what Miso was but it sounded better than boring tea.

"Sit, sit," Hatsumi pointed to the kitchen table.

Pop cleared his throat and sat down, drumming his hands on the table.

Hatsumi moved around the kitchen. Fin kept looking behind her, the hall was dark. There was no sound of boy or dog. Hatsumi placed a plain white mug in front of Fin and pushed a packet of Garibaldi biscuits towards her. The packet wasn't open. So Fin hung back waiting for Pop to start but he was still mesmerised by the bare walls. Hatsumi and Pop started to talk at once. Fin considered it was now or never. She leaned across and slit open the biscuits. She broke off two; three would look greedy, probably the boy and dog would finish the rest.

"Did you strip the walls?" asked Pop. Hatsumi poured boiling water into a white tea pot.

"Council did that and new radiators, but I did filling," said Hatsumi, smiling. She scanned the draining board for the tea pot lid. Fin spotted it on the table. She picked it up for Hatsumi. Hatsumi grinned. Fin felt good, in the past she would have been too shy to do that but since meeting lots of people in hospital she did more stuff. Hatsumi filled up their mugs but didn't add milk or sit down. Large tea leaves floated across the surface of the tea and a yellow flower unfurled. Hatsumi glanced about as if something was missing. Fin thought she looked more like a visitor than they did. Pop nodded. He slurped his tea. Fin decided to eat the Garibaldis while she had the chance. They were brittle then chewy.

"Well, I believe as senior caretaker you're my new boss, so I thought I should come over... I took a look at some of the taps this morning, hope you don't mind?" said Pop. "I suppose we'll need to meet and..."

Hatsumi frowned. "Maybe mistake?" She shook her head and fiddled with a teaspoon. "Old gentleman who lived here, died suddenly." Pop started to say something but Hatsumi put up her small hand to stop him.

"He old man, 97 or even 100. When I came two year ago, he my boss. I help him at home, in yard, but he got sick, he went hospital.

We stayed with Ty, dog; run the place," she waved a teaspoon towards the window. "He was boss... that make us co-workers," she smiled at Pop.

"Oh, OK," Pop said. For a moment they all stared out of the clean clear window, to the fir trees beyond. Fin liked the view it was like sitting in a forest.

5

FIN AND ZEN MEET AGAIN

Over the next week Fin saw Zen in the distance, usually up the hill. Zen's dog scroffled in the long grass. Fin put her head down and walked the other way a few times. However, as the paths either led to the main gate or up the hill she often found herself heading towards him again. He was long gone by the time she arrived. Once she caught him looking back at her, just before he turned towards Twin House. Fin thought they would continue missing one another. She was still too tired and ill to walk very far and he was obviously some sort of loser.

Early on a cold Sunday morning Fin discovered the Avenue of Victorian Inventors Pop had raved about for the last week. The Victorian Inventors' headstones had been chiselled in the shape of their inventions. But there were too many brambles to see what the shapes were meant to be. Fin pulled some of the brambles apart taking care not to catch her gloves on the thorns. This was tricky as the branches were springy. She tried standing on some but as she moved forward the brambles spiked into the bottom of her boots. She stumbled and scratched her face. Fin gave up in temper, her face smarting. She glimpsed a stone post box and a marble sewing machine. Not very interesting. Pop suggested there might be a Jelly

Baby or an Easter egg or even an ice-cream. But Fin listed the Avenue as another disappointment.

She headed towards the Mausoleums. She was nervous here on her own but she was also bored after the disappointment of the Victorian Inventors. And the house was so cold; walking was the only way to keep warm. The mausoleums looked like small stone houses with dark doorways, curving away up the hill. It was extra quiet. The stone boxes shut out the wind. It started to rain. There would be some shelter there. It was like living in a black and white movie. The world was so grey. She could see green and brown but she couldn't feel the colours, as there was no sun. Lord Basel's mausoleum was the biggest. It had a large gate made of twisted metal. Fin peered through. She realised she was being watched. Her neck prickled. She decided to pretend she didn't know. But she began to walk faster towards the end of the path. She was annoyed with herself. Mop and Pop had always told them if they were out alone to stick to well-lit streets with cars and people about. She was nearly there. However, the last lap was ringed with five open doorways black like broken teeth. Fin tried not to look inside.

She slipped on some wet leaves and almost fell but righted herself in time to come face to face with Ty. The giant dog stared. He was far bigger than she remembered. His head was wide and his body taught. He watched her. Fin stood very still, she knew from some book or other you weren't meant to stare directly at dogs as this was aggressive. So she narrowed her eyes and tried to look away. But she was too frightened. What if he sprang at her throat? She began to sweat. Her mouth went dry. She really didn't know what to do. Her legs wobbled. What if I faint? Don't faint, don't faint, don't. She remembered half a story about a woman who fainted. Her dog ate her face.

Ty didn't bark. Instead he made a giant yawn. His mouth got longer and longer. It made him look bigger and bigger. Maybe she could say "Hello, Ty." Would he even remember her? But her voice had gone. Her mouth was so dry even her lips were cracking. Then Zen appeared jumping on to the path, as if he had been running. Ty looked at Zen and shut his mouth.

"Bad boy," said Zen, raising his hand. Ty put his head down and put on a face that made Fin want to laugh. A sort of trying-to-look-innocent face; sheepish Gran would call it. Fin moved forward and stroked his wide heavy head. She was still shaky but she didn't want the boy, Zen, to know how scared she'd been. She moved her tongue to find some spit.

"He smells of wet biscuits, he was only yawning at me by the way," managed Fin, trying to sound confident. She was relieved the boy was there and in control. Ty now looked like a big stuffed toy; well one made in a factory where they hadn't seen dogs before. Ty enjoyed her scratching at his ears. He moved his greasy head around as if to say: look someone appreciates me.

Zen scowled. Fin wondered if Zen didn't want to share, probably a spoilt only child, who always had his own bedroom. Zen thrust his hands into his jacket pockets and whistled. Ty left, pushing past Fin stepping on one of her feet.

"Ow," she said. Zen turned and marched off. Ty followed without even looking back. "Jeez," said Fin "how rude." Boy and dog disappeared between crumbling pillars. Fin wished she had said something loud and rude. She headed off in the opposite direction.

Fin decided she wouldn't bother even being polite if she saw Zen, or Stig, as she was back to calling him. She didn't expect to see him again anyway. If she saw him or he saw her they would just go another way. However, that was before her accident.

Fin knew what hard meant now. Black, everything was black. Then her head really hurt. Her back hurt too. Odd shapes swirled and swam into the black, like deep sea creatures. Then there was an eruption from her stomach and mouth. She turned her sore head and was sick across a muddy marble floor. She sat up feeling very shaky. Her whole body was shaking; her head hurt, her eyes recoiled from the light. She squeezed them shut. Then, opened them again. She looked around. The floor was littered with rotten wood, splinters and sick. There was a Fin sized hole in the roof. She felt the back of her head. She imagined a hole but it just felt bruised. She stood up slowly. She had to bend over, leaning with her hands on her knees to steady herself.

She hurled again, this time forcing out bitter green bile. She thought she hadn't broken any bones but maybe she had internal bleeding. She could fill up like a bloated blood bag and burst. She'd fallen through the roof.

Fin glanced about moving her head slowly. Pain zithered across her brain, she felt dizzy. In front of her was an arched door, sickly pink glass filtering the daylight. Beyond there was a porch barred by a metal grill. To her sides were two small arched windows, pale green. Most of the panes were cracked. About half were missing; a cold breeze pushed its way in. Dead flies were piled up on the sills. She turned slowly. On the wall opposite brass plaques had been screwed to the wall:

Lord Peter Bartholomew Basel 1830-1900

Lady Anne Lily Basel 1840-1865

Peter Basel 1855-1866

Bartholomew 1853-1953

Mary-Bertha 1835-1910

Fin stepped over the wood and rattled the door. To her relief it opened easily. She stepped out into the porch. She could see the trees waving in the wind. She stepped on the dried leaves coating the floor. They crackled. She turned the grill handle, holding her breath. The gate was locked. The gap above was too small even for birds or bats to fly in. She was trapped.

"Help," she called in a half-hearted way. She felt a right fool. Her head throbbed. Ermine would crow about this: trying to bury yourself were you? Pop wouldn't be very happy about the damages. She tried again but her voice was swallowed by the marble walls. Fin called louder and rattled at the gate. She listened for the bin cart. Maybe Pop might suddenly appear checking obscure taps for leaks. But it might be the time of day he went to the D.I.Y store for supplies. Fin's head hurt too much to really yell. So she turned and went back inside pushing the door almost shut. It was cold and it was getting dark. She sat down with her back to the side wall. She used her trainers to push as much sick and splintered wood away from where she sat. She'd have to wait it out. When they realised she was late for tea they would come and find her. Wouldn't they? But that was hours away? She was hungry now with a very empty stomach. She tried to remember what

Pop had said about Lord Basel but she was too sore and hungry to concentrate, a bad sign.

Branches tapped the glass. There was a patter of rain. Drops fell on her face. Fin shifted about to keep dry. She had forgotten all about the hole she'd made in the roof. Pop was so gung-ho about the whole yard project he would probably get her to fix it. Now and again she heard scuttling. A mouse? A rat? The wind in the leaves? It sounded like a large rat with a crisp packet. Lucky rat. Fin liked the idea of rats. They were intelligent and friendly looking at least in her mind, but she'd never really met one up close.

The wind changed direction. Fin heard a weird yipping sound. When the wind changed again Fin was relieved to hear something normal: cars on the main road, or civilisation as Ermine called it. When Ermine went out Mop would ask where she was going.

"Civilisation," Ermine would shout slamming the door.

Fin was comforted by the city hum. She'd grown up with it like a distant sea. It reminded her of their old house in a *normal* road, in a *normal* street. Not this living in a graveyard. They all called it the yard now; saying graveyard took too much explaining to *normal* people. It was embarrassing. Fin worried about going back to school. She'd never hear the end of it. And with Zelda gone she'd be on her own.

It was dark. Mop and Pop were nearby or so Fin told herself. But why didn't they come with torches. It must be teatime by now. There was some glow from the hospital lights but they cast shadows through the trees so the light moved about. Fin wondered if they'd missed her. After all she'd been in hospital so long they might forget to miss her. Being invisible was overrated.

In a way they hadn't missed her. Pop and Hatsumi were on a roll. There was so much catching up to do. Hatsumi had made several bowls of steaming Miso while they spent the morning making a list of jobs. They'd spent the afternoon at the D.I.Y store then back to Twin House for more listing and planning. By teatime they'd moved onto research. Pop was even showing Hatsumi Lord Basel's Wikipedia page. It was only when Zen appeared looking glummer than usual, he was very hungry, Pop realised it was dark outside. He should head off.

Meanwhile Mop had been busy cleaning and unpacking the last of their stuff. Mop had a theory that once the house was really clean, they had their cups in the kitchen, Gran's samovar on the side board and the rugs out, the house would look different. It looked the same. Unless they won the lottery, which they wouldn't because they didn't bother to do it anymore, the house would continue to look the same. Mop felt it was scowling at her like an angry giant she'd disturbed. She stopped when Gran arrived with ginger biscuits and offered to brew up. Gran was in a good mood about the samovar.

"It just don't sit right in sheltered accommodation," she sighed. The warden, mad Maggie, as Gran called her, asked if it'd set the place afire. Mop sank onto a kitchen chair. Pop appeared looking sheepish. Everyone declared they were too tired to cook. Well Pop was too tired to cook and Gran was too tired to pretend her daughter's food was edible. Hot buttery toast was the only solution.

"Where's Ermine?" asked Gran.

"She's staying at Abimbola's, apparently," said Mop, "it's warmer there."

"Not surprised," shuddered Gran.

"They've got a bath which bubbles," Pop added.

Mop and Gran both frowned the same frown. "That sort of decadence gets you into trouble," said Gran darkly. Mop looked around, something was missing. Fat Bastard had been freed from his cat box. He'd spent the morning pooing in the corner of the kitchen rather than use the kitty litter. It was a dirty protest because he wasn't yet allowed outside. Mop went into the hall. Away from the kitchen fire the temperature dropped to very cold indeed. She pulled her cardigan across her apron.

"Fin," she yelled. "Fin, FIN."

"Did she help you with the taps today?" asked Mop, returning to the warm kitchen. Pop was miles away peering at the now black stained glass.

"I wonder what we look like from outside? What did you say?" he turned to Mop. "Did Fin enjoy helping with the taps?" Pop frowned.

"She didn't come out with me... I thought she'd changed her mind."

Mop was already in the hall. She took the stairs two at a time and burst into Fin's room. It was empty, the fire had gone out.

"Fin," Mop yelled again, checking the linen cupboard and bathroom.

Mop clattered up the stairs to Ermine's room, hoping to find Fin moping. Pop was in the hall with his torch. Gran limped to the kitchen door.

"When did you last see her?" she wheezed.

"She went after Pop... *this morning*," said Mop hurrying back down the stairs.

"*This morning?*" shouted Pop. "That was hours ago... Christ, go phone the police on the main road. I'll look for her."

Mop was pulling on her frayed coat. "Where?" she said, biting her lower lip.

"There." Pop pointed the torch towards the black yard.

"Maybe she's with her friends," Pop muttered jamming his feet back into his wellies. Mop was half way out the door.

"She doesn't have any friends," she said and started to cry.

"I'll stay here," said Gran. "When Fin comes back I'll burn her some toast."

Pop stared at Gran as if he had only just realised she was there. He nodded then disappeared into the night. The yard was very dark. The moon was buried by a blanket of cloud. The orange lights from the main road cast a hazy glow that seeped over the wall on a thin fog. Mop was already at the main gate, poking her phone. Pop shot past her.

"See if Hatsumi can help," he shouted.

Mop finished her call. It felt like forever, the operator had so many questions before Mop could shout "My daughter's missing just send someone now, please." By the time Zen answered the door Mop was sobbing. Hatsumi was in the bath. He stood there staring as Mop apologised and tried to stop crying. The oven timer went off.

"Mum's in the bath, eh come in?" He turned, left her on the porch, and sprinted to the oven. Ty sat by the door banging his tail on the floor, possibly looking friendly or looking for the best place to bite. Mop couldn't tell. She stepped in anyway and pushed the door shut. Ty padded off after Zen. The house was warm. Mop followed Ty into the kitchen. Zen was standing the other side of the table holding a large pizza.

"Fin's gone missing," blurted Mop. "We wondered if... you'd seen her *today*... in the yard?" Zen stared. Mop wondered if he'd understood her. She remembered she had never seen him speak.

She started again. "My daughter Elfin has disappeared..." she was interrupted by Hatsumi calling down the banisters:

"Hello, Zen, someone there?" Mop went back into the hall. Ty and Zen hurried past and out the front door.

Mop called up the stairs. "Sorry to get you out of the bath but..." Hatsumi came down wrapping a ratty man's bathrobe round her tiny waist, her long hair dripping down her shoulders.

"Fin's disappeared, we were wondering if..." Hatsumi turned round and ran back up the stairs. Mop decided she needed to get back to the yard.

"What a bunch..."

"Wait," Hatsumi yelled from the open bathroom window. A naked Hatsumi was jumping into jeans; dragging on a sweatshirt and wrapping her wet hair in a towel, all at the same time.

"Take keys," she shouted, fishing them out of her jeans pocket and throwing them to Mop. They landed on the ground. Mop picked them up.

"We take bin cart," shouted a breathless Hatsumi, banging the front door shut.

Ty kept close to Zen. He sensed the boy was tense. He kept looking ahead. Then up at Zen for a signal. Zen headed up towards the hospital. Zen had a gut feeling. Ty started to make quick forays in and out of the undergrowth, rampaging back and forth. Zen stopped at Mausoleum row. He usually avoided this place, too easy for an ambush, too closed in, and with all the carved, curling stone a bit too girly. Just the sort of place a dippy girl would go poking about, exploring.

"Hello, anyone there?" called Zen. He worried. Some bad lads hung about here smoking now and again. There was no reply, only the wind in the trees. Zen preferred to go round behind the mausoleums but it was too dark, too overgrown and too slow. He'd have to walk between them. Anyway Ty was with him. If he caught a whiff of fag smoke he'd leg it. Those lads had knives. Ty made his loud cough bark. A fox stared insolently at them from the path then trotted off.

"Come on," hissed a sweating Zen, starting down the isolated path.

Fin was very cold. She knew she should move around to keep warm. But her head hurt and she felt sick so she didn't. She'd shouted out as loud as she could. For a while now she had been curled up on the dry leaves. This was better than sitting in cold sick. Her bladder hurt. Maybe she was going to be here all night. Something warm and smooth touched her hand. Fin looked down and saw a snake. Or thought she did. She leapt up, flung open the door and tried to climb the grill.

"Help, HELP," she screamed.

Zen hadn't made it very far down the row. He was trying to peer into each mausoleum. They got gloomier as he travelled across the row from one to another. Sombre black marble contrasted with the mouldy white insides. It was like looking into the belly of a dead whale. Most were shrouded in ivy and brambles, urns ran round the tops like blocked chimneys. One or two contained life size figures lying down with their hands clasped together.

He jumped when he heard Fin yell. Ty shot ahead, and then stopped to paw the ground. Fin saw Ty. He pushed his nose close to her hand. She could feel his warm breath and smell his wet biscuit smell. His eyes were large; he seemed to be trying to figure out why she was there. Fin felt so happy she was about to tell him, when Zen appeared.

"Hi" he said, rummaging around in his coat pocket. For one mad moment Fin thought he had a key. She stepped off the grill. But Zen thrust a half-eaten Mars bar towards her. Fin considered it then took a huge bite. Thick, sweet, gooey caramel filled her mouth. Zen tried the gate and looked up for a way in. Ty opened his jaw. At first Fin thought he wanted some of the chocolate but she'd just rammed the last corner into her mouth. But Ty was staring at something behind her. His jaw continued to gape. His short hair stood up. Fin pushed herself into the bars and began to panic. Zen looked at Ty and shone his torch into the gloom.

"What is it?" squeaked Fin.

"It's..."Zen paused flashing the torch this way and that.

"It's nothing, there's nothing there." He stepped back. Fin tried to grab his coat. "Please," she said turning to half look round.

"Don't leave me here. I can't get out."

"I'm not leaving you, I was going to call out for your..." he stopped. Ty was pacing up and down his head held low, his eyes intent.

"Stop it," said Zen sharply. Ty ignored him. "How did you get in there anyway?"

"Fell through the roof."

Zen raised his eyebrows. He looked impressed.

"S' OK all we need..." said Zen, leaning back "is some rope and a ladder." He pulled Ty's neck. "Ty'll stay here. I'll get your mum."

Fin stuck her hand out. "Leave the torch." Zen pushed it through.

"Chill. I'll just go to the end of the row and yell. Someone'll hear. Ty'll stay."

Zen walked backwards. Then hurried to the end of the row and began yelling. Hatsumi and Mop arrived from one end and Pop the other. Fin was stiff with fear. She was convinced Ty had seen a ghost. He continued pacing. It wasn't until Fin had everyone's torches trained on every inch of the mausoleum she began to calm down. Hatsumi and Zen went back to Twin House for a ladder. Pop went back to Blind Twin House for rope. Mop stayed with Fin and suggested she used the pause to go to the loo in the corner but Fin just refused. Yuck.

After hours of nothing, everything happened very quickly. Pop rigged up a rope harness. Fin put her head and arms through. She needed no persuasion. Ghosts, snakes and Mop's pee suggestion all made Fin very keen to get out, fast. Pop used a tree trunk for traction. He balanced on the corner of the mausoleum walls and began to haul.

Hatsumi, Mop and Zen stood on the ground, pulling the rope taught, away from the mausoleum.

By the time Fin was standing on the brick path two bemused police officers had arrived. Ermine and Abimbola had shown them the way. The police officers were cautious at first, one held onto his radio. Mop and Hatsumi explained, filling in any gaps left by the other. Fin was taken to A & E for a check-up in the police car with Pop. After hours under bright lights she was allowed home.

It was a relief to shut her bedroom door and crawl into bed. Mop had made up the fire and put a hot water bottle under the quilt. Tea lights burned in jam jars along the mantel piece. There was a knock at the door and to Fin's surprise in walked Zen carrying two mugs of scalding hot chocolate. Fin was glad she had her good blue pyjamas on. Ty stood in the doorway looking sad. Zen put the chocolate down on her bedside table. The clock ticked and chimed 4 a.m. Fin hadn't been up this late or early since she first went into hospital. Zen looked round.

Fin thought he was looking for a chair.

"D'you mind if Ty comes in?" he said. Fin shook her head. Ty padded in and came right up to the bed. He looked at her, then walked over to the fire. He turned round several times then finding the right angle he lay down with his giant head on his large paws and fell asleep. Fin was proud of herself for not being nervous but she felt woozy after her hospital medication. Her eye lids began to close. She was fighting sleep. This was too interesting and weird to miss: a strange boy in her room and an even stranger dog. She made a note to ask Zen what sort of dog Ty was and why Zen didn't go to school? Did he have some sort of weird illness too? She hoped it wasn't cancer, perhaps Ty had cancer and Zen was keeping him company in his last painful months? Fin didn't know which question to start with. He was a boy after all.

6

HOME-SCHOOL

Mop helped Fin out of bed later that day, telling her the short walk to Twin House would be good for them both. This was how Mop used to be, always rushing about. In the last year she'd moved like someone in slow motion, even her talking was slow. Zelda said her mum should go to the doctor as it was probably a brain tumour. Fin asked Gran. Gran said not to worry it was just The Sorrow.

"We Russians are good at sorrow; it doesn't kill us, unlike the vodka. Fin worried less because Mop didn't drink vodka.

"It'll be easier to show you," said Hatsumi when Mop asked yet another question about Twin House. Fin had been waiting for the Miso but Hatsumi kept getting distracted around the kitchen. Hatsumi put her hands on her hips. Fin and Mop stood up again.

"Long story short, I live here with Zen and Ty. And you two are new neighbours. Very pleased." Hatsumi smiled. Her eyes crinkled.

They didn't get very far with the tour because Hatsumi stopped in the doorway.

"Now this is hall and this..." Fin followed. The rooms were sort off the same as Blind Twin House, except here all the walls were bare. No giant insect patterns to frighten the bejesus out of visitors thought Fin. Fin rubbed her hands over the filled plaster streams and rivers. It was like some sort of ancient map. Fin liked their rough feel. The old lino had been pulled back and thrown away to reveal black and white tiles. Three rooms were empty and echoed as they walked in. The room with the boy and dog in was different.

When Hatsumi opened the door Fin couldn't see the boy at first. It was getting dark again outside, the room was darker still. The only light came from an open fire, some dry twigs crackled.

"Zen," said Hatsumi. The boy raised his head and nodded. Mop said hi, the giant dog looked up. He was lying in front of the fire, like a lion. He started to yawn, his mouth grew. Fin thought he might dislocate his jaw.

"Stop it, Ty," Zen said. The dog snapped his jaws shut, his teeth cracking. Zen stood up. He waited for them to go, a pile of battered comics scattered the floor.

Here and there dark wood furniture gleamed. There was a scuffed leather armchair with a pile of newspapers on one side high enough to form a table.

"Do you like to read?" said Hatsumi.

Fin realised Hatsumi was looking at her, then back to the comics.

Mop jumped in: "Blimey does she, since she's been off school we've been to the library twice a week." Fin cringed. They had only been to the library twice because Mop forgot a bag of shopping.

"I bet you read novel not comic," said Hatsumi.

"Yeah but comics too," said Fin. She wasn't a complete nerd.

Fin was going to tell Hatsumi about the comic book she'd made with Zelda. Even the boys said it was cool. But Hatsumi continued. "Zen only read comics and he refuse school. I get visit from council, maybe court." They all looked at Zen. He looked a bit taller now he was a criminal. Zen returned a stony face. Ty lay on his side.

"Since father die." Hatsumi crossed the room and returned with a framed photo. Fin and Mop peered at it. Zen sighed and sat down, going back to his comics. There was a man in army uniform smiling. Fin thought he looked like an Inuit with his broad brown face. Hatsumi stood next to him like a pretty doll holding a small boy who scowled at the camera. Mop began to tear up.

"God I'm so sorry. Was he killed on duty?"

"Accident," whispered Hatsumi. Fin saw that tears were streaming down her face.

Mop took the photo frame and passed it to Fin. She wrapped Hatsumi in a giant hug. Fin felt embarrassed and glad at the same time. What if Hatsumi had cried without Mop there? Fin stood like a dufus. Zen stood up again. Fin stepped forward and gave him the photo back. He took it and placed back on the mantel piece.

Hatsumi tried to break out of Mop's hug.

"Sorry, so sorry, very pleased to..." she sobbed.

Fin felt her eyes water.

"Come and sit down" said Mop leading Hatsumi to the chair. Ty looked up and lumbered up out of the way. He pushed past Mop and put his head in Hatsumi's lap. She laughed and began to cry again.

"Not even my dog or my chair," she choked out.

Mop looked round and found a chair. She pulled it up to Hatsumi.

"Zem," she said "Can you make your mum a cup of tea? Fin you can help."

"It's Zen not Zem," muttered Fin.

Fin followed Zen into the kitchen. He didn't say anything, just boiled the kettle. Fin took some clean mugs off the draining board. Zen passed her a black plastic tray. When they returned Hatsumi sat quietly. Mop held her hand.

"We went to supermarket, very busy, very late," Hatsumi was saying. Fin thought it was the beginning of one of those: I'm so tired parent moans. It was not.

"I put Zen in car seat, safe. Load up boot. Husband drop off trolley and come back. Busy woman in Golf reverse into him, banged head, end of story. Never injured when Ghurkha soldier. So we come here. Now court maybe." Mop passed her the tea. They all drank in silence.

"I can help with the court letters if you like," said Mop. "And I've had half an idea about school, just thinking aloud..." She paused while Hatsumi sipped her tea. "Fin's off school and Zem. They could be home-schooled." Hatsumi frowned "Just for a while," added Mop. "But if you don't think that's..."

"No. Good idea, but is expensive?"

"Well," said Mop leaning in and warming to her subject. "It would be free, we could teach Zem..."

"It's Zen," said Fin "ZEN not Zem" before Mop could finish her plan.

"Oh sorry," said Mop. "Zen."

Fin and Zen looked at one another, both of them thinking fast. Fin needed to list as many objections as possible. Hatsumi sniffed and smiled "Is good idea."

The rest of the house was bare. Zen's room was the same room as Fin's but painted in pink undercoat. Fin had the better deal. Pink yuck. Fin was disappointed it had no other mystery door. But the ceiling swayed with origami birds: swans, cranes, swallows.

"That's beautiful," Fin said.

"We make them, I can teach, or Zen you can teach," said Hatsumi.

"Oh yes please," said Mop jumping in. Unusually Mop then stopped and looked at Fin.

"It'd be cool but it looks really difficult," said Fin.

"No is skilled but not difficult," said Hatsumi.

Fin was glad to admire the ceiling it meant she could politely pretend she hadn't seen the pile of dirty clothes strewn across the floor. Zen and Ty were following them like reluctant tourists in their own house.

"I was architect student in Japan. Then I meet Zen's Dad," said Hatsumi leading them out of Zen's room towards the dark narrow stairs. Fin didn't think that explained very much but Mop was nodding in sympathy even though Hatsumi couldn't see her. Fin had been banned from Ermine's room or the skip as she called it since they'd settled in.

In the attic, Hatsumi clicked on an angle poise lamp over a desk piled with folders, paper and a laptop. It was smaller than Ermine's room. The white walls made Fin feel as if she was standing inside a cake box. Again there was very little furniture just a large trestle table like the kind Pop used for wallpapering. A bare bulb dangled from the ceiling. In the dark Fin had the impression the table was covered in piles of paper but in the lamp light she could see the table was covered in an origami city.

Both Mop and Fin let out a wow. Soon they were peering into paper apartment buildings with roof terraces and herons. There were traditional Japanese paper houses with cats and several box houses where the sliding internal walls could be altered depending on the size of your family. Hatsumi was especially proud showing them these. They were her own evolving design, she said. The lamp light shone through the paper windows casting shadows and silhouettes across other buildings. Zen hung back by the door holding Ty's collar. Fin wondered if he was sulking because he wasn't used to sharing his mum.

"I have to work up here so Ty doesn't eat them," said Hatsumi.

Fin noticed in almost every street there was an animal you wouldn't find in a street even in London. There was a smooth elephant, a lion with a frilly main and a smiling whale.

"Do zoo animals roam about the streets in Japan?" asked Fin.

"What?" said Hatsumi.

Fin pointed to a tiny kangaroo waiting at a crossing.

"No, I made those," said Zen. They all looked at him. "It's for the scale."

Fin had the feeling he wanted to explain more but Ty was trying to pull him into the room. So he yanked the collar and dragged Ty down the stairs. Fin felt vaguely disappointed. She stared at the empty doorway. Mop and Hatsumi carried on talking.

"If I get good idea I design it on the computer but build it too with paper, like Gaudi. One of my designs won award in Korea, maybe they build it, garden library." Then "Sorry, sorry, sorry," Hatsumi was waving her hands "Been so long since I meet people, show work." She turned and glanced towards the dark portholes. "Yard work was too much, Zen good boy except school business..."Hatsumi looked very sad. She stared at the paper city as if she had lost something but couldn't quite remember what.

"Well we're here now, aren't we Fin," said Mop sounding a lot more confident then she had in a long time.

"Yes," nodded Fin. Fin didn't want to agree to home-school under any circumstances but if Hatsumi taught origami it wouldn't be so bad.

"Look, we've been here long enough. Why don't you and Zem, Zen come across to us for some food," said Mop. Hatsumi glanced up, she looked tired.

"Come over now to Blind Twin House for supper, dinner?" said Mop.

"Maybe another time, soon," said Hatsumi, leading them back to the stairs. Fin was glad Hatsumi had refused. God only knew what concoction Mop would stir up. Probably the sulky boy would refuse to come anyway.

Suddenly they were outside in the cold dark. Fin realised she missed the chance to ask Hatsumi why their houses had such weird names. She glanced back. The lamp was still on. The portholes glowed yellow through the bare trees.

7

SETTLING IN, ALMOST

Back at Blind Twin House things looked better, or rather less terrible. Ermine had invited Guy round. He was in the kitchen rolling a fag, a tobacco tin balanced on his knee. His floppy hair covered half his face. He nodded in their direction. The kitchen smelled of warm cheese. Ermine was at the sink washing up. She was wearing a spattered apron over her pub crawl gear. Her pink dreadlocks were wrapped into doughnut shapes above her ears showing her bare shoulders above a black leather corset. She glanced at Mop and Fin.

"I've made lasagne," she said "Ready in 20 minutes." She sponged the draining board rubbing off the lunchtime debris.

"Fin," she said, sloshing her gloved hands back in the bowl. "Can you find Guy a bin bag for all the laundry? We'll go to the launderette tomorrow."

Ermine always behaved better when Guy came over. She was also hoping to go out without any fuss. Helping softened up Mop and Pop.

"Sure," said Fin. She didn't give Guy time to finish his fag and store it in his tin. She didn't want him ramming her dirty knickers into a rubbish bag. Ermine ran the cold tap, rinsing plates.

Pop called that American washing up. He just dunked plates then left them on the draining board. So the next meal had a green, soapy taste.

Within a short time the kitchen was transformed. Though very little was said they all worked as if they were in some sort of television clean-up programme. Ermine washed up and cleaned the sink until the taps shone. Fin filled five bin bags for the launderette. Guy emptied and then filled the grate with newspaper faggots and chunks of wood. Pop joined in folding and cutting up cardboard boxes for recycling. Mop had a bath.

When Mop reappeared, a towel round her head; the kitchen was warm and cosy. Ermine dished out the lasagne with baked potatoes. The potatoes were soft and buttery. Mop rummaged around and found some tins of rice pudding. Guy took charge of these while Ermine and Fin hunted for jam and chocolate to put on top. Fin did better by finding a tin of golden syrup.

"Thank you," Mop said. "You've given me energy to make another list, at least."

"I'll do it," said Fin. She wanted to add golden syrup to the list. She loved the way it magnified the lumpy rice and its thick, burnt sugary taste. It stayed on her tongue long after she'd finished it. She hadn't finished the rice pudding. She was too full.

Over the next few days Pop and Hatsumi worked their way round the yard, checking taps, making lists about what needed to be fixed and shifted. They even spent a day down at the town hall seeing various people for forms, documents and contacts. Mop carried on setting up Blind Twin House.

Fin explored outside. Fin thought the less Mop saw her, the less likely she was to remember the home-school scheme. Fin was getting better though she still got very tired. The huge staircase didn't help. She was out of breath by the second turn. Why did the house have so many stairs? She was glad she didn't have Ermine's attic. Ermine was up there all alone. It was still spooky despite the three chains of white fairy lights Ermine strung round the walls. Fin suspected it was because she was afraid of the dark and didn't want to look a total wimp.

Fin woke up or thought she did. She might still be dreaming. Maybe the ceiling would turn back into melting ice cream dribbling on to her face. She rubbed her chin it was cold and slick with drool. Yuck. She yanked the edge of her quilt and began to rub her face hard. She was awake. She hated being awake alone at night. Whatever lurked about in corners and shadows was bound to pick on children who weren't asleep. Mop and Pop could wake up tomorrow and find her... a hand caught her quilt. Fin yelped. She half leapt, half rolled off the edge of her bed. She banged her elbow on the floor.

"Oww."

"Fin, what are you doing?" asked Mop

Fin sat up and rubbed her elbow. She was about to ask Mop the same silly question. But Mop was hurrying around the room, blowing out tea lights and picking up clothes. Fin frowned and stayed put. It was the middle of the night.

"Hurry up. There's been an explosion or gas leak or something on the main road. We're being evacuated..."Mop leaned back over the bed, dropping Fin's sweatshirt and trainers on to her lap.

"Oww" Fin said again.

"Sorry, but you need to hurry up. It looks like the Blitz on the main road..." Mop was heading off towards the door.

"Ermine, ERMINE," she yelled.

Fin stood up. She had a feeling Ermine was still out clubbing. She smiled in the darkness; ice cream and fear forgotten.

"Grounded much," she muttered, pulling her sweatshirt over her head.

"Ermine, FIN hurry up..." Mop shot up Ermine's stairs. Fin jammed on her trainers.

Mop clattered back looking scared. She was trying to ram her arm into her bobbly jumper. She grabbed Fin's arm.

"Where's Ermine?"

Before Fin could answer, Pop shouted from the hall.

"Hurry up, Radio says it's a sink hole..."

Within minutes they'd joined Hatsumi, Zen and Ty and most of their neighbours heading along the High Street. Fin shivered. It wasn't that cold but all these people moving fast made her scared. The street lights went out.

Fin stopped by a lamppost. The crowd parted around her. Zen stopped next to her holding Ty's collar. Why didn't he have a lead? Wasn't that illegal or something? They waited for Mop, Pop and Hatsumi.

"Where the devil's Ermine?" fumed Pop.

"Probably out with Guy or Abimbola," said Mop trying again to make her bulky bag fit her shoulder. Most people didn't have bags. Typical of Mop and Pop to overdo it and draw attention to themselves, thought Fin. And if she had a phone she could text Ermine, half her class had them now anyway. She fell into step with Zen and Ty again. Ty kept sniffing the air and looking at them as if to ask what the hell's going on? The streetlights flickered back on. The crowd relaxed, people began to talk, jokes were made and handed round.

"But it's 2 am." said Pop. The crowd slowed. Fin bumped into Mop's bag.

"Oww."

"Look," said Zen pointing at the curb. Beyond the curb was a big hole, really big, big enough to swallow several cars. As the crowd shuffled forward people pulled their bodies away while trying to crane their necks to peer in. Ty leaned right over. Zen pulled his collar to stop him jumping in to explore. Ty strained forward pulling Zen closer to the edge. Fin gripped the other side of the collar and heaved. The crowd was pushing past forcing them all closer to the jagged edge of the road. The hole looked like a big puddle without the water, just rubble and tarmac at the bottom.

"Sinkhole," someone said. Fin really pushed her feet against the curb. She didn't care she was pushing back into the crowd. She'd seen a programme on sinkholes. She could be sucked down to the earth's core, compressed into carbon or something awful. Ty looked at Fin and twisted round. Zen tripped up. Fin fell backwards into an old lady.

"Watch it, love, only got me slippers on."

"Sorry," muttered Fin.

There was another hole further on. There was some laughing and pointing at a car teetering on the edge. It rocked then pitched forward and disappeared, crashing and scraping its sides.

"Wey hey," someone clapped. But people began to speed up, pushing. Everyone wanted to get away from the main road. It was a relief to turn into Pump Street, round the corner from Fin's school. There were no more holes. Two more police officers directed the crowd to the main gates on Basel Road. People fanned out across the playground.

Miss Nomer, the head teacher bustled out of the main building as the school lights went on.

"Ladies, gentlemen, children welcome to Basel Road Primary. We want to welcome you all inside, slowly, slowly the doors are very narrow," she laughed. She was a big woman. She looked like a traffic cone in her orange raincoat.

"Tea and biscuits will be served shortly." She smiled again and ushered people in. Some of the P.T.A peeled off from the crowd. They had work to do. Inside it was noisy after the quiet streets. All the windows steamed up. Hatsumi sat down on a gym bench. Pop went in search of tea. Fin lost sight of Zen and Ty. She edged back towards the door where a thin breeze cooled the air. All she could see was a wall of backs in bathrobes, fleeces and leather. So she wandered outside. Zen was sitting on the ground on the far side of the playground. Ty rollicked around sniffing and squaring up to bins.

Fin hovered then decided to join them. Zen didn't seem to mind. He reached in his pocket and offered her some sour gum. Fin took one. It was like chewing purple flavoured cardboard. Her pockets were empty.

"Wonder if MacDonald's is open?" she said.

"Why you got any cash?" said Zen.

"Nah," said Fin, feeling silly. She tried to sound like Ermine, nonchalant, Ermine called it. "If I did I'd go for dhal and chapattis instead."

Zen nodded. "I'd go for milk ice-cream, or peanut butter ice-cream and..." He thought.

"You won't get that in Tooting," laughed Fin. "Fried chicken ice-cream?"

"Right."

A few stragglers shuffled into the hall. The caretaker, Mr Bunce began forcing open the windows. Fin and Zen watched. The steamy windows began to clear. At the far end, under the year one tin-foil robot a group of mums in headscarves was bustling about pouring tea into plastic cups. Pop and Mop joined the circle swirling around Miss Nomer. People began to share what they'd seen. Miss Nomer pulled out a chair and with Mr Bunce holding her arm she stepped up.

"Ladies and gentlemen, children," she raised her hand, and waited for silence. She was enjoying herself. Her big head teacher voice boomed across the hall and playground. Ty sat down and waited for more.

"Welcome again to Basel Road, I'm Miss Nomer head teacher," she nodded.

"This is Mr Bunce our..." a phone went off. Miss Nomer paused with a frown and waited for the fool to switch it off.

"Our caretaker. We have almost the whole P.T.A here making your tea."

There was a smattering of applause.

"There will be coffee and biscuits courtesy of Bhavin Brothers, shortly."

Loud cheers greeted this announcement. Fin didn't hear much more because the hall doors swung shut.

8

THE FIGHT

To Fin it was like watching a film except she was sort of in it. She was glad she hadn't left Blind Twin House in her old pyjamas. She'd seen Judy Royal and Ramona Spiteri-Downs standing at the edge of the hall snickering at everyone's clothes.

Fin did up her coat and rammed her hands into her pockets. It was raining softly. The tarmac was greasy. The wind blew an empty coke can across the playground. Some late evacuees wandered in off the road, laughing. Ty padded over. Fin rubbed his head.

A burst of rain and wind sent Ty, then Fin under the corrugated iron shelter. Zen joined them.

"Thanks for helping, well rescuing..." began Fin.

"S' OK... Ty did most of the work," said Zen.

"Well thank you, Ty," said Fin. She rubbed his head again, she was getting confident around dogs or so she thought. He pushed his big body against her legs, warming them. Fin smiled. In the past she'd have been terrified of a dog the size of Ty, with his giant gapping mouth, big teeth and bad breath. She'd have stuck close to Mop and Pop in the hall even if it meant putting up with Judy and Ramona making remarks about her wellies and Pop's ripped jeans.

"D'you think it's a sinkhole?" said Fin.

Zen shook his head. "Nah, council were digging up the road yesterday, probably just a cave-in..."

Fin thought he'd finished. Then he said "We were in an earthquake in Japan." Fin had a lot of questions about Japan, paper houses and Zen's dad. Her head was full. She wanted to get away so she could write them down in a list and empty her head. She chewed the cardboard gum. She was worried too much talk would put Zen off, send him back into his shell. So they just stood there. Fin's feet got numb.

"I bet your mum was really brave," said Fin. It was the best she could do.

Zen nodded, watching Ty watching the rain.

A football flew past and hit the wall. It was followed by Edge in full kit and a puffing Blimp in a fluffy purple bathrobe, silver tracksuit bottoms and green trainers.

"Jeez," Fin and Zen breathed at the same time. Blimp stopped, bending over his fat stomach, hands on his knees.

"Hi," he gasped.

"Hi," said Fin.

"Is he allright?" said Zen. Together they moved towards Blimp. Edge appeared with the ball under his arm. He smiled.

"Hey," said Fin. Edge and Blimp looked at Zen and Ty.

"This is Zen and Ty" said Fin pointing at Zen and Ty. Ty waved his tail. The two boys laughed at Ty.

"What is he half lion, half horse?" said Blimp stroking Ty's stripes, like a connoisseur. "More like half tiger," said Edge.

Blimp stood next to Ty. "I need a dog like this; he makes me look real thin."

They laughed. Zen smiled. Edge bounced the ball from knee to knee.

"Coming back to school?" asked Edge.

"Yeah," replied Fin with a sinking feeling. "Well eventually..." The boys waited. Edge turned and dribbled the ball into the playground.

"Come on guys we'll take you on... and win," shouted Blimp, chugging after Edge.

Fin had never been asked to play football before. She always hung back when teams were chosen in P.E. She was usually one of the last picked as she wasn't in the main group. The mainstreamers Zelda called them. Fin called them the herd. She wanted to look like she didn't care. Judy and Ramona were good at every sport. They could turn hand stands into cartwheels. Fin envied this skill even though she didn't like them. They were boring. But when she tried a forward roll her head hurt like her brain was loose inside her skull. She hated admiring Judy and Ramona for this, they were vile about anyone who couldn't do stuff.

Zen wandered out into the rain, his hands in his pockets. Ty looked at Fin, and then followed Zen. Fin pretended to follow Ty. The ball scudded towards the shelter. Fin took two quick steps towards it. The playground was greasy. She slipped falling on her side, hard. The boys made a boy sound half way between cheer and Ow. Fin got up and limped towards the ball, desperate not to cry. She kicked it towards Blimp, at least she didn't miss. Blimp blocked it, then tried to balance the ball from knee to knee but lost it. Fin made a half-hearted attempt to move in but Edge was there before her. Edge and Zen ran across the playground, leaving Fin and Blimp to shiver.

"Where's the goal?" asked Fin for something to say. Blimp shrugged. Fin thought it must be hard being a boy like Blimp. After all, the boys didn't expect her to be able to play. Ty tried to join in getting in-between Zen and Edge, grabbing the ball in his giant mouth and running off with it.

"Foul," shouted Blimp. Zen whistled. Ty returned looking sheepish with a punctured ball between his jaws. Edge laughed "Glad that ain't mine," he said.

Edge trotted off to find another ball. Zen, Fin and Blimp retreated to the corrugated shelter. Zen tried to pull the ball away from Ty but he pulled back. Zen left him to it. Ty sat down and began to chew.

"Don't you feed that monster?" said Blimp.

Edge ran back with another school ball, nearly crashing into Arden who was also running to the shelter. She was dressed in a tracksuit. Fin had never seen her in anything else. Arden was a tall quiet girl with perfect cane row hair. She ignored the rest of the class most days, preferring to run laps around the playground. She often missed school, because of training and winning competitions. Before Fin got sick there was an assembly with pictures of Arden winning a race in Oslo. Her cane row plaits flying out behind her as she crossed the finishing line while two very red faced white kids powered up behind her.

Fin suspected Arden was really about 28 years old. She was so mature she made some of the teachers look silly. The mainstreamers tried hard to add Arden to their gang but Arden just ignored them. Fin expected her to keep running but she stopped. The boys were chasing a new ball into the darkness.

"Jeez, Fin is that yours?" Arden pointed at Ty, who had his head to one side drooling and chewing the remains of the shredded ball.

"No," said Fin. "Ty belongs to Zen." Fin and Arden watched Zen take the ball briefly from Edge. Rain drummed on the roof.

"Zen?" Arden squinted at the boys.

"He doesn't come to school," said Fin.

"Don't blame him. You know we've got Miss Khan? Not missing much."

Fin shivered. There were three Miss Khans at Basel Road: Nice, Nasty and Know-all. Know-all worked in the library but Fin's class had Nasty this year. Home-school may not be so bad after all. Maybe make a list of what she and Zen "needed" to learn and present it to Mop and Hatsumi. But before Fin had chance to pursue this idea Arden began to bounce on the balls of her feet. She was impatient to get moving. The rain got heavier, the lads returned to the shelter. They were all shivering now.

"I'm going inside," said Blimp retying his bathrobe. Ty crouched low and growled, dropping the mangled ball. Fin felt scared of Ty. She decided she'd go in with Blimp.

Before she could tell the others, Ty sprang up. He shot out towards another dog, coming at them like a white bullet. They all froze.

"Shit, its Evil Eddy," said Fin, her mouth going dry. Ty stood very tall. Evil Eddy growled a horrible rumbling sound. Then he sprang at Ty's throat.

What happened next, went down very, very fast but to Fin and the others it felt like forever.

"Holy Toledo," gasped Blimp. They were now watching a giant ball of a dog fight, growling, mauling. Fin couldn't tell where one dog started and the other finished. Zen sprang forward and tried to grab Ty. But as he didn't have a lead it was difficult. Fin couldn't move and neither could the others. She wanted to help but didn't know what to do. She was terrified of Evil Eddy. Wherever Eddy was, Billy would follow. Fin wanted to run back into the hall and get Pop, hell, anyone who'd come out. But the ball of mauling, clawing dogs was between her and the hall.

Edge and Blimp moved forward. Arden grabbed Fin's sleeve. Blimp got round one side, his face slick with rain and sweat. His coffee coloured skin going white then green. Edge dodged around trying to grab at Eddy's studded collar. Edge was fast but the dogs rolled around snarling and biting and yelping. Eddy twisted his jaw and snapped at Edge's hand. Edge sprang back.

"Whoa," shouted Edge, staggering back. Arden began pulling Fin towards the hall. They turned towards the door only to find their path blocked by Billy Blatant. Fin realised they were on their own. She felt sick. Billy curled his lip. He stared hard, daring them to move. Arden straightened up; she was as tall as Billy. But against him she looked like a reed against a blade. Billy broke off staring first, to watch the dogs. Then he strode forward pushing through them barging Fin's side so she almost fell over. What happened next was almost slow motion Billy was so quick, graceful even. He lunged forward and grabbed Eddy's collar.

"Call off your dog, NOW," Billy yelled. Zen was out of breath and struggling to hold Ty by the scruff of his neck. His cheap collar lay broken on the tarmac. Zen gasped put both arms round Ty and tried to pull him away. Edge grabbed Zen's waist and pulled. Zen and Edge fell backwards pulling Ty onto his side. Billy let go of Eddy's chain, giving Eddy a chance to bite Zen's arm. Ty tried to stand but Zen had him down hard. Ty opened his huge yawning mouth. Blimp took one look at Ty's gape and hurtled round Billy towards the hall. Billy spat on the ground and yanked Eddy's chain. Eddy strained at his lead jumping forwards and snarling. Fin and Arden stepped back. Billy pushed a fag into his mouth, took out a heavy metal lighter, flicked it a couple of times and lit his fag.

"Well, what do we have here?" sneered Billy.

Zen rubbed his arm, his face obscured by his long hair. Both Edge and Zen were lying across Ty to stop him getting up. But Ty was strong. Fin wanted to help. The presence of Billy paralysed everyone. Arden stood behind Fin. But Fin felt alone, exposed. What if Billy turned and targeted her. Arden could run away. Fin's heart sat at the back of her throat.

Tales of Evil Eddy's reign of terror zigzagged across her agitated mind. The first day she'd been in hospital Zelda had bustled in to tell her about Evil Eddy cornering Charmaine's kitten in Basel Road and snapping its neck. This was witnessed by Year Five on their way back from the library. The police had been called apparently. Stories like this had a habit of growing; soon it became Charmaine's baby brother.

"I reckon," said Billy, drawling out his words for effect, "You boys owe me some com-pen-sation." Billy liked words like this.

"What?" said Edge. Zen shifted his weight.

"Look at the mess you've made of my dog," Billy hissed.

Billy let out the lead allowing Eddy another chance at Zen's arm. Zen flinched away. Edge sprang up out of range.

"Stop," Fin was surprised as anyone that she'd shouted out. It was a sort of reflex. Before her brain had chance to catch up with her heart she was shouting at Billy.

"That's enough. You want compensation we'll get the CCTV to sort it out," Fin pointed to the corner of the playground. The council had installed a camera to stop lead thieves taking down the school roof. Most playtimes found little boys making obscene gestures underneath it, then running away laughing hysterically.

Fin realised it was no good explaining Eddy had come at them. Zen got up. Ty stayed on his side, trying to raise his great head.

"Ty's hurt," blurted Fin. Then wished she hadn't. Billy mimicked, a classic bully manoeuvre.

"Ty's hurt, Ty's hurt, what sort of dumb ass name is that, *Jap Boy*?" Fin answered. "It's his name."

Billy was so powerful. It's like he could tell you to go shop lifting and you'd do it just to avoid his boot. Fin hated herself for answering.

Arden caught Fin's hand. Fin felt tears run down her cheeks. She hated herself more than Billy. How is it bullies are able to do this to you? How?

Then Arden stepped forward. "You're a bully and a racist and so's your dog," she said.

Billy smiled leaning back. He was enjoying himself. He dragged on his fag. He glared at Arden, blowing smoke in her face.

"I've seen you running by yourself..." He left that hanging. Fin realised several things at once. Arden could outrun anyone in London, but Billy didn't play fair. He'd ambush. His mates were scary. But he thought Arden was hot. She was. Fin had only ever seen her as an aloof runner but to a boy like Billy she looked like a beauty queen. Before Fin could process what any of this meant, if anything, Billy spoke again.

"You girlies witnessed this un-pro-voked attack. I reckon 50 quid'll put it right." Fin folded her arms. Arden did the same.

Emboldened by Arden, Fin said: "No Billy Blatant, the magistrate will fine *you*."

Arden nodded.

Billy threw his fag towards Zen who flinched. Fin realised it wasn't just her who was scared of Billy.

"We don't go to law. I know where YOU live, all you little boys and girls."

He let out Eddy's lead again. Eddy jumped forward barking. They all stepped back. Billy slid the lead through his hands till he was almost at Ty's throat.

"Back off" said Arden.

"Yeah," said Zen "Back off."

"Or what Jap-Boy?" sneered Billy.

Zen balled his fists. He was trying not to fight Billy with Ty injured on the ground and Eddy in the mix.

"Come on then, who's gonna stop me?" goaded Billy.

"We are."

Billy spun round. Fin had been so fixated on Billy and Evil Eddy she hadn't noticed Blimp's return with all five of his sisters. They stood in the rain, blue and pink saris billowing in the wind. They were all as tall as Billy and twice as wide. They stood there hands on hips, their scarves rippling and slapping in the wind: an Indian Armada.

Billy stepped back and laughed but he pulled Eddy's lead in sharpish. He was trying to go for scorn but it came out more like surprise. He muttered something obscene under his breath.

"Call your dog off and go home, Billy Blatant," Aruna ordered.

Fin and Arden moved closer to Zen and Ty, forming a protective barrier around Ty. Edge and Blimp joined them. The sisters glared it Billy. Fin half expected Blimp to start boasting about their Karate credits but he just stood with his arms folded. Billy considered.

"Sod this for a game of soldiers. I'm off."

And with that he yanked Eddy, pushing through them, still trying to intimidate. They turned to watch him go until he was out of the gate. Fin was shaking. Blimp gave a whoop and did a little dance, waggling his ass in the purple bathrobe. It broke Billy's spell. Baala and Chanda gently stepped up to Ty.

"Shall we check out your dog?" Zen nodded.

"We're used to people patients but..." said Baala. Edge and Zen tried to push Ty up. He stood wobbling. Chanda spoke quietly.

"This," she said pointing to Ty's stripy coat, "is probably superficial but that will need some stitches." They all leaned in. Fin winced. Ty's skin was ripped like an old coat. Blood caked on his side. Zen nodded.

"You need to get him to a vet for a jab." Here she rubbed Ty's head "Just in case of infection."

"Could be internal bleeding but if he's well over the next few hours I'm sure he'll be fine, won't you boy, girl, boy?" Ty tried to lick her face. The sisters laughed.

"Everyone OK?"

"They're med students," Blimp explained to Zen.

"No shit Sherlock," said Edge.

"And we aren't all med students, just three of us, Daksha's Physics, Hera's Bio-Chem."

"Wow," said Zen "Thanks anyway."

"It's the fire brigade," said Blimp. Three fire-fighters holding their helmets under their arms strode towards the school hall. A worried Hatsumi appeared in the doorway. She hurried over to the group, catching Zen by the shoulder.

"Where have you been?" After quite an explanation they slipped into the hall. It was bright and very warm, too warm. The school smell of stale pastry and bleach made Fin feel safe.

9

THE DAY AFTER

It was getting light or rather getting grey. Everyone was tired and ratty. When the fire fighters said it was safe to return home people began to shuffle out of the hall, leaving plastic cups, food wrappers and the odd sweater. Camaraderie evaporated. People just wanted to get home and check their flats and houses were as they'd left them. Not everyone had gone obediently to the hall. The situation was a gift for burglars.

Fin's legs felt like they were filled with concrete. Fin lost sight of Blimp and his sisters. She'd half expected them to walk back together but they'd stayed to help Miss Nomer clear the hall. Zen, Ty and Hatsumi had disappeared. As had Arden. The crowd closed in around Fin like a tide covering her head. There was less interest in the holes. They were old news and no deeper. Fin stared at the car. It looked like a toy chucked in by a toddler.

"Yo Fin," someone shouted.

It was Tolemy across the road. Fin wondered how Tolemy was the only person on the other side of the road. The police had been insistent they stuck to this side. He was standing outside his parents' furniture store, waving. He was wearing his fleecy leather coat. Other people glanced over. Fin didn't like Tolemy. He was spoilt. But the store was like the most luxurious sitting room in South London:

bouncy leather sofas sat around polished wooden tables. Paper lampshades glowed all night. Shiny chrome and sparkly chandeliers gleamed in the tea lights Tolemy's mum had placed on the tables.

Tolemy surprised her by shouting: "You OK?"

He had always been the class teaser, with a nasty streak. He made other kids feel small but was adept at buttering up adults. It didn't work with Miss Nomer, probably why she was head teacher. Fin nodded. Another Bolshevik, Gran called him.

"We're not, look." Tolemy pointed to the side of the shop. His mum and dad were standing there trying to argue without it looking like they were rowing. Tolemy carried on laughing and pointing. Fin now saw. The side road had gone. The tarmac ended abruptly in shadow. Tolemy's mum pointed something at the hole. Fin heard the expensive cheep of their black Audi. Some lights flashed on and off somewhere way below the pavement. Fin put her head down and trudged on, she needed to sit down.

Fin fell asleep after lunch and woke up with a stiff neck, her chin wet with drool. She'd been reading on her bed to escape Ermine banging about in the kitchen. Ermine was grounded for a week. Fin wiped her chin in her sleeve then padded to the loo. Then she remembered Billy. She opened her window and leaned out. Mop and Pop were walking down the brick path, stopping now and again, pointing. Pop was writing in his note book. Fin yawned. Billy wouldn't come here would he? She went downstairs. She pushed open the narrow black door to find Ermine wearing an apron. Abimbola was sitting at the kitchen table with a mug and a thick text book.

"Hey," said Abimbola. Fin's shoulders relaxed.

"Hey," said Fin feeling more grown up. The kitchen smelled chocolaty. Ermine was washing up.

"We had hot chocolate. D'you want some?" said Ermine. Fin thought she'd misunderstood. Ermine stared at her. She was about to dunk the milky pan in the washing up bowl.

"OK," said Fin and sat down. Maybe Ermine bumped her head last night? Fin decided she'd tell Ermine and Abimbola about Billy but she didn't get the chance.

"What's wrong with your hair?" said Fin. Abimbola's wiry black hair was grey and stiff like an old fashioned wig.

"Well," said Abimbola, shutting her textbook.

"You weren't the only person caught in the drama," said Ermine, stirring the milk.

Abimbola smiled. "I'll let Ermine tell you" she glanced over at the dribbling tap. "Now there's water. I'm going home to wash my hair." She jammed her book into her bag, stroked her phone and waved goodbye.

Ermine plonked the hot chocolate down in front of Fin.

"Sprinkles?" she said doing an impression of a very aggressive waitress.

"Since when did we have sprinkles?" said Fin.

Ermine waved the cheese grater in her face, took a chunk of chocolate and rubbed it over Fin's steaming drink. She then sat down exhausted by the effort. They sat in silence gazing around the kitchen. It looked different. Ermine had washed up. She'd cleaned the cooker, emptied the bin, put on their new second-hand washing machine and thrown the dead plants out the window. Weird. Ermine stared at Fin. Fin bent over her mug. The chocolate was thick and dark, like warm mud.

"We got caught down the Sump," said Ermine. Fin knew this was band night at the Pub On The Corner. There had been rows at home about it before. Fin sipped her chocolate.

"We thought the vibrations were the band," Ermine said. "Boy, were we wrong about that."

"Some of the punters got hit with plaster, people cheered. Bass guitarist stopped, the manager was shouting. Drummer kept going; he was out of it..." Ermine shrugged.

Fin nodded like she knew about drummers. Ermine didn't usually talk to her. Fin kept quiet. She didn't want to jinx it by drawing attention to the fact she wasn't Abimbola. She wanted to tell Ermine about Billy and ask what she should do, if she saw him again. Ermine was fierce, Billy wouldn't scare her.

"Then the stairs sort of sheared away from the wall, more shouting.

No way out..." Ermine stopped. The temperature in the kitchen dropped, in spite of the chocolaty mug burning Fin's hands.

"We shouted at every one to shut up and get the manager off the floor. He'd come down with the stairs, cut his eye," Ermine shuddered. "Abimbola made him a tissue compress... barmaid called the fire brigade but we had to wait. Then it got jumpy, idiots sharing phone stories about earthquakes and sinkholes.... That's an old building. We were waiting for the whole thing to come down on top of us. Fire exit," here Ermine held up her fingers to indicate quotation marks, "was locked. Chained from the outside, that's when it got ugly. Some of the patrons started abusing the manager with Abimbola standing next to him. Guy and me stood next to her. Band tried to calm things down even offered to finish the gig."

Ermine tried to laugh. "Ended up with us and the band backed to the wall, until the barmaid found a ladder, we let the thugs out first" Ermine twisted her fingers, her hands were shaking.

Fin looked at Ermine. Her face was pale. Ermine sighed.

"And to top it off, I'm grounded." Fin finished her drink. It was so strong it was almost beefy.

"Did you tell Mop and Pop what happened?" This was all Fin could think to say. She wanted to say they were brave but that felt silly.

"No I didn't want to get grounded for a year did I?"

They sat there listening to the washing machine swishing the clothes clean.

"I'm off for a bath," said Ermine. She got up slowly and trudged out. Fin noticed her satin skirt was ripped at the back. She looked smaller than usual.

The house was quiet. Mop had gone to check on Gran. Fin felt queasy after the hot chocolate. A large bag of salty crisps would cure that. There were no crisps in the pantry; only tins of beans, rice pudding and soup that they never ate and a box of sprouting potatoes. She slipped her wellies on, took her puffy jacket and headed out to find Pop. He may have cash for crisps. She couldn't see anyone about. The sun was warm on her face. The air was so still the bushes and trees along the tangled path appeared to be holding their breath after the drama of the night before. The air smelt of smoke. The main gates were shut. The main road was silent. They were cut off, shipwrecked. The yard had become an island overnight.

Fin peered through the rusty gate. Blue police tape crisscrossed the high road. Giant orange cones ringed the holes. Pigeons wobbled on the tarmac looking for chip boxes. A few people were wandering about, with shopping bags and kids. The schools were shut. Not that that was relevant to Fin yet, or so she thought. Fin heard the bin cart. Hatsumi must be on her rounds. Fin tried to crane her neck to see into the holes. They didn't look so deep or sinister in the sun. But the main road looked as if it had been hit by meteors. Fin was glad the gates were locked that meant no Billy for a while.

She turned to see Zen come out of Twin House, with Ty sniffing the air. Fin half expected Zen to ignore her. But Ty bounded over and jumped up. Fin stroked his big head trying to avoid the large scabs crusting his back. She scratched behind his ears then pushed him down and stepped forward. She walked towards Zen. Ty trotted alongside her as if he was her dog. This made Fin feel tall. Zen surprised her by falling into step. Fin found herself leading the way up towards the grassy knoll.

"What did the vet say?" asked Fin.

"S'OK, the vet said Ty's fine," said Zen rubbing Ty's head.

"He was a bit distracted, a man got bitten in the waiting room by his own snake, said Ty was an unusual dog. Mum said he was an expensive dog."

Fin glanced sideways at Zen. His trainers were cheap no-brands. He was the sort of boy Judith and Ramona would make fun of. But he was sort of cool, even in cheap trainers. Fin wondered how that worked.

"Does Ty have to go back?"

"Oh yeah."

Fin tried to think of something else to say.

"Mum asked me to check for damage, she gave me a book," Zen pulled out a small note book with a padded turquoise cover.

"That's pretty," said Fin.

Zen looked at her.

"Here, you have it." He thrust it towards her.

Did this mean she was making the list? Perhaps Zen couldn't write? "OK," said Fin.

They walked up towards the hill. This would give Fin a chance to prove herself by showing she wasn't a silly girl. The yard looked the same. The graves still leaned this way and that, apart from those that had given up and smashed face down or sunk deep into the mud. Mausoleum row was in shade. The only damage was a marble urn lolling on the path. Zen pushed it to the curb with his foot. They climbed higher, getting warmer. They stopped on the last path and leaned against the warm red brick wall. From up here they could see most of the yard: green grass and bare trees and out across the red brick terraces of Tooting. Seagulls wheeled overhead their giant wings slicing the air.

"Did you see the car in a hole?" asked Fin.

"Yep," said Zen.

10

A SURPRISE VISIT

Over the next few days Fin, Zen and Ty fell into a routine. Fin would hurry along the path from Blind Twin House. She timed it so she caught Zen as he left the house with Ty. Zen was usually falling over shoving his feet into wellies too big, while Ty jumped about eager to run. Fin was still a bit scared seeing Ty gallop towards her like a runaway pony. But he was polite now. He stopped before her and lowered his head. She would step forward and reach out to rub it. Sometimes he stayed and rubbed his greasy body against her jeans. Other times he'd dart back and forth saying come run with me. They would head up towards the grassy knoll. Zen disliked writing so Fin made the lists.

She listed: Things To Be Fixed:

1. Wire bin one side missing.
2. Blocked drain choked by leaves and detritus. Fin liked that word.
3. Angel: severed (another good word) arm.

Fin thought it was important to use strong words to show Pop and Hatsumi how important it was that these things got fixed. Other boring things like split plastic bin, broken light could fend for themselves. After finding three severed arms in one morning, at the grassy knoll and down the Avenue of Inventors, Fin had the idea of Zen sketching maps with compass directions. The arms were too heavy to carry very far.

One morning they caught sight of Billy, far below them. He sauntered in the main gate, stopped to light a cigarette then hung about on one of the paths while Evil Eddy sniffed around. Fin and Zen crouched down behind a tall headstone and waited. Ty sat next to them his eyes fixed on Eddy. Billy whistled to Eddy before heading back out towards the High Street.

Fin let out a sigh. Zen shrugged. As they made their way towards Twin House for elevenses Fin was relieved. It was like they'd been invisible. Billy didn't look like someone on a vendetta, just someone walking his dog. Fin decided to tell herself this several times that day.

They didn't talk much at first. Zen preferred to walk fast. Fin got tired. So not talking suited them both. Ty made noises: knocking his teeth together, barrelling through brambles and fighting billowing litter. Fin thought this would go on forever, until one day, they'd filled the small note book and Fin's diary. Fin hurried back to Blind Twin House with Zen and Ty.

Gran bought Ty dog biscuits when she heard about the encounter with Evil Eddy. Ty still had a nasty scab on his back but the vet said he was lucky. It was superficial. Fin ran into the kitchen planning to pick up some dog biscuits and grab a new notebook. She'd bought it with Pop at the weekend. She liked the feeling when she opened a new notebook, clean white paper waiting. This one had wide lines. Narrow lines cramped her thinking.

She ran smack into a broad belly. Miss Nomer was standing in the kitchen doorway.

"Well, Fin," said Miss Nomer, before Fin could apologise.

"I was about to leave but as you're here and..." Miss Nomer craned her neck into the hall. "Zen, come here. I hope that's OK with you?"

Miss Nomer smiled a steely smile. Fin stared around the kitchen. It was like she was seeing it through Miss Nomer's eyes. Pop and Hatsumi were sitting with chipped mugs, looking sheepish as if they'd been caught bunking. Mop was standing with her back to the sink, piled with dirty dishes. They'd had popcorn for supper, burning the butter first time around. Ermine had taken over, stating she didn't want to die from smoke inhalation. The dog biscuits had been opened and several were scattered across the table as if they'd been eating them. Pop had started a talk on the history of dog biscuits before they'd gone to bed. Zen joined Fin in the doorway.

"Sit down," said Miss Nomer.

Fin, Zen and Mop sat down. Ty opened his dog eyes wide and waited.

Fin and Zen sat down at the far end of the table. Mop took off her rubber gloves and refilled the kettle. Miss Nomer sat down, the chair creaking beneath her substantial backside. Pop cleared his throat. Hatsumi looked at Zen then at the open door. The boiling kettle got louder. Mop bustled about throwing cold tea away and opening another packet of biscuits. Oreos. The situation looked bad. Miss Nomer took a biscuit and passed the packet down to Fin. Fin had forgotten, or rather pushed, the idea of home-school to the back of her mind. However, she had come up with a list of projects she would be willing to do if pushed. However, they began to wilt in her head before the very solid Miss Nomer.

1. Learn origami; make an origami city and/or zoo. Fin estimated this would be one morning a week with Hatsumi then free time. After all if somebody really tried to origami a whole zoo that could takes years. She would show her parents when she was finished and not before, that would ruin the surprise.
2. Research the yard: maybe the life and times of Lord Basel? This would be a quick skim of Wikipedia and some Google images in a scrap book. Sorted.
3. English, well that was just reading. She did that anyway and Zen was big on comics.

But she got stuck on maths. She thought an argument could be made for origami being some sort of maths, Japanese maths. That made it two things at once: maths and learning another language, sort of. The list flashed before Fin as she slowly bit into the Oreo. She needed time to refine her arguments. A voice in her head that sounded a lot like Ermine hissed the word flimsy. Best sit tight and see what's what. She didn't want to put maths out there if Miss Nomer was just thinking about reading improving books.

No one spoke because the kettle was so loud. Steam rolled up the wall and curled along the ceiling.

"I was about to go," said Miss Nomer, scanning each guilty face in turn.

"It's fortunate I ran into both your families at the same time," she said looking directly at Fin and Zen.

"I'm concerned you two are *not* at school, the Education Welfare Officer and the Local Authority are also concerned."

Mop opened her mouth, then shut it. Hatsumi frowned and pressed her lips together. Miss Nomer put up a majestic hand.

"I've not come here to add to your stress, distress," she smiled at Hatsumi.

"I've a proposal. I suggest we take up your mothers' suggestion to home-school, at least," here Miss Nomer leaned forward and waited for both Zen and Fin to look at her.

"At least for a little while," she finished.

Fin and Zen looked at their mothers and then at one another. Hatsumi looked confused, Mop went red.

"Mrs Laurel, why don't you outline your proposed curriculum."

Mop grimaced and put her mug down.

"Well... Fin, Zem, Zen, I had an idea, not sure you'd call it a curriculum as such, but as you too like roaming about we could build on that..."

Mop paused realising she'd taken a wrong turn. She started again.

"I'm here in the day. Maybe I could teach you English for a morning..."

The clock ticked. Miss Nomer smiled, folded her hands in her lap and waited.

"Pop could take you out and about for History and Geography, umm and Horticulture, for another morning." Mop smiled pleased with the word horticulture. Pop had been reaching towards the plastic milk bottle. He stopped mid grab.

"Eh?"

"I do Math," jumped in Hatsumi.

Miss Nomer was no longer smiling.

"I propose you have a meeting, with Fin and Zen to come up with a rigorous programme for the next half-term, seven weeks. That will mean three mornings of school work with homework. I want to see your homework every week. Then we can try integration."

Mop picked up a chewed biro from the pile of old newspapers, in the middle of the table, and began writing this down on an abandoned shopping list.

Fin surprised herself by asking what integration meant. It sounded like some sort of exam.

"It means you go to back school," said Pop.

Fin felt her stomach slide down to a very cold place. Zen stopped jiggling his leg. They both sat very still.

"But not all at once," said Mop, turning to Hatsumi for back up.

"Yes Miss Nomer say maybe one or two morning a week, first."

"Well I said two or three but we can and should be flexible. You've both been through a lot and sometimes school must take a back seat, though learning itself must never stop."

She narrowed her eyes for emphasis. Fin rubbed the embossed surface of another biscuit. Miss Nomer dipped her Oreo into her tea before swallowing it whole. This gave everyone thinking time. Pop slurped his tea-minus-milk. Fin bit her biscuit in half. Zen tapped his on the table.

"And next time I see you, you can tell me why your houses have such," Miss Nomer paused choosing her words carefully, "strange names."

She made it sound as if it was somehow their fault.

11

BIG PLANS

It all started with big plans. Hatsumi, Mop and Pop sat late in the kitchen that night. Mop even suggested Ermine could teach art. Pop began to scroll through Wikipedia. Hatsumi made lots of notes. Zen disappeared with Ty for two hours, leaving Fin to answer questions and chip in with suggestions. Her parents were enjoying themselves. It was as if Miss Nomer had asked them to start a university.

It got dark outside. Mop finished the washing up while Pop nipped outside for a fag. Hatsumi went back to Twin House for books. Ermine came in with Guy. Mop asked her to make some dinner as she was so good at it. Ermine curled her purple lips but didn't disagree. Later after giant bowls of spaghetti, grated chillies and butter Fin and Zen were passed their curriculum.

"It's important it's Montessori, child centred," Mop explained to Hatsumi.

"Montessori," echoed Ermine. "Aren't you lucky."

Fin stared at the list. It looked like school but without break time, chat and the waiting for this and that to happen which was more chat time. Ermine leaned over her shoulder.

"That looks great, tell you what," she snatched the list. "Why don't you just give it a go, see how it evolves."

"D'you know that's a great idea. We can fit more in when we get into a routine," said Pop.

"But I don't want to... " began Fin looking at the word algebra.

Pop put his hand on hers.

"Don't worry plum; you're just out of practice, like Zen here."

"But I've never done algebra or Russian History or... " Fin felt her face go red and her lips wobble. Pop got up and enveloped her in a big hug.

"It'll be grand." Fin heard a chair scrap and bang against the wall. Zen and Ty swept off into the night. Hatsumi followed.

After a week of misery and broken pencils they all realised it was far too much. Fin looked up some new words to describe her feelings. She shouted them up and down the stairs. Home-school was grandiose, risible *and* egregious. She tried to slam her door in temper but it stuck. Guy offered to help but that wasn't what Fin wanted. She wanted a door she could slam herself. But she was pleased; Guy seemed impressed with her vocabulary.

He slunk down the stairs muttering: "Wow, egregious, dude."

Fin managed the week, Zen two days. Zen and Ty settled back into their old routine of roaming about. Fin wanted to go back to reading and wandering, pretending the yard was an overgrown secret garden but everything had changed since the incident with Billy and Evil Eddy.

Miss Nomer appeared at the gate on Friday on her way home to ask Pop, who was sitting in his van waiting for the traffic to move, how it was going. Pop said they were getting there but wasn't sure they would have homework to send in this week.

"Apparently," said Miss Nomer.

She caught sight of Fin who was trying to catch Pop, with the forgotten shopping list.

"Ah Fin," said Miss Nomer straightening up.

"Hello Miss Nomer," said Fin.

Pop got out of the van.

"I was expecting to see some homework, this week, young lady."

Shit, Fin thought. She glanced at Miss Nomer worried Miss Nomer could read her mind. Fin had to think fast. Otherwise who knew what programme they'd be put on next.

"Could I... I mean we, do a project instead?" asked Fin. "We could put all the homework together... in a holistic way."

Fin liked the word holistic. And why couldn't they combine all the homework? This might mean a lot less maths; maybe they could apply the maths to something interesting? Fin organised an argument in her head, while Miss Nomer narrowed her eyes.

"Go on," she said.

Pop waited, traffic trundled past, weaving around the holes and plastic barriers set up by the council. Fin glanced up the yard drive, looking at the tall spikey trees and stubby palms. Crumbling old graves were rudely interrupted by new shiny headstones.

"I'm interested in history," said Fin.

Pop beamed at this.

"So I thought Zen and I could do some research... on the yard and write about it, with pictures and graphs."

Fin thought she'd covered most of the National Curriculum, except P.E, but they'd be walking about, so that box was ticked too. Miss Nomer pursed her lips.

"If I agree you must promise to get it done to the best of your ability."

Miss Nomer gave assemblies each term explaining to parents and children her message was not work hard and suffer, but do your best. The school motto was: Only Your Best is Good Enough. Fin nodded. Pop came round the van and clapped her on the shoulder.

"But, that's a little too vague," said Miss Nomer. She scanned the drive, considering the yard. "I know," Miss Nomer nodded to herself, "my family has some connection with this place. You can research that, a bit of detective work." Miss Nomer smiled at Fin. "I know a little about Lord Basel and his work, you'll need to tell me more and see if you can find a link between Lord Basel and me." Miss Nomer nodded again as if she'd made a decision.

"Any clues?" asked Pop.

"Well my great Grandfather worked here. I've a picture of him; I'll send you a copy."

Fin decided she needed to do something. Otherwise Miss Nomer was going to return and drag them back to school. Fin began to wade through the boxes and carrier bags that had piled up around her room since they had moved in, blocking the still locked door. For the first few nights she'd worried it might open in the middle of the night but Pop assured her it was locked and painted shut.

"Probably just a cupboard or an extra loo?" said Pop, rubbing the back of his head. "When I've found the key, I'll sort it but its low on the list... mind you an extra loo would be damn useful."

Fin didn't like the idea of a loo crouching in the corner of her room. She tried to imagine a small square space with a blue porthole and a polished wooden floor. If it was empty she could drag a chair in and read in a circle of sun. This was unlikely. Since the gas leak explosion the lintel above the door was rammed down into the frame. Pop said it was now impossible to open without sawing through it.

"Good job you didn't shelter in there, plum, you'd be trapped."

Fin shuddered.

Most of the stuff in the carrier bags looked babyish, drawings stuck to stiff paper salvaged from old school displays and stories in loopy hand writing. There were lists in co-ordinated colours: blue and purple or orange and yellow, except those lists had faded, into the thick paper. They were meant to be the top 10 places her and Zelda would visit when they won the lottery or where they'd live. Back when they were going to be best friends forever.

Fin had started writing a series of detective stories about Aurora Starbuck but she got distracted trying to draw her, giving up each time Aurora didn't look quite right. Mop suggested Fin just write the story, using words to show who Aurora was instead. But when Fin started to write she found Aurora changed and got a poodle. Aurora got a mind of her own. Zelda said this was good news. Aurora was like a real character not made up. Fin didn't like little poodles so she changed it into a giant poodle that Aurora dyed a different colour each week. Both Fin and Zelda got bogged down in the poodle dying and soon forgot the mystery Aurora was meant to solve. Ermine read one instalment then made a fuss saying the pink poodle was meant to be her.

Fin got a recycling bag and began to chuck away her past. Zelda wasn't coming back and Fin thought Aurora had probably moved to Norway. Most of her old exercise books and animal magazines went in the sack. She kept one animal magazine about extinction because it had a black and white photo of a quagga on the front. It looked just like the stone quagga Ermine pointed out when they first moved in. Maybe she could use it for the project. It was research after all. Fin wondered if she would be doing all the work anyway.

"Where's the rest of the Addams' Family?" Gran asked, puffing into Fin's room.

Fin shrugged. She'd lost track of time sitting in the pile of dusty paper, old collages, silver foil and plastic wallets. Gran sat down on Fin's spindly chair. It wobbled. Gran settled herself.

"Having a clear out?"

"Yes, I'm… Zen and I are going to be home-schooled so I'm sorting out what we need." Gran nodded and waited for Fin to continue.

"I'm going to get some paper and history books together."

Fin leaned across the mountain of sacks and pulled out three heavy books she had completely forgotten were under her bed. She sneezed. Her face was itchy. Gran stared at the window as if she was looking out to sea.

Fin quickly pushed the books onto her bedside table. She felt bad; one was Gran's book on the last Tsar. Gran glanced down and looked surprised to find Fin in a pile of rubbish.

"Where is everyone?" said Gran.

"I don't know," said Fin, wondering if Gran hadn't noticed her earlier shrug.

"Back door wide open, you'll get robbed or worse living like this… I've locked it," said Gran holding up the key.

"But they won't be able to get back in," said Fin.

"Who won't? You don't want thieves coming back again?"

Gran passed her the key. Fin put it in her pocket.

"So you're having a clear out, good plan, travel light, that's what I've always said."

Fin got up. Her knees were stretched sore. She stooped over the bags to tie them up. They were heavy. She decided to roll them down the stairs and unlock the back door before Gran caught up with her.

She'd covered Gran's book with something Pop had bought at the library for 50p on *The History of London Plumbing* or something. Fin flicked through the pages debating whether to add this to the recycling. It was filled with diagrams of pipes and sepia photos of brick sewers and workmen in flat caps. Then she caught the title: *Lord Basel and the Workers' Spa*. Fin flipped again. Gran got up and rearranged the Imperial family humming to herself.

Fin sat back on her bed and pulled the big book onto her lap.

There was a photograph of a quagga with a boy about ten on its back. He looked serious despite the fact he was wearing puffy knickerbocker trousers. The caption read: Peter Basel with Bartholomew. Fin looked again, was that the quagga's name? But there was another boy in the picture. Because everything in the picture was faded and brown, it was difficult to see where the boys began and the trees behind ended. It was like they were all connected somehow. The other boy was tall. He was standing behind the quagga holding its reigns. He had on a flat cap but wore the same short trousers as Peter Basel. Peter had a spoilt face like Tolemy. He had a lot of white curly hair like a girl. Fin didn't like him.

Bartholomew looked black though it was difficult to tell. Fin stared. Most of the people in the history books at school were white. The Tsar and his family were so white they even wore white clothes. Gran continued to hum. Fin pulled the book closer and began to turn the pages one by one, until she was distracted by a banging on the back door.

12

IMPROVEMENTS, SORT OF

Things had changed a bit since the gas leak or gas event as Pop insisted on calling it. Gran had to walk to Blind Twin House. She preferred the bus because she always found someone to talk to or at. Her legs were less swollen and she was eating more. Mop was often outside cutting back the overgrown roses and brambles that ringed Blind Twin House. This started because part of the garden wall had come down so Mop had to clear the path for Gran.

Mop spent more and more time out in the winter sunshine. Guy stayed over most nights as it was too far to walk home. There were still no buses on the main road. Mop and Pop didn't mind as long as he slept downstairs on the sofa bed. This made Fin feel safer in the giant house. She disliked going to bed with all that cold empty space beneath her. Ermine and Guy cooked in the evening. Ermine couldn't stand waiting for Mop. It was simple stuff: spaghetti and pesto, roast potatoes with spicy tomato sauce, dhal and yellow rice and stir fry. But the pasta no longer shattered in your mouth, the dhal no longer had to be sliced out of the pan. There were no more jokes about save some bubble and squeak, to fill the hole under the sink.

Abimbola came over in the evenings to study with Ermine and Guy. And Abimbola really studied. Mop and Pop might wander over to

Twin House to review the day with Hatsumi or Hatsumi would join them. They would sit in Mop's study with the fire roaring.

One evening they moved all the downstairs furniture into the study, except the kitchen stuff and Guy's sofa bed. The room felt cosy and crowded like their old house. Things were really looking up for both families. The gas leak had been a blessing, said Gran. It had killed her indigestion, which had been killing her by the way, she said.

Fin often sat in front of the study fire dozing after tea but there was always a cloud at the edge. Sometimes Fin forgot what it was she was worried about, but she was still worried. And on top of that Mop, Pop and Hatsumi were getting carried away with the home-school planning again. Fin decided she'd have to start the project and get Zen on board otherwise it would be algebra or something stupid like knitting until Miss Nomer dragged them back to school.

Zen would disappear if Mop put her essay programme before him. Fin sat at Mop's desk listening to Hatsumi talk about the architect Frank Lloyd Wright. The word sequestered was used. Fin made a note to look that up. She liked the sound: sequestered. She left the room and hurried to the draughty downstairs loo. She locked the door, sat down and stared at the cracked tile floor. An idea began to form. The small black and whites tiles, and the draught cutting across her ankles began to recede.

She had it. Hatsumi could teach them some Maths through architecture; it must involve angles after all. They could do some origami too, that was about shapes. Fin narrowed her eyes. She needed to walk to figure out the rest. She pulled the flush. The water rushed from above her head down into the pan, loud. She grabbed her wellies and headed out towards the front door. Just in time.

She could hear Pop "No, not that one," he said. "I looked at that in the library, it's another exam board but they do text books too."

Fin paused.

Hatsumi joined in. "But it's GCSE exam? Maybe too advanced?"

"Oh no, the Home-Schoolers' Forum advise parents to go straight to GCSE, A' level even, if the kids are bright and why not?" said Mop. "Shakespeare, one family does Chaucer all week."

Fin didn't know what a Chaucer was but it sounded hard, like chemistry. She headed out into the dark, not even noticing she'd forgotten her torch. She was half way up towards the grassy knoll before she noticed the dark. She kept going. Her eyes readjusted to the darkness. She had to stop the adults, it was worse than she thought. She didn't notice the smell of cigarette smoke drifting lazily towards her.

It wasn't cold or even wet. Fin shucked off her coat, tying the sleeves round her waist. She passed the stone quagga with a quick glance. She usually slowed here. Sometimes when the sunlight scattered through the branches it looked almost alive, watchful. Fin didn't want to peer into the dark bushes beyond. In the daytime the grassy knoll was all odd shapes: Cyprus trees, stunted palms, stone pineapples and pillars. But by night it had a deep dark core. There was the black mausoleum in the middle with a rusty iron grill. Unlike the other mausoleums it had no peeling gold names. There was only a date in Roman numerals.

It was here Billy had stationed himself. He saw Fin head towards him, a faint trace of orange street light catching her hair. It looked like orange fuzz. Maybe she's a cancer kid, thought Billy. Eddy sniffed about. Billy bent down and caught Eddy's thick collar.

"Quiet," he hissed.

Eddy stopped and waited. He'd done his sniffing for the night. This new game might be interesting. Billy shifted his position to get a better view. He blew smoke slowly from his nostrils stubbing out the rest of his fag on a black pillar. He decided to follow the girl. Where was she going in such a hurry? Was there another house he hadn't seen? Or a shed maybe with expensive tools he could nick? Eddy strained at his collar, keen to give chase.

"Not tonight," Billy whispered.

Fin got to the top of the hill and turned to look back. Her eyes were used to the dark. There was a half-moon and the lights from the main road and the back of the hospital painted long shadows across the yard. Most of the tall trees had lost their leaves so she had a clear view. The lights of London, orange and white glittered beyond the wall. Pale wild grass stuck up between the dark shadows thrown by gravestones. Fin didn't see Billy. He kept close to the pillar, holding his breath. He was tempted to let Eddy go just to see the girl's face. But he'd lose the advantage. If he really wanted to be a mercenary he'd need to get the bigger picture. Wait, watch, wait some more, let his target do the work.

Fin wished she had her note book. Some good ideas were brewing. She rummaged in her pocket: an old shopping list and some stale peanuts. She needed to head back to get the ideas down before they evaporated. She started back the way she'd come noticing the change in the wind. For a moment she could hear voices and cars coming from the hospital. She went round to the quagga side of the knoll. The other side was just too dark. No one can hear you scream, Ermine said. She moved fast. It was creepy and too quiet now. Billy waited. Fin headed off towards Twin House she needed to talk to Zen. Billy watched her go, not the direction he'd expected.

Fin thought about Ermine. She didn't realise this was because she could smell the faint odour of cigarette smoke. She hurried on to Twin House before her confidence could ebb away. All the lights were on as usual but she couldn't see Zen or Ty. She banged on the door. There was no answer. She banged again. She thought she heard Ty clapping his jaws but she wasn't sure. She turned and leaned with her back on the door. A shadow emerged from the knoll. Fin stepped forward expecting Zen to appear. But it was Billy and Evil Eddy.

He strolled towards the gate, Eddy on his lead. At the gate he turned and tipped his head in Fin's direction. Fin shuddered, pressing her back into the door's worn wood panels. Billy disappeared onto the main road. Fin turned and banged the knocker until her hand hurt.

"OK, OK, where's the fire?" said Zen, heaving the door open.

Fin jumped in and shoved it shut behind her. Before Zen could say: make yourself at home, why don't you, or anything else. Fin blurted out "Billy."

Zen pushed his face to a small peep hole Fin hadn't noticed before.

"He's gone, but he had Eddy with him," Fin was shaking, what if Billy had jumped out?

"Did he hurt you?" said Zen.

"No," said Fin, too fast. "He's just creeping about, showing... trying to intimidate, probably been out there hours, just waiting to spit and swear."

"Yeah," said Zen. "But playing out in the dark by yourself... I mean..."

Fin gave him a look.

"I go out with Ty, when it's dark..."

"I wasn't playing. I was coming here, while your mum and mine are still drinking tea. We need to work fast on this home-school project."

Zen turned away and walked towards the kitchen. Fin followed. Zen shook out some Oreos. Fin picked one off the table and sat down.

Zen remained standing, waiting.

Fin chewed realising her mouth was dry.

"Can I have some water?" she said.

"OK," said Zen.

Fin watched him take a tumbler off the draining board. He didn't even check if it was clean, just swilled in water and plonked it down in front of her. Fin gulped. It had all sounded so clear in her head, now she was worried it was a bit silly. Ty padded in and nuzzled her hand, Fin handed him a biscuit. He dropped it, then licked it off the floor. He left a trail of slobber. Fin made a note not to slip on that when she got up.

"If we don't do something, Miss Nomer will have us both back at school before you can say Jack Robinson," began Fin.

"Eh?"

"We're stuck with home-school. But if we let our parents take over, we'll be doing A' level Maths and all sorts of ridiculous projects," Fin paused.

"So I suggest we plan it ourselves, that way we get to do what we want like a project that doesn't take all day, all week and we can... you can still roam about and I can well..." Fin tried to think of what she did. She could hardly fess up to playing or rather talking to the Imperial family. Since she'd been at home, and Zelda buggered off abroad, Fin used the Imperial family for company. She'd line them up and ask them questions and imagine their answers. Sometimes she wrote whole conversations down between the sisters. Though Anastasia wasn't very nice, chats turned into rows if Fin wasn't careful. Fin knew it was pretend. She wasn't mad after all. But she was so used to spending hours alone with her imaginary friends; it felt real a lot of the time. OK, Tsarevich Alexei was spoilt but Tatiana was really kind.

"I can sit and read etc..." said Fin.

To Fin's surprise Zen nodded. He took an Oreo which appeared to seal the deal. Fin was about to ask what sort of project he'd suggest but the back door opened and Hatsumi came in. Fin got up to go.

Hatsumi smiled "I thought you over there."

"I'll go back with Fin, Ty needs a walk," said Zen. Fin's shoulders relaxed.

13

BONFIRE

Home-school didn't restart right away. There was cleaning and clearing to do. The main road was closed to buses and cars. Metal fences with big warning signs were put up after a new hole appeared. At least there were no more gas explosions. The council called it historical subsidence. There were rumours about secret fracking and old mine shafts. Pop said it was more likely they were living on a honeycomb of Victorian sewers that were gradually giving way beneath their feet. Everyone called the holes the craters as if they had become a local landmark. The craters soon filled with Pepsi cans, greasy chicken boxes and torn newspapers. One night someone stole three metal fences. Four old mattresses were dumped in the deepest hole. Local shop keepers phoned the council. Surveyors and builders wandered the High Street taking measurements. The *Tooting Times* carried a different "expert's" view every day. There was a backlog of funerals.

Fin and Zen spent a few days wandering up and down the High Street at dawn, exploring. Fin checked for slippage but it looked like everything was stable. No one was about, so it felt like the yard, as if Tooting belonged to them. They figured Billy was probably too lazy to get up at this time, just to bother them.

After one such trip, Fin returned to find Pop making tea. Mop's face was red and puffy.

"The shed's fallen down a sinkhole," said Pop, over the boiling kettle. He seemed to think Fin and Zen would be interested. "It was rotten anyway and a magnet for thieves, not that I left tools in it, keep those in the basement. Muahaha."

Fin glanced at Zen. She worried what he might think of her family.

"Better get back," said Zen. "Feed Ty."

He rubbed Ty's head. Mop looked like she was about to cry. Fin saw Ty and Zen off then returned to the kitchen. Mop stood up.

"But a food bank, it's..." she said.

Pop handed her a mug of tea handle first, so he held the hot bottom.

"Look, we don't have to go, but the vicar said we were entitled on a low income. He was trying to be helpful. Send Ermine and Fin if you like."

Mop turned to Fin as if she only just realised Fin was there. She looked at her tea and went outside closing the kitchen door behind her.

"What's a food bank?" said Fin.

"Sit down," said Pop.

Fin didn't like his grown up tone, too polite. She sat down.

"You girls don't need to worry."

Fin started to worry. Pop frowned and glanced round the kitchen looking for something. Fin wanted to know right away, whatever it was, straight up like Gran's medicinal vodka.

"We're poor," Pop said simply. "Yes, I have a job, yes this house is cheap but the pay here is," Pop winced, "basic."

Fin felt a heavy cloud form above her head.

"Look love, we can manage, don't worry. The vicar thought he was being helpful, he was... but... it's..."

"It's humiliating," said Fin. She'd just translated Mop's expression. Pop nodded.

"The food bank's free food for poor families."

Fin wanted him to use another word.

"Supermarkets throw it all away, just cos it's a day over due."

"Out of date," said Ermine.

Fin wondered how long Ermine had been standing there, God what if Abimbola and Guy were listening too.

"I'll go," said Ermine.

"I'll help carry," said Fin.

Pop smiled and nodded.

The next day Fin wandered out into the autumn sunshine. Mop was already digging the earth inside the wall. A few red leaves drifted down from the trees. Pop was sweating in his boiler suit with Guy and Zen. They were attempting to push the remaining shed wall down.

"Let's do the other side, but mind the hole, it's not deep but you never know," puffed Pop. So they all went round the other side. Fin joined in. They began to push their feet against the rotten wood.

"Careful," shouted Pop as the side began to move. "Don't want any feet going through."

It was hard to stop. It was a satisfying feeling as the shed gave way, wood began to bend and splinter. They all stepped back when the corrugated roof banged down in a dusty heap. Guy bent over coughing. His jumper encrusted with dust and cobwebs. Fin was glad she hadn't joined in earlier. Zen tried to pull cobwebs off his T-shirt. Ty watched, lolling on a nearby grave. He scratched his back with his hind paw. Fin went over and leaned against the cold stone. Ty flipped his big bulk up, sitting up next to her, sniffing.

Pop and Guy began to drag the shed wall. Then Pop stopped.

"We'd better take the roof off," he said.

Zen knelt on the shed panel and began to pull nails out with the head of a claw hammer. The panel bounced a little and sagged. Pop rattled in his tool box. Guy came over to the stone and put a fag in his mouth. He didn't light it, the work wasn't over yet. He nodded at Fin. Fin tried out a smile. Guy blinked and rubbed Ty's back.

Fin used to worry about what Ermine told her friends, all sorts of made up stories about Fin. She was a conjoined twin, she had webbed feet. When Fin went into hospital Ermine hinted Fin had rabies.

"I never actually said rabies," said Ermine, when Mop told her off after the tenth phone call that day. But Fin just didn't care anymore.

Guy gave her a nod and Abimbola always chatted. Gran said if you've got any sense you judge people by what they do, not words. So has Guy got sense? Fin thought so, though he didn't speak. And Gran added if people didn't have sense they weren't worth bothering with anyway, end of.

Zen shouted. Ty jumped off the stone, leaping towards him. Zen disappeared through the rotten wood. Fin stood up, Guy lunged forward.

"Wait," yelled Pop. Guy stood at the edge of the shed panel.

"I'm OK," shouted Zen from somewhere beneath their feet. Ty ran backwards and forwards at the edge of the shed, growling. Pop, Guy and Fin began to pull and heave at the splintered panel. The wood was heavy and damp. Pop and Guy worked fast. Most of the sections were too big for Fin. It reminded her of her accident. Typical, they'd moved to an accident black spot.

Guy pulled up the last few boards like he was opening a lid.

"Are you hurt, bleeding?" yelled Pop.

Fin expected to see Zen sitting next to a skeleton. But he was standing on a slope of rubble. He wasn't too far away. Pop lowered his voice.

"Are you OK?"

Guy put out his hand and pulled him up. Ty coughed. Zen rubbed his head.

"S' OK." said Zen. "Bit weird."

They all peered at Zen. His face was coated in wood dust but he wasn't bleeding. He rubbed his face hard.

"Itchy," he said. Ty tried to lick him clean but Zen pushed him off.

Pop squinted at the rubble slope. "Well I'm not shifting that lot" he said. "We've got three funerals at 4."

They spent the next hour piling up the rotten wood for a fire, well away from the slope. Pop knelt on the ground and peered down into the gap.

"Not too deep, probably blocked by coffins, down the end," he said cheerily.

Ty barked. The old shed sat in a disgruntled heap waiting for a match. Fin rolled up some newspaper and began to light the ends. Guy wandered off for a smoke. Pop went in for a mug of tea. Zen pushed some dry twigs in the other side of the shed and lit them. After a lot of smoke and several false starts Fin and Zen stood back to enjoy the flames, crackling up towards the trees. Ty went back to the gravestone, keeping an eye on them.

"It'd be better at night," said Zen. Waves of heat rippled off the shed. The fire crackled and strange things curled in its orange heart. Fin wanted to find other stuff to add, sometimes things burned green or roared. Pop put his head out of the kitchen window.

"Well done, come in for some food, it looks safe enough."

Ty lumbered up and led the way.

After lunch Fin and Zen decided to keep the fire going. That was easier than asking adults if they could start a fire. So they spent the day collecting interesting debris. They added the brambles Mop had cut but they were too green; making billowing, eye-stinging smoke. There was plenty of dead wood along the paths. They had to work fast to stop the fire dying. Fin found some cans. Zen found an old carrier bag with oranges turning mouldy at the bottom. They hoped they'd make the fire smell orangey but they didn't. Ty kept his distance. Snapping his teeth if they went too close. Fin's neck itched. She rubbed it and realised it was her hair. It was growing back. She rubbed her greasy neck and smelled her smoky skin. Zen's face was smeared with ash.

14

TUNNELS

After dark, Fin and Zen returned to the fire. Ty kept watch from the grave again. Most of the shed was now grey and white ash but some wood still glowed red. Fin's hands got cold. She rammed them into her pockets. Her torch took up too much space so she took it out and began to sweep the undergrowth looking for rats and foxes. The beam caught the rubble slope and a curved shadow. Fin followed it idly. The curve moved with the torch. She decided to walk down the slope. Maybe there would be something interesting to burn?

Her feet slipped. She had to move fast so she didn't fall down. Ty, seeing her disappear, bounded to the top of the slope. Zen paused looking for sticks. It was chilly away from the fire. The slope was deeper than Fin thought. The air was damp and earthy. She shone her torch ahead. The beam caught the London clay but it was darker at one side. Fin jumped, expecting an up-ended coffin but it was just a dark rectangle. Weird. It was like a black hole sucking in the torch beam, returning no light. Fin moved slowly forward. It wasn't going to be a door into another dimension. She steeled herself for disappointment. She moved towards the rectangle. She was standing underground now. Her torch beam caught something. It was a gap and beyond she saw a tunnel.

Zen and Ty slithered down to join her. Ty started a big warning yawn. Zen peered into the gloom, his eyes adjusting after the fire.

"It's like a tunnel," said Fin.

"No," said Zen "It *is* a tunnel."

Ty began to pad forward. The gap was big enough to walk through. It was wider than it looked. It was sort of at a funny angle. Fin could only really see it when she was standing this close. It was invisible, or at least hidden, from the top of the slope. Ty edged through the gap. Fin shone the torch along his stripy back. Zen walked after Ty. Fin followed. She took the lead with Ty because she had the torch. She felt safe with Ty padding beside her like a small lion. And she felt a bit brave too.

The floor was dusty from the rubble. Ty left paw prints but soon the floor was smooth, bare and black. The walls curved around them like a tube tunnel. White tiles reflected the light. The ceiling was a very pale creamy green. It looked solid. Fin didn't think it would cave in.

"Maybe it's the Tube?" said Zen.

"Or a sewer?" said Fin.

They didn't speak for a while. It was like they'd break the spell and come to a dead end. They'd probably hit a wall or gate and that would be the end of their adventure. It was quiet and warm. They could no longer hear the road or the wind in the trees. Their sneakered feet made little impact on the black floor. Fin glanced back. She couldn't see the firelight anymore but the ceiling glowed.

"Wait," she stopped and turned off her torch. The ceiling continued to glow giving them enough light to see. Zen stared at the pale curves.

"Phosphorescent paint, cool. I had a phosphorescent clock once, dad took it away because the numbers frightened me in the dark," Zen said. "The 5 looked really evil."

Fin smiled and turned the torch back on, waving it about overhead. It was the most she'd ever heard Zen say. Ty padded ahead. He coughed and stopped. Iron bars blocked their way.

"Typical," muttered Fin, "to good to be true."

She joined Ty and peered through the bars. But it wasn't just bars. There was a gate in the middle.

She pushed the handle and pulled it open.

"I thought it'd be locked," said Zen stepping through.

Fin wasn't sure she wanted to go further. No one knew they were underground. But the tunnel was so smooth and clean, it was soothing. Ty jumped over the threshold, Fin followed. He ran ahead into the soft darkness. He wanted an adventure too. The tunnel curved gradually without them realising so pretty soon they could no longer see the gate behind them.

At the edge of the floor was a gutter. Ty knocked his teeth together and sniffed, his short brown fur standing up. He then hared off into the black. Zen whistled and hurried after him. Fin shone the torch after Zen. Then when the ceiling began to glow she flicked it towards the gutter. Bending down she caught sight of a chewed plastic bag, no, it wasn't that at all, but she couldn't understand what it was. Then she jumped. It was a sloughed snake skin.

"Yuck." Maybe time to go home, she thought.

Zen was calling Ty in the dark, his voice echoed along the tunnel. It was creepy. Fin just wanted to go back and tell Pop but she couldn't leave Zen and Ty in the dark. She began to walk fast to find them. She zigzagged the curved ceiling with the torch.

"Fin," Zen shouted somewhere ahead.

She wished he'd stop shouting. His voice echoed along the tiles. She couldn't hear Ty. She was too nervous to call back. Her mouth was dry, her hands were sweaty. The torch slipped and slid out of her hands. It bounced across the tunnel floor. The torch didn't break. It just rolled into the gutter. Fin checked for snake skin before picking it up. A weak light reflected in the phosphorescent paint giving the tunnel a dim glow. Fin paused. She listened to her pounding heart, and then wished she hadn't. The thumping sound made her afraid.

The tunnel stretched a long way in both directions. Which way should she go? She caught a sound. It made her neck prickle. Whispering? It seeped down the tunnel towards her. Fin clamped her jaw shut to stop her heart leaping out. Pop had taught her to run home fast in any emergency. But this would leave Zen and Ty alone in the dark.

"Zen, Ty, TY," yelled Fin.

The names echoed along the tiled walls. Something large came thundering down the tunnel. Fin let out a squeal as Ty jumped up pushing her to the wall and licking her face. Fin pushed him down but hugged his big thick neck. He was wet and smelly, like he'd been in a pond. Ty waited, looking up the tunnel and back at Fin. Was this a signal to follow? Maybe Zen was hurt. Fin grabbed his collar and tried to jog along while flashing the ceiling with her torch.

The whispering got louder. It was only her hand on Ty and the fact she didn't want to be left alone that kept her running. They rounded a corner fast and bumped into Zen.

"'bout time guys, can't see a damn thing. Gimme the torch something's odd..." said Zen, grabbing the torch.

Fin kept hold of Ty. Zen swept the torch about but didn't hit any phosphorescent paint. Ty shot towards the whispering, wrenching his collar out of Fin's hand. She screamed. Zen shone the torch in her face.

"What's the matter?" he said.

Fin didn't know where to start.

"What's the matter?" she parroted.

Ty barked and began to splash in the darkness. The tunnel had ended. Were they down a sewer? Fin grabbed the torch and shone it towards Ty but just caught the edge of the floor. Then the beam caught Ty's big eyes. He was jumping up and down, wagging his wide head, as if it was dog Christmas.

"I think we need a bigger torch," said Fin.

Fin and Zen stepped towards Ty slowly. It wasn't that either felt brave they just didn't want to be left alone in this weird dark place. With each step Fin told herself Ty wasn't afraid, so it must be OK. Except she knew Ty could run away fast. They'd be stuck or maybe she'd be stuck. Zen could probably run like the wind. Zen stopped. Fin bumped into him. He was standing at the edge of the floor. The black stone stopped. It was some sort of cliff.

Fin moved her torch towards the edge. Ty stopped splashing,

waiting for them to catch up. That was creepy, without the splashing, they could all hear the whispering. Fin was ready to bolt. The space around them felt big and cool after the tunnel. Then the torch caught water. They were standing at the edge of some sort of pool. Ty swished towards them. The water was clear, about two feet deep. The bottom was tiled, like the tunnel. Fin had half an idea. It was familiar like somewhere she'd been before. But that couldn't be right, or could it?

"That noise," said Fin, "It's water, like a swimming pool."

"Glad you said that," said Zen. "It was creeping me out."

"Well, I'm not sure," said Fin, keeping her voice low. She didn't want to add echoes as well.

"No, no a swimming pool is just fine, stick with that theory..." grinned Zen.

"OK," said Fin, "if I'm right..."

She felt better knowing Zen was nervous too. She always thought it was just her. Despite Gran saying she was comparing her insides with other people's outsides. Fin circled the torch around their feet creating a larger and larger area of light. At first all it caught was black floor but then the beam caught a phosphorescent wall and more water. The water rippled and sparkled. Ty tried to run in and out of the light.

Fin smiled in the dark, she knew whatever it was wasn't going to let them down. She moved away from Zen and began to follow the smooth floor. She waved the torch in front of her. It began to light half a wall. She moved methodically away from Zen following the wall as it curved.

"Wow," said Zen.

Ty stopped splashing and made a sort of yipping noise of encouragement. Fin kept going and going until her hand got tired. She felt like an explorer opening an Egyptian tomb. She stopped when she realised she'd left Zen a bit far behind. He didn't have a torch. But she needn't have worried. The walls here were phosphorescent too. Or at least half of them were.

"Woo hoo," shouted Zen, his voice bounced around, catching her up.

They were standing in a large round chamber. The walls glowed with smooth pale phosphorescent paint. The domed ceiling was too high for Fin's feeble torch. However, now the curved walls glowed more of the chamber was revealed. The ceiling was covered in a mosaic of blue and gold tiles. Ty started barking at something in the water. Fin hurried to the edge of the pool. There were dark shapes here and there. Ty pushed his nose into the water. He was trying to catch mosaic fish. Their green bodies appeared to wobble as the water moved. They were all ugly with bulbous eyes and open mouths. Some had long green whiskers and teeth.

"Yuck." Zen joined Fin. They spent some time peering at their bloated bodies.

"Who'd want to swim with them?" said Zen.

Zen left Ty trying to scare the tile fish and followed Fin. On the far side there were broad steps into the pool.

"I think I know what this is," said Fin.

She was excited. This was good because the next thing the torch caught made them both jump. Ty stopped playing and splashed over, hurrying up the steps with a worried face.

The torch light was swallowed up in a dark gap.

"What's that?" whispered Zen down Fin's neck, reaching for Ty's collar.

"It's another tunnel, look." Fin stepped under the dark archway and began to sweep the torch across the ceiling. She just knew Zen was impressed. He'd been scared too. Ty was keen to head down but Zen pulled him back. This tunnel was cold. Fin stepped back towards the pool and found another archway. This time her torch caught gold.

Zen laughed "What the?"

Ty barked. Fin inched forward to discover another chamber, much smaller with an oval white pool like a really big old bath tub. But the walls were covered in shards of broken gold mirrors. As Fin ran the torch up and down, the walls glittered and threw out crazy light patterns. The domed ceiling was plain phosphorescence. There was no water here. Zen poked Fin in the shoulder.

"Did you know this was here?"

"Not exactly, I read about..." Fin stopped, her torch began to fade.

"Shit, rechargeable batteries," said Fin. "They don't last very long."

They stared into the big chamber. It was pretty dim but there was enough light to see the big round pool. However, it looked a long way to the other side.

"We'd better go back, phosphorescent paint fades," said Zen.

Fin's torch went out. They walked back fast, the tunnel getting dimer by the second. They had to walk in darkness for the last leg of the tunnel.

15

DISCOVERIES BACK AT HOME

It was dark when they scrambled up the rubble bank, raising clouds of itchy dust. Fin caught sight of the red glow of a cigarette. Guy stepped towards them, waved and dropped his fag butt on the edge of the rubble. He wasn't fazed by them emerging from underground. The air smelled sweet. It reminded Fin she was hungry. Her belly rumbled.

"Let's get some tea at Blin... my kitchen," Fin wasn't keen to flag up their weird house name even if Zen did live in the yard. "I've got something to show you," gasped Fin, still out of breath.

Zen shrugged, whistling for Ty. They went towards the kitchen. The windows were open. Voices drifted out across the cold air.

"Hello," said Mop, when Fin opened the door.

Hatsumi and Pop were smoking in the house, though Hatsumi was standing by the kitchen window flicking ash in the sink. Pop smiled but carried on talking.

"No that was 1870. I'm sure. Last big Cholera epidemic." He waved his hands for emphasis, pointing his fag at Fin and Zen. Fin was really hungry. She didn't want to sit through a lecture. She wanted to get some toast and run upstairs with Zen to her overdue library book pile. Otherwise, Zen would probably lose interest and sod off with Ty. Pop was talking like he'd lived through the epidemic.

"Sit down, eat first," said Mop, sounding like Hatsumi.

Fin washed her hands at the sink. Zen just sat down. Ty waited by the door assessing the situation for dog friendly food. Mop slapped some crumpets under the grill. Fin poured water into their big red tumblers. Zen gulped his, like he'd not drunk for a week. Fin took an untoasted crumpet and pushed it under Ty's nose. He swallowed it whole, then sat down next to Fin's chair to wait for the next round.

Eventually, Mop passed round the crumpets, brown and buttery on top, burnt to charcoal on the bottom. Fin chewed her crumpet pushing her tongue into the holes soaked in melted butter. She'd dropped two more for Ty minus butter. She didn't know if dogs could eat butter. Zen ate four crumpets in the time it took Fin to eat two. Mop made a pot of tea.

"You guys are starving, playing with fire must be hungry work," she said.

Zen looked up blank. Fin glanced round the table. Pop was searching his pockets and the cluttered mantel piece for more fags. Guy drifted in, poured some tea then drifted out again.

Fin thought they'd been away for hours. Something big had happened but Mop, Pop and Hatsumi were trapped in the old time zone. Fin wanted to tell everyone about where they'd been but at the same time she wanted to keep it a secret. For now anyway. Zen's only concern appeared to be his belly. Ty led down by the fire after leaving a half chewed crumpet on the floor. He was leaving space for meat.

Before Fin could answer, Pop said: "You guys can use the last London cholera epidemic, in your project."

"Don't those bugs survive in the ground?" said Mop. "I heard they can't build on Blackheath because it's a plague pit, which means…"

"We should be careful about what we dig up here," said Pop.

"Doesn't the bug survive in water?" asked Fin before she could stop herself.

"Some do," said Pop.

Fin and Zen looked at Ty. He was dry now, just dusty. Fin was glad she washed her hands. She got up and washed them again. Zen did the same.

Pop ploughed on, oblivious. "There was a cholera epidemic, about 1848… Lord Basel, by then very rich, got tired of his workers dying off. So he started building sewers round here. Got into trouble with the House of Lords who thought it wasn't his business to improve London. So long story short," Mop smiled at Hatsumi, "He built his estate here, said he was a Londoner, entitled to protection under the law for civic amenities." Pop liked this phrase.

"He built this house?" said Hatsumi.

"Yes but this wasn't his mansion, these two houses came later. The big house was pulled down to build the hospital after he died. Pity really, but they did recycle the bricks." Pop stood up and refilled the kettle. Mop pulled the mugs across the table.

"When he died he left the estate for a workers' hospital and cemetery, in those days hospitals were a bit rubbish," Pop jerked his head towards the hospital.

Fin had heard all this before but now she was really listening.

Mop joined in: "Apparently he started the graveyard while he lived here, so he could keep his wife and son nearby."

"Cholera," Pop said. "They died of cholera."

"The Victorians were obsessed with death, they used to photograph dead relatives," said Mop.

Fin looked at Zen and Hatsumi. She remembered the photo of Zen with his dad. She wished Mop and Pop would shut up. Perhaps she could change the subject. Maybe she should drop a mug on the floor?

"We've got a book somewhere of whole families sitting around dead kids, propped up like they're still alive... Ermine's using it for her art exam."

This was news to Fin.

"How do you build a graveyard?" asked Fin, jumping in before the dead people story continued.

"Well, Lord Basel started getting customers, while these two houses were built. He actually lived here for a while; apparently he couldn't stand the big house without his wife and son. It must have felt pretty empty. His housekeeper lived in the other one."

"So let me get this straight," said Fin. "Lord Basel, lived in this house, while the graveyard grew around him."

"Yep," said Mop. "I think he wanted to stay close to Lady Anne and Peter. They both died about the same time."

"Very sad," said Hatsumi, still chewing her first crumpet. Fin wanted to point out she didn't have to eat it if she didn't want to.

"And ironic," said Mop filling up the kettle again. "Lord Basel did a lot to clean up London water. The Thames was so full of rubbish, you could drop a barrel in and it wouldn't move for a month."

Neither Mop nor Pop could resist an educational story. Fin glanced at Zen. He was listening. Even Ty was listening. Fin took a tangerine out of the carrier bag in the middle of the table and peeled it slowly. She held it up and caught Zen's eye, he shook his head.

"Lord Basel rebuilt sewers, lobbied for hospitals, he even had the scheme for a workers' spa," said Pop.

Zen glanced at Fin. Fin nodded.

"That bankrupted him, cost him everything."

"Very interesting," said Hatsumi, putting her crumpet down. She stood up. "Time to go." She glanced at Zen and Fin.

"You have big project on your hands. Start research tomorrow. Fire after."

Both Fin and Zen nodded. They did have a big project on their hands.

Fin hurried over to Twin House early the next day, early for her. Pop had already opened the gates, cleared up the cans and greasy chip paper blown down the drive over night. He'd moved onto cutting back some dead trees near the hospital. Mop had gone to Gran's. Ermine was probably still in bed.

Fin knocked at Twin House. It was too quiet, no-one was home. There was a note taped to the inside of the long window, next to the door. Large biro letters read: off to vets, back at 11. Fin wasn't sure whether it was from Hatsumi for Pop, or from Zen to her. She trudged back. The books she'd hurriedly rammed in her rucksack were heavy. It was sunny but cold. She decided to go and sit in the linen cupboard and read or at least look at the pictures. Maybe the Imperial family could join in, keep her company.

Mop returned mid-morning. She hallooed up the stairs.

"Fin we've got a hospital check, we'll take sandwiches for lunch..."

So Fin spent the afternoon eating banana sandwiches and a stale croissant waiting in queues for blood tests and for nurses to ask her silly questions. This meant walking along long corridors and then waiting for big grey lifts. By 5 p.m. a junior doctor suggested it might be better to admit Fin, to get all the checks complete, just overnight. Mop agreed and left Fin, promising to return with pyjamas and more food.

Fin sat on a hospital bed looking out of the window over rows of terraced houses and the trees that screened the yard from the road. She tried to catch sight of Zen and Ty but it was too far away. The ward was filled with noisy toddlers with broken arms and a little boy with a big bandage round his head. Fin spent two long days, waiting. Nurses came to take blood. Soggy food arrived on a tray. Mop returned with Oreos, Maltesers and Fin's rucksack. A student nurse showed Fin where she could make hot chocolate. Fin passed the time drinking the thick sweet goo with added Maltesers reading her way through the overdue library books on Lord Basel. By the time she was discharged she was an expert, she probably knew more than Pop.

It was odd having Zen in her room. Fin was so used to seeing him outside with Ty. Ty led across the top of the stairs, sniffing at the draught that snaked across the floor. Mop was washing up downstairs listening to the radio. Pop was banging about with nails and screwdrivers. Fin pulled the books in front of the fire. Zen tried to lean against the spindly chair then gave up and sat cross legged leaning his elbows on his knees. Fin had been excited but now she felt a bit silly. Her hands looked too big and her hair prickled. There was so much to show Zen but she didn't want to look like a total nerd.

"This," said Fin pointing to the cover "was Lord Basel's house, well mansion."

God now she sounded like Pop. Zen would probably never come by again. She'd be alone with just the Imperial family for ever. Zen whistled.

The sketch showed a large house surrounded by flat lawns and saplings. It had two turrets and a wide wooden door like a castle. Fin opened the book and flicked through hurrying to get to the map. But Zen put out his hand. He started to go through the book page by page. Fin had done the same thing. She hadn't been interested in Lord Basel or his grand plumbing plans. Pop had given her a lecture in hospital on that. However, she like Zen had been drawn into the large black and white photographs. They were so old they had a misty, foggy look around the edges. There were several photos of the house taken over the years, as the trees grew eventually hiding its façade. There were photos of the building of the brick sewers, with workmen in flat caps glowering with shovels and pickaxes. There was a painting of Lady Anne Basel. Fin liked this picture. It was in colour. Lady Anne wore a green velvet dress. She sat staring off towards a far horizon they couldn't see. She had lilies entwined in her long wavy hair. She looked sad. Fin could almost feel the soft velvet. Lady Anne looked like Rapunzel.

"Who's that?" said Zen.

"That's Lady Basel, Lord Basel's wife, she died of cholera in," Fin turned the book around and flicked several pages, "1874."

"That's her husband," Fin pointed to Lord Basel looking older than Pop with a handle bar moustache. "I think he was a lot older than her."

"Yep, wonder what she thought of his whiskers."

"She probably hated them but couldn't say as women had no rights back then."

"Is that why moustaches are extinct now?" said Zen.

"Maybe."

Zen rubbed his chin.

The next page showed the staff at the big house lined up on the steps, but they were too far away to see their faces properly. There were some sketches by Lord Basel of Twin House and Blind Twin House. Zen leaned closer. Some photos were taken during the Second World War. Fin knew this because the windows were covered in criss-crossed tape to stop flying glass during the Blitz. She felt like a detective working all this out, looking for clues.

The next chapters had more sewers and tunnels and a giant beam engine powered by the Thames tides. Zen began to flick, losing interest.

"Hang on you'll miss it," Fin took the book back.

Zen stared into the fire doing that boy thing, jiggling his legs. Fin couldn't find it. Zen was getting restless. He got up and walked into the hall to check on Ty. Fin began to sweat. The fire was hot on her face. Maybe it was in a book that went back to the library. Maybe she'd dreamt it?

"Here it is," said Fin, finally. Zen came back and sat down next to Fin. She showed him a hand drawn map by someone called P.B. There were little sketches of tunnels and pools. There was a border of coloured curly lines. But when Fin had looked at the books again she'd noticed they weren't lines at all.

"Those are snakes" said Fin.

"Corn snakes," said Zen. "They're all different colours."

They were. Pink, purple, blue, orange.

"I wanted one for a pet, they're not poisonous or anything. Dad was OK but mum said no."

"Not surprised," said Fin, shivering.

"No they're great: all warm and smooth..."Zen stared into the fire. "But when Ty came," Zen paused. "I don't think he likes snakes. He attacked the hose pipe last year, flooded the garden."

Fin laughed. She could just see Ty wrestling a hose pipe: water spraying everywhere.

The map was labelled Underground Workers' Spa and Sanatorium in long, looped handwriting.

Fin scanned the bottom of the page. She began to read aloud, skimming the boring bits.

"Lord Basel had plans for a Workers' Spa, blah, blah, blah... a recreational bathing area for workers on their Saturday afternoons off. Blah, blah, blah... He wrote pamphlets explaining the health benefits of clean water, blah, blah, blah... exercise... sympathetic to temperance movement but felt message was too straight laced... spa would allow workers and their families to let off steam, have fun and stay sober...." Fin turned the page.

"Here it is: The pools were to be fed, twice a day, by the Thames... beam engine to be powered by the weight of the Thames tide changes, to power fountains across South London. Unfortunately the Thames' water was still hazardous. The beam engine was installed. But by then Lord Basel was in so much debt the project was doomed. Some pools may have been constructed but they were probably incorporated into the sewers at the time of Lord Basel's death; when the house was pulled down to build the New London Hospital for the Sick and Dying."

"Great name," said Zen. "Bet people couldn't wait to go there."

"But don't you see, this is wrong," said Fin. "We've found the lost pools."

Zen took the book and flicked back to the map. The annotations were difficult to read.

"Does this say Battersea?" asked Zen.

"Maybe, not sure about the rest," replied Fin.

They began to turn the pages to find a better version of the map or more information but that was it.

"P.B might be Peter Basel," said Fin.

"Yeah," Zen turned to her "Didn't he die as a kid? Maybe his dad kept this map because his son made it."

"Maybe that's why it all got sort of buried and forgotten."

"What do you mean?" asked Zen.

"Well," said Fin thinking aloud. "It must have been awful for Lord Basel..."she paused she didn't want to upset Zen talking about dead people.

Zen got up and went over to the window. He leaned his forehead on the cold glass.

"I hate it when people do that," he muttered.

Fin waited, what did he mean?

"People keep stopping and looking at me, like I've got plague or something, cholera."

"Oh, sorry," said Fin.

"No, just carry on," said Zen.

"What before the cholera gets you?" Fin wasn't sure why she said it. She sounded like Ermine.

"Yeah, so you better be fast," said Zen. He turned round and leaned against the window sill, hands in his pockets. Ty padded in and resettled himself in front of the fire.

"Well, it doesn't say here, but all the spa sketches look like a kid's drawn them." Fin flicked back and forth. She found crude and delicate drawings. "I think this might have been a project for Lord Basel with his son. Some of these pictures are babyish but some are quite good. I think Peter dreamed this up. It's the sort of thing a kid would do."

"Yeah, underground pools," nodded Zen, "and snakes."

Fin found a sketch of upturned bowls.

"These bowls are fountain heads apparently," she said.

"I've seen those" said Zen. "Down the High Street and in…"

"Your right," jumped in Fin.

They were everywhere. It was just she'd lived in Tooting all her life so she didn't notice them any more. Most people thought it was some nuisance from the council. People cut their grass or moved their bins around them. In the school playground children would try to jump from one to the other, like stepping stones until a dinner lady yelled at them to stop.

"Do you know what this means?" asked Fin.

"Maybe," said Zen smiling.

Mop found them an hour later reading, a large pile of books scattered around them. Wikipedia was open on the battered laptop. There was a brief connection. Sketches, lists, coloured pens, rulers and biros, littered the floor.

"Great, you've started the project," beamed Mop.

Fin and Zen looked up with blank expressions, then returned to their research.

16

THE ADVENTURE STARTS

Fin and Zen hurried back to the tunnels the next morning. They both wanted to check it was real. Fin wanted to bring the Lord Basel book but it was too bulky. Besides if Pop saw them with the book he would try to join in and take them on a tap tour. Fin photocopied the map, and the beam engine because there were some instructions on the page. There was a table showing tide times for some reason and a list of what Victorian Londoners died of. Fin wasn't very systematic about the photocopying. She was rushing to finish before Mop asked her too much about what she was doing in the office, was it homework by any chance?

"Yes," yelled Fin. "Research for our project."

She wondered if she'd overdone it. Mop's head appeared round the door, she began to pull off her rubber gloves. Fin tried to rush past but Mop stopped her.

"I'm really glad you are getting into this... with Zen. He looked so sad when we first moved in," said Mop.

Fin was in too much of a hurry to get into this sort of conversation. She folded the photocopies and slipped her feet into her wellies, thinking: we all looked sad when we moved in. It's a graveyard, for God's sake.

She decided to grab a bag of supplies. She filled two plastic bottles that had been rolling around the draining board for weeks. The tap water was still yellow but very cold, which Fin figured would kill any germs. She took two flat packs of Garibaldis. That meant one packet each. For Ty there were some very stale croissants. She took two bruised apples just in case they got desperate and/or trapped. She'd read of trapped people cutting off their limbs to eat. Or was that to free themselves before they starved? Zen would probably know about survival as his dad was a Ghurkha.

Fin banged out the front door and headed down the brick path. The garden was bare now. Mop had cut back the brambles and dug the earth. The air smelt earthy. A robin hopped about on the wall. Zen was loitering in a patch of sunlight. Ty sniffed about between leaning headstones. The long wet grass tickled his nose.

Zen sort of smiled but Fin couldn't be sure, more an upturned lip. Fin squinted in the winter sun. Zen and Ty fell into step with Fin. They all knew where they were going. They didn't speak because the kitchen window was open. Mop wouldn't be able to see them through the crack. But if she heard them she might call out or catch a glimpse of them as they ducked down where the shed used to be. They walked fast but took care to tread carefully avoiding dry sticks and piles of leaves that might make extra noise. Fin wondered if they should go when it was dark next time. They eased themselves down the scree slope.

Fin took out her torch, now with new batteries, and Zen pulled out his.

"Fazers on stun," he muttered.

They didn't need them right away as the morning sun bounced down the loose rubble, reflecting light onto the tunnel ceiling. However, it soon began to get dark. The tunnel felt longer this time. They switched on their torches.

"Maybe we should use one and keep one in reserve," said Fin. "Just in case."

"Good thinking, Batman," said Zen.

They both switched off their torches.

"I'll start," said Zen.

He turned his torch back on and began to zigzag the beam across the ceiling making a pattern. They passed the spot where Fin saw the snake skin. It was still there. Ty spent a long time sniffing about and padding along the gutter.

"Come on, Ty" shouted Zen.

"Ty, Ty, Ty," reverberated along the tunnel.

"Shush, Mop's in the kitchen she might hear," said Fin.

"Sorry... Ty," Zen hissed. Ty lolloped after them.

"D'you think there are snakes down here?" asked Fin.

"Dunno," shrugged Zen.

They could hear the whispering water. It was creepy, even though now they knew it was only water. Zen made extra strokes across the phosphorescent ceiling to brighten the luminous paint.

When they rounded the last corner they were surprised to see the pool, light was coming in from above. It was still pretty dim but somewhere above there were windows, or holes, letting the light filter down. They stopped to stare at the domed ceiling. The blue and gold mosaic tiles made waves that went round and round. It was like looking up at a giant plug hole, water swirling down or rather up and away.

The round pool was almost empty. Ty licked the puddles on the steps. Fin sat down on the edge and let her legs dangle down into the empty pool. She shucked off her rucksack and took out her photocopies. Zen sat next to her and waited. Fin noticed his sweaty boy smell. She reached into her bag for the Garibaldis. She passed them to Zen to open. He took one whole strip and passed her the other. They crunched, then chewed. They swilled the last crumbs down with the rusty water. The Garibaldis weren't great survival biscuits as they made you very thirsty, realised Fin.

She opened the map. There was just enough light to read by. Their eyes had adjusted to the gloom. There were about six oval holes in the ceiling letting in shafts of sunlight. These slowly filtered down and sparkled on the puddles. Ty jumped about opening his jaw to menace the mosaic fish. Fin and Zen began to notice things they hadn't seen before. Opposite there were the three tunnels, dimmer but not the black holes they appeared to be last night. Ty ran round the edge of the pool to investigate. He stood on the thresholds and snapped his jaws. But he didn't venture in by himself. Fin and Zen decided they'd gone far enough for now anyway. Fin stretched her legs. She felt full after the Garibaldis.

"We must be, here," Fin pointed to the pool on the photocopy.

"No shit, Sherlock," laughed Zen.

It was a bit like a tube map but Fin wasn't sure they were looking at it the right way. She passed Zen the other sheets.

"What's this?" asked Zen, squinting at the tide times.

"It tells people when the Thames has a high and low tide."

"God," thought Fin, "I really do sound like Pop."

Zen turned the paper round in his hands.

"And it was in the Basel book?"

"Yeah," Fin remembered something about London bridges opening up to let tall ships sail up and down the Thames. But Lord Basel wasn't about boats.

"So maybe this is low tide," said Zen pointing to the empty pool.

"So last night, when there was water was high tide?" said Fin thinking aloud.

"Well, it wasn't very high. It's a bit rubbish for a swimming pool if it's only half full when everyone's in bed," concluded Zen.

Fin nodded. Ty meanwhile had started sniffing around the entrances of the other tunnels.

"Might as well take a look," said Zen springing up.

Fin folded up the paper and pushed it into her rucksack, mystery solved, adventure probably over. Or so she thought.

There was a draught on the other side of the pool coming down the tunnels. They hovered about on the threshold. They spent some time shouting rude words into the echoing darkness. The gold room glittered next to an archway leading to a square room. The tiles here were white and on the far side was a metal barrier. Behind the barrier was a very tall space housing the beam engine. They put their torches on to get a better look. Fin wasn't interested in engines. It lurked against the wall like a dinosaur. The beam and giant metal wheel cast shadows around the room. Zen leaned over a guard rail and stared down into some sort of pit. Fin's curiosity got the better of her.

"What is it?" she asked.

"It's just water, I think," said Zen. "Maybe it gets full with the tide?"

Fin looked down. It looked like the deep end in the pool except with no water. There was a rusty ladder pinned into the tiles which meant workers could go to the base of the engine for maintenance. Fin guessed. She shuddered. She wouldn't want to climb down past the big, black arms and wheels. The ladder was pretty close. What if the engine moved and caught your arm? Dragging you down, crushing you underneath.

Ty leaned over. Fin rubbed his back. She backed away from the edge. Ty watched her. He then pushed his head between Zen and the edge. Zen leaned away from the guard rail. Ty relaxed. But Zen changed his mind. He ducked under the guard rail. Then, slowly, he began making his way carefully down the rusty ladder. Ty's fur stood on end. He started to growl.

"That's dangerous," said Fin. "It might come off the wall."

"Then I'll be quick," said Zen jumping off the last rung, with a splash.

"Yuck, it's wet down here and smelly." Fin and Ty leaned over. Fin tried to catch Zen with her torch. Ty tensed his back muscles, knocking his great jaw together. Zen splashed about bending and peering at something Fin and Ty couldn't see. Neither of them liked this. There was a dark sludge around the base of the engine. Sometimes the torch caught a rainbow of oil on the water's surface.

Fin's knees were cramping, she shifted. She thought she heard something behind her. She turned quickly. The pool room looked the same, empty, quiet, waiting. Zen was climbing back out now, his trainers wet and slippery.

He re-joined Fin on her side of the barrier. He rubbed his hands. They were coated in small flecks of orange rust and tarry oil. He smelt like purple bubble gum, that heavy brackish smell of the dirty water.

"There's a grill down there, and quite a draught, might lead to the Thames or an underground river?"

Fin stood up. For some reason she wanted to go home. She hoped Zen would move but he rubbed Ty's head. Ty licked at Zen's hands.

"Didn't you say something about the Thames tide powering this?" said Zen pointing at the engine.

"Maybe," said Fin, "If the tide came in... it could start pumping up and down?"

"Perhaps it does, when no one's here," Zen put on a ghostly voice.

"No," said Fin, walking towards the pool. "No, if that was true, we'd see the fountains going, wouldn't we? Unless they clogged up years ago."

"Or maybe," said Zen, "the engine's broken down?"

They both stared at the engine, tall and proud, black and silver around its giant wheel.

"I don't think they break," said Fin. It looked too big and robust to break. Zen followed her out.

"Perhaps it's just rusted or maybe... Maybe if we figured out the problem we could get it going again?"

Neither of them believed this for one moment but they both enjoyed the idea: fountains springing up all over South London. However, if the fountains were dependent on tide times it might mean no one would ever see them because they would only work at high tide, in the middle of the night. Or so they thought.

17

SNAKES

There wasn't much else to do except explore the other tunnel. It was the same as the first except along the wall there was a line of green tiles with a raised leaf pattern. Fin rubbed her hands along the leaves. Zen took on illumination duties. Ty scuffled ahead. The tunnel was occasionally lit from above, like the dome. It twisted left and then right but it was difficult to tell after a while. Fin found it hard to keep her bearings underground. She took out her note pad. She wanted to make a map or keep some sort or record. She remembered Hansel and Gretel's breadcrumb trail. She wasn't sure what to draw. There were no landmarks. She could drop pages from her note book to leave a paper trail but Ty would probably gobble them up. She'd noticed dogs would eat anything. Or at least Ty would. Ty stopped on the next twist and stood very still. His short fur rising. Zen caught Fin's arm. She stopped, her hair rising on the back of her neck. Goosebumps ran up her arms.

They watched Ty. The ceiling began to fade. Ty did his big yawn gape. Zen stepped slowly forward. Fin followed. She didn't want to, but she didn't want to get left behind either. Ty had found a spiral staircase curling away towards a faint sound of traffic. Cars and lorries rumbled somewhere far above. A shaft of daylight caught a rusted hand rail. Damp green mould coated the walls and steps. The stairs were barred by a gate. Dry leaves, crisp packets and yellow newspaper had collected at the bottom. It looked like a nest.

Fin stared at the leaves. They were moving.

"Snakes," gasped Fin.

She was looking at a whole twisted mass of snakes coiling and recoiling around themselves and the leaves. Fin and Zen both stepped backwards very slowly until they had their backs to the far wall. Ty didn't take his eyes off the writhing pile, or move. Fin waited for one to rear up, puff out its neck and spit venom. She began to edge down the cold tiled wall. Zen stayed where he was.

"Ty," he hissed. Ty didn't move. "Ty."

Ty put his head down, closed his mouth and bucked his head towards the pile. The snakes coiled up tight then began to slither away under the steps. Ty couldn't reach them behind the gate. Fin thought the snakes knew this because they moved very, very slowly. Fin wanted them to disappear fast. She had time to see a thick green one curl around a short blue one. Then a red one almost got left behind. Ty put his nose to the edge of the gate and made a horrible growling sound in the back of his throat. His legs tensed ready to spring away. Zen grabbed Ty's collar and tried to yank him back. He refused to move until all the snakes were gone.

"Corn snakes," said Zen, releasing Ty's collar. "Harmless, maybe escaped pets."

"So they aren't poisonous?" asked Fin.

"Nope," said Zen "Good job, 'cos Ty's got no sense. You'd think he'd have some instinct or something but no sir."

"But they could still bite?"

"Suppose. Could have bitten Ty on the nose, serve him right."

They began to walk back towards the pools.

"Try explaining that to the vet," said Fin.

They walked back fast. Fin tried to time how long it took them to get back to the pools from the snake spiral. She also planned to look up corn snakes. What if Zen was wrong? They didn't bother swinging their torches across the ceiling as the tunnel was still dim enough to see by. Ty kept darting off to the sides of the tunnel checking for more snakes. Fin was a bit shaky. She'd had enough adventure for one day. She wanted Ty to stay close, to feel his warm fur and powerful back.

When they reached the slope Zen said he should give Ty a run to calm him down. Fin hurried towards Blind Twin House to log on.

Fin smelt cigarette smoke drifting around the bushes at the edge of the slope. She thought it might be Guy but she was anxious to get back to the house. So she didn't look around. She didn't notice Billy mooching about in the undergrowth, watching her. Billy had been out and about under the guise of walking Eddy. But he was really checking out the holes, and some busted buildings for loot he could sell. The splintered shed had been a possibility but the tools had been stored in the basement of Blind Twin House.

Eddy got bored mooching. He took off towards the hospital, hoping to catch a pigeon or a rat. Eddy never found any rats or pigeons in the yard. If Billy had taken time to think about that, he would have realised it was very odd. Eddy had caught and killed five rats on the main road, since the summer. Last week he'd caught a pigeon on the estate. Some old lady had shouted at Eddy. Animal cruelty, she'd called it as Eddy chewed the pigeon's wing. The old biddy even kicked out at Eddy, animal cruelty my arse thought Billy, they're vermin.

"Leave my dog alone, you sad old bitch," shouted Billy.

The old woman narrowed her eyes at Billy. Eddy made a swallowing noise and gulped the struggling pigeon further down his jaw. Billy bent and shook Eddy's collar. This could be an expensive trip to the vets. The old woman hurried across the road trying to hold her head up. But Billy could tell she was scared. He yanked the still struggling pigeon from Eddy's gob, getting his hands and new trainers coated in slobber.

He stuck to the yard because it was quiet, no busybody old ladies. Or at least he had done until people started moving in. What sort of freaks lived in a graveyard? They were poor, obviously; neither family had anything worth nicking. He'd had a look around when they moved in. There was the little woman who looked like a boy with her son who looked like a girl and a f'ugly dog. Then a hippy dippy family with a hot, pink haired daughter: some sort of misguided Goth, and the Chemo-kid.

Billy began to spy on the comings and goings at the yard. He wasn't really interested in other people but he wanted to hone his skills. When he was nine he'd seen a programme about mercenaries. This was his ideal job. He liked fighting, liked the feeling it gave him. It was like flying or lightning. He imagined news interviews, boasting about his successes, though he'd have to keep his identity secret to get more contracts.

At secondary school, he confounded his teachers, who all tried to get him expelled, for fighting, spitting, vile comments, intimidation, bullying, even a short-lived protection racket. However, the head teacher resisted for as long as possible. In Geography Billy was an A* student, even doing extra homework and presentations. No-one messed about, or even dared speak, in Geography with Billy there. They were all terrified including his Geography teacher. He was good at sport too. Basically whatever Billy thought was useful to his future career he worked at. He'd made a list. He needed to know about terrain, fighting, weapons, and telling people what to do, who you could trust. But he needed contacts and money. Pity Geography clashed on the timetable with Business Studies.

Billy was frustrated there wasn't any mercenary type work in South London. So he did some breaking and entering, with his mates Crime and Wave. They'd been excluded from school in Year 8. They spent their time roaming the neighbourhood, up to no good. He wasn't keen handling stolen property or mugging. Too risky. Billy needed a clean passport to travel. He was always looking for his break.

He'd been told off by the hippy dippy man about Eddy shitting in the yard. The man suggested Billy bring a bag and take the shit home. In the past Billy would have taken said shit and posted it through the man's letter box but he was keeping a low profile. He didn't even bother to menace the guy. He was saving himself for something bigger. However, he couldn't resist throwing a stone at the Chemo-kid to test his aim. He caught her in the back. She'd hurried on but rubbed her back with her hand, confused. Didn't know what hit her. Billy didn't do it again. He had to practice stealth, another skill for mercenary survival. Stealth and invisibility. Now he had some investigating or recon to do. Where had those idiots been all this time? And what was underground?

18

HOMEWORK

Fin rushed up to her room shutting the door. She had a lot of thoughts jumbled together. She just needed to sit and untangle them. The spindly chair was useful for this. She sat down facing the window. The chair was smooth and cool. She slipped off her coat. She pulled out a large note pad from under a sweatshirt she'd left on the window sill. There was a chewed biro inside.

A list was needed. And a lot of paper. Fin needed the white paper space to let her thoughts wander. She doodled for a while. Then started her list.

1: Was the underground spa safe?

Fin decided to write a note explaining where they'd gone with a map in future. She could leave it somewhere. So if they didn't get back for tea Pop and Mop would find it and come after them. Well that was the theory.

Fin leaned back and chewed the splintery end of the biro. Hmm, *if* she needed to do this maybe they shouldn't go at all? And where should she leave the note? She didn't want Mop finding it right away and stopping the adventure. That was part of a parents' job after all. The only children who ever went on adventures in her books were orphans. And what if she left a note and Fat Bastard ate it? Fin wanted to ask Zen for suggestions but then she'd sound like a total doofus.

2: Snakes: research: Wikipedia and Tolemy.

Tolemy had a Rock Python. He'd brought it to school. But she would need to be careful. She didn't want Tolemy to join in. He would take over. And probably blab their secret. She had some more thoughts. Before she could get them straight, she heard Mop yelling.

"Fin, Fin, FIN, Miss Nomer's here."

Fin closed her note book and stared at the wine gum glass. Miss Nomer?

Ermine rapped on Fin's door.

"Head teacher's come to see your homework," she sauntered off, cackling.

"Shouldn't you be at college?" Fin shouted back in temper.

"Photography trip was cancelled. I'm doing my work at home," Ermine called over the banisters.

"Bitch," muttered Fin.

She stared around, looking for something that wasn't there and didn't exist. Perhaps she could get into bed. Say she was ill. She caught sight of the Basel book, the black and white cover peeling. Fin picked it up, then ferreted about finding four other library books, two old note pads full of writing and the photocopies. This was a heavy, substantial pile. She caught the door with her foot and forced her way through. Ermine was sitting half way up her stairs.

"You and your boyfriend have had soooo long. D'you need me to help you carry it all down stairs?"

"Sod off," muttered Fin.

She walked slowly down the stairs partly because she had a lot to carry and she needed planning time. She could feel Ermine smirking behind her. Ermine decided to follow.

"This should be good," muttered Ermine.

Miss Nomer was sitting at the head of the table, smiling like a visiting queen. She was wearing a yellow and blue headscarf wrapped in elaborate folds around her head. It matched her long dress and jacket. Her expensive scent filled the kitchen. Mop was standing by the sink, holding a tea pot but looking like she'd forgotten what it was for.

Ermine blocked the doorway, behind Fin to add to the tension.

Before anyone could speak the back door flew open. Zen stumbled in with Ty chewing a dog biscuit.

"Whoa," he said. Miss Nomer's smile widened. She moved her hand to indicate the court should be seated. Fin found herself opposite Miss Nomer with the pile of books as a barricade. Ty dropped his half chewed biscuit and sat next to Fin. Zen and Mop sat down hardly daring to pull the chairs out. They were both squished against the table. Mop clinging to the tea pot, Zen holding a spare dog biscuit.

Miss Nomer smiled and nodded towards Fin.

Fin thought fast. "Zen and I have been doing research... research," Fin said again in a louder voice.

Zen frowned and nodded, before chewing on the dog biscuit. Fin pushed the pile out in front of her and stared. She decided to open the biggest book. It was the most impressive after all. As she turned the pages she realised she knew about this. They *had* done some research. She began to flip back and forwards if she could just find...Miss Nomer cleared her throat.

"I find it's better to use the contents page or if necessary the index," said Miss Nomer.

Fin looked up.

"The index is at the back," said Miss Nomer.

"Yes," said Fin. "But what I'm looking for may not be there. We've found out about Lord Basel's estate and how his wife and son died of cholera but the historians say his underground spa, the Workers' Spa, was never built (or bits were) and it was never finished but we've found..." Zen shot her a look. "We found some evidence to suggest the spa might exist but we've got more reading... research to do."

Fin finally found what might have been a page from Peter Basel's scrapbook; a child's drawing of the pools. "Thank you, Peter," Fin thought to herself. She pushed it towards Zen who pushed it on to Miss Nomer.

Miss Nomer scrutinized the book and began to turn the pages.

"Go on," she said.

"We, Zen and me," said Fin, willing Zen to join in.

"Found that Lord Basel not only built sewers but he designed and built a Workers' Spa. Some historians say it was never built but we have good evidence to prove that's wrong."

Fin stopped. She was repeating herself. What if Miss Nomer asked her what the evidence was? She didn't want to give the game away. Her face was getting hot. If this was a court of law the jury would find her guilty.

"Lead bowls... we trip over... in the street," said Zen, through a mouthful of dog biscuit. Miss Nomer looked up. Mop put the tea pot down.

"They're fountain heads," concluded Fin.

"We have those at school, you know" said Miss Nomer.

She continued flicking through the book. She went back to the beam engine several times, Fin noticed.

"The beam engine," continued Fin "is... was made..."

Zen joined in, looking at Fin "It was made to power the fountains, probably when the Thames tide is high, it might push the arm down and the fountains will work."

"So why don't they work now?" asked Ermine, coming into the kitchen and sitting down.

"Dunno... Maybe the engine just needs more grease... or a catalyst?" said Zen, thinking aloud.

Miss Nomer looked up, as a head teacher she liked words like catalyst. Fin was impressed too. Mop pushed her chair back and let out a sigh.

"Well," said Zen, "perhaps when the tide's high, like really high, the pool with fill up and it just needs someone, something to push the arm down."

"Arm?" asked Mop.

"On the beam engine," said Zen.

He leaned across the table and pulled one of the books open, looking for the beam engine. Mop got up and began to bustle about making tea. Ermine put some clean mugs on the table.

"What's that?" Miss Nomer was pointing to the map.

Fin pushed it down the long table.

"We are trying to create a schematic."

Ermine snorted, Mop gave her a look.

Fin continued: "of Lord Basel's world."

Miss Nomer looked at the map and began to compare it to the one in the book.

"What about the people?" she asked.

"The people?" asked Fin.

"Lord Basel... his family... and the workers?"

"That's our work for next week," said Zen.

"Or maybe an hour this evening?" said Miss Nomer.

Fin and Zen nodded.

"Now Ermine pour me some tea, and tell me how your art projects are going."

Phew, thought Fin. Zen caught her eye and smiled. Fin looked at the half eaten dog biscuit. Zen winced and passed the other half to Ty.

19

TY'S SECRET

Fin had done well. She wanted to tell ex-best friend Zelda. She hadn't heard from Zelda again. Well only once. Pop had shouted up the stairs, one evening, just as Fin got into bed. The fire was glowing, her book ready, her quilt pulled up, the Imperial family all facing the same way on the mantelpiece. Very cosy.

"Fin, FIN...."

"What, WHAT?" Fin yelled back.

Her door was wedged shut against the endless draught.

"You got an email, attachment. I'll print it tomorrow. I've run out of paper, TOMORROW," yelled Pop.

It was some days later when Fin remembered this "conversation." She decided to rummage around in the study. Mop and Pop had created a nest of newspapers, local newsletters, and paperwork that might be useful, one day. If they ran out of food and had to eat paper, perhaps.

"Getting ready for the siege of Leningrad," Gran had said. "Now that was tough."

Fin couldn't find anything with her name on, so she logged on hoping for a connection. It worked. Fin drummed her fingers on the desk, impatient. Their dodgy connection could disappear any second.

After, waiting for the computer to warm up she found Zelda's breezy "Hiya!"

Fin sighed. She wished she hadn't bothered. They'd had a pact not to use exclamation marks. Exclamation marks were for stupid people, not serious writers like themselves. Zelda was letting them down, big time. Zelda continued by "hoping school's going great," didn't Zelda remember Fin was ill?

"Say Hiya to everyone, did you tell them about Tod's pool party? Wish you were here! See my project, I did it with Tod, we got a double merit!!!"

Fin couldn't face any more. The exclamation marks were like being poked in the eye. But like picking a scab, Fin couldn't stop herself opening the attachment. She steeled herself for pool party photos and more exclamation marks. There was a big fake newspaper headline, above a black and white photo of Ty, or rather a dog like Ty. It looked a bit smaller. It stood in a concrete pen behind a wire mesh, a sort of dog prison. Fin read the caption:

Extinction: 1938
Trudi the last living Thylacine dies of neglect.

There were no more exclamation marks. Zelda and Tod had added R.I.P. Fin read the headline again. The what, what? She hunched forward, skimming ahead, then reading and re-reading. She began to shiver.

"Thylacines, native of Australia, were hunted to death by lazy farmers. Farmers blamed thylacines for sheep predation.

"Good word Zelda," muttered Fin.

The article continued.

"But it was feral dogs gone wild, that were attacking and eating the sheep."

Fin had a feeling this was Tod's work.

"There were bounties to kill as many as possible. Soon there was only one left. She was kept at Hobart Zoo but was left out in the heat and cold. So she died of neglect and despair, being so lonely."

There were some sketches of Thylacines next to some rocks. The caption said they were marsupial wolves that filled the gap in nature filled by dogs or wolves in North America and Europe. So it might look like a dog but isn't, this added by Tod or Zelda. It's an extinct marsupial wolf though one was reportedly seen in Australia, caught on camera in 1981. There was a link.

Fin tapped the keyboard. She waited, holding her breath, willing the link to work.

It did. Someone was filming an empty country road. There were spindly trees enclosing a few lean-to houses. Fin wondered why anyone would film an empty road. The sun shone on the scruffy bush and a battered truck. A yellow streak flashed across the road. The camera wobbled, blurring the animal. Fin watched it again and again. It could be a dog except it had a lion-like tail that swayed above its body. It was too blurred to catch any stripes. But the tail wasn't like any dog she'd ever seen, except Ty.

Fin spent the next hour researching and printing. She didn't want to go to Zen half cocked. She needed the loo but was reluctant to stop in case the internet connection was lost again. Her family moved about, in and out, doors slamming, random yelling, but short of another gas explosion Fin was glued to the spot. She almost missed the email from Miss Nomer inviting, or rather requesting, Zen and her attend the class school trip to the Natural History Museum. Fin replied both Zen and her were definitely coming whether Mop and Pop and Hatsumi had the £10 or not.

However, Fin wasn't the only person to have tripped over this extraordinary information.

Billy Blatant spent many a late night watching television. His father's drunken snoring kept him awake. He flicked idly, surfed channels, while stroking his phone. He stopped for international news and National Geographic documentaries. He hoovered up survival shows and programmes on dangerous fish that hid in muddy rivers. It was about 1 a.m. Eddy slept, farting on the matted rug. Billy sat with his feet on the coffee table, an empty coffee mug in his hands. His eye lids began to close. Then he jerked awake. His head had fallen back hurting his neck. Time for bed. He flicked one last time, catching sight of a man in a red cave. The man pointed to a bleached rib cage then he held up a picture that looked like the stupid girly-boy's weird dog. Billy leaned forward and turned up the volume. Within an hour he was a thylacine expert and he had a caffeine fuelled kidnap plan. He was going to make some serious money.

20

THE NATURAL HISTORY MUSEUM

The trip to the Natural History Museum was overwhelming. The school wanted to save money so the whole year was squashed onto the tube. Mr Savage then walked them the wrong way. When they finally got in it was like a natural disaster. There were school kids everywhere, mobbing exhibits. It was very stuffy. The air smelt of cheap cheesy crisps. The noise pressed down like a dense fog. Fin felt sick. Zen looked really fed up. Mr Savage suggested they split up and meet in the basement for lunch at their allotted time. Most of the kids took this as a free pass and melted into the crowd. Miss Khan tried to call them back while explaining to Mr Savage it wasn't a good idea.

Tolemy pulled Fin's sleeve. "Wanna see the giant tarantula?"

Fin didn't want to see a tarantula. Was it alive? But Zen was already following Tolemy down a side corridor that was less rammed. Soon they were away from the crowds. They slowed down and began to peer about. Most people headed for the dinosaurs but Fin had done that before. It was a recipe for a panic attack. They turned a corner and found themselves in a long corridor with stuffed birds, wings spread wide. Tolemy began to take pictures on his phone, laughing.

Zen walked along the cases towards the end of the gallery. Australasia was written in gold letters above the door. Fin was beginning to think that when you'd seen one stuffed animal you'd seen them all. The dust and the warm stale air made her sleepy and queasy at the same time.

Zen was hovering in the doorway. Fin joined him. This gallery was painted dark blue, so blue it was like walking into night. A recording of birds played above their heads. They made piping sounds, then twittered. There was a smell of new paint. The display cases had the same sad dusty animals trapped forever: trying to fly away, build a nest or in the case of the platypus, smiling on a curling piece of bark.

Zen leaned with his forehead on glass further down in the semi darkness, reading something. Fin thought he'd probably not been to the Natural History Museum before.

"No one actually reads those things," shouted Tolemy. "Come on we're nowhere near the spider," he added before heading off in the opposite direction.

Fin went up to Zen. He was miles away. Fin could see why. He was staring at a small stuffed thylacine. Its skin had dried so the taxidermist's stitches were straining across its neck. It was snarling at a small faded note: Thylacine specimen 1900, extinct 1930. It had Ty's black stripes and thick tail. Zen glanced at Fin but didn't really see her. He was shaking.

"I found out..." began Fin.

Zen looked very sad. Fin started again.

"How did you get Ty, where did he come from?"

Zen frowned as if he was trying to remember.

"It was the old caretaker, he had him from a pup... cub?"

Zen turned and slid down the glass. He sort of crumpled onto the carpet. Fin glanced around. They were alone. She sat down next to him and waited in the warm dark.

"He told us he worked at a dodgy pet shop, back in the day... imported parrots, and exotic animals, probably illegal." Zen rubbed his face.

"One night this box came from the docks. It stank. There were four dead dogs inside all the way from Portsmouth. Dog number five was almost dead."

Fin winced. She'd had enough of dead animals.

"The owner wanted to put it down, thought it was diseased. Mr Bill, the caretaker, said he couldn't bear it. Poor little beggar, he said. So he offered to deal with it. He wrapped it up in his coat. Said he didn't think it would survive the night. But when he got it home his missus took it on like a proper job, feed it milk and mashed up biscuits. They didn't have any kids, Mr Bill said, so it became like their baby. He quit the pet shop when he got taken on as caretaker, shopped it to the RSPCA, got it shut down."

"Glad about that," said Fin.

Zen dragged himself up. He stood in front of Fin as if he didn't know what to do.

"So why d'you call him Ty not little beggar?"

"I dunno. Just suited him I guess."

"Bit of a weird coincidence... as he's actually a thylacine. It's a bit like you kinda knew unconsciously or something."

"We called him Ty, not thylacine, we couldn't call him poor little beggar could we," said Zen folding his arms. "Too much of a mouthful."

"Very funny," said Fin.

21

QUAGGA

Fin walked with Zen to the yard gates. Now they had this huge secret she thought they'd chat about everything, like her and Zelda. But Zen was quiet, dark smudges appeared under his eyes. He just muttered goodbye, rammed his hands into his pockets and hurried off. Fin watched him go. He looked like the boy she'd first seen wandering about the twisting paths, disappearing between mausoleums; his head bent, his dog miles ahead. Dog? Ty wasn't a dog at all. Now he didn't even look like a dog. Good job he eats dog food, thought Fin. She walked back to Blind Twin House. Her legs felt heavy. It had been a long day. She needed a hot bath, some buttery toast then bed with a hot water bottle and books. The wind caught the trees above her head shaking dry twigs onto the path.

The storm woke her at midnight. Branches scraped the window, wind howled down the chimney. The fire had burned down to just ashes. The Blind Twin House sign squealed. Somewhere downstairs Fat Bastard swore. Cold air rushed over Fin's face. Her bedroom door was ajar. The hall beyond was black. Mop and Pop weren't far away. Fin wanted to call out but that was babyish. Besides if there was anything lurking outside her door it would know that she was there. She'd spent many nights stiff with terror at their old house pretending to be asleep so *It* wouldn't get her. Since hospital, she thought she had out grown nightmares.

Fin had liked being awake at night in hospital. She could see the other children sleeping, hear them breathing, and smell their warm breath. Sometimes the nurses padded in and out, or porters appeared pushing another child in a bed. Their tired parents followed with lots of bags and coats.

At the hospital Fin could turn towards the window. From her high hospital bed she could stare out across Tooting, orange street lights stretching away into the night. At Blind Twin House she was alone. Mop and Pop were heavy sleepers since they both started working the yard. Gran explained this was because they were the bourgeoisie: intellectuals not used to getting their hands dirty. Gran didn't think Mop or Pop could do very much. Fin had to agree. They meant well but often got distracted so didn't finish the job started; whether it was dinner or a business. Still they were both working on the yard for now.

Fin wished Gran was here now shuffling about, just making a night cap, she'd say to herself. Fin squinted at the door. It was moving, the draught was getting stronger, the wind louder. Thunder rumbled towards the house. Fin had a choice: lie in bed stiff with fear or take action. She lay there stiff.

She thought of Zen. Was he awake? Fin comforted herself by telling herself Ty was awake. She wasn't the only one left. Ty would be pacing, waiting for the storm to pass. Fin pushed her arm out from under her quilt and clicked on her lamp. The room looked friendly in the soft yellow light, she leapt out of bed, ran towards the door and barged it shut. Thunder shook the house. It felt like a giant skip of rubble being dumped on the roof. Fin jumped back in bed. She decided to read.

Half formed ideas swam about in her mind, as she plumped up her pillows and arranged her books. The thoughts were annoying. It was like being trapped in a room with a fly zigzagging across the ceiling; too stupid to find its way out. Fin began to go through the Basel book page by page, reading, scrutinising pictures, skimming text and folding pages to return to later. Soon she was making notes.

Lord Basel's son Peter died just after his mother in London's last big cholera epidemic. He was eleven years old. He liked animals so much he persuaded his father to start a small zoo. Together they were going to convert the estate grounds for wild animals to roam about unfettered by cages.

To practise Peter had some pretty exotic pets. There were pictures of him. He wore a white sailor suit and stood next to an evil looking parrot. In another he had a snake draped around his neck, while Bartholomew stood behind him holding the rest of the snake's thick body. Both boys smiled. Bartholomew wore white breeches; Peter wore black breeches.

Fin wondered if Bartholomew was a servant. His clothing was plain and his name wasn't recorded under most of the pictures. The next photo showed the two boys again. The caption read: Peter and Bartholomew with quagga. Bartholomew held the reigns. Peter was sitting on what looked like a cross between a pony and a zebra. It had a big head and stripes.

It began to rain, quietly at first then pounding. Fin rubbed her neck and pulled the quilt up round her body as far as she could. She wanted to know more but this book was mostly pictures and plumbing. She had to ferret about amongst the other books. The thunder rumbled again in the distance. The rain got heavier. Fin stopped to listen. She could hear water overflowing the guttering and cascading down onto some biscuit tins Mop had forgotten outside. It was noisy. Her room was now very cold. A damp draught whistled under the door.

Fin piled the books together, wrapped herself in her quilt and opened her door. She needed the internet but would it work? She pulled her door wide open so her lamp light caught the stairs. The hall was very dark. Darkness pressed down upon her head as she edged down the steps. She didn't want to wait for her eyes to adjust because she would lose her nerve. When she reached the study she turned on all the lights and shut the door. It took forever for the computer to warm up. The rain eased off. There were no curtains in here. So Fin had second thoughts and turned off the main light. She didn't like the idea that someone or something outside could see her, but she couldn't see them.

Fin sat waiting. She kept twisting round to check the door was still shut tight. What if the back door was unlocked? *It* would get her first. The computer screen turned blue. It was working, unbelievable. Soon Fin forgot to check the door. By the time the storm passed and the stained glass turned from black to wine gum colours again, Fin had quite a story. And she needed to see Zen.

22

GRAN'S ACCIDENT

Fin spent the rest of the day feeling listless. She was tired but not sleepy. Gran appeared with more complaints about the sheltered accommodation warden. She was a Bolshevik, apparently. Gran stubbed her fag out on a saucer. Mop sighed.

"Look this house is big enough for us and you. You're welcome to live with us, if you like," Mop added in a tone that said she really expected Gran not to like.

Gran narrowed her eyes, and said: "I could do with a walk. Fin take your old Gran on a tour of my possible new home, give your parents time to row."

Fin led Gran along the path at the edge of the yard. It was sheltered by holly trees and firs, fat fir cones littered the wet grass. Fin picked one up. Gran puffed behind. Fin liked walking with Gran. Gran wasn't like other adults who moaned if kids zigzagged about. Gran said life was like that. It wasn't a straight road. Gran was up for anything. Her family had survived the Russian Revolution after all.

They passed small, cheap headstones. Some families could only afford a few letters: Mable 1845-55, Thomas 1846-47, Elisabeth 1847-1850. Fin made up stories about how they died in her head. Gran hummed. Fin turned right along the Avenue of Mausoleums but Gran coughed and shook her head. So they carried on up the path. They walked in the direction of the hospital. This path was overgrown. Pop and Hatsumi had far too much work down below to get up here. Brambles like giant springs scratched Fin's trousers. Gran looked tired but carried on to the top of the hill. It was an achievement to get up high and look down on London, she said. Fin and Zen hadn't been here for a while not since they discovered the pools.

Just when Fin thought the brambles had blocked the path completely they burst through into an orchard, hidden by a barricade of overgrown hedges.

"Well I never," said Gran.

They stared at the gnarled, twisted fruit trees. The hospital wall loomed behind.

"This is like a secret garden," said Fin. She couldn't wait to tell Zen.

"It's like *The Cherry Orchard*," said Gran, nodding. "And no graves... this could be nice in the summer, maybe I'll come and stay after all."

Fin wanted to tell Gran about the pools and Ty but she wasn't sure where to start. Gran might warn her not to carry on exploring?

Gran took a step forward and stumbled. She fell flat on her face.

"Shit," said Gran.

Fin hurried over the uneven ground and waited for Gran to get up. She couldn't. Fin had to hold her arm while Gran bent one knee then pushed herself up, wobbling, nearly falling again. It felt like forever to Fin. She began to worry about the long walk back. Would they make it?

Fin led Gran back down the road. It was a longer walk but much smoother. Gran's hair was wild around her face. Her scarf slipped off. Fin had to leave Gran leaning on a tall headstone to run back and pick it up. There was mud on Gran's chin. She limped and winced, stopping now and again to take some quick breaths. Fin tried not to cry. She felt bad. It was her fault. Gran kept humming and stomping forward. She looked much older. Mop and Pop would be very angry.

Fin remembered the awful day she'd left the back door open at their old house. The snotty toddler who arrived with his mum (Mop's best friend), had crawled out and rolled in the compost heap. Mop had shouted at Fin.

"What if it was the front door?"

Ermine had spoken up for Fin that day: "Steady on Mop. Fin wasn't trying to kill anyone deliberately."

This had only made Mop angrier. It led to a rant about Fin's sloppiness and Ermine's smart mouth. And now she'd almost killed Gran. One person was an accident but two looked like a trend. Fin began to imagine a newspaper headline: Bad girl sent to Borstal. But Mop wasn't angry. Mop made up the sofa bed for Gran in the draughty sitting room, covered her in as many blankets and quilts as she could find and called the doctor.

"You did well to get her back, Fin," said Mop.

"She fell down," said Fin, again. Mop looked up. She was trying to comb Gran's hair, except Gran kept moving her head.

"Old people fall down all the time," said Mop, pulling a knot of hair out of the comb. "Tell you what, ask Pop to make some tea and get the Imperial family."

"Don't want *them*," said Gran, "They make too much noise. Old... bleedin' cheek."

"Too much noise?" asked Mop.

"Crying, complaining..." said Gran.

She looked tired and old. Fin hadn't thought of her as old before. Fin thought Gran should sleep but Mop said she needed to stay awake until the doctor came. She was snoring by the time Fin returned with the tea.

Mop was making up a fire. "The chimney's great in here," said Mop blowing on lighted newspaper.

Fin decided not to get the Imperial family. The draught could blow them off the mantelpiece. She didn't want Gran to wake up to see the Tsar burned alive.

"Zen came by today," said Mop, standing up.

Fin had forgotten all about Zen and Ty.

"Said he'd call back later."

For the next two weeks it rained. This was unusual for London. London rain is normally brief and grubby. Pop and Guy used the time to start the re-wiring which meant lots of cables, and don't touch that, and no there's no power on for a few minutes which usually meant hours. Mop was looking better. She went out most days, despite the rain. She liked cutting back brambles and digging. The earth around Blind Twin House was bare, ready for spring planting. Mop moved onto the orchard after Gran's fall. Mop and Pop said they didn't even know the orchard was there. They dragged Hatsumi into this conversation, talking in loud cheery voices, as if Fin had done something clever by finding it. Fin didn't want to be reminded of Gran's accident. She still felt responsible. Her cheeks burned whenever Gran or the orchard project was mentioned.

Mop sat at the table. Rain hammered onto the path outside the open kitchen window. The kitchen was dark. The stained glass would be great on a really, really sunny day but it was grey most of the time. So the house was dark, even in the middle of the day. There was no electricity but lots of swearing coming from the basement. Mop was making a list of things to plant. She chewed her biro and flicked through a thick book with coloured photos showing orange roses the size of dinner plates. Fin leaned over Mop's shoulder. Mop scribbled down the name of a pale yellow rose.

"That's probably somewhere warm, but it's worth a try..." said Mop.

"Yep," Fin agreed. "Do they have a section on graveyards?"

Mop looked up. She stared at Fin as if she hadn't seen her for a while.

"Your hair's growing back," she said.

Fin went to the downstairs loo. She peered at her reflection in the crackled mirror. Her hair was longer. It looked like someone had put a bowl on her head and cut round the bottom. The ends stuck out this way and that.

"Great," she muttered. "Fin the human loo brush."

Thank God she wasn't back at school. She sat on the cold loo seat and watched a small spider hurry towards the buckled skirting board. The spider had somewhere to go. Mop knocked on the door and pushed it open.

"Mop," protested Fin.

"Let's go visit Gran," Mop said pulling the door behind her.

Gran was back at home, but staying in bed longer than the warden liked, after her fall. Mop paused before she opened Gran's door with the spare key.

"Fin, I'm going to try some reverse psychology. I may need your help."

Mop turned the key and fiddled with the handle. Getting the door open was always tricky.

"Hello, it's just us," shouted Mop, nodding to Fin to join in.

Fin managed a weak "Hi Gran."

A growl from the beige bedroom greeted them. Gran hated the beige bedroom. Pop had promised to paint it deep red. Soviet style, he joked. The paint tins were still hidden behind Gran's sofa as the warden wouldn't approve. Not regulation. But they'd all been so busy. Fin felt bad. Gran's room was horrible, so un-Gran. Beige walls, beige carpet, with a pink dado rail. It smelt of shake and vac, the warden had been in trying to be helpful, Mop said.

"Maggie's so pleased you're taking it easy in bed," shouted Mop.

Gran pulled herself up and opened her glasses case. But she didn't bother to put them on. Fin thought Mop had overplayed her hand. Gran waved Fin over. Fin leaned over Gran. Gran gave her a wet kiss. She winked at Fin.

"Maggie says stay in bed. She can come in to clean and vacuum, not under your feet then."

Gran snorted. Fin sat down on one of the many chairs Gran had littering the place. Why did old people need so many chairs?

Gran was playing cat and mouse. Fin's face didn't burn. Gran was on the mend. Mop chatted on.

"Maggie says stay in bed. Take as long as you need, if you can't lie in bed when you've had a fright...?"

This was too much for Gran.

"I've not had a fright," she said. "Damn cheek. I could limp to the sitting room if I had to..."

Mop waited. Fin waited. Gran's frail hands smoothed out the red satin on her eiderdown.

"If there was painting going on I'd have to move wouldn't I?"

Mop looked at Fin with raised eyebrows. Gran leaned forward and Mop helped her struggle up.

So Fin, Guy, Ermine, Pop *and* Mop spent the next three days moving furniture, sugar soaping walls, undercoating, painting... all under Gran's direction. They had to sneak in when the warden was on her rounds so she didn't see such a large group going in and out and get suspicious. Three of Gran's sheltered accommodation friends staged fake falls to keep Maggie busy.

Finally Gran and Fin went out for chips. When they returned Gran had a deep red room. Ermine unrolled Gran's Persian rug to cover up the beige carpet.

"It's like sleeping inside a jewellery box," said Fin.

They were too tired to talk. They ate the chips munching in hungry silence.

"We make a good team," said Pop as they crossed the road home.

Ermine glared as if to say, just a one-off mate, but no-one actually disagreed.

23

BARTHOLOMEW

Fin wanted to tell Zen all about the painting at Gran's. Gran looked a lot better. Her accident meant she got her room decorated so it was a sort of a good thing. Fin imagined Zen missing her and wandering past Blind Twin House feeling gloomy when he saw there were no lights on. This was how Fin felt. Even when they went past a dark house and she didn't know who lived there. She felt sad and a bit put out, like she'd been rejected somehow. Zelda would understand. She would smile and say me too. Fin missed Zelda. Having Zen as a friend wasn't the same. Sometimes he'd call but sometimes Fin knew he headed out alone. Gran said he might be gloomy about his dad. Boys and men dealt with things alone, not like us girls, Gran would say pulling Fin into an awkward hug.

Fin decided she better get cracking with the Miss Nomer project. She had a lot of notes and photocopies piled up around her room. They blew about when she opened the door. She caught Mop using a rolled picture of the beam engine to light the fire. Who knows what National Curriculum task Miss Nomer would give them if they didn't get a move on.

Fin curled up with the Basel books and made some final notes on wide lined paper. As Zen wasn't around she used her girly felt-tip pens. They smelt of different fruit depending on the colour. She began to divide the project into sections, laying them out on her bedroom floor. She wrote questions in different colours on the plain paper she'd looted from the printer.

Section 1: The Secret Spa. Question: how could "someone" get the fountains working?

Section 2: Why was their house called Blind Twin House? Hmm, did she really want to know? Miss Nomer would urge them on, stating knowledge is power, or was it fuel?

Section 3: The Basels and Bartholomew? What was the connection with Miss Nomer?

Fin glanced at the pictures. OK Bartholomew was black and so was Miss Nomer but that didn't mean they were related, or did it?

Fin rooted around under her bed and pulled out *A Maths Problem for Every Day*. She shuddered. She better put this in the bin before Mop remembered it and suggested it was a chance to bond with Ermine. Ermine was good at Maths. In fact Ermine was good at everything. Even the cover was boring. Numbers marched across the front getting bigger. Fin reached further under her bed. There was a battered ring binder. Fin flipped through the plastic wallets, sneezing in the dust. She found the photo Miss Nomer had given her. It showed a man standing next to two black horses with thick feather plumes attached to their bridles. They were harnessed to a glass coach. Not like a fairy story glass coach. Fin had seen this before on the main road and at the yard. It wasn't for fairies but coffins. It was like a big glass box on spindly wheels with ebony edges.

Fin compared the man to Bartholomew. Was it an older Bartholomew? Fin didn't want to get it wrong. That was like saying all black people looked the same. Fin was sure it was Bartholomew because he stood exactly like the boy, tall and smiling, next to the animals, his animals?

She'd have to catch Zen. Even if he didn't want to see her, she had to finish the project. She needed his help. But first Fin had to finish organising her work and her head. She had too many thoughts banging around and around.

4. Why did the animals in the linen cupboard smirk?
5. What should they do about Ty?

Zen said the vet thought Ty was a dog. Zen said people were like this, taking things at face value, that's how the Jedi could trick them. And when they'd taken Ty to the vet someone had a pet tarantula in a plastic case. The vet was so excited you'd think they'd brought in a unicorn, said Zen. Unicorn, hmm, thought Fin. Ty was a sort of unicorn, which might mean if people found out about him he'd be hassled by paparazzi or even stolen. Fin remembered sad posters sellotaped to lamp posts showing kittens and expensive dogs that had suddenly disappeared.

Fin was tired. Her head was thick with words. She got up and rearranged the Imperial family. Then she decided they would make good paper weights.

Alexei stood on Bartholomew's picture, then Anastasia, Olga, Maria and Tatianna anchored a chapter each. She put the Tsar back on the windowsill.

His Imperial Majesty would have to remind Fin what number six was for. Fin picked up the Tsarina.

"You can guard the door."

She placed the Tsarina on the spindly chair. It was a long time since she'd spoken to them or asked them for their help.

Fin wiped down the draining board. She'd been left with the washing up. Mop and Pop had gone to Hatsumi's for a yard meeting. Ermine and Guy had gone out. She pushed the window open. She was sick of watching condensation run down the dark glass. It was cool and rainy outside. Now the brambles had gone from the side of the house she could see the yard. Zen lurched past in a raincoat under the dripping trees, Ty bounced ahead. Fin called out. But Zen was miles away. Fin yelled. Zen stopped and waved. Fin called him in. They left Ty in the kitchen with some cat food. Fin took Zen up to her room to show him the research. Fin waited for Zen to settle next to the fire. She was lucky, because she was ill Mop kept the fire going in her room most of the time, while the rest of the house froze.

Gran was taking it easy at Sheltered Accommodation, she still disliked the warden but she'd made two new friends since her accident, another Russian (what were the chances, everyone kept saying?) and an ex actress who was up for anything. Mop helped Pop in the yard and Ermine was either at College or photographing pink doors around London in black and white for her art exam.

Fin liked having the place to herself in the day. But as it got dark, it was creepy. Blind Twin House was just too big. When she was downstairs she'd shut the kitchen door and use the downstairs loo. The darkness at the top of the stairs was like an evil cloud. When she was upstairs she'd stay in her room, reading and staring at the glowing coals in the fireplace. She'd line the Imperial family up along the bottom of the bedroom door, like guard dogs. Fierce Anastasia stood outside in the hall just in case....

Zen crossed his legs and leaned forward. His long hair fell over his shoulders. Fin noticed he'd grown out of his ripped cords. They were about 5 inches too short. His hands looked bigger too. Could boys really grow that fast? It was at times like this Fin missed Zelda. Zelda had a big family so she knew stuff like this. Zen smelt of mud and damp and Ty.

Fin didn't want to look like a busy body so she said: "I did some work on the project, just in case Miss Nomer came by. D'you mind?"

Zen laughed and shook his head.

"Nope, not a problem." Then, he surprised Fin by saying: "I don't expect you to do all the work."

Fin began to lay the paper out in piles with pictures on the top, because they were more interesting. She'd folded the pages with questions on in half and used them to keep each part separate. Zen bent his head and began reading the questions upside down.

"This is Peter Basel with his pet quagga, one of the last ones ever. They went extinct in 1838. It was his pet. This is Bartholomew. He lived with his mum."

Fin showed Zen the picture of a tall black woman standing outside Twin House. Her arms were folded.

"I don't think the houses had names then. There's no signs."

Zen looked closer.

"The house looks new, like it's just been built."

Fin looked again. Zen was right there were no trees around the edges. She nodded and moved away from the fire. She was getting too hot.

"When Lord Basel died, his brother moved in. He tried to take over the estate but Lord Basel had left it to the hospital board. According to this," said Fin, opening the Basel book and turning to page 86, "he was ordered to leave by the council. It took them 20 years to get him out."

Fin continued: "I think he buried the workers spa. It says here he hated his brother and tried to derail his plans. When he was younger he wanted to be an artist. Lord Basel paid for him to set himself up, but they fell out big time when Lord Basel donated the big house to the hospital and built this one to live in."

They heard Ty lollop up the stairs. Zen got up and let him in. He pushed past and settled himself right in front of the fire blocking most of the heat.

Fin and Zen had to pull out some of the research from under his belly.

"Sorry," said Zen.

"S'OK," said Fin. "It's just rough work."

"Oh... does that mean we'll have to type it up?" asked Zen.

"'Fraid so, Miss Nomer's a stickler for proper work."

"What's a stickler?"

"No idea, sounds like an insect. Miss Nomer's an insect for proper work."

"What sort of insect?"

"Dunno, ants work hard."

"Or do they?"

Fin looked at Zen. Zen continued: "I mean you see them running about all over the path and round the kitchen but maybe it's all for show?"

Fin had forgotten Zen had lived here longer than her. She had only seen the yard in winter. She thought it was always winter here anyway, because of the graves. Maybe it was different in summer. She was getting cold. She shuffled next to Ty. Zen let the ant conversation drop. Fin thought Miss Nomer was more like a dung beetle because she'd read they worked very hard indeed, but that sounded rude somehow.

"Anyway, Lord Basel paid him to paint this house. He did the linen cupboard for baby Peter, except it wasn't a cupboard then. Years later he disappeared after a nasty row, cursing Bartholomew. Called him," here Fin picked up the book, "a devious bastard and swindler, threatened to come back and kill his mum."

Zen snorted. Fin read on.

"Lord Basel's housekeeper may have been his mistress and so that made Bartholomew his son. Bartholomew was left Twin House in Basel's will, while his brother was left Blind Twin House. Lord Basel's brother had the signs put up when he took over the estate. He was very bitter about not being left the land and the mansion."

"Not surprised," said Zen.

They both looked at Bartholomew, he didn't look anything like the curly headed Peter but he had the long, narrow face of Lord Basel.

"We need to find out more about Bartholomew," said Fin.

Zen nodded.

24

AT THE LIBRARY

The next day they took a wet trip to the library. The High Street was quiet. The shops were open but most of the road was still cordoned off. Workmen in high-vis vests were setting up tools around the holes. Fin and Zen didn't really notice the holes now. They had been there for so long they seemed to fit somehow. They did like wandering back and forth across the road. The High Street felt bigger. They could talk without shouting over the rumble of buses. Zen left Ty with Hatsumi. She said Ty could follow her on her bin round. In the past Ty would have come along but Fin and Zen worried he might stand out with his stripy back and lion tail, now they knew he wasn't a dog. Someone else might make the same connection.

The librarian frowned at them, removing her glasses where they dangled on a cheap gold chain.

"Shouldn't you two be at school," she said.

"No," said Fin "We're home-schooled... home-schoolers."

"Home-school?" repeated the librarian, nodding to a colleague, who was putting books away.

The colleague stopped. Fin could feel the man watching them. What did the library staff think Fin and Zen were here for, a raid?

Zen caught Fin clumsily on the shoulder.

"We got cancer, miss."

"Cancer?"

Fin pulled down her hood, revealing her choppy hair.

"I see," said the librarian.

The man went back to picking up books.

"So you want books on what exactly?" she said, taking a brisk tone.

Fin passed over the list she'd made.

"Wait over there," the librarian pointed to some tables. They went and sat down. It was draughty by the door.

"What d'you tell her we had cancer for?" hissed Fin. "We might need to come back."

"Dunno, I hate librarians, they're snotty."

Fin nodded. "Yeah and she was about to turn us out."

"You can put your head on the table if you want to," said Zen.

"No thank you, and by the way everyone hates librarians," said Fin.

"I wonder why?" said Zen.

After a brief chat with her colleague the librarian returned with seven books on local history, eminent Victorians and the Basel estate. She had a leaflet about how to search online for family trees.

"Thank you," said Fin.

Give her credit, it was a great pile. They took a book each and began to skim-read. The only distraction was a draught when the automatic doors swished open. After about an hour they found out that Bartholomew's last name became Basel when he inherited Twin House. Zen moved on-line. Bartholomew became a business man running a funeral business. There was a newspaper article dated 1900 outlining his family history. He had five children and 19 grandchildren. The librarian came back and leaned over the books. Fin had made some notes. Fin could smell her flowery scent, her glasses swung above Fin's head.

"Why the interest?" she asked.

"Well it's a history project on Tooting. I liked the picture of Bartholomew when he was a boy and thought it would be a good place to start." Fin didn't want to say too much about where they lived, just in case Mop and Pop discovered the cancer lie. Fin felt a bit bad about it now the librarian had found them so much.

"A boy?" The librarian considered this. "I haven't seen that photo."

Fin couldn't resist telling the librarian everything she knew, except the part about them exploring the underground spa.

"Alan, come over here," the librarian waved to her colleague.

"Well, I never," said Alan. "I'm a local history buff myself but you're filling in some gaps for me. But let me throw in what I know. It wasn't just a spa; it was an underground Victorian pumping station. So it's probably vast and under our feet as we speak."

Fin smiled at this. Zen wandered back from the computer and hovered at the edge of the table.

"I thought when the holes appeared we might even get to see some of it," Alan beamed, his round face red.

"Bartholomew's is still doing funerals," said the librarian. "They have the big B in gold letters on the side of their cars... Do you want to take all these books out then?"

"No thank you," said Fin

"They'd be too heavy," said Zen.

"Oh, yes of course," said the librarian, remembering they were sick.

"You can use the photocopier if you like, its 10p a sheet."

Fin and Zen decide to save their money for iced doughnuts on the walk back. Fin went for chocolate, Zen went for white, like that was a flavour.

"I thought you'd never stop yakking," he said, licking icing off his thumb.

Fin felt a bit put out, but Zen carried on.

"I found something very, very interesting," he paused and bit into his doughnut.

Fin waited, chewing her doughnut. The sugar overload gave her a headache but she didn't want to stop eating the gooey, chocolaty mess.

Before Bartholomew changed his last name to Basel, he had his mum's name," Zen paused and took another bite. He carried on talking through the dough. "It was Nomer."

"What?" said Fin.

"Nomer," repeated Zen, trying to shift the dough from around his teeth.

Fin had heard. But she was still digesting the doughnut and the information.

"So he's Miss Nomer's like great, great Grandfather?"

"Dunno about how many greats in there. Maybe go back and ask your new library friends," said Zen.

"Very funny," said Fin. They walked in silence for a while, savouring fried dough and thick icing. Fin had a mouth ulcer by the time they got back.

Fin's hands were cold and sticky. She couldn't wait to get in and run them under warm water. As they rounded the last corner, before the yard gates, they nearly bumped into someone coming the other way. Fin dodged the leather jacket. Zen stepped off the curb. The man muttered something but he'd didn't stop. Fin glanced back and realised it was Billy. He didn't have Evil Eddy with him and his hood was up but she just knew it was Billy Blatant. Zen had crossed the road.

"That was Billy," Fin said, catching him up.

Zen stopped and turned round. Billy was almost at the end of the High Street. Zen scowled.

"Maybe he's lost interest?" said Fin.

"Doubt that," said Zen. "Come on, I need a drink."

They went back to Twin House. Zen poured them pint glasses of water. He whistled for Ty from the kitchen window. Ty came bounding down the path. Fin remembered the day she'd shown Zen Zelda's project.

She'd sat back on her heels and watched Zen as he read it. His face intent, his hair pushed back behind his ears. She'd held her breath when he clicked on the link. He'd frowned. Then he got up and walked over to the window. He rubbed his face with the end of his grubby sleeve.

"Why Fin... why?" He hadn't used her name before. She'd looked at his dark eyes. They'd burned like coals in fire. Fin's stomach had wobbled. Zen began pacing the floor, his hair swinging back and forth.

Fin wondered if she'd done the right thing by telling him, showing him the film clip. The black and white film showed a thylacine pacing about in a small cage. Underneath the caption ran: *The last thylacine died a week later from exposure, shut out of its shelter in extreme temperatures, so zoo visitors could marvel at its stripy coat.*

Fin and Zen were soon leaning over Hatsumi's laptop on the kitchen table. They skimmed over the evil zoo, and stumbled on to some Victorian Naturalist drawings. The thylacines in the sketches seemed to leer through the long yellow grass. Zen leant against the radiator with his arms folded, chewing the inside of his lip.

Fin tried to order her ideas. She didn't want to say anything to make Zen feel worse.

"They got it wrong," she said.

"You can say that again," said Zen. "What sort of zoo was it anyway, more like a death camp."

"Zoos used to be terrible. They're much better now. There are even some animals they don't put in zoos, 'cos they don't cope..." Fin remembered Pop giving a lecture on bears.

Zen sighed. He was in no mood to hear about bears by the look of him.

"But they got it wrong about that being the last one, some survived..." Fin twisted around and re-found the blurred clip. "Look."

Zen came back to the screen but kept his arms folded. Fin was glad this film was sunny and only a few years old, not something from back in the day.

"It's not very clear, but look at that tail." She replayed the clip.

Zen unfolded his arms and leaned on the back of the chair.

"Could be a mongrel," said Zen.

"Maybe, but we've, you've got Ty haven't you?"

"Yeah, 'spose but he might be the last one, ever."

Fin considered this. It didn't feel like good news. She was tired.

Fin thought about the Ty situation but couldn't find any answers. Maybe he was like Peter's quagga, bound for extinction. They'd trudged over to Blind Twin House and headed for Fin's room as it was warmer than the rest of the house.

25

SECRET?

Ermine banged on the door. "Poison time, there's enough for you and your boyfriend." Fin cringed but Zen wasn't listening.

"I think we shouldn't tell anyone... for a while anyway," said Fin.

"But why would they treat animals like that... it was a zoo."

Fin decided it wasn't the time to mention the animal rights campaign she'd started with Zelda; before Fin got sick and Zelda buggered off abroad. When Fin thought about it now, she was glad Zelda was carrying on their work with Tod.

"I think we should keep quiet, because if other people find out..." Fin wasn't sure what other people might do. They probably wouldn't believe a couple of kids anyway.

Zen stared at the door.

"He's my d... mine. I'd like to see them try," said Zen, folding his arms across his chest. Fin just knew he was thinking about his father's knife. She began to worry. Zen began to rummage through Fin's books. He picked up her Survival Handbook and waved it in the air. Fin had forgotten she had this.

"I'm gonna study this, then we'll see."

He looked at Fin. "Can I borrow your book?"

"Yep, but it's for Brownie camp, it's for little girls in the woods."

Zen looked at the cover and flicked through.

"I've never read it," Fin continued "but if you want to knit a camp fire, or make rock cakes…"

"I may use it as a weapon then," said Zen. He sat down. "Did your sister cook the food?"

They were in luck. Ermine had made vegetarian lasagne. The kitchen smelt of warm cheese just as it turns brown.

"Sit, down then," said Ermine. She dolloped two giant chunks of lasagne onto plates and shoved them towards Fin and Zen. Ty pawed the back door.

"I thought we were having some," said Guy, opening the door to let Ty out.

"Nope, not enough time," said Ermine grabbing her camera bag and stuffing film into her parka pockets.

"Save me some," mouthed Guy, shutting the back door. Zen was already chopping his up to cool it down. Fin filled the jug with water and poured them both a glass. The water was still a bit brown.

"I don't think we should tell anyone, except maybe your mum," said Fin, thinking aloud. Zen winced. The lasagne was molten. He gulped some water.

"Everyone thinks Ty's a dog, he acts like a dog…" though Fin wasn't really convinced. Ty had always been odd. That was why she liked him. He didn't bark but coughed. He did huge yawns. This she now knew, from research, was a kind of threat display. Fin doubted it was very effective as other animals didn't know this. Or maybe they did instinctively? Come to think of it the High Street was filled with pigeons and she'd seen rats by the pub bins but there were no rats or pigeons in the yard. Could Ty have frightened them off?

Zen scraped his plate. Fin tried the lasagne. When Mop made it the pasta stayed hard like cardboard and she just grated cheese across the top. This was creamy and smooth. Fin bit into a soft, chewy courgette. Zen had finished.

"You can have some more, there's plenty left for Guy."

"What about your mum and dad?"

Fin thought it might be cruel to let them taste anything so good, especially if Ermine went off to Uni. They'd be back to burnt cardboard.

"They'll get chips later, after they've seen Gran."

Zen nodded and helped himself to another dollop.

"You've thought about this," said Zen.

Fin looked at the lasagne, then realised he meant the Ty situation. She shrugged.

"As long as your mum doesn't decide to move to Australia, or Tasmania, you'll be OK."

Zen nodded, his mouth full. Fin was pleased he'd noticed.

"Maybe avoid the vets," Fin added. "Gran says people see what they're told to see. They thought I was a boy in hospital because I had short hair."

Zen looked up and shook his head. "So that makes me a girl?"

They finished their tea. Ty scraped the door. Fin got up and let him in. Zen pulled Ty down and rubbed his head.

Pop returned with shovels and a rake. Hatsumi followed him in with a small chain saw.

"...'fraid so, a bit of a local thug, he's either gonna grow up and man up, or get into trouble with the police... I've moved him on a few times, said he was welcome to walk his dog but clear up the sh... Hello girly, Zen," Pop leaned over the sink and washed his hands.

Hatsumi smiled at Fin. Pop picked up the kettle, decided there was too much water in it, poured some away before clicking the switch to boil.

"Smells delicious," said Pop. Fin got a plate for Pop and Hatsumi.

"I thought you went to see Gran?" said Fin.

"No, too much on here," said Pop. "And I've got a plumbing job on tonight, installing sinks."

"Just little for me," said Hatsumi, sitting down next to Zen.

"Did you see Billy in the yard?" said Fin, trying to sound unbothered.

"No, just walking down the main road with that awful dog. It's the ugliest dog I've ever seen."

"Ty not pretty," said Hatsumi, shucking off her wellies.

"Ty looks like that dog on the telly," said Pop.

"What dog?" said Fin and Zen at the same time.

"Oh you know, that cartoon dog... Scooby Doo."

Hatsumi nodded nibbling her lasagne. Pop made four mugs of tea. This was good news in a way.

"What sort of dog is he anyway?" said Pop.

"Ty?" asked Hatsumi.

"No Scooby Doo."

"I think Scooby Doo made up dog." said Hatsumi. She turned to Fin. "Fin, how the project going?"

"Good question," said Pop.

"I'll show you our folder," said Fin. "It's not written up yet. There's more research to do but..."

She collected her folder from her room and passed it to Hatsumi. Pop leaned over the table, chomping noisily. Fin pulled out the notes on Ty. Best get another folder she thought. Hatsumi and Pop were impressed.

"I hope Zen does as much work as you," said Hatsumi.

"He does," said Fin. She counted walking Ty twice a day as work.

Fin went out later to buy milk and bread from the corner shop. It was one of those milky London days. Anywhere else the sun would be shining. There was a bright grey light. Migraine weather Gran called it, best stay indoors. Gran stayed in more since her fall.

The heavy air pressed down on Fin. She was sweating. She saw Billy on the other side of the road. He had Eddy on a long chain. They were walking next to a short white woman with scraped back hair carrying two bulging shopping bags. Fin decided if Billy crossed the road, she'd head back fast. She pretended to tie her laces; glad her hair was long enough now to cover her face.

While she fiddled with her trainers, Billy carried on oblivious. Fin stayed in a half kneel just in case. Watching Billy from behind made her feel better. It occurred to her that Billy wasn't as old as she thought. She thought of him as some sort of man, a dangerous man but he was probably younger than Ermine. She watched them turn into Bleak Street. Weird to think someone like Billy had a mum. Billy's mum looked mean like she'd shout at someone if they bumped into her by accident. Someone else to avoid, glad they lived on the other side of the road. She couldn't imagine his mates Crime and Wave had parents. They were just too vile.

Billy was helping his mum out today. He'd run out of cash. He was hoping she'd take something out of her purse at the shops. She didn't. Billy borrowed her fags later and went for a walk. He avoided the yard. Since the new people moved in it was too busy. Before, he'd been able to get away from everything there. The funerals stuck to the main path by the chapel. The new caretakers were everywhere: emptying bins, plastering stone angels, clearing paths, burning leaves. It was a disgrace. If anyone had asked Billy which no-one ever did. Shouldn't the dead be able to rest in peace? He knew what his Granddad, God rest his soul, would call them.

Billy wasn't sure where his Grandfather was. The prison had taken care of his cremation, cheapskates. There had been an urn on the kitchen table for a week then his dad took it to the pub. He claimed he'd scattered the ashes in the yard by the fir trees cos it's like a real forest. But his mum reckoned his dad got blind drunk and lost it, probably ended up in the gutter somewhere. Billy shuddered. There'd been an awful row that night. Someone called the police. The urn and his Grandfather were not mentioned again.

He missed the yard. There he could get away and think. He enjoyed spending hot summer days lying on a mausoleum roof planning his mercenary future. Last year, he'd used it as a getaway. He'd joined Crime and Wave breaking and entering. Stealing to order, they called it, like a reverse Amazon.

They had an old step ladder, hidden in brambles and a roll of heavy duty bin bags, with small rubber gloves. After dark they'd climb the wall, into the yard, head over to the ladder and choose a dark garden with no dog. They'd put on the gloves, tight, so they were easy to work in. They'd crack glass with a brick and push and pull it out of the frame. In 15 minutes they were done. They had a list: phones, tablets, PCs, fancy kitchen knives, and anything new. Most of this was thrown away later, dumped in someone's wheelie bin.

The real game was to go back when people had replaced their stolen stuff with new. This went to Sven. He picked up the bin bag, paid them for the weight. This annoyed Billy as the haul was worth a lot more than they got but Crime and Wave didn't care. Chill, we got a system was all they said. Billy realised the real money was to be made at Sven's end. But that meant more risk and contacts. Wave said Sven would pay fair if Billy had something interesting. Now Billy had something. Wave said Sven had paid 700 quid for a Burmese cat but Billy bet that was exaggeration.

26

ZEN'S DAD

Fin and Zen put together a short presentation about Ty for Zen's mum to offset any possible hysteria. There were three PowerPoint slides and the clip showing the possible outback sighting. Fin wanted to ask Zen what happened when Zen's Dad died. She knew that must have been huge. She wondered if Hatsumi had just stopped working like a broken toy. Like when Mop was ill. Then Fin found out.

She wandered over to Twin House in the dark. She made herself small, trying to blend into the shadows cast by the trees but she felt bigger by the time she arrived at Twin House. The yard gates were locked after dark, so probably the worse she would face was a fox. It hadn't occurred to her that while she wandered along the path towards the lights of Twin House, Billy might be watching her, waiting to pass so he could finish another burglary.

As usual all the lights were on. Fin paused. Twin House was beautiful at night. Clear light bulbs dangled from the ceilings.

Hatsumi was gradually covering all the windows in delicate paper snowflakes for Christmas, though that was ages away. Fin saw Zen lollop down the stairs. His shadow lurched up the wall behind him. Fin's breath made a fog in front of her mouth. She heard a fox cry up on the hill, another answered from the estate. It was cold but the air felt clean and clear: thinking air.

Fin bounced around past the kitchen window. She waved but Zen was sitting staring at Hatsumi. His eyes burned. His face was red. Hatsumi turned. She saw Fin. She tried to wipe her red face. She was crying. Fin froze. Hatsumi pulled a tea towel off the draining board and wiped her face. She beckoned Fin to come in. Fin cringed but followed the command.

Hatsumi tried to say hello but burst into tears. Her tiny shoulders bobbed up and down. Fin frowned. She was starting to cry herself. She bit her wobbling lip. Zen kicked the table. Fin stepped forward and put her arms around Hatsumi, like Gran did. Just hold the space, love. Fin wasn't sure what that meant but someone needed to hold Hatsumi in. It was like her stuffing was coming out.

She thought Hatsumi would swallow the tears like most adults and shake her off saying I'm fine. Hatsumi just kept crying. Fin patted her back. She'd seen a nurse do this at hospital. Her shoulder was wet. She realised she was a bit taller than Hatsumi.

She thought she should try to sit Hatsumi down. But at the moment they were stuck to the spot. She heard the chair scrape. Zen moved but Fin couldn't see where. Had he left the room? Was he putting the kettle on? This was Pop's answer to any upset. Fin held on and tried not to mind that her face was squashed.

Soon they were both covered in sweat, tears, and Fin suspected, snot. Hatsumi sniffed and sniffed again, into the tea towel.

"Sorry." She broke away from Fin and sat down.

Fin rubbed her face. Zen surprised her by handing her another tea towel. It was white and very clean. Fin went round to the other side of the table and sat down. Zen eyed them both as if they were mad and sat back at the end of the table.

There was a new white candle in the middle of the table. Hatsumi pulled out a box of matches.

"I wanted to light candle for Zen's Dad..."She looked out of the window. She looked like someone had scraped out her insides. Bereft. Fin had read this word but didn't know what it meant until now.

"Every time I see bloody carrier bags, I want to scream head off. So tired, being this angry."

Fin waited.

"My dad was sort of killed by a supermarket," said Zen.

Hatsumi snorted. Zen sighed. Ty padded in through the door. He looked surprised. He walked over to Fin and put his giant head in her lap. Fin rubbed his greasy fur, smelling his biscuit smell.

"I don't remember it. I was in the car," said Zen.

"I only worried when he was away," said Hatsumi. "Not when he home."

Fin nodded. She was still biting her lip. It felt bruised now. She tried to unbite while still looking serious. But her teeth were stuck to her dry lips and they were bleeding. She didn't want to stain the white tea towel. She tried to wipe her lip with her finger. Now her face smelt of Ty's fur.

She imagined Zelda's gleeful face as the drama unfolded for some reason.

"Dad was fine. He knew what he was doing in Afghanistan," said Zen. "We were in the car park. I was belted in. Mum was loading the back of the car. Dad took the trolley back. Some woman reversed into him," Zen paused.

Fin felt the temperature drop in the kitchen. It was odd, though, they seemed to have forgotten she'd heard the story before. It was like they were stuck, like the town clock in *Back to the Future.*

"He was OK, but he'd banged his head which lead to a subdural haematoma."

"He died 20 minutes later, in back of ambulance, before it left car park," finished Hatsumi.

Fin re-bit her lip. Ty's head was heavy now. She didn't want to cry. It was their story not hers. They seemed to be waiting.

"I'm really... sorry," Fin wanted to kick herself. It sounded like she'd spilt a drink. "I'm sorry I never got to meet him." She'd heard Gran say this once.

"Thank you," said Hatsumi, sounding American for a moment.

"He was kind man, with big feet." Hatsumi put the matches down.

"Some days, emptying the bins... seeing carrier bags, I was loading car..." She sighed. "Sorry, Fin. You come for homework."

Zen and Fin looked at one another. Did Hatsumi think all the time they spent roaming about they were doing homework? Zen got up and came round the table. He went to put his hand on his mum's shoulder but didn't quite get there. He didn't know what to do either

Fin realised. Fin pointed to the matches. Zen leaned over and picked them up. He lit the candle.

"I want us to remember him, not plastic bags," said Hatsumi.

Fin pushed Ty off, got up and turned out the kitchen light. Odd, Fin felt as if Gran had padded in.

"Well what are you waiting for?" Gran would say. Fin cleared her throat and licked her split lip. Her tongue tasted rusty.

"You could tell me about him, if you…"

They all looked at the candle.

Hatsumi smiled. Zen shrugged and left the room. He returned with a photo album and plonked it in front of Fin. An hour later they were still only half way through. They'd stopped for tea and fig rolls. They kept the light off.

Zen walked back with Fin. Fin wanted to stay longer in the kitchen with just the candle, but Ty got bored and began to pace about, nudging Zen and Fin with his wet nose reminding them he wanted to walk. Hatsumi looked up once as if she was expecting Ty to bark like a dog.

They made their way along the path. It was even colder now. Frost coated the ground making it slippery. The dead leaves crunched. Ty zigzagged ahead. They didn't bother with torches anymore. They knew the way. Pop and Mop had cleared the path for Gran. A dim orange light seeped over the boundary wall.

"I used to be scared of dogs," said Zen. Fin found this hard to believe.

"Dad took me on a long walk," Zen stopped to pick up a frosty fir cone. He fired it into the undergrowth. Ty shot after it.

"It was weird. There were no houses, it was really windy."

Fin shivered. That sounded like The Countryside. She'd been there once, all hills and mud and no shops. What was the point of a place like that?

"We cut along this farm track, some sort of short cut. There was a green bus at the end, dad thought it was the bus stop," Zen glanced at Fin. "A double decker, but it was in the field. It had curtains." Zen paused listening for Ty. He reappeared behind them without the fir cone.

Zen shuddered: "All the curtains were moving about, the bus was sort of wobbling. We kept walking because the road was on the other side. But the bus was full of dogs, barking, snarling, fighting to get out. There must have been at least 30, real wild."

"Feral," Fin said.

Zen nodded. "One was so desperate it was all twisted up in the curtains," Zen half laughed. "It nearly hung itself trying to get out and kill us."

It was meant to be funny but Fin didn't laugh. They passed the war memorial. Ty sniffed the paper poppies. Zen called him back.

"Couldn't breathe, any minute they'd bust out, eat us to death. Dad held my hand. Just kept walking, the same pace. I wanted him to pick me up and run. Then we heard a man shout at the dogs. They sort of relaxed, got back from the windows. But those windows," Zen shuddered "were covered in blood and slobber."

Fin wished Zen hadn't told her that. That was the kind of thing that stayed with you, long after a story had finished.

"Didn't go near a dog until we got Ty, and now he's not even a dog."

They were standing outside Blind Twin House, under the creaky sign. Fin's feet were numb. She wanted to say something about Zen's dad but couldn't think of anything. Zen whistled for Ty, and turned away.

"See you at homework club," he called over his shoulder.

27

BACK TO SCHOOL

Everyone said it was going to snow. Fin knew it wouldn't. It never snowed when everyone said. It only seemed to snow in London well after Christmas. It was Monday morning. Fin was being herded along the pavement with Zen, and Ty. Ty moped about behind Hatsumi, causing her to stop frequently to yank his lead. Mop kept up a brittle conversation. A cutting wind blew grit in their eyes. Zen and Fin were going back to school. Just mornings to start. After Christmas: all day.

Fin half hoped Zen would sprint off. He'd done this in the past but he just trudged on. Fin wondered if he'd got bored with her and their trips. He'd really enjoyed the game of football with Blimp and Edge. And he'd had a long talk with Tolemy about snakes on their trip to the Natural History Museum. Fin was glad Zelda was in Australia. Zelda was competitive. Tod and Zelda were probably still great mates.

Hatsumi had to wait at the gate with Ty. So Mop signed them in at reception. A smiley woman in a bright green sari welcomed them back.

"Fin and Zen, follow me, everyone has been expecting you." The lady tipped her head forward. Fin tried to smile. The lady rustled ahead. They followed the swishy green scarf up the stairs and round the corner. The school still smelt of bleach and stale pies.

The green swishy lady knocked on the classroom door. Edge yanked it open.

"They're back," he shouted.

Blimp jumped up waving his hands for silence. The trainee teacher Miss Roebuck nodded.

The whole class chanted "Welcome Back Fin and Zen." They all clapped.

The smiley lady put her hand on Fin and Zen's backs and gently pushed them towards the noise, shutting the door behind them. The classroom was very warm. Condensation ran down the windows.

Blimp waved them forward to an empty desk, set up in the middle of the room. There was a tin of Celebrations.

"Sit, eat," said Blimp, imitating his dad, pulling the lid off.

Some of the boys laughed. Arden raised an eyebrow at Fin. Fin felt better. She'd forgotten about Arden.

"We made cakes," said Truelove, plonking a large Tupperware container next to the chocolates.

"Thank you," said Fin.

"Yeah, thanks" said Zen.

They sat down. Arden reached up and shoved a window open. Fin felt the draught. She could breathe. But she felt all wrong being inside.

"Now," said Miss Roebuck taking charge, "Everyone sit down."

Blimp squeezed around the room with the chocolates. Edge carried a tray around with plastic cups filled with very cold Coca-Cola. Fin could hear it fizzing.

"Now," continued Miss Roebuck, swigging some Coca-Cola. She stopped and took another swig. "Hmm, that felt good," she laughed, "Not that we do this every day. We need to look after our teeth."

"Amen," someone said.

Miss Roebuck frowned: "Welcome."

There was another cheer. Miss Roebuck glanced round to let everyone know that was enough.

"We want to welcome you guys back. We thought we'd have a small party, so when everyone's settled, you can tell us a bit about yourselves. The rest of the class will fill you in on what we've been doing while you were away."

"Too much Maths," someone shouted.

"Not enough football," said Edge, pouring out more Coca-Cola.

"Don't worry, you'll be able to catch up, it's not that bad," smiled Miss Roebuck.

Fin liked her. Zen was staring at the walls. They were covered in essays, maths problems, and laminated photos showing a class visit to the sewerage farm.

Truelove started. She'd been chosen to sing a solo at her church and she'd done all her maths homework for the last two weeks. Edge was captain of the school football team. Blimp made everyone laugh saying he was manager. Miss Roebuck said Arden had won two half-marathons and was training for her third. Arden folded her arms, whatever, she seemed to say. Eventually, they got back to Fin and Zen but the bell went.

"OK, guys, clear up and go outside," said Miss Roebuck.

Blimp and Edge hovered with a ball, for a while, but Miss Roebuck kept Fin and Zen in for most of break.

"I know this is all a bit much. You can go outside or stay in the library. After break we're doing some poetry but if it's all too noisy you can join Mrs Ahmed in the library until lunchtime."

Fin wanted to run to the library. It would be warm and quiet. If you took a book Mrs Ahmed left you alone. Fin guessed Zen wanted to play football and she knew the girls would be kind today. They were like trophies after all. So she spent the end of break being quizzed by the girls, mostly about Zen.

Zen joined the football, like he'd always been there. Tolemy arrived at the end of break and slapped Fin on the back.

"Dentist," he grinned, a bloody wad of cotton wool dangling from his lip. The girls screamed and ran off. Fin was relieved. She'd forgotten just how boring they were.

Tolemy pushed the bloody cotton wool back into his mouth. Fin had a headache. She wanted to sit down in her room. The bell went.

Later Fin and Zen walked back along the busy main road. Most of the holes were now filled. Cars roared past. They had to keep dodging shoppers and mums with giant buggies. As soon as they turned into the yard they both began to relax. The road was behind them. The walls and bushes shielded them from the cold wind. Fin had that feeling, the one where you think you forgot to do something, but can't remember what it was. Something was bugging her.

She was relieved when Zen said "Bye, then" and sauntered off.

Fin needed to be alone in her room and just think. Her head was too full of school. Mop gave her a hug in the kitchen. Fin took off her coat and washed her hands. She sat down at the other end of the table. Mop put the kettle on, and pushed bread in the toaster. Fin got up and decided to watch the bread. The toaster smelt good, as all the old bread crumbs burned.

"Well done by the way," said Mop. "Hatsumi and I were worried you'd both run back." Fin was annoyed. She didn't realise that was an option.

"I've made casserole, for tea" said Mop, glancing at the oven.

Fin pushed up the toast. It wasn't ready. She pushed it down again.

"Was it OK?" asked Mop. "The trainee teacher looks very nice, brighter than the last one." Mop put the tea on the table and sat down.

"It's too noisy and hot," said Fin. She felt bad tempered all of a sudden.

"Was Zen OK?"

"Yep," said Fin, collecting her toast.

"Can I take this upstairs," said Fin, buttering her toast. Mop raised her eyebrows.

"Oh... OK."

Fin felt mean. She flung her plate and mug on Gran's flowery tray. She took the stairs two at a time. She didn't want to bump into anyone else.

Fin chewed her toast staring at the pink and blue and red stained glass. Zen had fitted in well, like it was his old school, not hers. He'd played football at break. She knew nothing about football but even she could see he was as good as Edge. And Edge was Captain. They'd been tackling one another most of the time leaving the other boys to shout from the side-lines. Still Arden had spoken to Fin. Arden usually spoke to no-one.

Fin balanced on the spindly chair and rubbed her jeans. Her room was cold with no fire. She tried to make a list of thoughts but she was too tired. She ended up staring at the Imperial Family. Fin began to tune into their conversation. Gran had told her how to do this. Just relax and ask them questions. You'll soon see or rather hear answers. Of course they all had an opinion about school.

Anastasia said she'd join the football, why let the boys have all the fun? Tatianna said she wouldn't bother; take a maths book, make numbers your friend. They don't let you down. Tatianna explained numbers were like good servants, there when you needed them. Alexei just sighed. He was sad. He wasn't allowed to play wild games like football. Fin imagined him leaning against an icy window watching Cossacks playing football in the snow. Jumping and sliding in their thick boots.

Fin sat on her bed. It was more comfortable. She pulled the quilt over her cold legs. Her eyes were sore. She shut them slowly trying to sooth them. She really needed to put a warm flannel on her face. The Imperial family chattered on. Fin lost the thread.

She woke up in the dark. She was very hot. Someone had covered her up. There was cold drool on her chin. She wiped it off. The fire was still unlit. A warm smell of chicken and carrots drifted up the stairs. Her clock said 6.15. She'd slept all afternoon.

Mop and Pop were banging in and out. She could hear Guy, Ermine and Abimbola talking on their way up the stairs. Fin curled up then stretched. The Imperial family waited. Fin's bladder hurt. It must be tea time.

28

A NEW ROUTINE

They had bowls of casserole. It was too runny for a plate. For pudding Fin started on some Madeleines. After the soft hot potatoes and chicken, she savoured their lemony sponginess. She listened to everyone talking at once. Ermine was trying again to explain to Mop and Pop about her art project aided by Guy and Abimbola. Ermine planned to photograph all the pink front doors in London. She got tip offs from friends on Facebook, when she could get a connection. Ermine rolled her eyes. She got last minute tip offs when a door was about to be painted over too. Hence the rushing about and demands for train fares. The photos were all in black and white. Ermine and Guy developed them at college but Pop and Mop had to pay for the supplies.

"But it makes no sense," said Mop again.

"Why not colour, if it's called *The Pink Door Project*?"

"This is why I do science," said Abimbola.

"It's just art," said Ermine, grabbing Guy's arm to indicate it was time to leave. Abimbola stood up.

"Thank you for the chicken soup."

"It was meant to be casserole, but thank you," said Mop. "Only 5 hours late, it was supposed to be lunch." Mop looked at the empty casserole dish.

There was a pause. Pop opened his mouth and shut it. There was a knock at the door. This gave Ermine, Guy and Abimbola the chance to head off upstairs. Fin expected Hatsumi but when Pop opened the door Zen stood on the step with Ty. He caught Fin's eye.

"Hello, come in," boomed Pop. "We were just having cakes, if... is your mum OK?"

Zen nodded his head.

"Thought Fin might want to come out, walk Ty."

Pop frowned. It was late and dark but Ty was big.

"I'll get my coat," said Fin grabbing the rest of the Madeleines for Ty.

They didn't walk far. They were both tired and scratchy after the first day back. However, it felt good to be cold, then walk fast to warm up, then slow down and listen to the big, dark, quiet around them.

Over the next few weeks Fin and Zen went to school just for the mornings. It was a bit of a con because that was most of the school day, the afternoons being very short and devoted to Art and P.E. Zen sat with Edge and Blimp now. Fin sat next to the wall with Arden quietly tapping her pen next to her. Arden was OK. She talked sometimes but not all the time. Miss Roebuck thought they'd work well together.

However, at break Arden put on her running shoes and disappeared along the edge of the school field. The other girls still saw Fin as a novelty but when she didn't want to do their hair at break time they soon left her alone. Fin was fine with a book in the library but often Mrs Ahmed shooed her out for "fresh air." Something Mrs Ahmed didn't need herself apparently.

Fin felt like an empty mug or maybe a spare shoe. She liked the books she found but she felt odd in the playground. She had to stand and read most of the time. Little kids ran round screaming, balls bounced past. Girls giggled. Fin missed the Imperial family. She had half an idea to bring them in or at least one of them. She could sit with Olga in a warm corner of the library. But her family looked weird enough as it was.

"Fin," boomed Miss Nomer bearing down on Fin as she tried to find a place outside that wasn't cold. "I haven't forgotten our project. I've heard great things from Zen's mum. So I want you both to put together what you got this weekend for a presentation on Monday, nothing too fancy, just for me and your class." And with that she blew the whistle. Fin shuddered.

29

SWIMMING POOL

Fin told Zen on the way home. He grimaced. They decided to go back to the tunnels to figure it out. They didn't get out until very late. Pop was reluctant to let Fin out.

"It's almost bedtime," he said, glancing around for his watch. "Aren't you tired after school?" Fin shrugged.

"We'll only be half an hour," she said.

Pop picked up an apple. He didn't so much eat them as attack them with his mouth. Fin decided to leave before the crunching started. They walked slowly. It was warm and quiet in the tunnels, soothing after the windy, noisy playground and clanging bell. They could hear Ty up ahead, lolloping. He'd be no good as a hunting dog, thought Fin. Then they heard a loud splash. Fin and Zen looked at one another, then sprinted towards the pools. They didn't bother to illuminate the ceiling. Fin held her torch out in front of them. This slowed her running down. Zen streaked ahead. He stopped dead standing in the dark domed room. There was loud splashing and thrashing. Fin arrived puffing and waved her torch across the void.

It sounded like Ty was fighting a sea monster. In Fin's head she saw a giant fish with bulging eyes swallowing Ty whole. Zen caught her arm and directed the torch. The pool was full. Dark water came right up to the curved lip. They couldn't see Ty but Fin thought she could see a black shape moving towards them in the dark rippling water. She took a step back, ready to run. Zen did the opposite. He leaned forwards.

"There's something in the water..." he said.

Fin wished he hadn't said that. It sounded really creepy and made whatever it was real. Zen didn't have time to finish. The something leapt out of the pool, causing an explosion of water to drench them both. Zen toppled backwards and fell over, bashing his elbow on the hard floor. Fin screeched, jumping into the air. Ty stood over Zen, dripping and shaking himself dry. He wagged his tail and looked quickly from Zen to Fin and back again. Zen swore and sat up. Fin slid down the wall and sat down. Zen pretended to check his torch. Ty panted and waited. He couldn't understand why they weren't joining in.

"Jeez," said Zen. "I thought that was a shark or something."

Fin tried to smile but her face was stiff. She crawled over to Zen.

"I thought it was a killer fish, a big killer fish..."

"D'you get those in the Thames then?" asked Zen.

"All the time, they swallow boats and sharks."

They got up. They were both wet. Ty began to pad round the other side towards the steps. Fin and Zen followed tiptoeing around the lip, shining their torches across the water, then illuminating the walls. They couldn't sit on the steps because they were now under water so they hung about watching Ty plough across the pool.

Now they had more light the water didn't seem as scary. It wasn't clear like swimming pool water but they could see the bottom. It didn't smell of chlorine, more like puddles. There was some silt at the edges that clouded up when Ty paddled by. Now and again they saw a finger sized fish that darted away from the light.

"I think they're called sprats or sprackals," said Fin. "Something like that."

"Sprackals, eh?" said Zen. "Are they poisonous, could they like eat us if we got in?"

"No, they just..." Fin didn't finish. Zen was laughing. He put his hand in the water.

"It's kinda warm."

Fin rolled up her wet coat sleeve and splashed her hand in the water. It didn't feel warm to her, more like tepid bath water. Ty galloped up the steps. Fin and Zen stepped back to avoid being sprayed with water again.

"But why's it full, it was empty before?" said Zen sitting down.

Fin began to pace along the pool side. She remembered something important.

"In the Basel book there was a list of the tide times. I thought it was there 'cos the book was about London... the Thames... but I think Lord Basel built this to use the river."

Zen frowned.

"Don't you see," Fin continued, "the Thames is tidal. It'll fill up the pools twice a day. Last time we were here must have been low tide."

"So if you come at high tide... you can swim?"

"Suppose," said Fin though she couldn't see who'd want to swim in Thames water.

"But you'd need to check the table; it changes all the time, so sometimes you'd swim in the day and sometimes in the middle of the night."

"Sounds like a crap idea for a swimming pool. I mean imagine if your school came and there was no water?"

"Yeah, but if you hadn't been to a pool you think an empty pool was what you got, you'd play football instead?"

Zen shook his head. Fin took the torch and wandered over to the beam engine. Ty followed. The trough was full here too, except the water was dark and dirty. Fin was glad there was a barrier. Ty sniffed and padded away.

When Fin returned Zen was hopping about from foot to foot. He shucked off his trainers and socks, then his sweatshirt and trousers. He had sort of shorts on underneath. Fin was glad about that. He waded down the steps.

"Not bad, sort of..." Zen waded forwards trying to remember where he'd been in water like this before. He held his arms above his head. Ty ran towards the steps and wagged his head from side to side. Then he jumped in. He looked a bit like a horse trying to keep his big head above water. Zen began to splash about. His T-shirt gradually got darker and darker as he walked towards the middle of the pool. Ty banged his jaw together. Then he stopped as he was getting water in his big mouth. Zen began to swim to the far side of the pool. He stopped and tried to touch the bottom disappearing under the water. He came up spluttering.

"It's deep," he shouted, his wet hair plastered to his face.

He lent back and began to backstroke, his arms long and fluid. He was a good swimmer. Fin hovered like a spare thumb. She envied Zen's confidence. She wondered if she should mention legionnaire's disease and dysentery but she didn't want to be a kill-joy.

She took off her trainers and balled up her socks. Next she rolled up her trouser bottoms above her knees and dumped her coat near the glowing wall. She listened to her bare feet slapping towards the steps. The steps were broad and shallow. Mica glittered in the white stone.

Fin could only go down three steps before she felt the ends of her trousers get wet. She stepped back up. Ty and Zen watched her for a moment before swimming around the pool.

Fin wished she was a wild sort of girl, like Aurora Starbuck, who'd strip to her expensive underwear and jump in. Perhaps next time she could wear her swimming costume and bring a towel?

Now there was the presentation to worry about instead. Fin decided to make some PowerPoint slides by typing up her notes and adding some pictures. She explained to Zen they could sit in the dark with the rest of the class, just click the slides and read from the notes.

"Fine by me," said Zen.

They were walking towards the pools again. Fin had printed out the London Water tide times. By the time they got there the pools would be half full, maybe, if she'd understood the maths. She'd promised Zen she'd get in the water.

"Can't you swim?" Zen had been talking to Blimp at school. Blimp couldn't swim but he had a plan to build a coconut raft to sail around the world.

"Sort of scheme a non-swimmer would come up with," said Zen.

Fin remembered school swimming lessons at the leisure centre. She'd been in the deep end trying to avoid being drowned by Tolemy, Zelda and some boy who left to go to a better school, his mum said.

Blimp and the rest of the class doggy paddled in the shallow end, while a bad tempered life guard shouted instructions.

Fin had put on her swimming costume. But she had grown. It was stretched so tight it felt like her shoulders were being pulled down. She wanted to stop to snap the Lycra away from her skin but with Zen she felt self-conscious. She didn't want him to look at her.

When they finally got there Fin had run out of chat about school. She'd told him all about Zelda and how Blimp liked to listen to the giant billboard nailed to the outside wall of his flat. When the picture changed, the wooden slats slapped making a sound like the sea which was where Blimp got his idea about the raft. Though, Fin couldn't explain the coconuts.

"He needs to learn to swim, it's dangerous. Kids drown," said Zen, pulling off his sweatshirt.

Fin was warm. The too-tight costume had rubbed her skin. Her shoulders burned. The water was almost to the top step. Fin dipped her hand in. It was cool not cold. It would sooth her skin. She got undressed quickly, flinging her clothes in a pile. Zen still beat her. By the time Fin made it down the steps, bending forward slightly to loosen the costume's grip and to hide her chest from Zen, he was splashing around with Ty.

She sat down, feeling the water press against her skin. Then she leaned forward again to push off from the step and swam towards Zen and Ty. Her hair fanned out from her head, catching on her neck as her head moved up and down. She forgot to keep her mouth shut, as usual. She'd probably get diarrhoea tomorrow. The light was dim. Fin wanted to come back when it was light outside, but they were at school in the day now. A plan was needed.

"It," said Zen poking Fin in the back and splashing away.

Fin half ran, half swam to catch him. He'd poked her hard. They tried to get Ty to join in but he just followed them around rather than swimming away. They chased for ages because they couldn't think of anything else to do. Then they both felt tired, shaky and very hungry. They got out, rubbed themselves down with their sweatshirts and pulled on their clothes. Fin wished they had a flask of hot, hot chocolate. She promised herself she'd make some, next time.

They hurried back but it took a long time. Fin's feet were wet so they squelched about in her socks. Her costume began to rub again. This time it was worse as her skin was wet. She'd have to persuade Mop to get her another one.

30

ANOTHER WORRY

"You may have to wait for Christmas," said Mop. "Sorry. But if the school's taking you swimming you'll just have to borrow Ermine's or something."

"Yuck."

"Let's talk about it this evening; you've got your presentation today anyway."

"What? You know about that?"

"Yes, Miss Nomer sent us an email, said we could go."

Mop looked at Fin. Fin bit her lip. She hadn't expected that. She imagined the whole class pressed together with their parents and babies crowded at the back. Zen would probably escape out the window. She'd be trapped. Her chest felt tight. Mop frowned then smiled.

"Fin, FIN."

Fin stared at Mop. Black stars swam before her eyes. She grabbed a chair and sat down hard. Great now she felt really sick. She clamped her teeth together.

Mop rubbed her shoulder. Fin was suddenly very hot, then very cold. She shivered.

"It's OK, we aren't going, neither's Hatsumi. We thought you guys wouldn't want us around."

"Oh," said Fin, wondering if she'd just had a panic attack. She'd seen panic attacks on television. Some people couldn't even get on a bus. They thought they were about to die and the world was going to end. Gran said that would be the right time to die. God how many more problems did a person need?

"Look, if you guys don't want to do it that's OK… Miss Nomer's been pushing you both, well you really, because she says you're bright, we know that… she thought you were in Zelda's shadow… a bit…we…" Mop stood up. "You could really shine but if you don't want to do it…" Fin got up and picked up her rucksack. Yep she was scared. But she hadn't realised it was OK to get out of stuff. They made their way down the wet path towards the main road. Cars swished through the rain, buses rumbled past. Fin heard Gran's voice in her head.

"If you're scared of something and you avoid it, it just gets bigger."

Gran had taught her this on the day she and Ermine made a terrible fuss about a spider. It had run down the curtain and across Ermine's hand. Both Fin and Ermine had screamed and run out of the room. The spider was at least as big as Ermine's hand, maybe even her face. Gran trapped it in a glass with an old birthday card over the top. She marched towards them. They both cowered on the stairs ready to run again.

"Look, it's harmless. You've turned it into a tarantula."

"But it's the size of a tarantula," shouted Ermine.

Gran considered the point.

"Maybe. Maybe it's a tarantula but it's not a giant, bird-eating spider is it?"

With that Gran disappeared into the garden.

"I could have been bitten…" yelled Ermine. "Bitten and died frothing at the mouth, biting Fin in a poisonous frenzy."

"That sounds like rabies," said Fin.

"Yeah, like I said: dangerous."

Best do the assembly so it didn't turn into a bird-eating spider. Though, Fin wasn't sure she'd be able to persuade Zen with this argument.

Fin's mouth was so dry by the time Blimp turned out the classroom lights she thought she wouldn't be able to speak. She'd hoped Zen would run off but he sat quietly by her side, waiting. Fin looked at her seat in the corner of the classroom. She wanted to go back there or even go home. Arden caught her eye and smiled. This surprised Fin. Then they were off. Zen hit the slide button and Fin told the story. They didn't get very far because the bell went. No-one moved.

Miss Roebuck cleared her throat and leaned forward in her chair.

"Tell you what, why don't we finish this after break, if we lose some Maths it's not the end of the world."

There was a yell of appreciation. Blimp flicked the lights back on and chairs were scraped back. Miss Roebuck put up her hand. Everyone stopped.

"That's if you don't mind?" she said.

"No," said Fin. Zen just nodded.

Blimp and Edge waited for Fin and Zen on the stairs. Fin thought it was about football.

"Right, you've got to make it last, as long as possible," said Blimp, putting his arm round Zen's shoulders. Edge went to do the same to Fin then changed his mind.

"It's really good, so we don't mind listening all morning," said Edge.

"All day," said Blimp.

"All week," said a voice at the bottom of the stairs. It was Arden. She was bent over tying her laces. She stood up. She was as tall as them even though they were still two steps up. Her thick hair fanned out around her shoulders.

"Tell you what," she added, "we'll ask loads of questions to keep you going." She pulled her hair into a tight bun and turned towards the playground door.

By the time they were all sitting in the dark again the message had gone round. The class sat very still. Some like Truelove had written their questions down on their hands so they didn't forget. Miss Roebuck scanned the room. She sensed there was an atmosphere but she couldn't put her finger on what it might be about. Had she been given a broken chair? Had someone smuggled in a pet hamster? Did the class know about a fire drill? The Q and A went so well,

Miss Roebuck abandoned the Maths lesson completely. The Maths'
teaching assistant came in, went out and came back to join in. Fin and
Zen forgot to be nervous and told almost everything.

"D'you know you describe it so well, it's like you've been there,"
said Miss Roebuck when the clapping died down.

Zen shook his head vigorously from side to side. Fin looked down.

Tolemy leaned back on his chair and muttered something to Edge.
Edge raised his eyebrows. Fin didn't like the look of that.

31

BILLY AGAIN

Fin and Zen had spotted Billy a few times when they came back from school. He was usually on the other side of the road, walking Eddy. He didn't go to school. Probably excluded, thought Fin. He had indeed been excluded again for menacing a teacher. The head regretted using this word. But it was accurate. Billy's mum kicked up a fuss. How was she supposed to know what menace meant? How was poor Billy supposed to know too?

The head said they could only give Billy a good report in geography, so it was better if she took Billy elsewhere. A fresh start. The teachers whooped when they heard Billy was finally going, especially the geography teacher. He felt the other staff avoided him as his subject was sort of keeping Billy there. Billy's mum made a fuss and appealed to the governors. They considered Billy's thick file with distaste.

"Leave it," Billy's dad said. "There's no money in it. He's a shit. They've had it up to here," he waved his hand over his head. "Billy, you get a job. You can drive by in a new car, show 'em. Teachers drive shit cars."

Billy's mum tuned out. This wasn't about cars. Billy wasn't too bothered. He could smoke, run Eddy and plan. If he needed cash there was Crime and Wave. Billy ignored Fin and Zen. He was playing a long game. He watched and waited. He'd seen Fin, Zen and Ty rambling about and he'd seen them disappear behind the house. He thought there might be a short cut or a gap in the wall taking them to the High Street. So late one night when everyone apart from Fat Bastard was asleep Billy let Eddy off the lead and under the gate. He climbed over. Eddy shot off towards Blind Twin House and disappeared. Billy hurried after him until he nearly fell into the tunnel. He used his phone light. He could just see Eddy sniffing about ahead.

"Well, well, well," said Billy to Eddy, straightening up and walking into the tunnel. He didn't figure out the phosphorescence because he kept his phone light close to the ground. But being Billy he kept going.

Fin was in bed. The doctor said Fin had overdone it, being back at school for five mornings. Mop and Pop agreed. It rained most days so Mop stopped clipping brambles and digging. Pop did a lot of work before breakfast. So after breakfast he'd come and read to Fin. Mop would come in when Pop went back to the yard, looking tired. Fin pretended to doze to give Mop a break. Mop had put on some weight. Her jeans fitted her now instead of hanging down ragga-style. Fin worried Mop would go back into her shell. Fin was glad she was at home to keep an eye on Mop. Ermine was busy putting on a pre-Christmas exhibition with Guy. They'd been in and out to photograph the yard. And they'd spent some time listening to Fin explain her presentation on Lord Basel.

"So he used snakes?" Guy asked again.

Fin leaned over and pulled a box from her bedside drawer. She pulled out the snake skin. Ermine began snapping away.

"I'm gonna call this picture: hobby-girl," she said.

"Cool," Guy leaned towards the skin.

"Lord Basel... well it was his son Peter's idea really," Fin continued.

Guy peered at the translucent skin. Fin passed it to him. He took it carefully. But it was much stronger than it looked.

"London had a big problem with rats and pigeons spreading diseases."

"Probably, still does," said Ermine, adjusting her camera lens.

"Anyway, Peter came up with the corn snake idea. They're harmless and pretty. They could be used as pest control. Down the tube and for the Spa tunnels, pipes, wherever." Fin stopped. She was worried she had given too much away. Ermine perched on the spindly chair and leaned towards Fin.

"Well go on," she said, taking another shot.

"That's it really," Fin stopped. She wasn't used to the attention.

"But where did this come from?" asked Guy, holding up the snake skin to the light. Ermine clicked some more photos. Mop kicked the door. Guy got off the bed and wrenched it open.

"Tea," she was balancing a tray with three steaming mugs and a packet of Jaffa cakes. Guy took the tray, draping the skin on Fin's bed. He decided the windowsill was the best place to put it.

"Everyone OK?" asked Mop.

"Yeah," said Ermine, "Just getting educated. That one's scary." Ermine pointed to Fin. It was a compliment. Mop smiled in her distracted way. She wasn't listening.

"We're off to the garden centre," said Mop by way of reply.

"Woo hoo," said Ermine. "Remind me not to get middle-aged."

This had given Fin thinking time. Guy passed round the tea and dropped the Jaffa cake box on Fin's quilt. Ermine put her camera down, grabbed the box and tore open the biscuits.

"Peter had pet corn snakes, so they tried an experiment in one of the tunnels, maybe a sewerage tunnel. Anyway, it worked. Snakes like it warm and dry."

"But sewers aren't warm and dry, well they're not dry," said Ermine, looking from Fin to Guy.

Guy tried to hand Fin her tea by holding the mug on the flat of his hand. It got too hot.

"Shit," he said.

Fin took the mug, a little tea spilt on her quilt. The mug was very full.

"Exactly, sewerage tunnels would be wet and full of shit" said Ermine.

"Maybe the snakes were just for the spa then?" said Guy. "But there are water snakes aren't there. Where did you get this one?" said Guy, wincing at his hot tea.

"I think the snakes did so well, they're still about in the yard when it's warm, sort of feral," said Fin. Ermine got up and slurped her tea. She was unaffected by the boiling liquid.

"Well, I think we should keep an eye out," said Guy.

"Too right, I don't want to get bitten," said Ermine.

Rain pattered against the window.

"We probably wouldn't use snake photos anyway, a bit of a cliché. Too Gothic?" added Ermine putting her camera back in its case.

"I don't think they'll be out in the rain anyway," said Fin.

"Rain or no rain, we're off to photograph the quagga. Was that one of Peter's pets?" asked Ermine.

"I dunno," Fin was tired.

Ermine was blocking the heat from the fire. Fin put her mug down and pulled her paperback over. Ermine didn't take the hint. She stayed talking to Guy about the light and photography this and photography that. Fin's eyes began to burn. She shut them. When she woke up they'd gone, leaving the dirty mugs on the window sill.

32

ZEN'S BETRAYAL

The doctor decided Fin could stay at home as long as she stayed in bed. This meant she missed the build-up for Diwali, Eid and Christmas at school. Pop dragged a big tree back for the sitting room but decided to leave it in the hall, where it was lashed to the banisters. It scratched their legs as they went up and down the stairs, pinging pine needles across the floor. Pop was busy in the yard by day and spent most evenings at some new flats installing bath and shower units. Some of the flats had two bathrooms and an extra loo. Lots of plumbing work.

This meant cash for Christmas. Mop helped out more in the yard. She'd been going round in circles for a while re-digging the earth around their house. Now she was often out on gate duty, directing funerals. Bartholomews paid her to open the chapel, put the heater on and make tea. Mop spent a lot of time greeting mourners in Gran's black coat with the astrakhan collar. Bartholomews loved her. It gave the drivers a chance to escape the claustrophobia of the overcrowded limos.

Ermine shouted as another pine needle pierced her foot as she hurried up and down the stairs. Ermine's friends banged at the door. Fin often heard shouting and laughing then silence. She settled back expecting Zen and Ty to appear but they didn't.

She was fed up. She wanted to go downstairs but the kitchen seemed too far away. Her room was warm. Mop left the little lamp on because it was always so dark outside. She had plenty of books but her head hurt if she read for too long and her mouth tasted horrible. She didn't even fancy biscuits. They were too dry or sickly sweet. And where was Zen? Fin imagined him playing football or talking with Tolemy, turning into Tolemy. Maybe she'd try writing to Zelda again?

But when the school holidays started Fin heard Zen shouting. She struggled out of bed and opened the window, leaning as far out as she could. The trees were bare so she could see Zen on a wide path, running with Ty. Fin waved her arm. But then she saw Zen and Ty weren't alone. Zen was being chased by Edge, kicking a ball with Blimp puffing behind. Even worse Tolemy was shouting from the gate. Zen tore off his sweatshirt, threw it on the grass and began moving a wire bin. Tolemy shouted something about the main road. Zen ran back and with Tolemy's help pushed the gate shut. Blimp bent over out of breath. They were setting up a football pitch. Fin felt as if she'd been slapped. For one mad moment she'd thought they were coming to see her.

She yelled something very rude and slammed the window shut. Over the next few days Fin heard the lads play football. It didn't matter how grey or drizzly it was. They'd moved further into the yard. She could no longer see them. Pop had probably moved them away from the main gate. Fin drew some pictures in her diary. They weren't very kind. She made the boys really small playing on the open grass above a mass grave. She drew skeletons waving their skeleton fists at the noise above.

When Christmas finally came it was a bit flat. The best part was waking up to a fat stocking filled with chocolate buttons, oranges, walnuts and a thick animal action magazine. There was some soap that smelt of toffee and lots of little things Mop had spent ages wrapping up, like Hello Kitty pens. Fin sucked the chocolate watching the watery sun make coloured patches across the floor. Then Gran arrived. They all argued about the chicken-not-turkey cooking and how to fit in a quick walk before the sun disappeared. Gran said she'd walked enough for one life time. She plonked herself down next to the samovar. Ermine and Guy started peeling potatoes. This left Mop, Pop, and Fin to "enjoy" a walk. They only got as far as the corner shop. There was no-one about, except the odd car. Pop bought them all crisps. They headed back to a huge roast, and present unwrapping. Fin had hoped Zen, Ty and Hatsumi would join them but they'd gone to stay with some architects Hatsumi met on a course in Brighton. Odd to think Hatsumi had a life outside the yard. Fin thought Christmas day by the sea sounded cool.

After lunch everyone was very full and a bit sick. Fin ate about twenty crunchy ginger star shaped biscuits. That was Guy's present. He called them leeber-chuken, which sounded weird. Fin felt weird. It was like she'd been poisoned but was yet to find out how she would be ill. Puke, headache, diarrhoea? It turned out to be a mixture of all three. She was sent to bed with another hot water bottle. When she woke up it was dark. Christmas day was over. But the holiday sort of dragged on.

She began to talk to the Imperial Family. They were a bit standoffish at first. Fin had neglected them after all. But soon they lined up on the window sill and made comments about the boys. But the flat boredom was making Fin feel worse.

"Why don't you get back to your project," said Mop, bustling in to open the window. Fin pushed her Aurora Starbuck mystery onto her bedside table.

Mop had a carrier bag. She passed it to Fin. Fin reached inside. There was a big wide-lined A4 pad, box of crystal blue biros and an expensive packet of four highlighters in neon pink, turquoise, orange and purple. Fin was pleased and annoyed at the same time. This meant Mop knew she was feeling down and left out.

After Mop cleaned out the grate and built up the fire, she suggested Fin got out of bed.

"I'll light this later, we need to get you up," she said, sweeping out.

Fin didn't want to get up. She felt dizzy. Her legs were very stiff. She piled all the Basel books with the new stuff and went and sat in Peter's cupboard room. Mop returned with the laptop.

"You'll be lucky to get a connection but you never know."

Fin doubted it unless she climbed on to the roof and leaned out at a dangerous angle. Usually Mop and Pop had to go to Twin House as it was nearer the main road to get a connection.

The cupboard was empty and warm. There were lots of pipes. The small window was clear glass with red edges so lines of pink moved across the floor when it was sunny. Fin pushed an old bean bag under the window. She had her back to the wall. From here she could see along the wide empty shelves, the painted animals appearing in-between.

She arranged the books, paper and new pens around the sides of the bulging bean bag. She's shut the door to cut out the draught. Fin half hoped Zen would come to visit and not find her, like she had somewhere better to be. She flicked through the books. The big pictures drew her in and soon she was miles away. There were drawings of the Workers' Spa and lots of diagrams of fountains. Fin caught a photo of an upturned lead bowl with plants behind it. Then there was another diagram: the bowl had been cut in half. It was connected to a pipe travelling underground; this eventually led across several pages to the beam engine. There was some text in what Pop called copperplate handwriting, all swirly and curly. Fin had to read it several times. She was bored by yet another plumbing story but the curly writing drew her along. It looked so good it made you want to read it, even if it was a list of pipes.

A watery sun broke through the rain clouds. The white linen room glowed pink. She read on, she had all day. The beam engine was to be powered by the Thames at high tide. It only needed pressure. Here there was a diagram with arrows showing a man with a flat cap pushing it down. Just as Zen had nearly done and almost fallen in. At high tide once set in motion the beam engine was designed to work like a water wheel powering the fountains of South London. Fin thumbed through but found nothing else. She needed to think about this. The bowls were everywhere: along the edge of the school playground, along the High Street, in the backs of people's gardens.

Now and again there had been local news stories where residents complained to the council to get the bowls removed. Stuff Victorian heritage, when your old mum's fallen over and broken her hip, people wanted them gone. The council always responded with some guff about tube vents. But they weren't vents. They were fountain heads. Fin wanted to jump up and tell Zen. If they went underground when the tide was high, they could push the beam arm and start the fountains. Maybe?

Fin would need to get to grips with deciphering the tide timetable again. But then Fin stopped. There was no Fin and Zen, like there was no Fin and Zelda. Fin wanted to go back to bed and pull the covers over her head. But she knew she'd feel worse She went back to her room and got dressed. She'd finish this project by herself. Though, she wasn't sure how. But it was the sort of thing Aurora Starbuck would be up for. She didn't think she had the nerve to go to the spa by herself. And after Christmas she'd go back to school and sit next to Arden. She may even go back to school all day. Zen could look after himself in the afternoons.

It was only when she plonked herself back down on the bean bag, after lunch, she noticed scratched writing on the bottom of the back of the door: Peter Bartholomew Brothers in Arms.

Fin heard Zen yelling outside. Since when did Zen yell?

"Bye, later."

"Later."

Voices veered off into the distance. They were on bikes by the sound of it. Fin thought she heard Ty snapping his jaws together. She rammed herself further down her bed scattering books and pens across the floor. Tatiana had been keeping her company. She toppled off the bed-side table and rolled under the bed. Fin grabbed her pillow and pulled it over her ears. She shrieked in frustration. But it didn't make her feel any better. Her stomach churned.

She wanted Gran to appear, pull back the covers and tell her a comeuppance story. Gran was good at these. One day a very fat man had pushed in front of Ermine and Fin at the bus stop, knocking their crisps into the gutter.

"Oh, he burst," said Gran. "It's made the local paper, very little the hospital could do about that one, a nasty case," Gran had shivered.

Fin actually remembered seeing blood oozing down the dirty bus window and a woman fainting at the bus stop. But this was probably what Ermine called false memory syndrome.

To make things worse Zen was now hurtling up the stairs, Ty at his heels. Fin turned her back to the door and shut her eyes. She kept the pillow near her face so when Zen came in he wouldn't be able to see whether she was faking sleep or not. There was a knock at the door. Fin imagined Ty standing on his back legs putting his lion paws against the wood. Fin waited. Zen waited. He knocked again, less confident now. Fin saw them in her head. Both standing there, facing the shut door. Fin waited expecting Zen to push the door open and walk over to her bed. Zen said something to Ty. And before Fin could figure out what it was they left. Seconds later they were away across the yard racing for Twin House and tea.

Fin was disgruntled. She shrieked again and banged her fists up and down on the bed. This made her more angry, not less. She was annoyed with Zen. But she was more annoyed with herself. She was turning into Ermine. She sat up and pulled at her hair. It hung round her neck in greasy strands. She was too angry to lie in bed any longer.

She got up and rearranged her papers on the floor, picked up Tatiana and put her back with the Imperial family. Alexei was standing in a patch of green light. This made him look very ill. Fin moved him along to join Anastasia in a pool of blue light.

"Well what would you do?" asked Fin, using her best Imperial sounding voice.

She felt better. She pulled her diary out of the book pile, took a biro off the mantelpiece and waited, pen poised. For as long as Fin could remember she'd been writing things down. She'd just start with a rant, raving about something that annoyed her or her and Zelda. Then she'd drift into a story or a conversation. Including the Imperial family had been Gran's idea.

"If you listen, when it's really quiet they'll talk to you. They kept me company for years," said Gran.

Anastasia was the first to speak. "Find some new friends, I would." Fin sat back on her bed.

"I thought I had," she wrote. She glanced back at the Romanovs. The Tsar looked very sad.

"As well he might," Fin heard Gran now.

"You guys only had each other. When it came down to it you didn't have any friends either."

Gran had often told Fin the Romanov story. They had asked their friends and relatives, including the King, if they could stay with them to escape the Russian Revolution. Their days were numbered. They were ignored, left to the Bolsheviks, who killed them. Fin always hoped the story would end differently but it never did. A family lined up for a photograph in a basement were shot until they died. Fin shuddered. Ermine's first photography project had been lining families up in their garages; as most people they knew couldn't afford basements. She then took a picture of the empty garage. The pictures won an award but they just creeped Fin out.

Fin had drifted off thinking of photos and families. She put her diary down and opened the window. A cold breeze whistled in. Fin pulled the window shut and tried to peer through the coloured glass. The bare trees were dark red, the sky a sickly pink. Because the glass was bumpy she couldn't see if Zen was about still. Mop and Pop began rowing on the stairs about manure.

33

AVENUE OF VICTORIAN INVENTORS

Zen didn't give up. He reappeared the next day and ran into Fin as she came out of the bathroom. She'd finally washed her hair. She was wearing her ratty too short pyjamas and an old jumper of Ermine's with long matted sleeves. Fin scowled. Zen smiled and stood back waiting for Fin to lead him into her room. Fin wished she'd cleaned her teeth, her breath probably stank.

"I came yesterday but you were asleep. Mum wouldn't let me come before..."he said.

Fin kept her back to him, fiddling with the window. Zen came over and put his warm hand on her's. Fin thought he'd gone weird.

"I'll do it, they're so stiff at our place we can't shut them. Mum made like a... like a" Zen cast around the room for the word.

"Like a draught excluder?" said Fin, no longer able to wait. Zen frowned.

"Yeah, she did what your Gran did." Zen indicated by rolling his hands around.

"Like those, only long and thin," he pointed to the Imperial family who were lined up waiting for Fin's next move. Looks like a Bolshevik to me, the Tsarina seemed to be thinking. Fin looked at Zen. He did. His cheeks were pink, his face tanned and his dark hair looked like he'd brushed it with thistles. In fact he had thistle or something caught in his hair.

"You've got something in your hair," said Fin.

"Have I?" He crinkled up his eyes, the room was getting dim. "Maybe you should get back to bed. Your arms are deformed," he said, then laughed. Fin looked down. She'd folded her arms across her chest. The extra-long sleeves were hanging lose over her elbows. Zen really wasn't picking up on the atmosphere. He turned around and picked up Olga. Then, he carefully put her down.

"Are these your relatives then?"

Fin couldn't resist this question. She flicked off her slippers and tucked herself into bed, to hide her old pyjamas. Zen perched on the spindly chair but soon got up and sat with his back to the wall, next to the door. Fin thought it was odd to see him without Ty. Like there was something missing. Like seeing people without their glasses, they looked sort of wrong.

Two days later Fin found herself following Zen and Ty along one of the many winding brick paths. They pushed past brambles and ducked under twisted trees. Headstones leaned towards them or lay in broken halves on top of flat graves eroded by acid rain. Zen wanted to show Fin what Mop and Hatsumi had been working on. It looked like no one had taken this path for at least 100 years. Perhaps Mop and Hatsumi had used the main path riding the bin truck instead?

Between the graves, however, Mop and Hatsumi had been clipping wild rose bushes and clearing stinging nettles for weeks. Zen helped some afternoons. Guy had joined in with a blow torch. This hadn't worked terribly well because the undergrowth was damp. Guy made a smoke cloud that hung about for hours drifting over a funeral. An officious vicar complained mourners couldn't hear his prayers because of all the coughing. Zen thought this was funny.

Fin began to puff and sweat. This path was really steep. The stumpy trees poked branches in her face. Eventually they rounded a corner past a white marble mausoleum coated in green mould. Its pillars leaned towards the path as if it was about to fall and crush them.

Fin guessed very few people would risk passing it. More tombstones, like broken teeth, disappeared in the dark spaces under the trees. Fin couldn't help but read the curling lead letters: Mary 1826-27. Fin winced. She tried to peer over Zen's shoulder. He walked fast. Then he stopped. He bent over to retie his laces. Fin stopped and stared. She couldn't quite take it in. She shut her eyes and opened them again. The red brick path was bordered on either side by grey stone furniture.

Zen turned and smiled. Ty sniffed about around the base of a stone sewing machine.

"This is the Avenue of Inventors, it's... well look."

Zen ran up to a black marble post box. He pushed his hand in. Then he stiffened and shouted for help. Fin lunged forward but by the time she got to Zen's arm he was laughing, pulling it out. Fin's face was hot.

"Very funny," she muttered.

Fin walked down the row. There was a white marble gramophone. The earth had sunk on one side, so it appeared to be sliding off its plinth. Fin thought of sticking her hand in the trumpet but decided the joke had been done. Zen jumped about.

"Some of them are obscure but I think this is a loo," he said, sitting down on a curved block of grey stone.

"Obscure?"

"Well... more weird really."

Zen moved ahead into the thin winter sunshine. Ty nudged a gnawed fir cone with his nose.

"What's this?" Fin stopped, staring down at a wide flaky plinth. Three shapes like melted babies led across the top. Their features dissolved by acid rain. Zen came back.

"They're the Jelly Babies."

Fin looked at Zen. Another joke? They looked like dead triplets. God what was it, with this place? Zen smiled and laughed.

"No, they really are. I've looked them up."

"Really," said Fin, folding her arms.

"Really, I found some boring website on great Victorians. They invented loads of stuff. Jelly Babies, the flushing toilet..." Zen pointed and hurried back to the seat. "The gramophone... ice-cream and Easter eggs."

"Where are they then?" said Fin, turning.

She wanted to see the Easter egg but she still wasn't sure if Zen was winding her up. She began to walk down the avenue. She couldn't see very far because there were the usual bulky, boxy mausoleums, jutting up like ugly, abandoned houses. If Zen was right would she find a penny farthing? Now that would be cool. Zen caught up.

"Look, Ty found this," Zen peeled off his sweatshirt and spread it across a patch of stinging nettles. He then pushed his hands down carefully, crushing the nettles. Fin leaned over under a thorn bush. Sitting in the weeds was a white marble typewriter. Fin wanted to touch it. The keys looked waxy and smooth.

"Obviously, it doesn't work," said Zen, crouching down, pushing a key. Fin leaned over and did the same. The key was gently concave. A drop of water cooled Fin's finger.

"I tried to move it," said Zen. "Put it back where it was meant to be, but it's really heavy."

"How did it get here?"

"Dunno, vandals maybe?" said Zen, dragging up his sweatshirt. "You didn't believe me, did you?"

"Well," said Fin. "It's a bit far-fetched."

"Not really... Victorians were mad about inventions and death."

Fin waited for Zen to continue. It was his turn now to tell her stuff.

"They had photos taken of all their children. Even the dead ones."

Fin screwed up her face. Zen continued. "Yeah, they sort of propped them up or made it look like they were asleep. I'll show you later, we could add it to our project."

Fin hadn't thought about it as *their* project, more *The Project*. But she was glad Zen said: our project.

"So where's the Easter egg?"

"I didn't find an Easter egg or ice-cream, they might have..." Zen looked around. Ty looked around too. "Dunno, we could look... probably somebody nicked them."

"What, a giant stone Easter egg?"

Zen shrugged.

"Maybe," said Fin, arriving at the end of the Avenue, "they weren't all buried here." She hadn't seen a penny farthing. Zen nodded and whistled for Ty. There was a gate at the end but it was jammed shut. Mud had built up around the bottom, burying the base. Zen climbed over. Fin cut around the side. There was no wall. Ty followed. Fin liked it when Ty followed her. Sometimes when Zen was out of sight, she'd pretend Ty was her dog.

34

AN EMPTY HOUSE

Later Fin hurried over to see Zen, Ty and Hatsumi. Zen could show her the Victorian death photos. Ermine loaded her up with tins and a large glass bowl. They'd been washed up weeks ago but still not returned. Ermine said it was time to take action. So Hatsumi had enough containers to deliver more food parcels. Things were better now Ermine did most of the cooking with Guy playing sous chef and Fin as washer up. Usually Mop went to bed after supper, tucked up with a book, a hot water bottle and her blue pills. Fin missed Mop in the evenings. But she liked the way Mop left her bedroom door ajar. Her light cast a friendly path down the dark stairwell. Pop would have a fag outside, planning his next job, if he wasn't installing more baths. He'd come in, make some notes with a stubby pencil and find a quiet fixing sort of job. This usually involved a lot of noise and swearing in the basement or lying under radiators with pliers.

It was cold with a smattering of drizzle. Fin could feel her bulky torch whacking her hip. She walked fast but she wasn't frightened. She stopped once to rebalance the tins and bowl on a handy headstone. A breeze blew her hair in her face. It was getting long now. It made her nose itch. Damn, she really wanted to rub her face. She planned to really, really rub her face when she got to the back door at Twin House. She could lean against the door to support the tins.

She thought about when she'd first moved in. She would never have dared wander about in the bushes. Now she found it soothing, well not the bushes part, but being out at night alone in the yard. She could hear the faint tide of traffic on the main road. The air smelt of damp earth but other things too: cigarette smoke, warm soy sauce, beer and urine. It wasn't too bad when it all blended but sometimes when one smell took over, like urine, it was bad.

Fin looked up. Twin House loomed up out of holly and crazy old rose bushes. But the windows were all black. All of them. It looked different, as if the insides had been sucked out. Fin had only seen the house like this when they moved in. She thought it was empty then, derelict.

Fin felt like she'd been kicked in the stomach. Had Hatsumi, Zen, and Ty gone? The tins felt heavy, awkward. Fin was on a ridiculous mission. She kept going. Crossing the road she caught a shadow to her right. But when she looked all she could see were the dark firs forming a thick wall around the back of the house. Usually the lights shone across the road. Fin would catch sight of Hatsumi going upstairs or Zen running down stairs. Sometimes Ty's shadow leapt up the walls. Fin was proud she wasn't scared of the monster dog. She'd seen little kids on the High Street cry when they saw Ty. One old man called Ty an ugly bastard because he stepped on his foot in the post office.

Fin kept her eyes on the firs. She had to go round the back to leave the tins. She wasn't going to carry them all the way back home. She was spooked. The firs looked like a good hiding place for someone or something. She glanced at the main road. The occasional car swept past beyond the gates. She could always run to the gate and yell. It was chained but there were some uneven bricks, she'd seen Zen use as a foothold to get over when Ty's ball rolled under the gate. But she couldn't see them in the dark.

Where were Zen and Ty? They were always there. And when they came over to Blind Twin House, Hatsumi always left the kitchen light on. Fin walked past the empty windows and around the back. The trees shivered in the breeze. Fin jumped and almost dropped the bowl. She stopped. Her heart pounded. She felt silly. She told herself Hatsumi probably went out earlier and forgot to leave the light on.

Fin left the tins on the step. Not the best plan, a passing a fox might piss on them. A dog barked, a bus rumbled past. Fin just wanted to get back. Was she being watched? Fin didn't like the fact she couldn't see into the house. Something might be able to see out. She walked away fast. She didn't look back. What if she saw a face?

It was windy. Bushes roiled around her. A plastic bag rustled, caught in the bare branches overhead. Fin scraped her hair behind her ears. She swung her torch in a wide arc across the path, then stopped. She was scared she'd pick up something she didn't want to see. Something white appeared on the path ahead: the snarling snout of Evil Eddy. He made a low growling sound, drool poured down his jaw. Fin stood absolutely still. She waited expecting Eddy to jump at her throat. She was going to die and it was going to hurt. Her mouth went so dry she couldn't move her tongue, let alone shout for help. Her arms shook making the torch light wobble. Then a white hand appeared and grabbed Eddy's collar clipping it to a chain. Billy bent over Eddy yanking the lead. Eddy didn't take his eyes off Fin. But he was now tethered to Billy. The next move was Billy's. Billy straightened up. He looked at Fin with a frown, like he wasn't sure who she was. Fin waited. She knew she should run back to the main road and yell through the gate. Billy appeared to be considering, waiting for Ty and Zen? He bent down and patted Eddy pushing his rump down into a sitting position. Taking his time, letting Fin know he had all the cards. Eddy turned his big ugly head quickly. For a moment Fin thought Eddy would bite Billy. Billy and Eddy eyed one another. Billy held the chain. Then they both turned to stare at Fin.

"S'alright, he won't bite, come on," Billy beckoned her forward.

Fin annoyed herself by following Billy's command. She wobbled towards them, then passed them, close enough to catch Billy's fag smell. Billy laughed and slapped Eddy's rump. Fin shot off at the sound and didn't stop until she was leaning with her back against the inside of their kitchen door. She wanted to tell Pop all about it, but all about what? Billy hadn't threatened her. Evil Eddy wasn't pissing down the side of someone's grave. Pop encouraged dog walkers when he saw them. As long as they were respectful, he said, liven the place up a bit. He'd even put some old bowls by the taps so the dogs could drink.

"Encourage people to take an interest in local facilities, otherwise we'll lose them," he said.

"The council can't close a bleedin' great graveyard," snorted Gran.

"You'd be surprised," said Pop.

Gran nodded "Maybe not," she said.

Fin stared around the kitchen. It was empty. The coals glowed in the grate. Fin locked the door and shucked off her coat. The almost darkness was warm and comforting. Fin was glad of the wine gum stained glass. Billy couldn't see in. She steeled herself to cross the cold darkness to the sitting room. The door was shut but she could hear the television on the other side. She turned the brown Bakelite nob. Guy and Ermine were curled up on the sofa under Ermine's quilt. Their faces looked blue. Ermine leaned over and picked up the remote. She turned the television down. The sofa made a weird island. There really was no other furniture in the room. Mop had given up trying to make the house cosy.

The house resisted. They couldn't light a fire in every room. It was too much work, and too expensive. Pop had the radiators working but they were so far apart the rooms stayed cold. Hence, the quilt. Guy pulled a hot water bottle out and tested it with his face.

"Get a refill, love," said Ermine, sounding like an old lady. She considered Fin. "You look like you've seen a ghost, or are a ghost."

Guy got up on one leg, giving his other leg time to wake up.

"Join us if you want," said Ermine.

"Yeah," said Guy pulling the quilt back for Fin to take his warm spot.

"I saw Billy," said Fin. Ermine curled her lip. Guy walked past with the hot water bottle. He was wearing thick purple hiking socks. Ermine patted the sofa. Fin went and sat next to her sister.

"Make us some tea," Ermine shouted after Guy. "This could be an all-nighter. What do you mean, you saw Billy?"

Fin explained. Her bottom lip wobbled. Ermine being kind had thrown her. She let her guard down. But at least she wasn't blubbing like a baby.

"Look, stay away from him. He's a menace."

"What d'you mean: menace?" Fin asked.

Ermine flicked channels. She looked at Fin. "Well he's probably all talk and criminal damage, but that dog's dangerous and he runs with a bad crowd."

It was odd to hear Eddy referred to as a mere dog. He inspired supernatural fear. She wondered about what other dogs Eddy ran with, until she realised Ermine meant Billy. Guy returned with mugs of tea for all three of them and a hot, hot water bottle.

"Did you lock the back door," said Ermine

"Oh yeah," said Fin.

"Good, Pop forgets. I've taken to checking it before bed," said Ermine.

The television showed a man talking in front of a beach. Then he was walking round a ruined castle. The stone was yellow in the sun. Back in the yard it was always winter. Fin and Ermine stared at the screen. Guy slurped his tea. Ermine tutted.

"Sorry," said Guy. "But you girls wanna get treatment for your misophonia."

Ermine leaned forward and picked up her mug.

"It's not misophonia; you just make too much noise." Ermine sipped demonstrating how to drink tea without slurping. Guy passed Fin her mug.

"Do want me to take a look?" asked Guy. "Outside?"

"No, I bet he's gone," said Fin, balancing the mug on the quilt. The tea was too hot, even the mug handle was too hot. "He was just showing off."

"Probably," said Ermine. "But we need a game plan. I'm not trying to be patronising but I think you and Zen and those others should stick in pairs; not go alone especially when it's dark and there's no-one around. I know you like to ramble but maybe stick to the time Hatsumi's out doing the bins?"

Fin thought this was a good idea. She didn't plan to wander back alone after dark again. But she'd lost something. Billy had taken something, stolen it from her.

"I can walk you around. He's very cocky with his f'ugly dog, like to see him on his own," said Guy.

"Some hope. He's just a bully. No wonder he got kicked out of school, probably tried to take Eddy in," said Ermine.

Fin knew Guy and Ermine were trying to help but all this talk of Billy was stressing her out. She wanted to forget Billy and Eddy. The man on the television was now standing in a dungeon pointing to chains. Fin wanted Ermine to turn it over.

"What's this, the Discovery Channel?" said Guy, taking the controls. Ermine took them back. She flicked past a horror movie; someone was being strangled, until she found Grand Designs. Kevin McCloud stood grinning in front of a building site. Ermine turned it up a little so they could hear what he was saying, but talk at the same time. Kevin chatted to a man with a beer gut and hard hat.

"What others?" said Fin.

"Eh?" said Ermine.

"You said Zen and me and the others should stick together. Did you mean Blimp and Edge?"

"Blimp and Edge, who calls their kids names like that?" asked Ermine.

"The boys with the football, with Zen, the other day," said Fin.

Ermine was watching an architect explain the many problems of the building job.

"What? No. I've seen some others." Ermine turned the sound up.

Fin sipped her tea, it was cooler now. What others? She'd never seen any others. Had Ermine seen ghosts? Fin really wished she hadn't thought this. The room felt very dark with just Kevin McCloud's face to light it up. Fin didn't want to go to bed. She planned to stay with Ermine and Guy even if they sat there all night.

Fin decided she'd try not to be frightened by Billy but rather appalled, as Gran would say. She'd have to work at this, was it really possible to swap one feeling for another? One you would rather have?

35

A DANGEROUS TRIP

The next day there was no intel on Twin House. Pop said he hadn't heard anything. Hatsumi did have the weekend off, so perhaps they'd gone away? Maybe to the seaside? Fin thought this was a ridiculous idea. And if true, very risky. Anyone could be wandering about on the beach. Someone wildlife nut might spot Ty and where would that leave them? Fin was sore about Zen not telling her about the trip. In her head it was a trip where Edge and Zen played football while Blimp tried to swim in the shallow surf. Fin sat on her bed with nothing to do. She imagined Zelda at the seaside. Everyone but her.

"This is ridiculous," said Fin, getting up and rearranging the Imperial family. They seemed to agree. No-one's gone to the seaside. Maybe Zen and Hatsumi had been attacked and were lying hurt instead. Fin decided to check out Twin House again. The path was spooky after Fin's encounter with Billy. The sky was very grey. So even the daytime felt dark. Bushes looked like good hiding places. Fin glanced left and right and sometimes behind. She began to worry she might see "the others," Ermine had seen. A car swished past the end of the path causing Fin to jump. Then she felt glad, at least someone was about.

The Twin House windows were empty and cold. Something was missing. All the paper snowflakes had been taken down. Fin felt as if she'd been punched in the stomach. Had Zen and Hatsumi really gone? Fin pushed her face close to the glass. She was relieved to see Hatsumi's checked shirt over the back of a chair and Zen's old trainers by the back door. Fin didn't know this was the sort of tat that got left behind when people moved house. Her parents were hoarders, so took everything with them.

Fin couldn't see the bin which had been stuffed with all Hatsumi's paper snowflakes, screwed up and rammed in the top. She wandered away towards the grassy knoll to stare at the quagga. Then she had an idea. Something she could tell Zen about when he came back. Something she might even send to Zelda. She decided to visit the spa alone, but in the day time. It would be lighter. Just a quick trip. She felt nervous, a bit shaky, but she'd check no one was around, leave a note on her pillow and run there and back. Once Fin had the idea she had to make herself do it. The sooner the better. Otherwise she would get more worried. The sun slowly broke through the clouds.

Billy had the same idea but Fin didn't know this at the time. After a quick trip back home Fin took a detour by the wide path above Blind Twin House. This way Mop and Pop wouldn't spot her. The thick cypress and fir trees were like a mini forest of green surrounded by bare winter trees. She skirted round the back of the charred wood remains of the shed. There was still an acrid smell of burnt stuff. Then, she was down the scree slope and into the tunnel. It was nicer in the day. The tunnel felt warm; the thin sunlight spilled ahead lighting the floor and the curved ceiling. Fin didn't need her torch at first. She jogged towards the spa. When she got there, a little out of breath, it was full. She could smell the water, a kind of powdered metal smell. It was high tide. And the chamber was light.

Fin tipped her head back and studied the dome. There were oval shaped holes in the mosaic ceiling filtering in sunlight. Fin wondered where they came up. Maybe there were some grates hidden by crumbling graves and long grass in the yard above. The water wobbled, the sunlight flickered. Fin went over to the edge. A small almost transparent fish darted away. She walked around to the other side. The gold spa had no skylight. However, some of the glass tiles caught the sun off the water throwing back the light. The jagged edges sparkled. Fin wished she had her swimming costume. The beam engine looked the same. It waited in silence, like a museum dinosaur.

Fin wanted to share it with Zen. It felt a bit flat being here by herself. She sat down at the edge of the pool staring at ripples and sunlight. If she had a phone she could take some pictures. But Mop insisted she wait till secondary school. She'd probably be the last kid in London to get a phone. Zen didn't have one because they were poor. But somehow it didn't seem so bad for boys. Fin drifted off. She stopped thinking about anything but the water. Then she heard a noise. She instinctively looked towards her exit but it was coming from there.

"Hold on."

Someone was coming down the tunnel. Fin jumped up and ran. She ducked into the dark tunnel that led away from her exit. Her feet echoed up round the curved walls. She forced herself to stop. She held her breath. She stepped very close to the tiles. She was relieved she hadn't illuminated the ceiling here. That would give her away. This tunnel curved from the spa. So even if someone shone a torch in her direction they wouldn't see her if she stayed where she was. She began to breathe slowly and waited. She was shaking but she forced herself to count five long breaths. This calmed her a bit. Aurora Starbuck did the same thing when hiding from the Hooded Claw. Fin had to think, otherwise...Maybe there was no other way out. She could hear someone, a bloke talking to himself? That was scary. The someone was probably mad and dangerous.

"Eddy," shouted Billy. Eddy echoed round the dome.

Fin realised she had been kidding herself, when she told herself she wasn't scared of Billy. Her body was telling her she was very scared indeed. Billy's voice got nearer echoing down the tunnel then further away. She heard the clank of Eddy's lead. Thank God he wasn't roaming free. He would have caught her scent and come after her. Fin turned slowly and began to walk as fast as she could, trying to make no noise. While Billy amused himself by shouting down the tunnels listening for echoes.

Fin wanted to punch herself for being so stupid to come here alone. And no one else knew where she was. She stopped. She couldn't hear Billy anymore. Fin realised she was walking in almost total darkness.

Her legs wobbled. She leaned on the wall before sliding down to sit on the smooth floor. Billy had gone. She'd had a lucky escape. She shuddered to think what could have happened. Her adrenaline began to evaporate. She was getting tired and stiff. Should she wait for Mop to read her pillow note? That might not be until tea time and by then the yard would be dark.

She had to go back. She got up and began to creep towards the spa, her heart in her mouth. She stopped every few yards to listen but she couldn't hear anything except the lapping of water as she got closer to the pool. There was another sound too. It was like being inside a shell. Fin realised this was the wind across the skylights. It sounded like the wind across the chimneys at Blind Twin House. She breathed out, relieved. If she hadn't known this, she would have really freaked.

Billy was probably long gone but what if he was waiting with Eddy at the mouth of the tunnel? Seconds felt like hours. Fin kept her torch off. She couldn't risk a glowing tunnel. Billy might spot this and return for another look. She padded on. Usually she walked noisy as Zen called it, to frighten away corn snakes. They'd seen three cross their path on one trip. She knew they weren't poisonous but she didn't want to be bitten. Even though Zen said they were more afraid of her than she was of them. Fin hated it when people said that. And she wasn't convinced it was true. They probably didn't know they were afraid. Snakes had such tiny brains. They'd probably bite first, think after. She imagined catching her toe in the jaws of a big one, as it lay across the tunnel. She felt it bite down, its long fangs sinking into her trainers. She stopped. She could hear an ambulance on the main road, not far now.

The scree slope was bright in the sun. Fin paused one more time, then made a noisy run for it. She scurried past the kitchen window. It was half open. She could see Hatsumi sitting at the end of the table. She looked like Mop did when they first moved in, before she started gardening and got the blue pills from the doctor. Hatsumi looked like a lost child. Fin stopped. Hatsumi put her head in her hands. Mop got up and put her hand on Hatsumi's shoulder, picking up a bulky letter from the table. Fin wasn't sure whether to go in or stay put. Mop might send her upstairs, out of the way. And then she wouldn't know what was happening to Zen or Ty. But she didn't want to be caught listening like a creep. So she carefully let herself in. Mop looked up and smiled.

"Put the kettle on," Mop said. Fin went to the sink. She washed her hands with the coal tar soap, smelling its strong tarry smell. She always expected the bubbles to be orange like the soap. But they weren't, why was that? Hatsumi sighed and shifted in her seat. Fin busied herself with the tea bags, mugs, getting the milk carton from the fridge. She didn't look at Hatsumi. Mop and Hatsumi resumed their conversation.

"I can't understand it, why now?" said Hatsumi, with the air of someone who'd said this a thousand times. Mop sat down next to Hatsumi and put her hand on Hatsumi's tiny arm.

"Listen to me; we're going to fight this."

"But they say I can't stay here because my husband dead. But Zen can stay because he born here, make no sense." Fin noticed Hatsumi's accent got stronger the more upset she became. "And not to work, then I lose house." Hatsumi looked at Fin. "You look after Ty."

Mop squeezed Hatsumi's arm. "No, you're going to carry on working and living here because you need food and shelter. Zen will look after Ty and go to school... English law is based on what the man in the street considers reasonable. That's reasonable. A judge will agree. This letter hasn't come from a judge but Immigration..." Mop stopped. It sounded like she'd considered this before. She leaned forward to catch Hatsumi's eye.

"Your husband was a decorated soldier, killed..." Mop paused, choosing her words. "Killed by a... in a terrible accident. He had permission to stay, so do you and Zen."

Hatsumi nodded and sniffed.

"Boy, I can see the headlines on this one," said Mop. Her eyes burned like the coals in the grate. There was a popping sound and the kitchen light went out.

Fin picked up the matches and lit one of the large white candles in the middle of the table. There might be some sun outside but the kitchen was always dark. Fin decided to open some biscuits.

"Thank you," said Hatsumi, her eyes large in the candle light.

Fin wasn't sure whether the thanks were for her or Mop. Pop bumped through the kitchen door on his way to the basement.

"Sorry," he shouted.

Mop caught his sleeve and passed him the letter. Pop took a while to read it. His glasses were smeary as usual and the candle wasn't too bright.

"We need a plan of action. Fin get paper, pens and light more candles. I'll fix the fuse later," he said.

Fin set up the candles. She decided the situation called for five. So she opened a new packet with no complaints from Mop. She placed each one in a chipped holder and pushed them towards Mop who already had a note pad in front of her. Hatsumi looked dazed. She just stared at the candles.

"Zen back to roaming all over. He not go back to school."

"Right, Fin can help with that part of the plan... and with Miss Nomer. Come to think of it Miss Nomer might write a letter to our M.P," said Mop. "We can fight this."

"Yeah," said Pop "and just let them try and come here." He bent down and pulled a giant padlock from his tool box. "D'you know, I've found chains the size of boa constrictors in that basement. We could hold off those b... Immigration for weeks."

Hatsumi tried to smile. She sort of coughed like Ty.

"Where's Zen?" asked Fin.

Hatsumi frowned and started to get up.

"Sit down, I'll go," said Mop.

"I'll go," said Fin. She hurried out before anyone could object. She had half an idea that might make Zen go back to school. But she was worried about Mop's headlines. What if Ty ended up in the paper?

36

BAD MOODS

Fin was pretty stoked as she hurried out of the kitchen. If she saw Billy near the house she'd just storm right past him. Show him she wasn't bothered, maybe. Mop and Pop were nearby. And so were Zen and Ty. There was no wind. It was just cold. The sun had gone. Why was it always cold here? She didn't remember it being cold back at their old house. Even their street always felt warm and muggy. Maybe she was confused. It had been too warm in hospital.

She had a feeling Zen would walk up to the back of the hospital, perhaps climb the wall and sit on top. She'd seen him there after they'd moved in, his face sullen. She walked fast. She wasn't sure what she'd do if he wasn't there. She stopped now and again to listen for Ty. Anything crashing about in the brambles would be him, not a monster.

Ty surprised her by running up behind and rubbing her hand. Fin jumped then struggled to keep her balance as Ty pushed past on the narrow the path. His greasy back rubbed her jeans as he took the lead through a canyon of narrow, pointy graves. She reached the top by climbing over a fallen tree trunk and sliding down the other side. The tree was rotten. So chunks of wood flaked off against her jacket. Fin paused. She liked the sweet woody smell.

She looked up. The sky was almost dark. Some light from the

hospital streamed over the wall lighting the tops of the graves and angel's wings. She could see some stars, a clear night, no wonder it was so cold. Ty turned along the path that followed the boundary wall. It was very dark. The hospital light didn't reach the bottom. Ty disappeared. Fin waited, should she follow? Then he returned panting. Zen wasn't there.

Ty looked up at her. He expected her to lead the way. But she had no idea where Zen was. She was worried. It wasn't like Zen to abandon Ty. Had Billy got him? Fin had to do something. She decided to head down the main path. If she didn't find Zen she'd get Pop to help. Billy might still be about, lurking, spoiling for a fight.

"Right Ty, this way," she said. She tried to whistle. But Ty took off down a side path, Fin hadn't noticed before. She got out her torch. The path twisted between the graves and then opened out becoming a circle. Ty cough barked and bounded forward. Zen was sitting on a wooden bench. He was miles away, staring at a stone girl carrying scales in her outstretched arms. Fin stared too. The girl was about her size. She had a smooth face and long hair that rippled down her stone back. Ivy smothered her long skirt.

Fin plonked herself down next to Zen. The bench was damp.

"Hi," she said, searching her pockets for supplies. They were empty.

"Hi," said Zen. He sounded tired. Ty sniffed the ivy. He stood on his hind legs and put his head up to the stone girl's face. Fin waited. They sat there. She could feel the damp seep into her jeans. Her feet began go numb.

"My parents may look like idiots but they've got a plan. They're in the kitchen now with your mum coming up with a plan."

Zen kept staring ahead. There was a smashed dovecote rotting in the long grass. Fin wondered if Zen had knocked it down in temper. There was a splintered post nearby. She shone her torch over it, then let the beam drop. Fin couldn't sit here all night she was shivering.

"It's something legal. Knowing Pop it will involve writing to our M.P. and the prime minister and all the newspapers... he's been stock piling chains so we can seal ourselves off and become an independent country... if we need to. But we probably won't," Fin wasn't sure where all this had come from. She must take after Gran's melodramatic side of the family.

"Except they'll probably make us go to school, over the wall..." Zen looked at her, raising his eyebrows. Ty padded off down the hill. Zen pulled himself up after Ty. He rammed his hands into his pockets.

"And I suppose we can live on biscuits the rest of our lives?"

Ouch, Fin thought.

"Well if you don't believe that my parents and your mum can take on Immigration and win, your... your just being rude." Fin was annoyed. She sounded silly. Zen turned. His eyes locked on her's. Fin felt her stomach squirm. His eyes were so dark and warm.

"Rude?"

"Yeah," said Fin her face going red. She got up. I'm not going to hang around here, she wanted to say. Zen walked over to her. She could smell his dirty jeans and clean hair. Something had changed. Fin couldn't read his mood. She looked past him at the stone girl. Why were they fighting? Ty surprised them both, barging back through the undergrowth, his head low. Zen bent down and pulled Fin's sleeve. They crouched in the middle of the brick circle, not a great place to hide. There were voices.

"Billy," hissed Fin.

Zen caught Ty's collar. Fin grabbed the other side. They waited holding their breath. Billy had someone with him. The other person grunted or laughed but didn't speak. They were on the path that led to the back of the hospital. There was a wooden door in the wall. Pop had emailed the hospital to try to get them to pay for a proper gate they could lock, to stop the likes of Billy using it as a short cut or getaway. Billy kicked open the flimsy door. The other boy or boys laughed. Then they were gone.

Fin, Zen and Ty headed down the hill, fast. Fin realised she hadn't told Zen anything important about Billy and her idea. She decided that could wait. They headed to Blind Twin House in silence.

"Well," said Pop, pushing his hands into his pockets.

"I think we go home now," said Hatsumi. She stood up, and headed over to the door. Ty tried to walk between Hatsumi and Zen, stepping on both their feet. Zen didn't notice.

"Thank you," said Hatsumi.

Then they were gone. The draught from the open door blew out the candles. Mop began to clear up. Pop went over to his tool box and began to rummage for fuses and screwdrivers. Fin relit the candles.

By tea time the next day it was very, very cold outside and pretty chilly inside.

"We might have to call an electrician," conceded Pop, dropping the last box of supermarket candles on the kitchen table. Fin helped Mop outside. They'd moved beyond the garden to tidy the path leading to Blind Twin House. It was the best way to keep warm, moving about turning over the earth and clipping, endlessly clipping. The feral roses seemed to grow back overnight. Fin looked out for Zen and Ty. It was easy to cut back the undergrowth in winter. Branches were stiff and snapped with a satisfying snappy sound. Fin took the secateurs and cut away around three big headstones. She found a stone lion sitting on its haunches. Further along they discovered two angels that had fallen or been pushed over about 50 years ago, judging by the amount of ivy and brambles entwined round their wings. Fin was pleased with the finds. She worked hard to cut back the ropey ivy. Then she dragged some spikey holly onto the wheel barrow. She stopped now and again. Even though she was wearing old gardening gloves the thorns pierced her fingers if she moved too fast.

Mop was really pleased. She passed Fin a nylon brush and a bucket of soapy water.

"Try scrubbing, it might take off some of the earth."

Fin scrubbed. At first mud and little bits of vine fell away but the stone was stained. It was as if the angels had absorbed the earth through their pores. Fin wondered if they could paint them white.

"In the spring I thought we could get Ermine to take some photos and you can write something. We could upload it on the internet... start a website."

Fin wondered where this scheme was going.

"Then," said Mop, smiling at Fin, "I could open Blind Twin House as a B and B. It's big enough."

"B and B?" Fin turned the words round in her mouth.

"Hatsumi's keen too, if they, well if things work out..." Mop glanced in the direction of Twin House. She looked like she was staring across an endless steppe. Fin considered the wonky grave stones strangled by ivy, stinging nettles and brambles.

"Well they'll need to like biscuits," muttered Fin, bending a wiry branch under her wellingtons. She dropped the brush in the bucket. It was hard work and it wasn't really making any difference. The light in the yard was dull and yellowy, even the air was stained. Fin took off the damp gardening gloves. She undid her coat. She was too warm now.

Mop tapped her on the shoulder. "Look," said Mop. "It's snowing."

Fin looked. Mop put out her tongue. A few small flakes like bits of shredded loo paper whirled about before settling on the muddy path. They melted. Fin blinked. A few snowflakes caught her eye lashes. It felt good, like a tiny burn. But it wasn't settling. The snow disappeared into the mud.

Typical London: warm and grey, cold and grey, nothing kind of weather. Fin tipped the water out of the bucket across the path. It washed some of the mud away. She finished loading up the wheel barrow and yanked up the handles. Mop picked up the secateurs and headed back to the house. Before Fin reached the gate the snow had stopped.

For lunch they had tinned soup and chunks of brown bread. The soup was supposed to be chicken but it tasted of skin and tin. Mop kept the window open, just in case there was more snow. The sky was cloudy, the air still yellow. Fin didn't want to hope for snow. Then it definitely wouldn't happen. Hatsumi surprised them both by tapping on the window.

"Come in," shouted Mop.

Hatsumi came in smiling.

"Stay for lunch," said Mop.

Hatsumi smiled, shaking her head. She was wearing a big green fleece. It looked like a man's fleece, perhaps Zen's dad's?

She wasn't carrying anything. Fin was disappointed. Hatsumi often brought some macaroons or something they could all share for pudding. Fin could leave the adults to talk snow and eat them by the fire. Mop shut the window. They were getting cold. Their exercise warmth had worn off.

"I supposed to work but I spent morning sending emails; getting information, spoke to very helpful man. War Office."

"Whoa, whoa," said Mop. "You need to explain, how was he helpful?" Mop was on her feet now moving towards Hatsumi. Fin decided to wash up in case Hatsumi started to cry again. She could pass her a clean, cleanish tea towel. Hatsumi waved her arm.

"Too much to say now, funeral in," Hatsumi looked down at her bulky man's watch. "Funeral in 10," she grimaced like a naughty child. Mop picked up Pop's fleece and followed as Hatsumi opened the door.

"I'll give you a hand. Blimey what do we look like? Care in the community on work experience."

Fin heard them laugh as they passed by the kitchen window. She enjoyed washing up. She liked to put her hands in the too big rubber gloves then push them into the hot water feeling the gloves close in, in warm folds. She looked at the bubbles, oily rainbows sliding across them. Wash up, everything was clean, wipe the table, sweep the floor, empty the bin, collect more coal and pile up the used newspapers next to the grate. It was soothing when you weren't interrupted. Like she could make everything better, somehow.

She was interrupted by a loud banging at the front door. She went to answer it, hoping it was Zen. But he'd come round the back. It was a man in overalls with a tool box.

"Electrician?" He seemed to be asking Fin what he was. Fin just nodded to be polite. The man waited. Fin heard Mop on the path behind. She arrived breathless, her hair stuck to her sweaty face.

"Sorry, I saw you drive in."

"Yep, with the funeral," the electrician laughed.

"Sorry about that," said Mop.

Worse for the corpse, thought Fin.

"It's this way," said Mop pointing towards the cavernous hall. The man raised his eyebrows. Fin was glad she'd cleaned the kitchen.

"Looks like snow," the electrician said, rattling his box, wiping his clean boots on their dirty mat.

Fin decided she needed to talk to Zen.

37

WATER FOOTBALL

She glowered at Zen through the clear windows at Twin House. He was bent over something, sitting with his back to the door. Ty was probably in the other room warming his belly in front of the fire. Hatsumi always had a fire in the sitting room. Fin thought of the big framed photo of Zen's dad sitting on the small table next to the fire. Maybe it was Hatsumi's way of keeping him close, almost like he was keeping an eye on his little family.

Fin burst through the door, barely knocking. Zen turned round. Fin narrowed her eyes but decided not to speak until she was standing in front of him. She marched round to the other side of the table. Zen started to open his mouth. Fin put her hand up. She'd seen Gran do this. Apparently this was a popular gesture of the Tsar when all his children rushed him at once, competing for his attention.

Zen closed his mouth and sat back.

"I hope you'll hear what I have to say and not go roaming off, some might say sulking." This wasn't what Fin meant to say. She sounded like someone from the telly.

"I've a good idea and Mop and Pop and Hats... your mum, have some good ideas about how to get you out of this. But if you just wander off with Ty, then... then... it makes us feel like you don't care."

Zen opened his mouth again. Fin remembered how Billy had called him a girl. He had such big dark eyes and browny-pink cheeks. His hair was so thick. But a girl would brush her hair. It wasn't fair. Here she was a girl and nearly bald. OK her hair had mostly grown back and she wasn't a girly-girl, but all the same. Fin got distracted by what was in her head. She tried to rearrange her thinking. She needed to get back on track.

"Look just don't wander off, we all get worried. Then there's less time for the campaign." Fin decided to sit down. She pulled out the chair next to Zen. It was covered in books, newspapers and an open box of coloured drawing pins. She tried to pick them up but they slipped and cascaded onto the floor. She had to kneel down to root around under the table. Zen half got up to help. Fin put up her hand again to stop him. She began to stack the papers and collect the pins.

"Your mum has really got it going, Mop's made a list. And I thought we could go to school together. Get Miss Nomer and well, everyone to help... as you guys love football you could invite them to the spa on say Saturday for, for water football." Fin finished and put the pins on the table, shoving the papers on another chair.

Zen smiled: "Water football?"

"Yes, water football or whatever that game's called in the water with footballs." Fin was scowling. "Edge could come and Blimp, Arden could run the tunnels..."

This time Zen put up his hand. Fin paused, shaking. She sat down. He might tell her to clear off. After all she didn't have a dead dad and deportation hanging over her. He was allowed to feel bummed out.

"Only if you join in the water football," he said.

This was unexpected. Fin nodded. Zen went to one of their clean, orderly cupboards and opened it. He took some time scanning the shelves, before rummaging about in the back. He took out a rainbow coloured packet.

"Japanese biscuits." He cut the packet open with a sharp knife and slid half over to Fin. "Deal?"

"Deal."

Fin pulled one out. It was a round wafer with a whirl of pale gold icing on the top. It was crunchy and chewy and tasted of coffee, then chocolate with a dollop of raspberry jam in the centre.

"These are good," said Fin, still chewing.

"Yep," said Zen, taking another one. "They're called Bunyan."

"Wait you do know that bunions... "

"Yep."

Fin hopped around pulling on her jeans. She had on one pair of stripy socks. She planned to put her hiking socks on top, then her wellingtons. Otherwise, she would be cold all day. It was warm at school but when she came back, she soon got cold. Blind Twin House was down to fires and candles again. The electrician had taken one look at the two brown twisted cables that ran round the house and laughed.

"Rewiring: urgent," he wrote on his call out bill.

Pop reckoned he could do most of it himself but that meant spare evenings and weekends. It would take a while. Fin dragged a bucket of coal up to her room in preparation of the big freeze.

At Basel Road School it was like stepping into the future. There was electric light, hot radiators, and computers that worked. Fin tried to ignore Mop and Hatsumi who both insisted on going with them. Ty was stuck at Twin House looking sad at the kitchen window. Miss Nomer spotted them in the playground and beckoned them into her warm office. Fin kept her head down. It looked like she and Zen had committed some sort of crime. Which in some ways they had: trespass. But she knew Mop and Hatsumi wanted to canvass Miss Nomer for their campaign. Miss Nomer listened, her eyes narrowing. Then she walked over to a filing cabinet behind her desk. She pulled open the bottom drawer and pointed.

"I've had dealings with these people before. And," she straightened up "I've not lost a pupil yet, or their parents for that matter."

Hatsumi burst into tears and sat down. Mop put her hand on Hatsumi's shoulder. Miss Nomer sat down behind her desk and pushed a box of tissues over. They all waited for Hatsumi to stop sobbing. Zen took a step closer to his mum. Fin stepped closer too. They heard the bell go. The playground noise quieted down. Kids were lining up for class. Miss Nomer paused listening. Excited voices rushed up the stairs, book bags and coats were dropped, classroom doors were pushed open then closed.

Hatsumi sounded as if she was going to choke, trying to stop crying.

Miss Nomer sighed "Let it out, let it go."

She turned to Zen and Fin. "I'll need your support. You'll both need to buckle down and show real improvement, no coasting. It'll all go in my report."

"No pressure then," said Mop, trying to smile.

"Well a little," said Miss Nomer.

At break there was the usual crowd wanting to know what was going on. Fin didn't feel they'd earned the information. She wanted to make something up.

But Zen said "Immigration are trying to deport my mum."

Everyone agreed this was unacceptable and probably illegal. But they gradually drifted away calling for Edge to join the football. Edge kicked the ball but stayed along with Blimp, Arden and Tolemy. They shivered and tried to think of things to say to make Zen feel better. Fin looked at them. They were all keen to join Pop in barricading the yard, turning it into an independent country. Blimp even started to dream up names.

"It'd be like Lichtenstein or Monaco without the money and the sun," he said.

The others laughed. Fin and Zen tried to join in.

"You made it sound a bit crap," said Tolemy.

"Craptenstein?" asked Blimp.

"Yep," nodded Zen.

Fin was annoyed. She felt Zen was being disloyal. Yes it was a bit shit, but that was for her and Zen to say, not Tolemy or Blimp.

"Yeah, but imagine if it snows," said Arden.

"Whoa, yeah," the boys agreed. "It'll be the best," said Edge. They all looked towards the thick white clouds. For a moment the cold felt good, like a harbinger of snow. Fin decided it was now or never. It probably wouldn't snow but they had something better or at least nearly as good.

"Why don't you guys come over on Saturday morning, bring your footballs and your swimming stuff." She caught Zen's eye. She felt a bit guilty. She hadn't quite owned up to the fact that she wanted to include everyone because of Billy. This way they'd outnumber him, if he reappeared.

Fin wasn't sure how they would get away with it. But she'd been thinking about this for a while. She knew they would need something to go on. She felt in her pocket and drew out a tatty photocopy of the workers' spa. She unfolded it. The others leaned over.

"Zen and I found this. It's sort of a secret. So don't tell anyone. Just say you're coming over for football, and then we'll show you." She could tell they didn't believe her but they were keen to come if only to knock about.

"We better make up some water football rules," said Zen, on the way back to class.

38

WATER FOOTBALL FOR REAL

Fin couldn't believe it was actually happening. Pop nodded when she told him she'd invited Blimp, Edge, Arden and maybe Tolemy around Saturday morning. To be fair he had two screws in his mouth. He was measuring a white cable along the floor. Guy was half way up the stairs with more cable. Fin was nervous, but happy. She wanted it to go well. Zen was going to ask Hatsumi to make macaroons. Fin decided to add croissants to the shopping list Ermine stuck up in the kitchen. Croissants were great picnic food in Fin's opinion. No-one really hated them. And when croissants got squashed in a rucksack you could always re-inflate them by pulling them about. There had to be crisps and biscuits too.

Mop was distracted. She thrust £10 into Fin's hand, shouting as she went up the stairs, she wanted change.

"Don't we all," shouted Ermine, who was trying to write an essay around Pop's hammering.

Saturday came. It rained. No-one appeared. Fin was already in the kitchen with carrier bags of food and a plan. The rain got heavier. Fin opened the kitchen window trying to look down the path but she could only see as far as the bushes. However much they cut back there were more. She'd planned to take everyone to the top of the yard. There was a grassy mound like a small hill. The graves stood in rows around the edge with the paths forming a sort of border. Gran said it was a plague pit but Pop said that was unlikely, more like a mass grave for poor people. Same difference, said Gran.

The yard was started by Lord Basel in Victorian times. But Pop couldn't explain why the council was reluctant to dig graves here. Locals assumed it was contaminated. Even the dog walkers avoided it. Ty sniffed about there, so Fin told herself it was safe. There was a stunted tree and one headstone. But it may have just been thrown there by vandals.

Fin knew better now. She'd made some rough walking calculations and suspected it was the top of the dome. She hadn't seen any chimneys but perhaps they were hidden amongst the graves lower down?

Mop came in and out collecting nails and tape. She was helping Pop rewire. Fin pretended to read last week's newspaper. She wanted to drag the bags off the table. She was starting to feel upset. The bulging bags highlighted the now doomed trip.

"I expect it's the rain," said Mop, "keeping them away, or their parents."

"Yep," said Fin, turning the pages, trying to sound not bothered. OK probably Edge and Blimp decided they couldn't play football in the rain. And it wasn't like anyone could phone, most days. Arden probably had her mother leaning over her pushing her on with more homework. Tolemy was probably stuck in front of a video game. And Zen? Zen came out whether it was raining or not. Mop came back into the kitchen and looked at the bags.

"Tell you what, if your friends don't come, because of the rain," Mop added, "why don't we try the new café on the High Street? They've homemade Battenberg in the window." Fin winced at the word friends. And the homemade Battenberg sounded made up. There was a knock at the window. Fin went over and peered through the gap. Zen was standing there, his wet hair plastered to his head. He looked past her to the bags.

"Is that all food?" he said.

"Yep," said Fin. "And Coca-Cola."

"Woo hoo," he smiled and ducked round towards the back door. He went straight to the table to pick them up.

"Sorry, we're late but they wanted to see our house and Ty. Then they wanted to see this house but I said best wait in the tunnel. So I left them shivering in the dark. Unless you want them to come round."

Fin shook her head. Ermine was shouting and Pop was banging.

"They'd been waiting at the gate in the rain."

Zen hoisted the bags off the table and waited for Fin to open the door. But a very wet Blimp barred their way. Within seconds the kitchen was full. Everyone was wet but excited. Zen put the bags down and Fin decided to light the fire. She shut the kitchen door. Maybe all her family noise would sound like a telly programme. They all crowded around. It looked like they weren't getting very far today. And the bags were pretty heavy too.

"Wow," said Blimp, "your house is cool and big."

Fin broke open some Garibaldis and when everyone was warm she gave them a tour. No one turned their nose up. Everyone said hello to everyone else except Ermine who stayed in her attic.

"This is all weird but in a good way" said Tolemy. Then he asked "Do you have a secret tunnel or something?"

Fin even showed them the basement. The rain continued. Fin wished it was sunny so they could all see the patches of colour cross the old floors.

"Well if you are all ready," said Fin.

Tolemy narrowed his eyes and said it sounded like a school trip.

"Well, you're gonna learn stuff you didn't know before," answered Zen.

Fin shared out the bags and some extra torches and they left. The rain had dwindled to a fine spray. Zen and Ty led the way quickly and quietly around the back of Blind Twin House. They passed the dead bonfire, then down the scree slope. They stopped when they were all out of the rain.

"Where are we?" Blimp shouted, his voice echoing down the dark tunnel.

"You'll see," smiled Fin, shining her torch on the curved cream ceiling "You need to be quiet," she whispered. Blimp, Edge and Tolemy crept along. Arden strolled, she seemed very comfortable in the smooth tunnel, probably because it would make a great running track. But she hadn't said anything so far apart from thank you for the Garibaldis.

As they moved further down the tunnel everyone got quieter and quieter. The plastic coke bottle got heavier and heavier. Fin wished she'd given this bag to someone else. Ty padded ahead like some sort of tracker lion. He looked huge. They kept an eye on his rump. With everyone shining torches on the curved ceiling the tunnel was very bright. Fin was bursting with things to say but she thought she might sound like Pop. She didn't want to put them off. Zen made the decision for her.

"Fin, tell them about the snakes."

"Snakes, SNAKES," said Blimp, he stopped. Tolemy, Edge and Arden stopped too.

"It's OK they aren't dangerous." Fin shone her torch across the floor just in case she hit a snake. "Ty's good at sniffing them out." They all looked at Ty. He'd carried on walking. He was disappearing into the darkness. Blimp stepped closer to Edge. Was he thinking about going back? Fin had to work fast.

"Lord Basel, well his son really, had a good idea to use *harmless* corn snakes to keep the tunnels free of rats and mice..."

"And pigeons," added Zen.

"What like pest control?" said Tolemy. He began to shine his torch towards the narrow drainage channel at the bottom of the tiled wall. He leaned forward showing off. He wasn't afraid of corn snakes. Edge and Blimp stayed put.

"Look, we've only ever seen one or two," said Zen. This wasn't quite true but it was far better than fessing up to a writhing pile. Arden stood with her long arms folded watching Tolemy and Fin.

"They're shy," said Fin. "The noise of our feet probably scares them off."

"You'll be lucky to see a snake..." said Tolemy shining the torch at Edge, then in Blimp's eyes. "But I can see a couple of chickens."

Edge made a lunge at Tolemy's torch. Tolemy jumped aside and hurtled off down the tunnel into the darkness. He disappeared into the gloom. Arden shrugged and began to follow shining her torch overhead like she did it every day.

"Chicken my arse," muttered Edge, following Arden, bouncing his ball aggressively at walls. The sound rang around their heads. Zen looked at Blimp.

"Ty frightens the snakes off with his bad breath."

Blimp nodded. It didn't feel like they were all in it together anymore. Fin wished they didn't have Tolemy along. He was such a brat.

However, soon they were all together again. Tolemy wasn't quite as cocky now. He stopped. The black arch loomed ahead. There was a whispering, swishing sound. Blimp grabbed Fin's arm.

"Is that the corn snakes?"

"Nooo," said Tolemy. His voice carried into the chamber and bounced around. He'd tried to sound big but he looked as worried as Blimp. Ty shot forward unable to wait any longer and leapt into the dark.

"He disappeared," said Edge, tensing his body, gripping his football.

"It's OK. It's water," said Fin. She stepped forward and began to move around with her torch. Zen followed. The others slowly followed him. No-one wanted to stay alone in the tunnel. They could hear Ty splashing about below them. The newbies had no idea how far below. Gradually everyone got the hang of lighting the walls round the chamber. It wasn't great. The chamber had a dim murky air. But it was enough. Fin was worried the others would be disappointed. But they weren't.

"Wow," they all kept saying, except Arden who just looked and looked.

Fin, Zen and Ty were disappointed the tide was out. The pool was more like a puddle. Fin tried to explain what it was like when it was full.

"You mean like a swimming pool?" said Tolemy.

Edge joined in. "Is it like a swimming pool then?"

"Where people swim?" said Blimp. They smiled. Fin was being teased.

But they were all too excited to take it all in.

"Sometimes it's light in the day," said Zen.

Ty was running back and forth across the pool floor sniffing, hoping for fish.

"So why isn't it light now?" said Arden.

"It must be the rain, making it too dark up there." Zen pointed up towards the domed ceiling.

Fin and Zen took out the supplies. They were all hungry. They sat down with their legs dangling down into the empty pool and began to crunch their way through the crisps. The Coca Cola was soon swigged which meant less to carry on the way back. Fin stuffed the rubbish in one carrier bag for the return trip. Zen jumped down into the empty pool and pretended to swim, flailing his arms. Edge and Blimp joined in. Soon the boys were kicking the ball across the puddles. They tried to get one another as wet as possible. There was a lot of shouting and some swearing. Fin showed Arden the beam engine and the gold tiles.

"You're quite brave aren't you," said Arden looking at Fin, then back at the tiles.

Fin was pleased that Arden had spoken to her but she wasn't sure about brave.

She shrugged. Did Arden mean the snakes?

"You found all this... most people wouldn't have got past that dark tunnel."

"I came by myself once," blurted Fin.

Arden waited for her to continue. Fin really wanted to fess up about Billy but she didn't want to scare Arden off.

"That was a bit scary."

"Why?"

Fin hadn't expected this question. She thought it was obvious: alone, dark tunnels, whispering water and Billy. She wasn't sure where to start. A wet football bounced past them. Edge and Zen tore up the steps after it.

"Hey," shouted Blimp. He was stomping up and down, splashing. Tolemy began to splash Blimp. Blimp tried to splash back. Zen and Edge tackled one another for the ball darting around Fin and Arden.

"Your pool's filling up," yelled Tolemy.

Edge kicked the ball out from under Zen. It sailed through the air and landed splat in three inches of water. Tolemy hurried up the steps. Blimp picked up and ball and followed. Tolemy slid off his wet trainers.

"Yuck."

They all sat back down on the edge of the pool. They waited. Slowly the water returned. Ty amused them by running in and out. But it was a slow process. After what seemed like forever the pool bottom was covered. Two small fish darted about. Somewhere above the winter sun shone casting ripples across the surface.

"If we sit here for a year it might fill up, then?" said Tolemy.

Zen nodded. It looked like they weren't going to play water football today.

Fin worried they may not come back. After all they hadn't played the water football. But everyone was in a good mood. All the food had been eaten, all the coke drunk. Fin's bag was light. The tunnel still glowed dimly. So they decided to try getting back without using the torches. Edge dribbled his ball. Zen, Blimp and Tolemy made up plans which hinged around someone understanding the tide timetable. Fin found herself walking with Ty and Arden.

"He's a weird dog," said Arden. "When I told dad he had stripes, he didn't believe me. Just said dogs don't have stripes and went back to reading the paper... if he's so certain that would mean I was hanging out with two kids and a tiger. Maybe he should look into that."

"My dad would give me a lecture on the history of the tiger."

Arden nodded. She knew about that sort of dad.

"Imagine coming back minus an arm because you really were playing with a tiger."

"Hmm... I'd probably get another lecture on the way to hospital," said Fin, thinking about the last time she was in hospital. She imagined her and Arden in beds opposite one another. She was very near telling Arden that Ty wasn't a dog at all. But she kept her teeth clamped together. She and Zen had an agreement. Fin got the impression he'd told Hatsumi. Every time Ty came in and out of the kitchen she'd frown and start to say something. Though, that might be because she was distracted by Immigration.

"I could run here," continued Arden, stretching her long arms above her head. "This would make a great track in winter, when it gets icy, up top." She pointed to the ceiling.

"Well, yeah," said Fin "but..."

Arden stopped bending down to adjust her trainers.

Ty sniffed along the drainage gutter, hoping for a snake.

"Look, it's OK." said Arden glancing up at Fin. "If this is your place, you and Zen and the monster dog, that's OK. It's part of your garden anyway... but if we all come back. I could run."

"It's not that," said Fin. "It's... well it might be dangerous by yourself. I saw Billy here."

Arden stood up and stared. "Billy Blatant?"

"Yep and Eddy, but he was on his lead."

"What about Billy Blatant?" said Tolemy turning around.

Edge stopped bouncing his ball. Zen and Blimp stopped walking.

"I came down here by myself." They all stared at her as if she was mad. Fin didn't look at Zen. "It was just once to see, to see if I..." Fin paused.

"To see if you could do it alone?" said Arden.

"Yeah, it was a bit scary without... Ty" Fin wanted to say without Zen too but she was too embarrassed. Her face was really hot.

"Well," said Tolemy. "Get to the Billy part."

"I heard him talking to Eddy, at first I thought it was some nut talking to himself."

"Billy's a nut," said Blimp.

"I hid in the other tunnel because it's pretty dark. Billy just poked about. Then they left."

"Probably nothing for him to steal," said Tolemy.

"Or smash," said Arden.

Fin looked at them. She expected them to be cross. Tolemy shrugged.

"Shame we didn't bump into him today," said Blimp.

"Eh?" said Edge.

"Well we could have set up some sort of ambush. Wacked him round the head with the coke bottle."

"Yeah, then he'd get real mad and set Eddy on us," said Tolemy.

"But we have Ty, super dog."

They looked at Ty. He was sitting on his haunches trying to lick his back.

"He probably won't come back," said Arden. "There's nothing down here to steal or break."

They nodded.

"We saw him off the last time," said Blimp.

"Yeah but we had your scary sisters for back up," said Tolemy.

"They're not scary, just Feminists," said Blimp.

Arden had begun to bounce on the spot. The tunnel was dark now. Tolemy turned his torch on, lighting his face from below.

"Race you back," he said. He turned and sprinted off. Arden shot past Fin. Edge followed. Blimp began to sweep the ceiling with his torch. In the pale glow Fin saw Zen staring at her. Ty stopped licking and hurried after the others.

"You're a bit of a nut yourself" said Zen.

Fin smiled. It felt like a compliment.

39

BLIMP'S PLAN

They headed towards the scree slope. The sun had gone. Fin stopped them.

"You can all come back to Blind... my house but you have to promise to keep this secret for now and not come back alone."

Blimp was already lumbering up towards the back of the house.

"Fine. Just show me the taps." Edge laughed. They were all very thirsty again.

"Fine," said Arden.

Tolemy put his head on one side.

"Why? You don't own it, Fin."

Blimp stopped and turned round. Fin didn't like Tolemy's tone or the fact that Blimp was now drawing attention to their location. Zen walked up the slope and for a moment Fin thought he was being disloyal, and going off. Zen put his arm round Blimp's shoulder and guided him back down the slope. They stood around Fin and Tolemy.

"Look, we didn't lie about the swimming pool, when the tide's high. It's a great place but what if you ran into Billy, alone..." said Fin.

Edge bounced his ball then stopped because of the noise.

"Fin's right," said Zen.

Edge nodded, bouncing on the balls of his feet.

"Fair enough" said Tolemy "But why do I have to get your permission to come along?"

"You don't," said Zen exasperated. "If you've got the confidence to hang out here alone good luck to you, but we always go with Ty, just in case."

Ty had been sitting on the slope licking his paw. He stopped at his name and waited. Tolemy frowned.

"What's Scooby-Doo gonna do?"

Arden sighed. "They found it, their rules." With that she marched up the slope followed by Edge and Blimp.

Tolemy shrugged but did a nasty laugh when he walked passed Ty.

Over the next few weeks they did form a sort of club. They never managed to get to the spa when the tide was high but there were a few games of water football when the pool was half full. The boys stripped down to their boxers and T-shirts and played rowdy. Zen would beckon to Fin but she just didn't fancy it. She wanted to swim. Tolemy, Edge and Zen were fast and strong. They got so wrapped up in the game. They'd crash into one another and struggle for the ball. Rules were made and broken. Blimp blundered about, trying to teach himself to play water football and learn to swim. Fin hated watching from the side-lines but she couldn't bear to be seen in her too small costume. Borrowing Ermine's would be worse; it fitted at the bottom but puffed out where Ermine's boobs had been. Yuck.

Fin envied the boys. It looked so easy they just got longer, bigger but not puffy with periods. It was like back at school after Zelda left. She'd wait on the side-lines. Some of the girls would smile as they came out of the door after lunch, then hurry over to their friends, stopping only to pull up their socks. It never occurred to them to include her. Fin took to reading more and more. Books she'd read before, books she'd found in the library about boarding school and pixies, anything, just to give herself something to look busy. Thank God Ermine dumped a pile of her old books in Fin's room. Fin felt less bothered now she had books she actually wanted to read.

She told Gran, when Gran caught her looking sad. Gran organised a trip to a very large library, so then Fin had even more books. That was when Gran gave her the Imperial family to keep her company.

"Leave the Cossacks to their rough games. If you can't beat them, do something different," said Gran.

Fin had even started writing her own stories but she didn't want to go back to sitting at the edge. Arden would join them when it rained so she could run in the dry. She'd persuaded her dad to buy her a head torch so she could run alone in the dark. Fin wondered if she should try to be more like Arden, minus the running and the head torch.

Sometimes Blimp sat out and Arden would stop. Fin liked that. Blimp kept checking the beam engine and the water levels.

"What is it with you and that engine?" asked Arden.

"I think with my superior weight, I could lean on it and get it going," he said, spreading his arms wide. "It might pump and power up the fountains."

He heaved himself up and tapped Fin on the shoulder.

"Follow me," he said.

Fin and Arden followed. Tolemy tried to splash them as they walked round the edge of the pool. Blimp pointed to a line of blue tiles, Fin hadn't noticed before.

"I think when the tide's there, its high."

"What, where it says: high tide?" said Arden, laughing. She pointed to the back of the engine. High tide was painted in black letters above the blue tiles.

"Wow, I never noticed that," said Blimp. "Anyway, when's the tide high, once a year?" Blimp looked at Fin.

"Actually it's twice a day but we're never here at the right time. We could work it out from the tide timetable but it's maths," said Fin.

Blimp pulled a face. "But *if* we worked it out, we could come back, get it going or at least try."

"What would you do exactly?" asked Arden, folding her arms.

Blimp went round to the barrier and put one leg over. He wobbled, then decided to climb back.

"We just need to push that down and let the tide do the rest."

"I dunno," said Fin. She wasn't sure she could read the tide timetables and it looked dangerous.

"I've got it worked out in my head," said Blimp. "I can stand on there," he pointed to the thick black arm, "push it down and hang on. Then when it comes back up, get off." He grabbed the safety rail. Fin and Arden leaned over looking down into the dirty water. They couldn't see the bottom.

"What if you fell in?" said Fin. "You can't swim and the, that," she pointed to the thick metal down rods, "that could push you under."

Blimp wasn't listening. "You teach me how to swim then. How long can it take?"

"A week?" said Arden.

Arden probably learned in a week. Fin looked at Blimp. He might take longer.

"Hey, fat Indians can swim, you know," said Blimp, slapping his belly. He laughed and walked towards them putting his arms around their shoulders. "Why should those clowns have all the fun?" They turned to see Zen, Tolemy and Edge wrestling one another under the water. Ty was jumping about trying to join in.

"He's got a point," said Arden. "Why don't you guys come to my house after school and we'll work it out."

Fin and Blimp were surprised. They had only ever seen Arden running. The idea of her at home doing normal stuff hadn't occurred to them. And they had never, ever heard of anyone actually going to her house. Blimp shuddered.

"Doesn't your dad make coffins?"

"Yes and no, he has carpenters do that in a workshop, not in our house, dumb-ass."

After school the next day they waited for Arden at the gate. Fin usually went home with Zen but he was playing football with Edge. He didn't seem to notice. They stood about while Arden filled a form in requesting time out for another competition. This time she was off to a training camp in America.

"Cool," said Blimp.

Arden shoved the forms back at the school secretary.

"Not really," said Arden. "All we see is the track, manky cabins, and ants... oh and mosquitoes."

"Bet they're better than London ants," said Blimp.

"Oh yeah," said Arden. "You've no idea."

Fin wondered if this was banter and should she join in. She tried to think of an ant related remark. She hadn't read any books on ants. She'd read a book about spiders when she was six. That was a mistake she'd had nightmares for a week. She'd had to sleep with Gran then Ermine. Fin shivered. She'd wait for the banter to move on.

They walked along in silence. Blimp cleared his throat and pointed to his flat.

"That's my bedroom..."

They waited to cross the road.

"My bed's next to the wall. All night I can hear the bill board changing."

They looked up. Blimp's room was at the end of the terrace. When Fin was small she liked it when they drove down the High Street. Pop would shout out "the picture's changed." It was usually a beach with blue sky advertising expensive holidays. In the winter it might be a new bedroom. Fin wanted to walk into the pictures and live there. The board had been upgraded. It was made up of moving wooden slats that flipped over to the reveal another advert. Usually the edges of the picture peeled away, the paper flapped in the breeze. This ruined the walk-in effect for Fin.

"It sounds like the sea... waves. That's where I got my idea." Blimp paused waiting for them to ask what it was.

"Well?" said Arden.

"I plan to make a coconut boat, or raft whatever floats best and sail round the world. So I need to learn how to swim."

They stopped to cross another road. A small dented car turned the corner. Fin thought of Blimp in striped pyjamas on a coconut raft looking out across the sea.

"Promise me, you'll come and pick me up if I'm stuck in America," said Arden.

"Yep, but I need to know your weight and volume as that'll affect my navigation and ration supply."

Usually by now Fin would be at home drinking scalding tea in front of the fire or walking Ty to the grassy knoll with Zen. Arden surprised them both by cutting down a side street, then sharp right onto a lane running along the backs of the terraced houses. It was quiet here. There were a few green wheelie bins, two parked cars and a cat but that was all. Most of the houses had low walls so Fin could see gardens, washing lines and giant flat screen televisions.

"I like to get off the road," said Arden. "But you can reach the house by Basel Drive, if your parents are collecting you by car."

Blimp shrugged. "I thought we'd walk back together."

Fin nodded, she didn't want Pop turning up in his dirty van. The lane sloped down towards some trees. They followed Arden past the last terraced house. Fin was surprised, from the main road she thought this was all houses but it wasn't. They were walking down a hill with allotments spread out on either side. There were rows of bamboo for summer beans. Wooden huts were dotted about next to plastic water butts. An old man was bending down. He straightened up when he saw them pass but didn't smile. He watched them go.

"We're not stealing vegetables," Fin wanted to shout but she just put her head down and kept going. There trees thinned out and then grew thicker again. The path got very steep. The allotments finished at a sagging metal fence.

"Not far now. I usually run up this lane in the morning," said Arden.

There were brambles then another fence, this one made of sturdy wood. A farm gate barred the road. Arden vaulted over, leaving Blimp and Fin to wobble over at the same time. They were on gravel now. The grass was mown under the trees and there were no brambles. Fin could see a brown track further down, where the ground levelled out.

Arden stopped and pointed. "That's my track, that's the workshop, that's our house."

"Wow," said Blimp wiping sweat from his face with his arm.

Fin took off her coat and tied the sleeves round her waist. She couldn't believe what she saw. Arden had her own running track. It circled under the trees and past the workshop, a big corrugated iron shed. Someone was sawing inside.

A wide wooden sign announced *Waker and Son's Funeral Carpenters*. Wooden planks were stacked neatly around the doors and side walls. There was a small mountain of sawdust piled up at the back. But it was the house that really struck both Fin and Blimp. It was like something from a Sunday Newspaper. It was all wood and plate glass windows. It looked like a series of wooden boxes piled on top of one another but each one turned to face a different direction.

"Is that really your house?" said Blimp, laughing.

"Yeah, my daddy love wood," said Arden, enjoying Blimp's enthusiasm.

"Come on, we make coffins but the bodies go in them later, not here," said Arden.

"What a neighbourhood," said Blimp, hurrying to catch up. Fin couldn't help glancing towards the open shed. She could see two men talking, surrounded by more piles of wood. She was glad she couldn't see any coffins. The house looked very expensive. Arden took out a key and let them in. Inside it was more wood. Fin and Blimp took their shoes off without being asked. The dark polished floor looked like it had never been walked on. The walls were wood too but sort of rough looking like they weren't finished. There were paintings, real paintings of fields and seas and some just colours. All the furniture was wood or leather. Blimp plonked himself down in a big arm chair and began to sniff the arms. The house smelt of sandal wood and polish and pizza dough. A door opened and an elderly black man approached. Fin thought he looked old because he had white hair and a beard. He was wearing an apron.

He smiled. Arden turned to Fin. Blimp jumped out of the chair.

"This is my dad." The man nodded and smiled again.

"This is Fin. She lives at Blind Twin House. This is Blimp. He wants to build a coconut raft."

"Well that's very, very interesting. You can tell me all about it over pizza." He gestured to the door. Arden led them into the kitchen. The dough smell mingled with toasting cheese. Fin could taste the air.

The pizza was thin and crispy. It was expensive. Everything they'd seen in Arden's house was expensive. The plates, the glasses, even the taps were well-made and smooth. For a while they ate in silence. They were all very hungry. Fin tore the pizza with her hands. Blimp looked around for a knife and fork. The cheese was very hot. Fin had to flick it back on the dough to avoid being burnt. A phone rang in another room. Arden's dad disappeared to answer it.

"Mum," said Arden, glowering.

"Is your mum as old as your dad," asked Blimp, picking up a giant slice of pizza and folding it in half, like a sandwich. Fin used the ends of her fingers. She remembered she hadn't washed her hands after school. Arden laughed.

"No-one's as old as my dad. Mum's thirty-eight but she doesn't want people to know she's nearly forty."

"Does she build coffins too?" said Blimp. Arden raised her eyebrows at Fin.

"No, she's a lawyer for the EU. She spends most of the week in Brussels. She gets back Friday night just to supervise my homework schedule, *and* my training *and* my clarinet."

"She's a lion mum," said Blimp.

Arden frowned.

"I think, he means tiger mom," said Fin. "There was one on television. She made her daughters do school work all the time."

"My sisters do school work all the time, but they like it. They're good at it," added Blimp.

"Probably because they do it *all the time*?" said Arden.

She pushed a bowl of small purple grapes towards them. Fin took a few. They were very sweet and made her feel thirsty. Blimp shook his head. Arden started to say something but her dad came back.

"Your mother says hello. She won't be back this weekend. She has another case."

Arden looked at her father. They didn't comment on the news, but Fin felt the atmosphere lighten.

"You'll still be training," said Arden's dad, crinkling his eyes. "Now," he said. "I know you don't want old folks hanging around but let me make you one of my specials. You can tell me about your plans." He pulled the fruit bowl towards him, looked at it, and selected some grapes. Arden got up and began opening cupboards. She got out four blue glasses, shaped like vases. Her dad opened the giant stainless steel fridge. Arden went through a side door and came back with five brown cartons of ice-cream. She carried them between her hands and her chin. She began to line everything up.

"Can I use the loo?" blurted Fin.

"Certainly," said Arden's dad.

Arden dropped the cartons on the table, one rolled towards Blimp. He grabbed it.

"Wow, Cherry Garcia, cool."

"That's nearly empty, but you can finish it off if you want," said Arden's dad.

"The loo's just there," Arden pointed to the hall.

Fin went into the hall and stood looking at the front door.

"No here," said Arden coming up behind her and pulling a handle in the wood wall.

Fin slipped through the gap and for a second stood in darkness. Then a light and a fan whirred on. The room was very small like a box made of polished wood. The loo was white with a dark wooden seat, opposite a big mirror and an old fashioned sink with gold taps. It was like a posh cabin on the Titanic. Fin felt a lot better with clean hands. They now smelled of almonds not school.

"Now," said Arden's dad is there anything you don't like?"

Blimp and Fin surveyed the ingredients. Fin wasn't sure.

"As long as there's no fish flavour, I'll be fine," she said.

"No, no fish ice-cream," said Arden's dad. "And if there was I'd throw it away. However, you may want to try the noodle ice-cream. It takes some getting used to."

He pushed over a carton. Arden passed them spoons. Blimp and Fin scraped out the hard, caramel-coloured noodle ice-cream. Arden and her dad went to work. They crushed ginger nuts, and dropped chocolate coated raisins, into the bottom of the glasses. Chocolate fudge ice-cream, chocolate sauce, banana ice-cream, more chocolate sauce, a small scoop of coffee ice-cream, not too much, said Arden's dad, were layered on top. Then white chocolate sauce with some chocolate coated peanuts, brown bread ice-cream and finally a dollop of buttery cream.

They were out of cherries, so Arden put Maltesers on top.

"Good, I'd forgotten about those," said Arden's dad.

There was no room for wafers. Arden just put those on the table for them to munch or use as an ice-cream scoop.

Fin and Blimp forgot the noodle ice-cream because they couldn't stop watching. When they did try the noodle it tasted of caramel and salt and something yellow that Fin couldn't put her finger on.

"If it's OK with you, I'd like to move in," said Blimp.

"We'd love to have you," said Arden's dad. "Some people are put off by our business."

"Eh?" said Blimp.

"The coffins," said Arden.

"No. I could use the wood. Well some of the wood for my raft."

"Tell you what when you've finished. I'll show you around, leave the ladies to clear up." Arden's dad smiled and raised his hands. "Just kidding, it all goes in the dishwasher."

The cream began to run down the side of the glasses. Arden collected some spoons with very long handles. She gave them three each.

"Eh? Have you got other visitors?" asked Blimp.

"No I just like to use different spoons for different bits so it doesn't get too muddled up."

Fin thought if she had a phone she would take loads of pictures right now.

Blimp nodded, as if he did this all the time. Arden's dad swept up the cartons and took them back to the freezer. Fin started slowly trying to catch the cream before it ran all the way down the glass. Blimp dug straight into the middle trying to excavate all the flavours at once. Arden worked her way round the edge.

"I think I liked the noodle ice-cream," said Fin.

"Where d'you get it?" asked Blimp.

"Dunno, dad looks them up on-line, sort of his hobby."

"Isn't he having ice-cream?" said Fin.

"No too much cholesterol or something. He has a spoonful when a new flavour arrives."

"You guys should open an ice-cream place," said Blimp, through a mouthful of sauce and peanuts.

Arden nodded.

"No seriously, you should."

Fin nodded too. The ice-cream was too good to talk through. It was thick, heavy like fudge. It didn't melt fast like cheap ice-cream. They were aiming for the bottom but about half-way down they were all flagging.

"You can finish it later if you want," said Arden.

"I'll show you the workshop and you can work on your appetite," said Arden's dad, returning without the apron. Blimp left the table reluctantly expecting the ice-cream to vanish like a dream.

Fin wasn't sure what would happen when Blimp left but Arden became quite chatty. She talked about her "tiger mom", the endless homework and running. Fin surprised herself by telling Arden about Gran.

Arden said "I'd like to meet her; she sounds a bit like my dad and probably nearly the same age."

"Maybe," said Fin. "Gran would say this ice-cream is good enough for the Tsar."

"No," said Arden getting up fast. She shot off. Fin worried she'd said something wrong. Arden returned with a Tupperware box. She slowly peeled off the lid. Fin peered inside. It was nearly empty but in the corner was a chunk of pale ice-cream with gold flecks. Fin imagined Blimp shouting: no way. Arden passed her a tea spoon.

"Go on, it's edible... it's one of dad's experiments." Fin dug her spoon in.

"This really *is* good enough for the Tsar, guess the flavour," said Arden, moving the ice-cream across her tongue.

Fin felt so full her stomach hurt, but she couldn't stop herself taking another spoonful. She felt like she was going to explode.

"It tastes of..." Fin chewed the thick ice-cream, trying not to let it stick to her teeth, that hurt. It tasted of a picture Fin had once seen of a house on stilts surrounded by big green leaves and pink flowers. The gold melted in a crinkly way on Fin's tongue.

"It's pistachio with rose jam," said Arden. "Finish it, you might get lucky and find a petal."

"Can we save some for Blimp? He'll never believe us."

"Or let us forget it, if he doesn't get some... Let's go in the other room," said Arden. She resealed the Tupperware and thrust it back into the freezer. She looked a bit sick herself. They left a sticky mess. Fin decided she would never, ever eat ice-cream again. They plumped down on the cool leather sofa overlooking the trees and the grassy hill.

Arden and her dad insisted on walking them up the hill and along the lane. It was dark and cold. Fin remembered the pistachio ice-cream, too late for Blimp to try. They waved good bye on the road. As Arden disappeared down the lane, Blimp let out a huge fart. He sighed.

"My sincere apologies, but I fear something has disagreed with me." He laughed. Fin laughed. "Tis best I voyage alone."

40

SNOW

Fin saw Zen as she rounded the gate. Pop had pushed it almost shut. Fin felt pleased to be back, it was like living in a secret garden. Mourners and visitors could wander about with their dogs and plastic flowers during the day, but come dusk the gates were chained shut and they had the place to themselves. Fin didn't want Mop and Hatsumi to start a bespoke *B and B*. It was her, Zen's and Ty's territory now. Fin didn't want to make polite and stupid conversation at breakfast about doilies or whatever. What if the visitors didn't like Ty coming into the kitchen? What if they asked too many questions about Ty? What if some loud mouth came from Australia and recognised him for what he really was? Fin started to get wound up.

She walked faster to catch Zen. He was out of sight now under the trees in the long avenue. Fin got angrier thinking about the rude couple in her head, saying Fat Bastard should be put outside in the rain. She didn't even like Fat Bastard. Fin heard Gran's voice.

"Calm down Fin, it's all in your head."

"As is that comment," said Fin, out loud.

Ty ambled out of the bushes. Fin rubbed his head. Together they walked up to Zen. He was fiddling with his torch.

"Hi," said Fin.

"Hi," Zen didn't sound pleased or annoyed.

Fin wanted to tell him all about the ice-cream but she still felt a bit sick. And she didn't want to do a Zelda and show off. She imagined Zen with his head pressed against the window waiting for her. Zen continued to fiddle, then swore and rammed the torch in his pocket.

"Up to the wall and back?" he said.

For a moment Fin thought he was asking Ty. Fin looked at Ty then back at Zen.

"Oh, yeah," said Fin.

They walked fast. It was very cold. Fin's hands were raw. She didn't have her gloves and the fancy soap at Arden's house had dried her skin. Fin just wanted to go home, sit on the loo and think about her day. Then she wanted to get into bed with lots of Nivea on her lips which were chapping. Zen's lips were always chapped. Fin wondered what they felt like. She rubbed hers. They were sore and crinkly.

She slept badly. She had to get up twice to go to the loo. It was very quiet outside, too quiet. This meant leaving her warm room and padding over the cold floor to the dark bathroom. Mop got annoyed if Fin put the big lights on when they were trying to sleep. Fin took her torch but that made scary shapes across the banisters. A big shadow would move towards Ermine's narrow staircase. Fin jumped every time. She rushed back to bed leaving the loud flush till morning. A fox cried across the yard. Another answered further away. That was the only sound apart from Gran's old clock ticking on the mantelpiece. Fin looked at her door. It was shut tight but it was so warped it looked like it was cracked open. Fin left her lamp on and decided to think about Arden's house and the walk home. But the walk changed. She was in the dark lane, feeling like something was behind her. Something that shouldn't be there.

Her eyes burned so she shut them and eventually fell asleep. She was woken by Mop.

"Wake up and look outside," said Mop, hurrying over to the window. She shoved it open as far as it would go.

"Snow," she said.

241

Fin jumped out of bed. Cold air pushed through the open window. The sill was covered in about four inches of snow.

"No school today," said Mop, twisting out of Fin's way.

Fin pushed her fingers into the snow. It made a soft crunchy sound like a wafer biscuit. She leaned out. Black bare branches were coated in a layer of snow like new icing. A thick blanket covered the path and garden. Everything was smooth and clean. The air tasted of wet stone. Pop crunched out of the back door and round the side. Fin wanted to be the first one out. The yard was white. She wanted to be the first one to make foot prints, to sink into the magical crunchiness.

Pop looked up.

"No funerals today," he said. "May not even open the main gate."

He stood looking at the graves or rather where the graves had been. Most of them had disappeared. They were now uneven bumps under the snow. A few sparrows hopped about.

"It's so quiet," said Fin.

"I know. It's bloody brilliant. No buses. And no bloody tube, I shouldn't wonder."

Pop leaned through the kitchen window. Mop passed him a mug of steaming tea. Fin looked at the pale yellowy-grey sky. It was going to snow again. She just knew. Maybe it was the Russian in her. She left the window wide open, jumping around to get into her jeans. Then she was downstairs. It was only 7 o'clock but she just had to get out.

"I'll be out later. Tell Pop to open the gates, so the others can get in."

Fin wasn't sure who these others were. She was already crunching after Pop. She didn't want others to come and spoil the snow with dirty footprints and dog shit. But then she thought of Arden and Blimp and Edge. But they'd probably stay inside and watch the snow on television that was what her class usually did. The snow was deep. It almost came over the top of her wellies. She had to find the path. There were snow drifts on either side. The snow could pour into her boots then she would have wet feet and that was a recipe for misery.

Crunch, crunch, crunch. There was no other sound. No cars, no buses, no planes, no sirens. Once she heard someone talking into a phone on the other side of the wall. Then crunching footsteps, then nothing. Pop had gone back inside for a leisurely breakfast.

Fin stopped and looked around. Fir and cypress trees had great dollops of snow all over the tops like ice-cream. The mausoleums had at least a foot of snow on top. They looked like small houses. Fin's face was stiff with the cold and her lips felt sore. But she didn't care. She could see Twin House. Hatsumi had all the lights on. There were new paper snowflakes in the sitting room window. They looked cool, next to the real thing. Fin walked across the yard road, then back again just to enjoy her boot prints. She stopped. She wanted to leave room for Zen and Ty. What would Ty think? Fin banged on the front door. From here she could stare through the gates at the snow covered main road. Two commuters slipped past their breath fogging the air in front of their faces. Hatsumi answered the door with a giant smile. Zen was jumping into his wellies behind her.

"Come back for cookies," said Hatsumi, pulling on another sweatshirt. Ty was pacing the hall. When Zen jumped out into a snow drift, on the porch, he bounded after him. Ty landed in a cold white world. He looked surprised. He jumped about yipping. He ran back towards Hatsumi, then round the road as if he wanted to leave tracks too.

"Since when does Ty do that?" asked Fin.

"What?"

"That, the yipping."

Zen shrugged. "Since it snowed, I guess. Ty, TY." Zen looked at Fin "Quagga?"

"Quagga."

They weren't disappointed. The stone quagga looked beautiful. Snow lined its back like a blanket. Zen ran up to it then stopped. Neither of them wanted to disturb it. It had icicles hanging from its nose and under its fat belly.

Ty pranced about in the snow. It was deeper here. It had melted a little in the night then re-frozen. They crunched on. There was a cracking sound. The snow was too heavy for an old fir tree. They watched as one of the branches slowly leaned down onto the snow before it snapped.

"Better watch out," said Zen, pulling up his collar. They tramped on through the middle of the snowy knoll. This was a mistake. The snow was really deep. They were wading through it. Ty watched them.

He ran round the edge instead. The snow soon came over the tops of their boots. Fin's got stuck and her foot came out. She had to grab a head stone to keep her balance.

"Thanks, Maud," she said.

Zen fell over and disappeared in a giant drift. He pulled himself up by another stone.

"Thanks, Maud," he said, red in the face.

"They can't all be Maud," laughed Fin.

"Oh you'd be surprised," said Zen. "There's Maud Smith, Maud Jones, she's Welsh and Maud Basel and Maud Ahmed."

"And old Maud and Maud junior..." added Fin.

They were heading up the hill. The snow was so deep it wasn't even slippery. When they got to the top it started to snow again. Big, flat flakes. Fin put out her tongue and tried to catch one. Zen was better at this. The snow got heavier but the flakes were smaller. Flakes whirled about making their eyes sting. The air was thick and foggy with them. They tried to stare out over Tooting but it was disappearing in a blizzard. Ty clapped his jaws together. Neither Fin or Zen were ready to go back. Fin knew this could all be gone by tea time. She kept repeating: please last, please last. There was so much of it. They could just see Pop and Hatsumi talking by the gate. Mop struggled towards them. They all went into Twin House. A man and his dog peered through the gates and pointed his phone at the yard.

Fin felt different. She felt good about her new home. The snow lasted for a week. There was no school. The school boiler broke so even after two days when the buses drove down the gritted main road there was no school. Pop took the chain off the gate and left it ajar but it wasn't until day three it occurred to any of the city kids the yard would be a great place to visit. Arden arrived first with a freezer bag filled with noodle ice-cream that they decided to eat outside. Fin and Zen had tried squirting chocolate sauce onto snow mounds then licking it up, but real ice-cream was far better. The snow tasted stony. Blimp and Edge arrived after lunch led by Tolemy. They finished off the ice-cream inside by the fire then went on a tour. Ermine and Guy were out taking photographs in black and white, as usual.

There was a big snowball fight as the snowflakes got bigger and thicker. Ermine, Guy, Mop, Pop and Hatsumi joined in. When some of the snowballs hit ears and eyes they all began to wind it down.

"It's getting dark," said Pop "You'd better escort your friends to the gate. It's tea time."

Fin was sad. She could tell everyone was disappointed. Tolemy looked surly. He had to leave the yard. Fin felt pleased she lived somewhere cool. She could carry on exploring the snow. All the other kids had was the main road, and maybe a small back yard. Apart from Arden, but she was alone, with a pile of homework.

Five days later, Fin was finishing off her diary. She was rushing to write everything down.

"Look how much has changed," said Gran, standing in Fin's room. Gran had escaped the Sheltered Accommodation under cover of the snow. Mad Maggie had been too busy hustling the council to clear the paths to keep an eye on Gran's movements. Fin agreed. Things had changed and in ways Fin couldn't have predicted. She put her diary away. She remembered to watch her head. She was taller now. She kept bumping her head on the angle-poise lamp, if she didn't shove it out of the way first. Her hair fell in her eyes. She pulled a band from the table, stuck it in her mouth and pulled her hair back. It wasn't a pony tail yet but she couldn't stand not being able to see. She watched the sun on the floor boards, lozenges of colour wobbled through the radiator heat. Pop finally got the heating working now the snow was melting. Usually she put her feet or hands in the colour to watch the changes but today the boys were waiting.

Gran was already half way down the stairs. Pop had used some of the snow holiday to set up the samovar. This meant no more boiling the kettle. It was also a ruse to tempt Gran out and about. Since her fall she'd stayed inside too much, said Mop. However, Gran had outdone their expectations by getting out and about in the snow and ice. This worried Mop even more.

Outside Zen whooped. Arden flashed past, she was training again. They saw her most evenings because after track she'd do a circuit of the yard. Then they'd all explore. The snow was mostly over. It had been shovelled into dirty piles along the High Street. In the yard it melted slower. But it was thinning. Foot prints started the great dissolve.

However, there were still plenty of icicles. The angels had fringes dripping from their wings. Crosses that lent to one side appeared to be pulled down by icicles. The taps were the best. It looked like water had exploded then frozen in bulbous blobs that mushroomed around the old pipes. Tolemy had tried to prize them off. He planned to freeze some ice for the summer. But they were too hard, too slippery. Pop yelled at them to leave the taps alone. They hadn't been back to the spa. It lay forgotten, quiet, waiting.

"Do you think the pools are frozen over?" asked Zen, after scooping up some snow and trying to push it down Fin's back. She was keeping her distance, just in case he tried again. Why did boys do things like that? Arden said it was good preparation for ruling the world, *badly*.

"Dunno, we could look?"

Zen looked surprised. "Yeah" but then they didn't go. There were large black-ice slicks to skate across. Fin slipped and banged her elbow, time to go home.

Then the snow was gone. It was grey. They went back to school. The High Street went back to boring normal. Fin decided to get the Basel project back out. Maybe Blimp was right about the beam engine and the fountains. Fin made notes. She'd need a team to pull it off. She'd ask Mop if she could have everyone over for tea. As long as Mop bought pizza, they'd survive. Fin made a list, this was the sort of thing her and Zelda imagined and talked about: big schemes. But Fin never ever thought she'd get to have a go at one.

Eventually over slightly burnt pizza, Blimp said: they could invite more children and charge them to swim. Fin thought this was a bad idea. Too many kids would mean Pop might notice. But Tolemy was keen on Blimp's idea, possibly just to disagree with Fin.

"Don't worry," Blimp said. He'd made an inventory of the kids they could trust not to blab or worse bring younger brothers and sisters. "By then the trees will hide our comings and goings anyway, your family won't suspect a thing."

Fin was uneasy. Ermine already gave her odd looks when Fin and Zen had been at the spa. They'd been swimming one night. Fin wore a T-shirt over her new black costume. Ermine caught her coming in with wet hair.

"It's possible," said Zen, chewing a pizza crust.

"Fin," said Blimp "Admit it's possible."

Fin got up to pour out more coke. She needed thinking time. The coke fizzed up over the edge of the glasses. Zen grabbed his and began to slurp up the bubbles. This was the best part. The others did the same.

Fin nodded, sucking up her own bubbles. It was possible but unlikely. Blimp had made an unofficial start, he admitted. He'd been getting younger kids to unclog the fountain heads whenever they saw them. He told them one of them was full of gold coins. It was just a question of unblocking the right one. Two of his aunties had even joined in the search.

"They'll spread the word," said Blimp.

On school trips to the town hall, and the local park, little kids had come back with hands coated in grease. The teachers couldn't understand the fascination with the dull upside down metal basins.

In the meantime Fin, Zen and Arden got to grips with the tide times. Fin didn't think they'd ever bring it off. But somehow they kept going anyway. The beam engine was stiff, not stuck, but it would need more than a couple of kids standing on the arm to get it moving. And then what would happen if it moved? Whoever was on there would have to ride the arm down under the dirty water. Then try to jump off when it came up again. If it came up. It was just too dangerous. Blimp was the heaviest but he couldn't even swim.

Fin carried on reading the Basel books now rather than just looking at the pictures. She combed the internet when they had a connection. It was possible the pipes were blocked or broken. After Ty's walk she sat with Zen looking out over Tooting. It was twilight. The colour had faded from the yard. Lights were beginning to come on along the main road. Some birds flew home overhead. The long grass felt damp beneath her jeans. Ty jumped about snapping at moths. Edge, Blimp, Arden and Tolemy had to leave before Pop locked the gate.

Sometimes they'd wait until he began to swing it across, then race down the hill, trying to get there before he picked up the chain. They'd turn and wave from outside the gate. Fin and Zen would flash their torches at them to wave goodbye before heading off themselves feeling lucky they lived there.

41

FIRE

As the summer came the little band drifted apart, despite all their plans. Arden had track. Edge went to Cromer most weekends to stay in a caravan when he didn't have football. Tolemy went to a crammer. Blimp helped in his dad's shop though he would appear now and again with packets of broken biscuits. Fin and Zen spent their evenings following Ty through the long grass. The council didn't cut it in the summer to save money. The sun got hotter. The grass got longer. It began to turn yellow. After a few weeks most of the gravestones disappeared beneath the long swaying grass. One evening after the hot steep climb Fin turned to look back across the yard.

"It looks like the Russian Steppe," she said.

Sometimes on a very hot Saturday afternoon Zen and Fin would take Ty to the pools but mostly the tide was too low to even splash.

"Good job we didn't invite half the neighbourhood," said Zen.

"Yep," said Fin.

Ermine had asked if they were going away, not because she wanted to go anywhere with her family, but because she wanted the house to herself for parties.

"No money," said Pop. "Besides who wants to go away when you have all this?"

Ermine frowned and spent more time at Abimbola's. She just shouted she was going out. Gradually the tide turned and the spa began to fill in late afternoons. Fin caught sight of Edge and Blimp on the High Road and Tolemy in the furniture shop window. But it was like they'd forgotten they were friends. Fin half-heartedly suggested to Zen they invite everyone round for tea or something but Zen was distracted. There'd been some official looking envelopes for Hatsumi. He was worried it might be Immigration again. Fin felt a bit silly really. Probably the new school year would mean every one teaming up with new friends or old friends, leaving her and Zen alone or maybe just her if Hatsumi got deported.

But then there was the fire and everything changed forever.

Fin saw the fire first. She was going to bed. She heard some fireworks in the distance. She opened her window to look out through the trees. The colour had gone. The birds called to one another above her head. A crow swooped low across the yard. The cars on the main road were a distant tide. Fin thought about the Thames. If she'd understood the tide times there was a high tide coming. If it was really hot tomorrow, it would be cool to swim underground. She planned to go with Zen and Ty. She missed the others. Their shouting in the echoing tunnels, the ball games, and the surprise snacks from Blimp's shop.

There was a glow near Twin House. Fin leaned out smelling the warm air, trying to catch the sun's gold through the trees. The sun was usually behind Blind Twin House at this time of day. Her room lay in shadow. She could smell smoke. Fin breathed it in. She liked the smell. Then she saw something move. She couldn't see what through the thick leaves. There was a crackling sound. Fin watched the long grass by the road catch fire.

A line of flames ran along the edges of the paths fanned by the breeze. Smoke billowed from the direction of Twin House. Her eyes began to sting. An acrid smell began to fill her room.

Fin slammed her window shut and ran down stairs. She barged into Ermine who was coming the other way with a pile of photography books crowned by a mug of tea. The mug went flying spraying tea up the wall. Ermine swore and flung the books down trying to grab Fin. Fin dodged and headed for the kitchen door.

"Shut the windows, there's a fire outside."

"What?" said Ermine leaving the tea and the books to stomp after her into the kitchen. The downstairs windows were shut. The kitchen door was locked. Mop and Pop had finally decided to treat themselves to a curry night out.

"What do you mean, freak?" said Ermine.

Fin pushed open the kitchen window. She was actually glad when smoke billowed in.

"Shut it," Ermine shouted.

Fin banged it shut. Ermine lent over and opened it again to see what was going on. Fin wished she hadn't done that. The wind was stronger now, blowing towards the house. They could hear it across the chimney. They could also hear a roaring sound. The fire was getting stronger. It had eaten through the long grass and was now running up the dry ivy wrapped like accelerant around the trees.

"Shit," said Ermine.

"Phone the fire brigade," said Fin. "I'll check the windows."

Fin ran up the stairs. Ermine overtook her and clattered up her rickety staircase. Her phone was in the attic. They both noticed they could see the air. A pale smoke was seeping into the house. Fin slammed the bathroom window. She could hear crackling and snapping. Everything felt very warm. Fin held her breath. She could hear Ermine clomping about above her head. Fin wasn't sure what to do. They couldn't leave, or could they? Should she fill the bath with water? What if they got their clothes wet? But that wouldn't protect them against smoke. Ermine thundered down the attic stairs.

"Typical, it doesn't bloody work," she said, waving her phone.

Fin stared at Ermine. Ermine stared back.

"Right," said Ermine. "We've shut all the windows, someone will notice from the main road and call the fire brigade. We can sit tight... worst case scenario..."

They made their way slowly down the stairs. Worst case scenario meant them both burnt to a crisp, to be found like twiglets the next day.

"Yeah, worst case scenario," said Ermine, "we go to my room, push my quilt under the door."

There was a loud splitting crack. The dead tree behind the house was going to fall. They both waited looking up at the ceiling expecting the roof to fall in and branches burst through. The tree didn't fall but the roaring was loud and near. It was like standing in a chimney.

"Quickly, what do we need?" said Ermine.

Fin shot off to the kitchen to grab a jug of water and the loaf of bread. They rushed back up to Ermine's room. The smoke was thicker in the house. Ermine pushed her quilt under the door. They stood back and looked at their supplies. Then they went to the windows. It was difficult to see. It was almost dark and smokey fog hung heavy in the trees. Between the leaves they could see an orange glow.

"If the house catches fire we're trapped," said Fin. "Your stairs will burn."

Ermine stared at Fin.

"Well, I'm waiting, genius."

"I know," said Fin. "The fire's there," she pointed in the direction of Twin House. "We could try walking in the other direction, away from the house. We can shout or climb over the wall... there's a few graves we can stand on."

Ermine chewed her lip. Fin coughed.

"To hell with this, let's go."

They left the bread and water on the floor. They made their way back down the stairs. They were fast but quiet. It was like they didn't want the fire to know they were leaving.

It was windy outside. The sign squealed. Fin opened the front door. Smoke swirled across the path but there was no fire here, thanks to Mop's bramble clearing. They stepped out and shut the door behind them. No return, they both thought, but didn't say so.

Fin remembered Fat Bastard. She worried should they go back. But the door was shut and the smoke was getting thicker. Ermine stepped into the smoke. Fin followed.

They hoisted themselves over the low wall. Then they turned down a path they never used and fought their way along bumpy bricks towards the boundary wall. It didn't take long but they had to climb over a tree trunk, and past a row of graves with enamelled photos.

Fin felt they were being watched and judged. Was the fire their fault? Had Ermine thrown a fag out of the window? When they got to the boundary wall Fin realised it was higher than she remembered. The crumbling headstones were about two foot from the wall. The gap was too big. How would they manage? Fin tapped Ermine's shoulder and pointed in the direction of the gate. It was cold and damp here. They were surrounded by old trees, even older graves and ivy. There was smoke but no fire. They'd left that behind. They began to walk slowly towards the gate. They were coughing hard now. Fin was finding it difficult to breath. It was like her lungs were shrinking. It was taking too long. There were brambles and stinging nettles. Sometimes there was a path. Sometimes they had to step over graves or climb onto a plinth and down the other side. Ahead they could hear crackling. The smoke was black now. Fin wanted to hear someone, anyone shouting. Maybe no-one else had noticed.

When they finally reached the gate Ermine tried to use her phone. Pop had chained the gate. But they'd skirted the fire for now. They stood as close to the gate as they could. They tried to breathe the cooler air blowing down the main road. Ermine was finally through to 999. An old man walked past and stopped seeing Fin. He frowned.

"You shouldn't be in there. It's shut," he barked.

"No shit Sherlock," said Ermine, breaking off her phone conversation.

"We need..." began Fin, but the old man matched off.

Fin looked round. Through the smoke she could see fire whipping up towards the grassy knoll and the back of the hospital. Twin House stood in swirling smoke. Did Zen know there was a fire? She'd only spotted it by accident.

She left Ermine and ran towards his door. Hatsumi surprised her by running round from the back of the house and shouting at Fin. She looked very worried.

"Ty's gone missing, Zen's gone looking but..." blurted Hatsumi. She stopped to stare at Fin and then Ermine. Fin hadn't noticed the smoke had blackened their faces and hair. Their clothes were greasy and sooty. Hatsumi grabbed Fin's shoulder. Thicker yellowy smoke seeped towards them. Ermine shouted something and waved her phone. She shouted again and started to run towards them. This panicked Hatsumi who looked like she might run off.

"Hatsumi, can you open the gate?" said Ermine. "The fire brigade's on its way but you need to let them in."

Hatsumi looked dazed. Hatsumi felt in her pocket and brought out her keys. She had to walk to the gate. The keys were attached to her dungarees.

"I don't know where Zen is. He missing, looking for Ty."

"Where did he go? Which way?" asked Fin.

Hatsumi looked towards the smoke. The wind changed direction. For a moment it was cool and pleasant on Fin's face. Then the flames turned and rolled towards them.

"There," said Hatsumi, wild eyed, pointing towards the wall of smoke.

Ermine was trying to push the gate open. But with her phone trapped between her ear and shoulder she was struggling.

"Lift," shouted Fin. "We need to lift not push."

Fin helped Ermine and Hatsumi heave the heavy gate. Just when it got too heavy it began to budge. Cars slowed down as the smoke began to drift across the road. Tolemy popped up the other side of the gate.

"Fin, Fin," he gabbled.

Fin ignored him. She had enough on her plate. Tolemy grabbed the gate and pushed it back with Fin as far as it would go. Ermine backed off, dropping her phone. Fin picked it up. Ermine marched out towards the main road and stood on the curb. Fin turned to fetch Hatsumi. A small crowd had formed on the other side of the road pointing at the smoke.

Tolemy ran after her. "Fin, hold up," he puffed.

Hatsumi had disappeared. Fin hoped she had gone back inside. Fin went around the back of Twin House. Hatsumi was pacing the kitchen, talking at her phone.

"Fin, Zen and Ty are in trouble," shouted Tolemy.

"I know," said Fin, wrenching the kitchen door handle.

"No, you don't get it. It's not the fire, its Billy."

"Billy Blatant?"

"Yeah, I've been trying to tell you. I think Billy did this, started the fire, he's kidnapped Ty, down the tunnels."

Fin coughed. The yard was being smothered in smoke. She almost expected to see Billy dragging Ty towards them. Instead, the grey wall parted disgorging Zen. His face was sooty and weirdly blank. At first he didn't seem to see them. Tolemy yelled and waved.

"Over here, mate."

Zen limped. Hatsumi banged on the kitchen window.

"I think I know where Ty is but we'll have to work fast. Billy's taken him down the tunnels to Battersea," yelled Tolemy.

"What?" said Fin.

They could hear sirens now. Ermine was yelling Fin's name over and over again. Zen turned and ran off into the smoke. Hatsumi screamed. Fin pushed open the kitchen door.

"It's OK. Ty's down the tunnel..."

Hatsumi clearly didn't understand any of this. Tolemy stepped behind Fin. She felt better now the fire brigade were on their way.

"We know where Ty is. It's a tunnel. Zen's gone to get him, we'll help." Fin said this because Hatsumi looked like she was going cry. Fin had no idea how to fix this.

"And there's no fire there," shouted Tolemy, turning to run after Zen.

"I need a torch," said Fin. She took a liberty and ran into Hatsumi's kitchen and grabbed a torch from the drawer. When she got back outside Tolemy was gone. Fin would have to get there by herself. Ermine was still shouting, walking towards Twin House. Hatsumi followed Fin asking questions. The fire truck was stuck behind a van, the sirens blared. Fin caught sight of Blimp puffing towards them. She had an idea. She had seconds to bring Blimp up to speed before the fire brigade pulled them all out. Within a minute Fin was running back through the undergrowth along the boundary wall.

42

KIDNAPPED

Fin had seconds to get her idea together though it had been germinating for weeks. Billy on the other hand, had been planning for months.

Billy had been well pleased with his plan. He'd leaned back in his dad's easy chair, flicking the foot rest up to celebrate. Eddy put his head on his paws and glared around the room.

"Well, we're ready," Billy muttered, savouring the moment. Eddy watched Billy's face. Billy smirked. Eddy sulked. He didn't know what Billy was up to. Billy went over the plan one more time. He was going to enter the yard via the hospital. Crime and Wave would join him later with a Sainsbury's shopping trolley nicked to order. They might have to lift it over some of the tatty paths, the terrain was uneven. However, Billy calculated from the rendezvous point it was all smooth sailing. Billy liked words like: terrain and rendezvous. He was seeing this as a pilot mission; test some strategies for future mercenary activities. It was all training for the real thing in the Swat Valley or Central Africa.

He picked up the taser supplied by Sven. Then, he counted the steps on his fingers.

1. Check yard is empty of busybodies, hostiles, gate keepers etc.

2. Empty petrol can in a zigzag, double rations for dry trees and full rubbish bins.
3. Wait until targets leave house for their stupid walk.
4. Move into position.
5. On signal: light fires and bangers. Frighten target 1. Target Gold? Billy ruminated on possible code names but stuck to target 1. He didn't want Crime and Wave laughing or worse getting confused.
6. Net target (Ty) taser, put into transport (shopping trolley).
7. Run to tunnels.
8. Get to Battersea Park rendezvous.
9. Close deal with Sven.
10. Return on foot via road.

Billy didn't want to get caught on CCTV. He knew Crime and Wave would make a fuss. They'd put their hoods up like a big sign to the police. Arrest us now we're thugs on a rob. Lovely Jubley. Billy needed to work on that phrase. He wanted something better but this plan took all his brain for now. Just getting the right net had taken three weeks.

Billy wasn't taking Eddy. He couldn't take Eddy to Central Africa. And if he needed anyone bitten he had Crime and Wave. Eddy was too easy to identify. Without Eddy Billy was just a teenage boy in a baseball cap. Billy had enough on his plate with a taser, a shopping trolley, a bleeding great thylacine and Crime and Wave. Everything had gone to plan. So far.

"Text book," Billy kept muttering under his breath.

Crime and Wave were stealthy he'd give 'em that. Though, Wave enjoyed the petrol trail too much. He'd turned up early to cover a wider area. He'd even added petrol and rags to the back of the hospital where scaffolding and building debris butted up against a new wooden hoarding apologising to patients for any inconvenience.

Wave only caught a glimpse of his handy work when he jumped off the scaffolding and ran towards the rotten yard gate. The flames ran up the petrol towards the hoarding like a firework display. The yard went up shortly after. Crime set off some bangers near Zen and Ty. In the smoke and confusion Billy's crew was able to net and taser Ty who had ran towards Billy, away from the bangers, leaving Zen alone in the smoke.

Ty had been very heavy to lift. He'd made a blood curdling sound when electrocuted. He'd thrashed about until Billy stuck him again. The shopping trolley didn't really work over the uneven ground. They had to carry it and it was damn heavy. It banged into their shins. But Billy couldn't see any other way to move Ty. He was much bigger than a regular dog. And he wasn't a dog. For all Billy knew he may have poisonous fur or something.

Billy was angry with Wave. He'd bring every pig in Tooting down on them. The guy was insane. Billy silently vowed never to work with the brothers again. Every time they turned and saw the fire, Wave cackled, until Crime shouted at him to shut it. They got lucky hitting a narrow concrete path. This led to the main path, then passed round the back under the trees and down the scree slope. They slipped on the slope. The trolley tipped. Ty began to thrash about. They nearly overbalanced but by brute strength they got the trolley onto the smooth tunnel floor. Billy tasered Ty again. Ty convulsed and thrashed, then lay stiff with his tongue lolling. All three lads held their breath. Billy put his hand next to Ty's great jaws.

"No, still breathing," muttered Billy, relieved.

Sven promised two grand in used 20s for a live specimen. They paused listening. Nothing. No sirens, no shouting, nothing. The tunnel was black. Crime and Wave looked doubtful. Billy got out a small torch.

"Here," he passed it to Crime. "Shine it up there."

Crime took the torch directing the beam towards the ceiling.

"Shit," he laughed. The ceiling lit up. Wave got out his phone and did the same.

The brothers tramped ahead, trying to tag the ceiling with obscenities. Billy pushed the trolley. They passed the pools which were almost full. But there was no time to stop and gawp. They had to get to Battersea. Sven wasn't the type to hang about. Billy didn't slow down. No-one had followed. But that could change. There was a rusty gate, more a grill really, covering the end of the tunnel. They came up in an overgrown circle of bushes and an abandoned brick shed. From there they'd take the path along the Thames towards the zoo. Sven was going to meet them with his security van. If anyone saw him hanging about they'd assume he'd come to check on the zoo. Sven was to wait under the trees, well away from any CCTV.

Billy swore now and again at Crime and Wave who acted like a couple of toddlers with the lights. Billy wished he'd gone alone, keep all the cash. His next job would be a solo.

43

BATTERSEA PARK

When Fin heard the words Billy and Battersea she couldn't take it in. The fire filled most of her brain. Battersea Power Station? Why would Billy go there? Was he planning to throw Ty off? She'd been there on one of Pop's education tours: a giant brick building squatting by the Thames. Four white chimneys pointing at a glowering sky. She'd been inside. There was no roof. It was all shivering puddles, pigeons and too much sky. It was all too big. Rust ran round the building like cancer, trapped by green tiles. Mouldy bandages over an open wound. Battersea. She didn't want to go there. But the idea of Ty and Zen there alone with Billy was terrible.

She had to do something.

"Think, Fin, think," she heard Gran telling her to stop, think and check your gut feeling.

"If the Tsar had done this he'd still be alive or at least his children would," said Gran.

The trouble with the Tsar was he had people do the thinking for him, like kids today. Gran had said scowling as Mop fiddled with the microwave. Fin knew Gran meant Mop and Pop when she said kids today. Fin could see her point.

"Right," Fin had said.

Fin couldn't run fast after Tolemy. There were too many broken headstones and spikey bushes but she kept going. If she tripped over here the smoke could smoother her. It was already difficult to breath. She gashed her leg on a snapped branch. It stabbed her leg like a knife. She stopped and rubbed it. She hadn't even got to the tunnels yet. Zen and Tolemy would be long gone.

When she got to the scree slope, her eyes were streaming. She could hardly see. Sirens wailed along the High Road. What if the tunnel was filled with poisonous smoke? She really should go back but how? Fin couldn't see the way she'd come. If there was smoke in the tunnel she was trapped. She'd been stupid. She started to shake. She had to do something before panic took over. She darted down the slope, expecting to have to run back up but the tunnel was clear and quiet. She ran headlong into the cool semi-darkness. She just kept running. She imagined smoke snaking its way after her, curling and coiling around her legs. She didn't think to question why the ceiling glowed. She just ran and ran. She had to stop when she reached the pools. She had the stitch so bad, she thought she'd split. She leaned over, panting, fighting to get her breath back, to run on. She could hear running feet. Fin lurched towards the dark arches. But which one? Shit. Then she saw it: a faint glow in the second tunnel. Choking in air she sprinted forward.

As she hurtled off, Edge, followed by Blimp and his sisters arrived at the pools.

The sisters stopped for breath too, leaning on one another. They waited, panting for Blimp to lead the way. Blimp tried to explain about Ty despite being totally out of breath. Edge put his hand on his friend's arm and took over. He wasn't out of breath. Blimp stared at the water. His eyes were red and streaming, from the smoke.

"It's full," Blimp interrupted Edge, "the fountains... If we get the beam engine to move... We can put the fire out." Edge and the sisters stared at Blimp. The noise of someone else running fast made them all turn. Arden appeared.

"Where's Fin?" she shouted.

Edge pointed to the darkening tunnel. Arden ran past and disappeared into the gloom.

Blimp had done running. He led his sisters towards the beam engine. Their phones created a feeble path of light. The engine looked bigger and uglier than he remembered it. The water was deep and dark. Blimp blew out his breath and glanced at Edge. Edge was too small. His body just didn't weigh enough. Aruna and Lakshmi on the other hand were broad and heavy. And they could both swim.

"OK ladies," said Blimp. "We need to stand on the arm to push it down. When it gets going it'll keep going..." He looked at his sisters.

"What?" said Aruna.

"I'll go first," said Edge, climbing over the barrier. He stepped neatly onto the broad arm, holding a rail above his head. For a moment Blimp hoped Edge was enough. He wasn't. But he'd made it look easy.

Blimp stepped forward. He wobbled a bit, the gap between the floor and the dank pool below was wider than it looked.

"Don't look down," he muttered. "Right," he shuffled along to be next to Edge. He needed to sound confident. He talked over his shoulder. All his sisters gripped the barrier, appalled.

"By my calculation, we'll go under the water once but as the arm comes up we can jump off." Mentioning going under the water was a mistake. Big time. He could feel his sisters step back. But he had to let them know so they could hold their breath.

"What kind of crazy scheme is that, Bhupindar?" hissed Aruna.

"You can't even swim, what happens if you slip off?" said Lakshmi, staring into the abyss. Blimp gripped the rail tighter.

"It'll start the fountains and stop the fire..."

"Probably," said Edge.

Mia sighed and unwound her scarf.

"Mia," the sisters chorused. But she stepped on in a business-like way.

"Well, come on then," she said, bending her knees as if she was on some sort of park ride. Nothing moved.

"We need one more, we're too light," said Blimp.

This was the cue for the heaviest sister to step forward. Blimp worried they'd have to jump up and down. But with Aruna's weight, added to their own, the beam gently moved down. It was slow. Blimp and Edge smiled at one another. Blimp was about to whoop when the beam gained speed. Before they were ready it plunged them into the cold, greasy water. They just had time to close their mouths and eyes. Then, they were up again, gulping for air. Down again. Repeat. Edge sprang for the rail on the first rotation. Blimp and his sisters were gripping tight, frightened of slipping into the black water under the machine. It was only now they were riding the beam engine they realised how dangerous it was. And that they had no idea how to get off.

"Get off," shouted Edge.

The other sisters joined in. This added to the noise and panic. The creaking beam and the splashing water was deafening in the small space. Mia was crying. Blimp's hands were cold. Soon he would be too cold to hold on. Mia jumped next and was grabbed by Edge and Lakshmi. Just.

They hauled her over the guard rail like a rag doll. Aruna hung on. She was as inept as Blimp. She couldn't figure out how to get off. Her whole body was shivering. On the fourth go round, she moved one foot off and tried to step onto the brick parapet. She let go too slowly. The beam was too high. She leaned down hoping to catch the rail. She missed, her feet slipped. She tumbled down into the churning black water. She banged her head on the tiles. Someone screamed. The scream echoed above the thrashing water. Edge swore. Blimp looked down. He couldn't see his sister. He couldn't grab her. She was just too heavy. He took a depth breath and as the beam dipped under the water he stepped off. He doggy-paddled away from the machine. There was just a bath-width of space between him and the metal arm. The choppy water kept sucking him back. He pulled at the water, crawling himself away. Down came the beam again.

There was Aruna. Her head was bleeding. Her eyes were wild. She'd backed herself against the tiled wall by holding a metal ring. Blimp paddled over and caught the ring.

"You OK?" She nodded. But she wasn't OK. She was shuddering. Shock. If she went onto shock he wouldn't be able to move her.

"They're OK," shouted Edge. He was climbing over the rail to catch the beam again. Blimp wanted to shout no, but he was too cold and winded to speak.

"We need to get back on," said Blimp, using the last of his strength. Aruna shook her head.

"Aruna, I can't lift you. You have to move with me." She nodded. Edge meanwhile went past them, riding the beam under the water. He made it look easy and bloody dangerous at the same time.

"When you see my head," Edge shouted. He went under the water. But when his head appeared neither Blimp, nor Aruna could let go to join him. Blimp felt he was welded to the metal ring. Edge got off again but he was pretty wobbly. The sisters shone their phones down.

"It's OK. Jasmine's gone for help, hold on."

As the light danced around them Blimp caught sight of some metal pins in the wall on the other side of the engine.

"Look," he pointed. "Aruna, look over there." Aruna slowly turned. She looked confused like she'd just woken up. She didn't seem to know where she was. The pins formed a sort of basic ladder. As the beam went up she let go and swam in a quick jagged motion towards the rusty pins catching it just before the juddering water swept her under the arm. Blimp was too shocked to be surprised. Then she was hauling herself up with the last of her adrenaline. Blimp doggy-paddled his way round. Aruna was now balancing on the parapet holding the wet guard-rail above him. The pins were rusty and very thin but they didn't give way. He heaved himself up one at a time. His legs shook like jelly. Soon he was lying in a wet heap next to Aruna with Edge slapping his back. His sisters cried around them.

44

SHOW DOWN

Soon Fin left the smooth luminous tunnel behind. She was jogging and stopping and walking fast. This tunnel was narrow and untiled. Damp bricks closed in around her. There was a strip of phosphorescent paint she tried to illuminate but it was too high. The torch beam was too feeble. She kept going. She was scared she'd bump into Billy each time the tunnel curved. The darkness was a relief. She felt invisible. But she dreaded Evil Eddy. He'd smell her. She couldn't out run a dog.

The walls were wet with green slime. Sometimes the phosphorescence had fallen off the ceiling. It lay chipped and dissolving on the greasy tunnel floor. Fin felt a cold breeze slice her legs. She must be near some sort of exit. If Billy had come this way he might be at the end of the tunnel. Fin slowed down, listening. Her legs wobbled but she kept going. At least Zen and Tolemy were somewhere up ahead. Or were they?

The phosphorescence ended. She began to edge her way forward by following the thin torch light across the slippery floor. The tunnel smelt of dirty water and dead pigeons. She stepped over crisp packets, leaves and rotten newspaper. This meant an exit was close.

Fin stopped, listening. There was no sound of Billy. There was no sound of Zen and Tolemy either. She crept forward. She put her hand on the tunnel wall.

"Yuck," she rubbed slime off her hands onto her jeans.

The tunnel tipped up a little. She was standing on mud surrounded by bushes rustling in the wind. It was cold and breezy. Fin could hear London traffic in the distance. She began to push herself through the bushes, crunching over empty coke cans and old water bottles. It was almost dark.

Fin crouched down. She edged towards a chain of white lights, suspended from lamps, above a wall. She tried to keep low in the bushes. She bumped into something warm and solid, lost her balance and fell back onto her bum.

"Look, where you're going," hissed Tolemy.

Fin was so glad she wasn't alone. She rubbed her hands and started to stand up. Tolemy grabbed her arm and pulled her back down. He didn't even look at Fin. He kept peering through the bushes. Loud crunching on the coke cans and the sound of someone slipping and swearing announced Arden's arrival. Fin doubled back to find her before she broke their cover.

Fin made a shushing sound. Arden nodded. The white lights cast a faint glow over her thick hair, like a halo. Fin wasn't sure what they were hiding from. She couldn't see anyone.

"There he is," said Tolemy. He shot out towards the lights. "Zen, over here mate."

Arden caught Fin's sweatshirt. They couldn't see where Tolemy had gone. Fin and Arden stood up and fought their way through the bushes. But what they saw made them duck down and crawl back in. Fin felt empty like the Russian doorstops. Maybe she was just made of cheap rubbish.

Tolemy had seen Zen standing under a lamp with his back against the wall. But he hadn't seen what Zen could see. The tree branches swayed in the breeze. The leaves scattered the white light. Now, Fin and Arden could see three other figures lurking under the trees. Zen was surrounded with his back to the wall. Tolemy ran slap bang into an ambush. He looked at Zen, then at the three figures as they closed in around them.

"Whoa," Tolemy jumped back. He raised his hands as if to say hold on. Fin felt sick. Her stomach went cold. Arden gripped Fin's sweatshirt tighter. They held their breath. They didn't dare move for fear of giving away their position. That was their only advantage. Fin couldn't see Eddy. She was scared he'd get behind them, blocking their escape.

"This isn't Battersea power station," whispered Fin. "It's the park." She stared at Arden. Arden stared back. It occurred to Fin that Arden had never been out with other children. She might think all this was normal.

"Arden, you need to phone the police. Tell them Zen and Tolemy are being attacked by thugs...or will be soon in Battersea Park."

"Where?" whispered Arden.

"Battersea Park," repeated Fin.

"No," hissed Arden, "I know that, but it's a big place. Where's the call box?"

"I don't know."

Then Fin had an idea.

"I can't see Eddy..."

"Eddy?"

"Billy's dog Evil Eddy."

"Is that his real name?"

"Dunno... look you run towards the road but away from here," Fin pointed behind them. "They can't see you in the dark, keep under the trees."

"Then what?"

"Find a phone on the road, or stop someone," Fin was exasperated.

"OK." said Arden. "What'll you do?"

"Dunno. But if they run off. I can tell the police where they are, or be a witness or something." Fin didn't know. She was making this up as she went along.

"Can do," said Arden. She turned and slipped out into the black park.

Fin thanked her stars that Billy didn't have Eddy otherwise it was game over. Fin waited. She needed to get a better look at where Ty might be. Why couldn't she see him? She heard an engine nearby and almost broke cover. It couldn't be the police already, could it? No. There were no sirens. It was a small white security van. Its headlamps swept the scene, illuminating a sign that read: Battersea Park Zoo. The engine stopped. A man in a baseball cap and a heavy jacket got out. Fin stood up slowly. Her legs were stiff. The man shouted something. The three figures rushed Zen and Tolemy. They were dragged towards the man. Tolemy's phone smashed onto the path.

Fin sucked her breath in and ducked down again. She needed to think. What if Tolemy gave her away? At least Arden hadn't been spotted but could she get help? Should Fin stay where she was or run back down the tunnel to Ermine. Her sister would know what to do. But Ty would be gone by then. She leaned her hands on her knees and peered at the scene. She needed to get the van registration but that meant crawling closer.

Her eyes had adjusted to the faint light from the lamps. She could see Billy Blatant and another boy holding Zen by his arms. Another shorter, thicker lad had Tolemy. Tolemy was twisting about making a ruckus and pointing to his phone. The lad let Tolemy go. Then, so fast Fin had to replay it in her head, he swung at the side of Tolemy's head. Tolemy's knees buckled. He fell down hard, banging his head. The boys laughed. One of them picked up Tolemy's phone and hurled it over the wall. Fin heard a splash. It must be the Thames. The river was high. High tide.

Fin expected the security guard to stop them. He watched and said something. Fin crawled closer on her hands and knees. The thick lad dragged Tolemy up and marched him towards the van where he flung him down on to the ground. Tolemy winced and held his nose. Blood gushed down his face. Zen was white with anger. He started to shout something but Billy just punched him. The boy on Zen's other side complained to Billy and let Zen drop. He was on his knees while Billy argued with the lad. The man stepped towards Zen, asking him something. Zen didn't reply. He was too winded.

Fin was crying. She only realised because her face was wet.

"Where's Ty?" She whispered. "Must find Ty." She had to focus on Ty or she was going to lose it.

Billy grabbed Zen's hair and yanked his head back. Fin had the crazy idea that if she saw Ty perhaps she could get him away but where was he? What if he's already dead?

Billy left Zen and walked back towards the river wall. He wrenched a shopping trolley out of the shadows and wheeled it towards the man. Something was thrashing about inside. Billy took something out of his jacket pocket. He poked it towards the thrashing thing. There was a crackle, then a terrible yelp. It was Ty. Fin shuddered so violently she thought they'd see her. She was at the edge of the bushes with only a few twigs between her and the park. But she had darkness on her side. As long as she kept away from the river lights she was covered. She did something that surprised her. It was instinctive. She began to crawl nearer Zen. She had to do something before they killed Ty. Slowly, silently she elbowed her way along the damp grass until she was near enough to hear what was being said.

The man was called Sven. He inspected the trolley, ordering Billy to unwrap a net. Billy tried but the net was caught. Crime had a knife. He ambled over, pulled up some of the net and began to slice. Ty lay very still, too still. Sven leaned over and whistled.

"Stay there." He went back to his van. He ignored Tolemy and Zen. He got in and started the engine. Tolemy got up and staggered away into the darkness. He didn't get far. Fin heard him fall and retch. But Fin had no time to worry about Tolemy. Sven drove the van towards the trolley. He left the engine running, jumped out and wrenched open the van doors. They couldn't push the trolley along the grass. Ty made it too heavy. All four figures crowded round Ty. Fin couldn't see what they were doing but she thought they must be trying to get Ty out and into the back of the van. Fin edged closer to Zen.

"Zen," she hissed. "Zen," Fin wasn't sure Zen could hear her but she carried on. "Arden's gone for the police."

Zen was on his knees trying to stand but he was holding his side. Sven reached into his van and humped out a metal cage, barking instructions. He banged it down, fiddling with some sort of catch on the top. They planned to tip Ty in. Fin couldn't stop them but she could get the van number plate. She couldn't see from this angle. Zen or Tolemy probably wouldn't remember, even if they'd noticed. They'd both taken a beating. Fin tried to hiss again but Billy looked over. She put her face down to avoid the light.

Billy hadn't seen her. She kept her face near the cold earth. She made a list.

She was still invisible.

The police had been called.

Billy didn't have Eddy.

Fin turned and began to crawl away from the boys. The grass was long. Her jeans were damp and heavy. This slowed her down. Now and again she caught the awful smell of dog's shit. She kept going. Then she was behind the van. She had no pen to write down the number plate. She repeated it several times: a white ford van, number plate: SV8 4NB. When she looked away to test herself she couldn't remember all the numbers. She tried some mnemonics. Snake van 8 snakes, 4 cakes-no that was leading her astray but once she's thought of them she could see snakes curling round the cakes. It was a bit crap. It wouldn't work. Ty would disappear because she was too stupid to remember 6 digits. A loud dispute interrupted her worrying. The man was opening the cage and waving his arms about indicating that he wanted the boys to tip Ty in. Fin got it, why didn't they? A row had broken out over Zen and Tolemy and money. Fin was too close. She wished she'd stayed in the bushes.

"You said two grand, this merch is worth more," said Billy. "Now you try to stiff us?"

He had his hand on Ty's head pushing it down. Crime and Wave leaned on Ty's legs. Most of the net had been cut away. Ty began to thrash about. Zen wobbled up. Tolemy staggered back towards the trolley. Tolemy watched the trolley scene as if he'd just woken up in the park and didn't know how he got there. He was too confused to run off. The row continued. Fin took a big risk. She moved nearer Tolemy. She whispered as loud as she dared.

"Tolemy," she wasn't sure what else she was going to say. She had no plan. Tolemy jumped. He looked round wildly into the black park. Then he tried to leg it towards the lights on the main road. He crashed into Fin.

"Quiet," Fin said.

Zen saw Tolemy go and heard Fin. He didn't try to escape. That would give the game away. Fin needed a plan. A siren sounded far off across the park. Billy ignored it, as did Sven. Fin and Tolemy watched a police car sweep along the main road and disappear round a bend.

"Shit," spat Tolemy.

"Shut up," said Fin.

"You owe me two grand," demanded Billy.

"Two grand?" shouted Crime. He let go of Ty's legs. Ty tried to claw his way up. Billy rammed Ty down.

"You said One."

Billy just glowered.

"I'm not paying a grand, you muppets," snarled Sven. "Look at this mess: a mad dog and tourists. TOURISTS."

With this he let the cage lid fall. He took out a roll of bills.

"You'll get 500. *If* you get it in the cage, *and* in the van, pronto."

Billy began to argue. He was angry but didn't want to lose it. Sven was vicious. And Billy couldn't let go of Ty's head. Sven had the advantage.

"Worth more dead, than alive anyways." Sven leaned back. "My customer's only interested in stuffed animals. He's a pervert. Don't want anything that bites. 500 to whoever gets it done."

Sven slipped the roll back in his jacket. Fin was confused. Tourists, a pervert, stuffed animals? Where they going to kill Ty? Surely he was worth more alive? Maybe Sven was trying to... but Fin didn't get to finish the thought.

There was another siren on the main road. Zen sprang towards Billy. He threw a punch that caught Billy on his nose. There was an awful crunching sound. Billy roared. He let go of Ty. Blood spurted from his nose. He grabbed Zen. He began pounding Zen in the ribs. Zen tried to keep his fists up. Crime opened the cage. Then Crime and Wave tried to lift Ty out of the trolley but he was very heavy. Sven shot into his van.

"I called the police," shouted Fin. Her voice was so loud Sven glared round. Ty was too heavy. Crime dropped Ty's back legs. Ty struggled twisting away from Wave and leapt free. He bounded away, trailing net, towards the zoo. Zen and Billy were rolling around on the ground. The siren was getting nearer. Sven reversed fast. Fin had to run back towards the bushes to avoid being hit. He roared off with the back of the van hanging open. The sirens got closer. Crime and Wave looked at one another and shot off in the opposite direction of the van. Fin's heart was in her mouth. Fin ran towards Billy and Zen, Tolemy followed. The sirens were loud. A police car was coming across the grass. Billy was up kicking Zen in the ribs. Zen was curled into a ball.

Fin screamed stop, stop, again and again. Billy ignored her. He didn't even hear the police sirens. He'd entered another dimension. He just wanted to kick and kick and kick. Tolemy took a flying leap, kicking his feet into Billy's kidneys. Billy staggered but stood his ground. Tolemy tried again. Fin grabbed Billy from behind his knees. Billy ended up on the floor for a moment with Tolemy and Fin on top of him. But he was mean. He punched them off. Fin staggered away into the headlamps of the police car. Billy twisted round and ran off along the Thames path. Zen started after him but slipped on the wet grass.

"Stop, we know where he lives," yelled Tolemy.

Zen looked round for Ty. Ty had gone.

45

WHAT HAPPENED NEXT

What happened next was a mess. Fin was sick in the back of the police car. The police officer told her not to worry; his mate was on clean up duty. Fin tried to get out of the car. Her legs were wobbly and the blue flashing light was making her feel more sick. She had to look for Ty. All the windows were open so the car was very cold. What if she had to sit next to Billy?

Then the car was moving. One officer was holding her head.

"OK love, just let it out. We're on our way to hospital."

Fin leaned back on the seat, balling up soggy tissues. The roads were almost empty, black and orange. Whenever, they approached a junction the police driver flicked on the sirens. They ploughed through red lights.

Then Fin was sitting on a hard plastic chair under white strip lights. It was noisy, people milled about. Some held their arms; others had bandages around their heads. Everyone looked tired and sort of flattened. A toddler scampered about trailing crisps. The police officers laughed with an ambulance driver in a green jump suit.

A nurse came up to her with a clipboard, pushing a wheelchair. She spoke to Fin. Fin looked at the police. She couldn't understand what the nurse wanted. Fin's ears didn't seem to be working. She needed to tell the nurse about Zen and Tolemy. They were hurt at Battersea

Park. She struggled up. She had to phone 999. Stars fizzed before her eyes, then she was wrapped in black velvet. Now she was in the wheelchair. The police were talking to the nurse.

"We've called your mum and dad. They're on their way and your friends are just ahead of you..." The officer leaned towards her holding a plastic cup of Bovril.

"Well done, you did some of our job tonight; just don't make a habit of it." He smiled and nodded. His radio crackled. The Bovril smell made Fin retch.

The nurse wheeled Fin through some white doors. The other side was warm and quiet. A blue corridor stretched away into the distance. On either side were little bays like beach huts where children lay in hospital beds or families sat on plastic chairs. Fin caught the sway of doctors' coats and the murmur of voices.

The nurse wheeled her into an empty cubicle, yanked the curtains closed and left. Fin sat there looking at the wall. She waited, nothing happened. So she got up slowly and turned the chair round. She sat down. She felt sick and her shoulder hurt. All she could see was the wrong side of the curtain. It looked like apples and pears. She got up again and pulled the curtain open slowly, until she had enough gap to see most of the corridor.

She could see other children. A baby started to cry, like it had a very sore throat. There were two toddlers, and a boy about Ermine's age in a torn football shirt. The swing doors opened. Mop appeared. She looked very, very tired. She had puffy bags under her eyes. She looked older. She hugged Fin. This was awkward as the back of the chair got in the way. She stank of smoke. Fin remembered the fire. Had their house burned down? Mop looked around and pulled up a red plastic chair. She sat down.

"We're all OK. Everything's OK." Mop nodded, trying to reassure herself as much as Fin. "You kids gave us a scare, running off like that. We thought..." said Mop. Pop put his head round the curtain. He smiled and waved three bags of salt and vinegar crisps.

"Found a vending machine that works and one that dispenses hot pies."

"Jeez," said Mop, sounding like Ermine.

Fin got up and went to the tiny sink. The water was warm and the pink soap smelled like pink would smell if it had a smell. She dried her hands in a big green paper towel. She felt a bit better.

"You can eat them. You're just here for observation," said Pop, crunching a giant crisp. Another nurse pushed in a hospital bed for Fin to lie on. After some checks she turned the overhead light off and closed the curtain.

"Your friends are just down the next corridor," she said.

Mop got up. "You stay with Fin. I'll see how they are."

A male nurse appeared with a paper carton with some pills for Fin to swallow. He had to go off in search of a cup and jug of water. Fin just took the pills dry.

"I'll go to the loo," she said.

Perhaps she could catch up with Zen and Tolemy. But all the curtains were shut now. Fin could hear someone snoring. When she got back Pop helped her take her trainers off. She felt too tired to take off her socks. She leaned back on the stiff, clean pillow and fell asleep without even eating her crisps.

A woman police officer came back the next afternoon as Fin was being discharged to ask her about the events of the night before. Fin went through it all slowly. She was still very tired. She had to backtrack. The police woman waited patiently while Fin rearranged her thoughts.

"Thank you, we've a good idea who those boys are."

Fin thought it odd that Crime and Wave were boys to the police woman. It made them seem smaller but more vicious somehow.

"Your friends are doing fine but your dog's still missing. But don't worry. I've got all my colleagues looking for him..." She looked down at her black note book. "Last spotted running towards Battersea Park Zoo..."she broke off here and gazed across the children's ward. "I wonder if he made it into the zoo? Could be worth a call." She shrugged and got up to go.

Fin's lip wobbled. She began to cry. Once she started she couldn't stop. The police officer gave her a hug but Fin could feel her pulling away. She had to get on.

Fin remembered the zoo sign. She also remembered Sven driving off with his van open. He could have caught up with Ty or run him down. Fin felt bad. She felt even worse when she saw Tolemy. He came limping along the corridor with a black eye. His face was swollen. He nodded his head indicating she should leave Mop and Pop talking at the nurses' station. They didn't speak. Tolemy turned and led her towards the lift. They went up to the top floor and followed a sign to the ICU.

Nurses and cleaners bustled about. Tolemy pointed to a glass wall. The room had four beds in it under a giant window covered by a flimsy blind. All Fin could see were lumps under sheets with equipment and tubes coming out here and there.

"Zen's in the end bed," said Tolemy. "But we can't go in because of germs."

"No, you can," said a bright voice behind them. A chubby nurse was snapping off some gloves. She had false eye lashes. Fin wondered if that was allowed. After all they might drop off into patients' wounds.

"Come on, I'll take you."

Tolemy looked at Fin, as if to say she thinks we're five years old. However, they followed her in. Zen was asleep. He looked sort of green. A buzzer went off. The chubby nurse left them standing there.

"D'you think he's got brain damage or something?" said Tolemy.

Fin moved to the end of the bed. There was a clip board with notes and lots of Biro initials. She tried to read it. Tolemy came round and hooked it off. It was some sort of list. Tolemy pulled the page up. He'd seen this done on television.

"Suspected rib fracture," he read. He pointed to a diagram of ribs, one scribbled on.

"Why don't they do an X-Ray?" said Fin.

The chubby nurse returned. Tolemy snuck the notes back fast.

"Time to go," she smiled, waving her arm at the door.

They headed back to the lift.

"We've got to find Ty, if it's the last thing we ever do," blurted Fin.

Tolemy looked at her. "The state we're in, it will be, but we've got every single kid at school behind us."

"Even Mad Matthew?"

Tolemy nodded and winced. "Especially Mad Matthew." Then he

tried to smile. "You don't know about the fountains do you?" he croaked. "You've got a lot of catching up to do."

46

BACK HOME

When Fin got home, everything was different and the same. The yard smelled of smoke. Most of the tree damage was superficial. They were too full of sap to burn properly. Pop pulled over outside Hatsumi's.

"We'll walk, like we did the first time," he said. Fin struggled out into the cold day. She felt empty, like there was nothing left inside.

Four dead trees were charred stalks. Pop looked up at them.

"I'll have to take those down but the rest are fine, may even encourage new growth." Pop really was a glass half-full sort of person.

"Like a bush fire, like in Australia," said Fin.

Pop zipped up his fleece and pulled a tool box out of the back of the van.

"Yep, what made you think of that?"

Fin wasn't sure. She had half an idea. Maybe, she wasn't so empty after all.

"What happens to the animals? In a bush fire," asked Fin.

"Well, I dunno. They sort of run away, or burrow just before it happens, they sense it before we do... probably pick up on vibrations, smell... bears can smell..."

But Fin wasn't listening. She balled the tissue up in her pocket.

"Do they come back?" she asked.

"What?" Pop was distracted. They were standing in front of the stone quagga. It was black and cracked. Its fat belly split. Fin almost expected its entrails to tumble out. She looked underneath. It was just stone.

"Damn. The heat must have been intense..."said Pop. He looked sad. "Come on. We'll get you home then I can make a list, start fixing things again."

Some new graves were scarred by smoke but the black marble ones looked the same. Ermine and Guy were out taking photos. Fin could see Ermine's pink hair bobbing up and down in the distance. Guy said something and Ermine laughed, bending over her camera, shaking.

Abimbola had left a gooey ginger cake on the kitchen table before heading off for another study day. Blind Twin House still looked too big for their furniture. Fat Bastard had spent the last few days in Ermine's attic room, refusing to come down.

Fin dragged up to her room. She opened the window and leaned out. She strained her eyes for Ty. Nothing. She was too tired to cry. She wandered round picking things up and putting them down. Eventually she sat down with Anastasia. She felt slowed down, listless. She was meant to phone Tolemy with the plan to get Ty back but she had no idea where to start. Someone banged on the front door. Fin was too tired to hope it was the police. After all they would hardly come all the way here to announce they'd found "a dog."

Mop yelled up the stairs. "Fin, it's your friends."

Fin got up and looked at the Imperial Family. There was a knock at her door. Fin opened it. Arden, Blimp, Edge and Tolemy stood in the hall.

"Hi," they all spilled into her bedroom.

"Wow, this is really cool," said Blimp. The sun shone through the stained glass casting colours across the bed and the floor. They spent some time putting their hands in front of the different colours. Then, they were all tucked up in the linen cupboard guzzling coke and chewing ginger cake.

"Well, tell her what happened," said Tolemy.

Arden and Edge sat back and folded their arms. Blimp laughed, coke coming out of his nose.

"Not again, my sisters phoned the paper, some blogger phoned last night. Mum's not so pleased." Blimp retold the terrible story about nearly getting killed by the beam engine. He put in lots of sound effects.

"You should go to the doctor. You might get dysentery," said Fin.

"Dysentery, doctors, that's for wimps," Blimp batted this away. "With three sisters studying medicine, I'll be fine."

While Blimp thrashed about in the water the beam engine began to power the fountains. It happened slowly at first so no one noticed. Water bubbled up over the top of the lead bowls. Just enough to wet the sides like rain. When Blimp was hauled limping and soaked back along the tunnels, the water began to jump up in leaps and starts. It looked like an overflow. Besides, news of the fire had spread. People were shutting windows, pulling in washing and turning on the news. Shoppers ignored the fire engines and the wet bowls on the High Street. This was London after all.

However, Lord Basel had done his job well. Thames water was forced up pipes and out of the upturned bowls. Fountains erupted across the yard dousing some of the flames and creating a sort of water break against the others. Soon steam filled the air like a warm fog.

Blimp was wet already but his sisters got drenched getting him to the main road. At first they thought it was the fire brigade. But fire trucks had moved further away from the main road, to tackle the hospital. With a loud choking sort of noise and a few more spurts the fountains burst into action. Suddenly there were fountains all along the High Street, in back gardens and across the park. People stopped. Pub goers and dog walkers took photos. Strangers started to talk to one another pointing out higher jets of water. Little kids escaped flats to run in and out of the spray. A local news team wasn't sure whether to follow the fountains or the hospital. The hospital story won. There might be casualties. No one was ever killed by a fountain, they decided.

It would take the Saturday Guardian and Gazette to sort the fire from the fountains. It was big news. Blimp's parents were interviewed over the phone and a reporter was coming to their flat that evening.

Fin was happy for Blimp. "Better tell them your name's Bhupindar," said Edge.

"Nope, I'm gonna put Blimp out there, that's my stunt name."

"So you turning professional now?" said Tolemy.

"Oh yeah."

"How's Zen?" asked Arden. The atmosphere changed. Fin felt the emptiness return but she updated them.

Blimp waved his arms about stopping Fin's tale. "I'll use my interview to get people to look for Ty."

Edge and Tolemy both nodded.

"Great idea, you could hold up a picture," said Edge.

"No," snapped Fin.

They all looked at her with surprise. "That's not a good idea..." she said. She sounded mean. Fin felt as if she was hovering. She put her coke down. Her hands were sticky. She wanted to wash them and forget all this had ever happened.

"Why not?" asked Arden.

"Because... it'll be like *Jaws...* "

"*Jaws*?"

"Did you bang your head last night?"

"No of course not. Everyone'll go out and look for him for the wrong reasons."

"The wrong reasons?"

The others looked confused. Fin felt the wood panels digging into her back. She was trapped. She paused. They waited. She told them. She wished she hadn't because then no one knew what to do. They had no plan.

47

MAYBE, JUST MAYBE?

Over the next few days things went back to the way they were when they first moved in. Fin followed Pop around the yard helping. Pop tried to cheer her up by letting her run the bin cart around the paths. Hatsumi was still at the hospital with Zen. Fin and the others had been on a tunnel run, not to enjoy the pools but to leave some of Ty's favourite food at the Battersea end. They tried calling too.

They had to be careful. The council now knew about the tunnels. A wooden barricade and a padlock had been erected at either end. Pop provided the padlock for the yard end which meant he had a spare key. At the Battersea end they'd just pried the wooden door from the frame with a screw driver, borrowed from Pop's tool kit. Pop was in his element traipsing along the tunnels. Blimp and Edge gave him a tour. Ermine and Guy took more photos. Abimbola even had a tour with Blimp's sisters. Fin just felt tired. Everyone was very excited about the fountains. Pop and Blimp began working on a plan to start the engine at high tide without anyone risking their life again. Blimp tried to get Fin involved but it wasn't the same.

Fin hung about by the gate in a raincoat. It wasn't raining but Pop, Guy and Blimp had disappeared underground to re-start the fountains. They wanted her to time how long it took for the water to appear topside, as they called it. Fin fiddled with her watch. She stood in the middle of the path because there were lead bowls on either side. She didn't want to get soaked.

A tatty mini cab pulled up. Hatsumi got out frowning. She went around and opened the roadside door. Zen hopped out. Fin was so pleased, she shouted.

"Zen," then she felt a bit silly.

She hurried to open the gate. Hatsumi surprised her by giving her a huge hug.

"We stay. Immigration scared of Miss Nomer," she whispered, as if saying it out loud might jinx the good news. Fin felt better. Had the awful tide turned? Zen nodded and winced. Hatsumi paid the cabbie. She shouldered Zen's hospital bag and pushed her way through the gate.

"Fin, why don't you and Zen go for walk? I set up tea."

Zen didn't look pleased. Fin guessed the hospital said he needed exercise. Hatsumi hurried in. Zen stood staring round. He didn't look at Fin. There was a spurting sound.

"Look out," said Fin. She grabbed his coat pulling him into the middle of the path. Jets of water shot up on either side blotting out the main road and the yard for a moment. Water sprayed and slapped the tarmac around them. A fine mist coated their faces. Zen looked surprised.

"Pop, Guy and Blimp," said Fin.

Zen nodded. The jets coughed and spluttered and sunk low. They became small bubbly fountains, just covering the lead bowls. It was all over, for now.

They walked towards the grassy knoll. Zen rummaged in his pocket. He stopped. Fin rummaged in her pocket and found some stale gum. She passed it to him.

"Thanks," he said, taking the paper off slowly and pushing it in his pocket.

Fin wanted to tell him they were still looking for Ty. But they hadn't found him. So what was the point? Zen began to speed up, cutting off onto a side path. Fin walked behind. Did he want to be alone? Then she realised he was looking for scat, tracking. She slowed and willed him to find something, anything. Why hadn't she thought about this? Ty could have been wandering about the yard at night looking for them? Though, she wasn't sure why. The last sighting was Battersea Park. He'd run off into the night. What if he'd come back down the tunnel?

After half an hour they gave up. Zen was too tired to continue. He sat down on a bench. They watched the sun on the flat windows turning them gold then a pinky-red. Fin's feet were cold. The fountains trickled. Fin could hear the water bubbling and hissing nearby.

"I saw Billy," said Zen. "Well a police mug shot. He looked really pissed off..." Zen rammed his hands into his pockets. "He's been arrested... probably out on bail..."

Zen turned to Fin. Fin realised he was warning her. She might see him. Fin didn't feel scared. The fact that Billy was unhappy made him seem a lot smaller. He probably wouldn't ever bother them again. Too much trouble. There was no profit in it.

Their faces were cold and stiff. It was getting dark. Fin heard Hatsumi calling. They got up and trudged back down the brick path cutting through stinging nettles. Hatsumi had every light on in the house. She left the kitchen door open and clattered about. Soon they were drinking Miso and munching brown bread and butter. Hatsumi opened cupboards and shut them again looking for some sort of pudding. Zen had dark circles under his eyes. He'd probably go to bed after tea. He did. This left Fin and Hatsumi to talk about the fountains over the washing up. Fin was surprised. Hatsumi was usually quiet but tonight she made a lot of noise talking and rattling. She kept glancing at the open door. Fin realised she was hoping Ty would hear and come bounding in. Eventually she sighed and gave up. It was just too cold.

Fin decided she should head home. Hatsumi offered to walk her but Fin wanted to be alone. It was all too sad. Fin knew she didn't want to see them tomorrow. This made her feel disloyal but maybe the next day would be better. Perhaps Ty had found a new family who were stuffing him up with treats. Fin wandered back the long way. She wasn't sure where the fountains were in the dark. They may still shoot up. She heard a blackbird in the tree above her and a rat rustled in the bushes. Cars swept by on the main road. Should she try one more tunnel trip? Pop met her on the path. Tea time again.

Fin was asleep. Then she was awake. She looked around her room in the moonlight. She'd left the window cracked open. Her back was cold. She sat up and began to untangle her quilt. She heard the low rumble of a lorry. Then something like a cough. Someone on the main road, probably. Noise carried a long way at night for some reason. She got up and ran her fingers through her hair. The knots hurt. Her hair was past her shoulders now. It made her neck sweaty at night. She found an elastic band and tied it up. A sharp draught caught her by the window. She shivered and grabbed her sweat shirt. She pushed the window open and leaned out. There was a shadow by the gate post.

"About bloody time," hissed a voice.

Fin leaned further out. It was Zen. And Ty.

As she jumped into her jeans she felt full, like she'd eaten something really good. Within minutes Fin was walking with Zen and Ty in the moonlight. Fin kept rubbing Ty's giant head. He butted her legs and made his yipping sound. They followed the brick path all the way to the main gate. There were no lights on at Twin House but the windows caught the moonlight. There was no traffic on the main road. The only sound was the wind in the trees. Ty padded ahead then stopped and turned round waiting for them to catch up. Zen and Fin took long leisurely strides. It was good to walk. The air smelt of damp earth and pine. They ambled towards the quagga.

Fin squinted trying to imagine the live quagga with Peter and Bartholomew on its back. She was glad Peter and Bartholomew were sort of nearby. Though, Peter was only 11 and Bartholomew an old man.

"So when did Ty come back?" asked Fin, as they pushed past giant weeds and thistles onto Mausoleum row.

"Last night, I think," said Zen. "Something big got into our bins... mum put out every treat we'd ever given Ty. She even tried to get some snakes from a dodgy pet store but they don't deliver."

"Really?" said Fin.

"Mum was chopping up steak, dropping it along the path when Ty came jumping through the back door. 20 quid's worth of steak for the foxes."

Ty looked at Zen. Zen rubbed his head.

"We did that all along the tunnel, all sorts. Blimp's dad donated a lot of broken biscuits," said Fin.

Zen stopped by the Basel mausoleum and looked at the moon.

"I know, I saw the mess," Zen said.

"But where was he?" said Fin, sitting down on the cold marble step.

Ty sniffed about before settling down by Fin's feet.

"I think he came back, but was sort of waiting for us... me to come out of hospital."

"Good job you weren't in there any longer," said Fin. She wished she hadn't said that out loud. She didn't want to think about losing Ty ever again. She'd lost and found enough for one year.

"So, Ty you were scroffling about in the bushes, the whole time?" said Fin rubbing his head, behind his ear.

"Not exactly," said Zen. He pulled out a torn page from the local paper. He passed it to Fin. She opened it up. She had to stand up to catch some moonlight to read: "Battersea Park Zoo Mystery: Keepers at Battersea Park Zoo are excited and confused. Two of the Tasmanian Devils appear to be pregnant. Blood and urine tests, carried out by London Zoo experts, confirm pregnancies, keeper Anwar Choudhry is mystified because the Devils have been kept in isolation. All the Devils at Battersea Park Zoo are female. Tasmanian Devils can be very aggressive..." Fin looked up.

"So you think that was Ty?"

Zen nodded. Fin sat down, then stood up again. She began to pace about.

"If he's a close relative, like a horse and a donkey, it's possible, and he did go off in the zoo direction. This might mean..."

"I know," finished Zen. "He's no longer extinct."

ACKNOWLEDGEMENTS

I owe a great debt to the following people: Patricia Borlenghi my publisher and editor; Ken Wilson-Max for my cover illustration; Judith Bryan, Ariel Kahn, Louise Tondeur and Eleanor at the University of Roehampton for teaching me to focus on the process of writing not the product; Fred Botting, James Miller, David Rogers and Brycchan Carey at Kingston University for opening the door to more writing; Laura and Smudge; Anique Rehal; Richard and Karen Morris; my friends who held my hand in the dark; everyone at *Chalk the Sun* for dynamic workshops and great company; the *No Pens* wherever you are and the team at *Fisher and Co*, we rock; and Hannah C.

Most of all: thanks to my husband David Vowles who is always kind, generous and wise. And of course Phoebe, Tatum and Andrew.

Reprint of # - C0 - 210/148/24 - PB - Lamination Gloss - Printed on 03-Nov-16 08:18